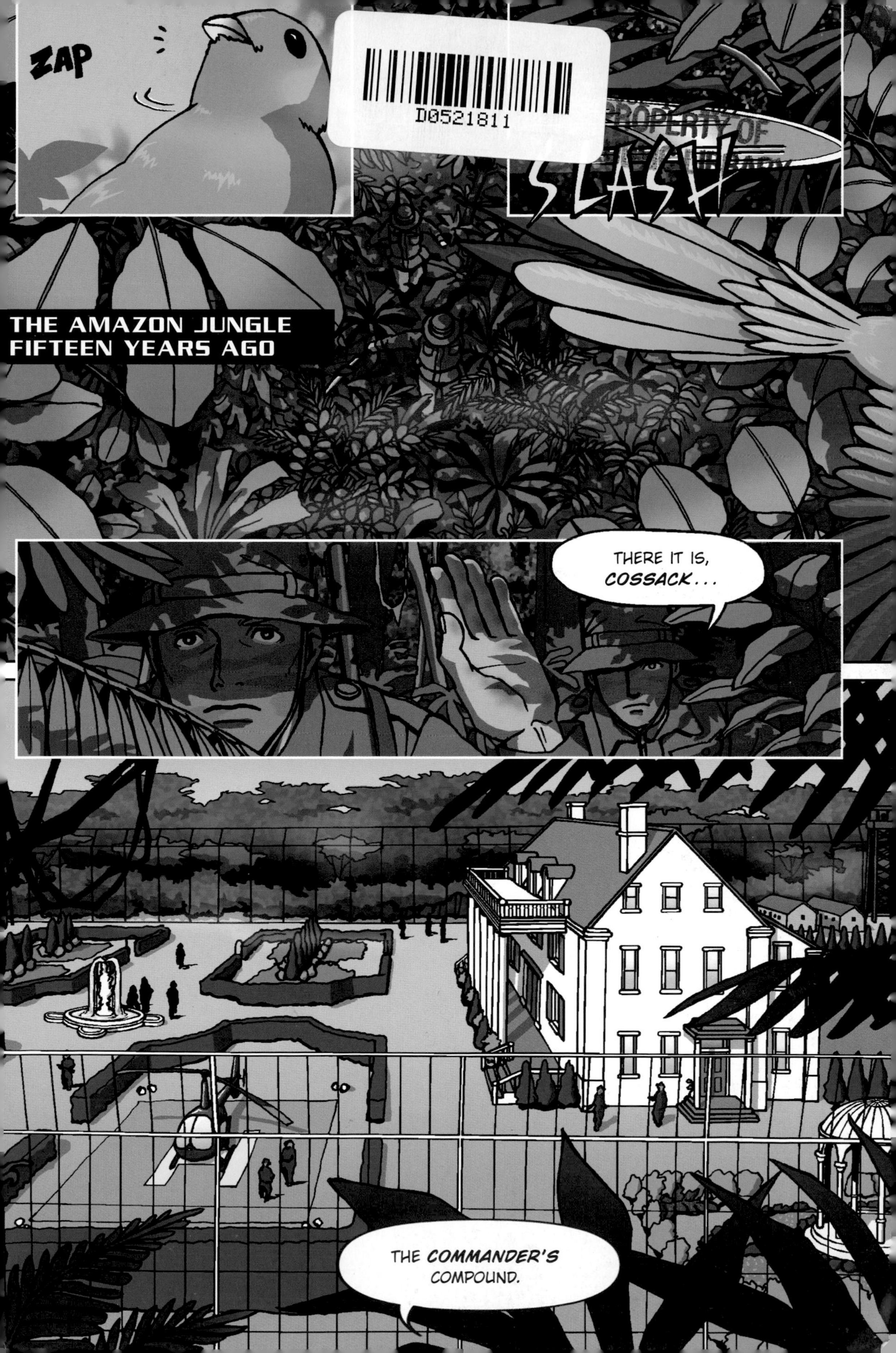
ZAP
SLASH
THE AMAZON JUNGLE
FIFTEEN YEARS AGO
THERE IT IS, COSSACK...
THE COMMANDER'S COMPOUND.

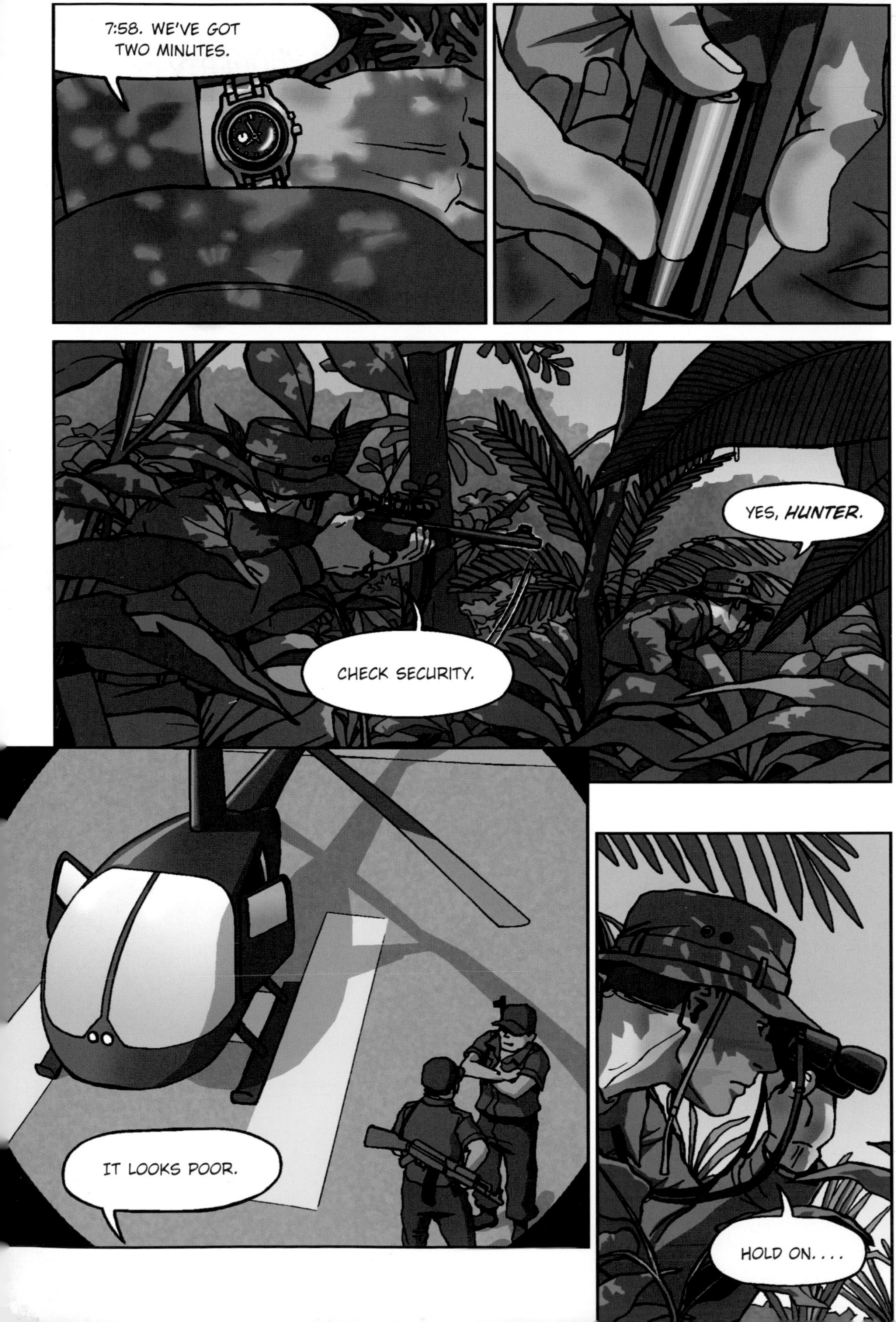
7:58. WE'VE GOT TWO MINUTES.
CHECK SECURITY.
YES, *HUNTER*.
IT LOOKS POOR.
HOLD ON. . . .

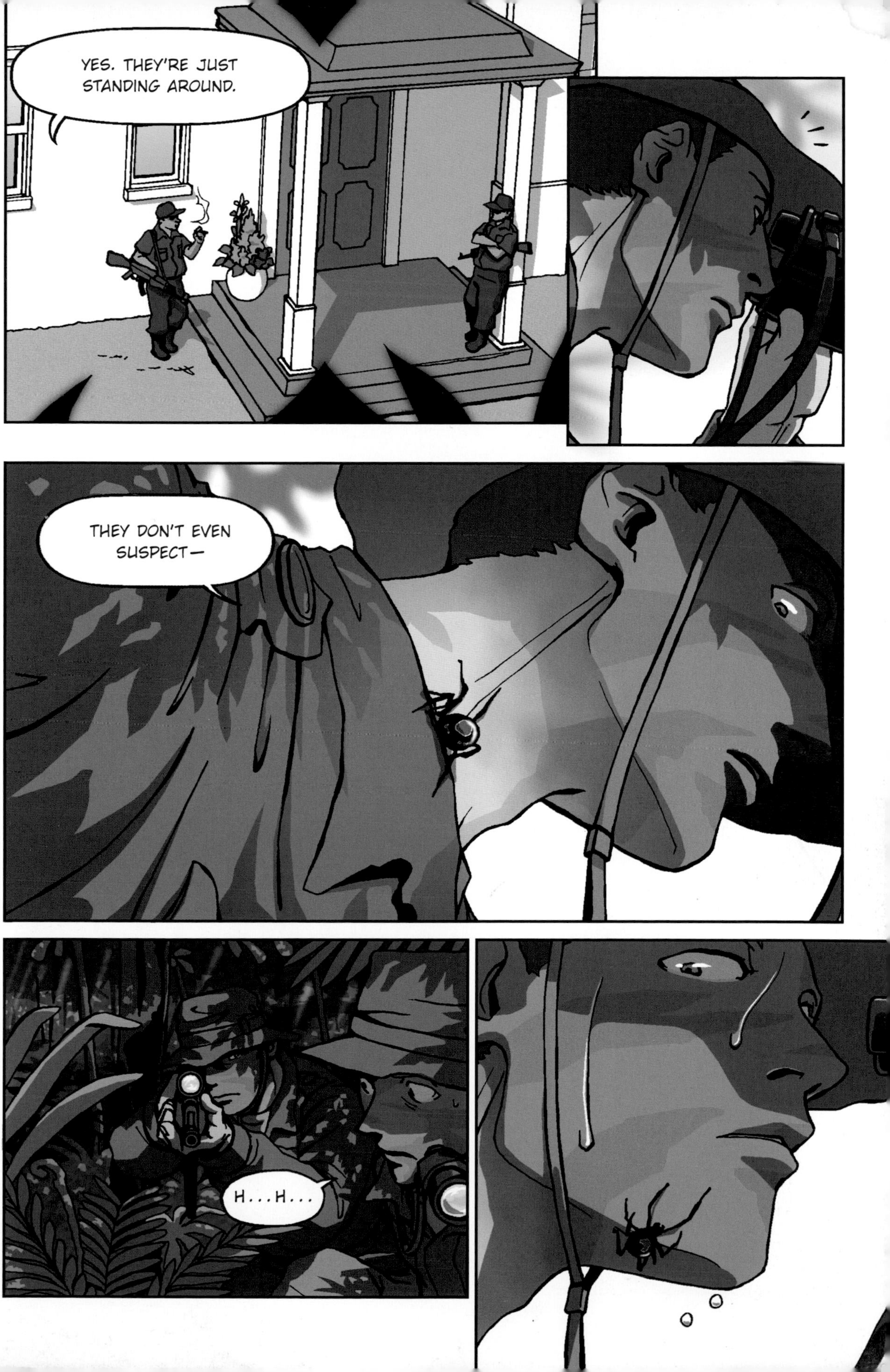
YES. THEY'RE JUST STANDING AROUND.
THEY DON'T EVEN SUSPECT—
H...H...

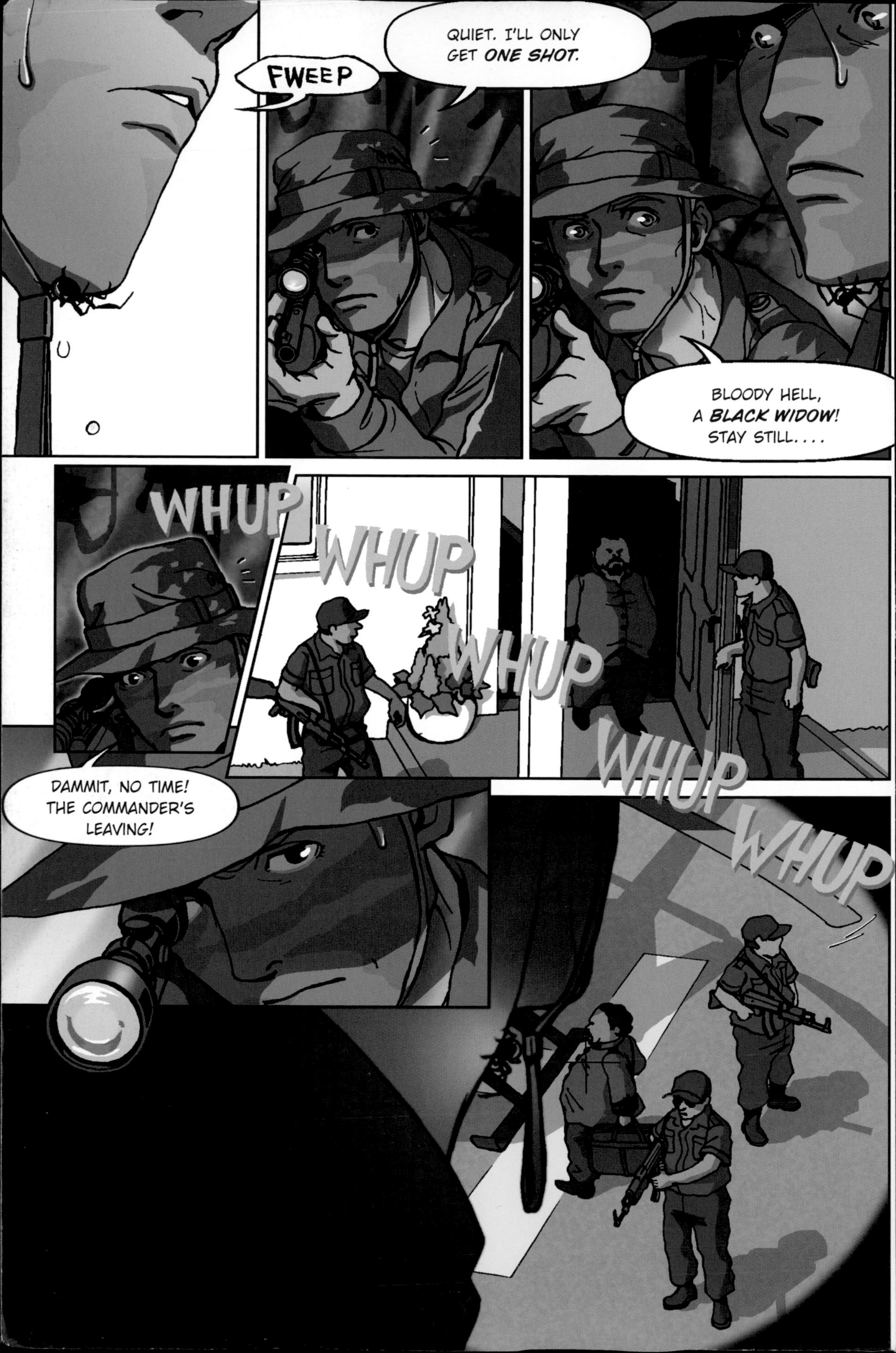
FWEEP
QUIET. I'LL ONLY GET ONE SHOT.
BLOODY HELL, A BLACK WIDOW! STAY STILL. . . .
WHUP
WHUP
WHUP
WHUP
DAMMIT, NO TIME! THE COMMANDER'S LEAVING!
WHUP

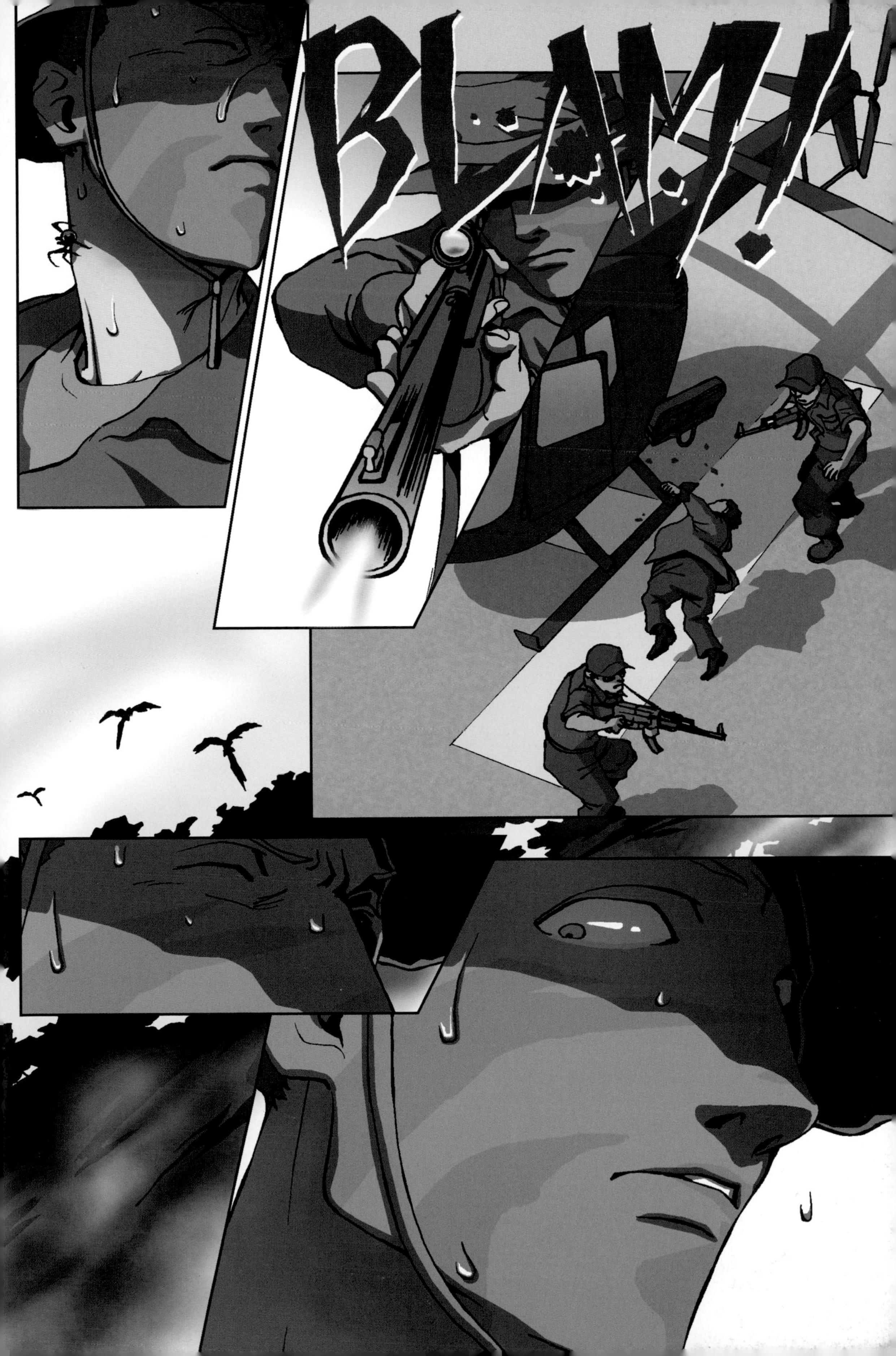
BLAM!!

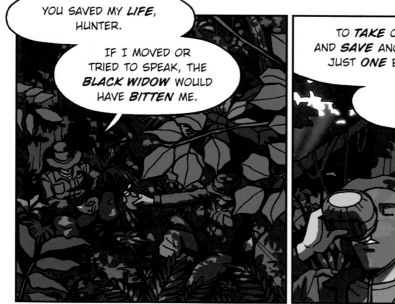

RUN!

YOU SAVED MY **LIFE**, HUNTER.

IF I MOVED OR TRIED TO SPEAK, THE **BLACK WIDOW** WOULD HAVE **BITTEN** ME.

TO **TAKE** ONE LIFE, AND **SAVE** ANOTHER, WITH JUST **ONE** BULLET . . .

NOT BAD, IF I DO SAY SO MYSELF.

I WILL **NEVER** FORGET THIS, MY FRIEND.

DON'T MENTION IT, COSSACK.

LET'S GET OUT OF HERE **ALIVE** BEFORE WE START COUNTING **DEBTS**, SHALL WE?

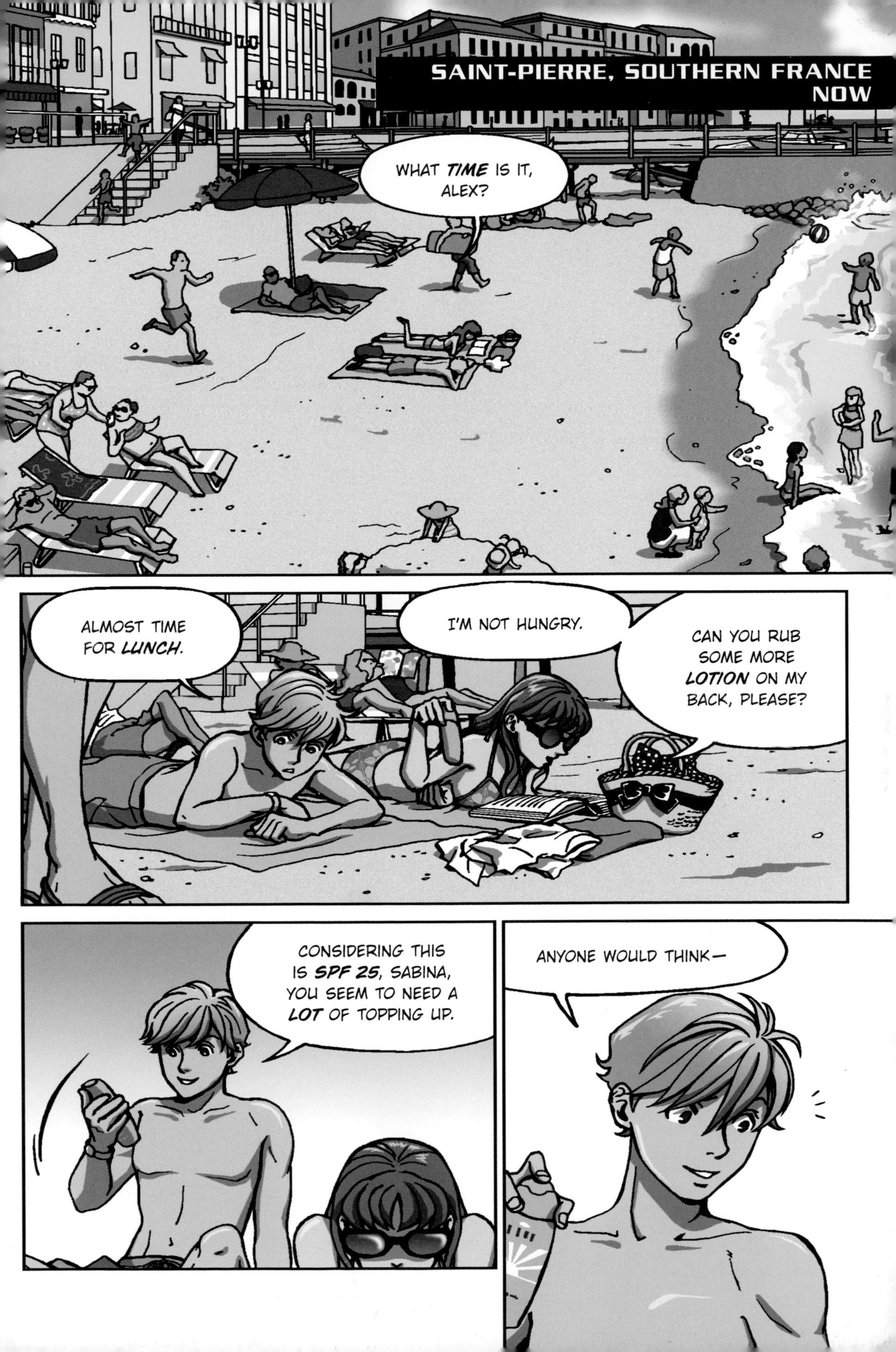
SAINT-PIERRE, SOUTHERN FRANCE
NOW
WHAT TIME IS IT, ALEX?
ALMOST TIME FOR LUNCH.
I'M NOT HUNGRY.
CAN YOU RUB SOME MORE LOTION ON MY BACK, PLEASE?
CONSIDERING THIS IS SPF 25, SABINA, YOU SEEM TO NEED A LOT OF TOPPING UP.
ANYONE WOULD THINK—

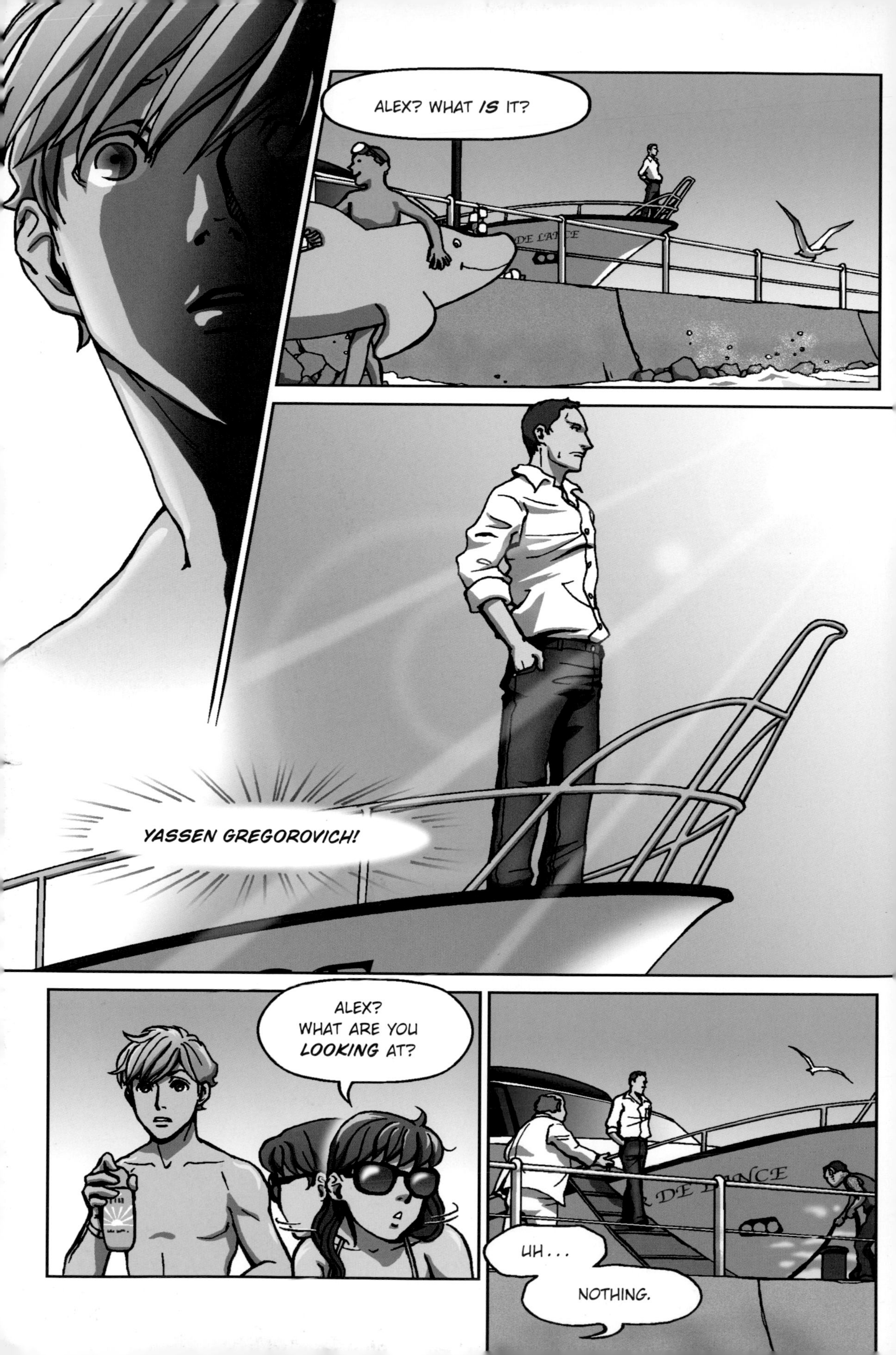
ALEX? WHAT *IS* IT?
DE LANCE
YASSEN GREGOROVICH!
ALEX? WHAT ARE YOU *LOOKING* AT?
UH . . .
NOTHING.

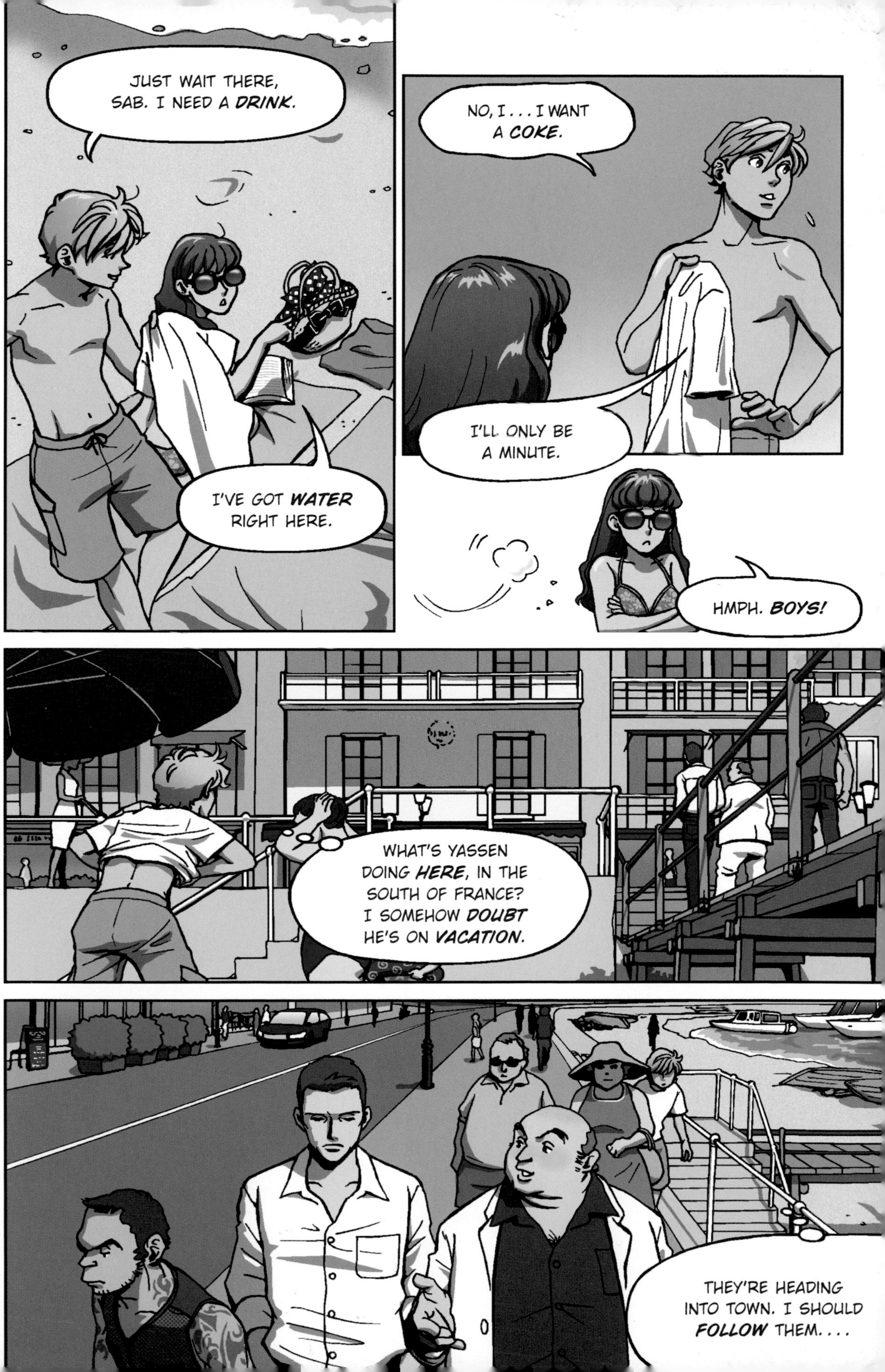
JUST WAIT THERE, SAB. I NEED A DRINK.
I'VE GOT WATER RIGHT HERE.
NO, I . . . I WANT A COKE.
I'LL ONLY BE A MINUTE.
HMPH. BOYS!
WHAT'S YASSEN DOING HERE, IN THE SOUTH OF FRANCE? I SOMEHOW DOUBT HE'S ON VACATION.
THEY'RE HEADING INTO TOWN. I SHOULD FOLLOW THEM. . . .

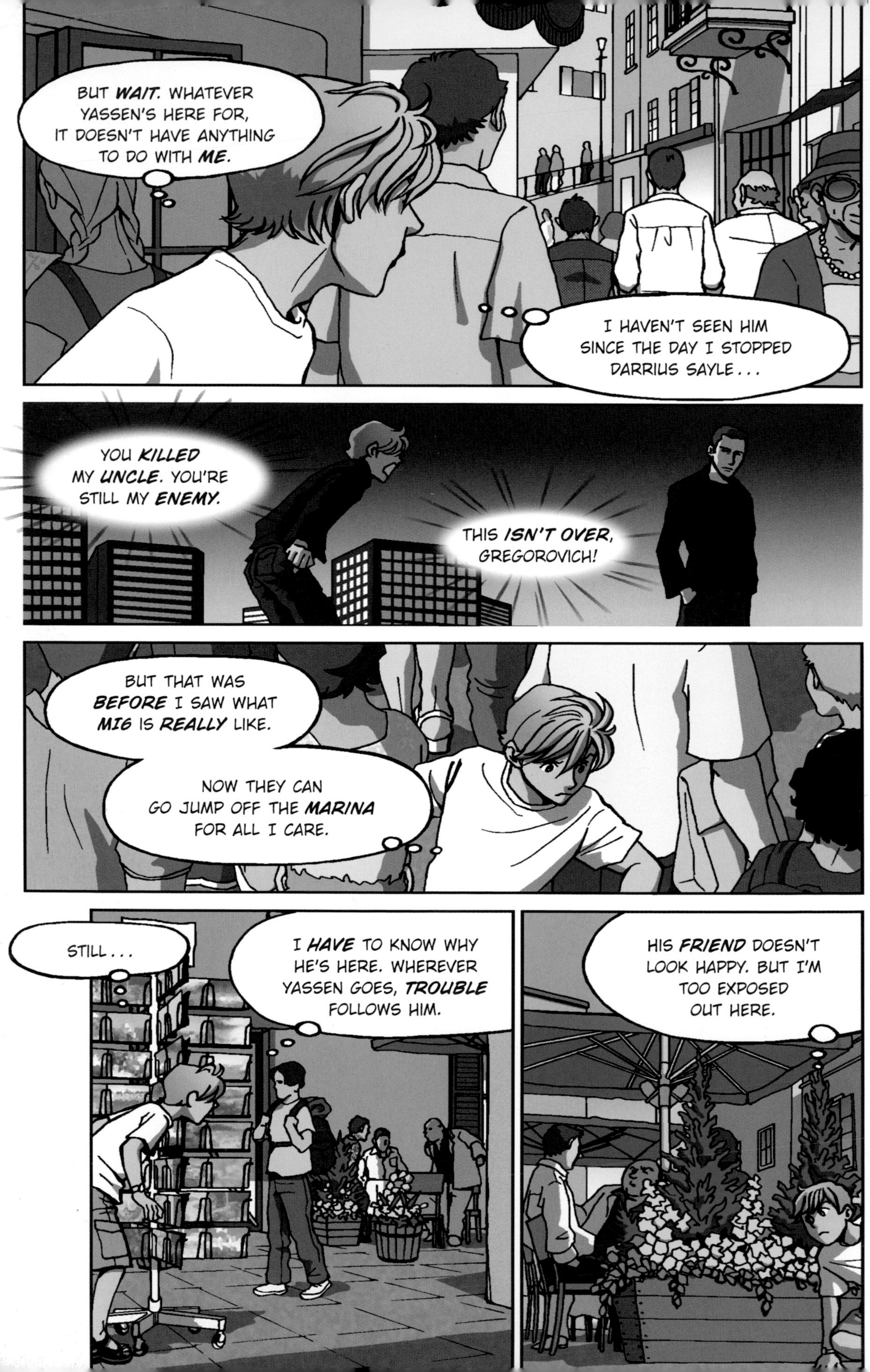
BUT WAIT. WHATEVER YASSEN'S HERE FOR, IT DOESN'T HAVE ANYTHING TO DO WITH ME.
I HAVEN'T SEEN HIM SINCE THE DAY I STOPPED DARRIUS SAYLE . . .
YOU KILLED MY UNCLE. YOU'RE STILL MY ENEMY.
THIS ISN'T OVER, GREGOROVICH!
BUT THAT WAS BEFORE I SAW WHAT MI6 IS REALLY LIKE.
NOW THEY CAN GO JUMP OFF THE MARINA FOR ALL I CARE.
STILL . . .
I HAVE TO KNOW WHY HE'S HERE. WHEREVER YASSEN GOES, TROUBLE FOLLOWS HIM.
HIS FRIEND DOESN'T LOOK HAPPY. BUT I'M TOO EXPOSED OUT HERE.

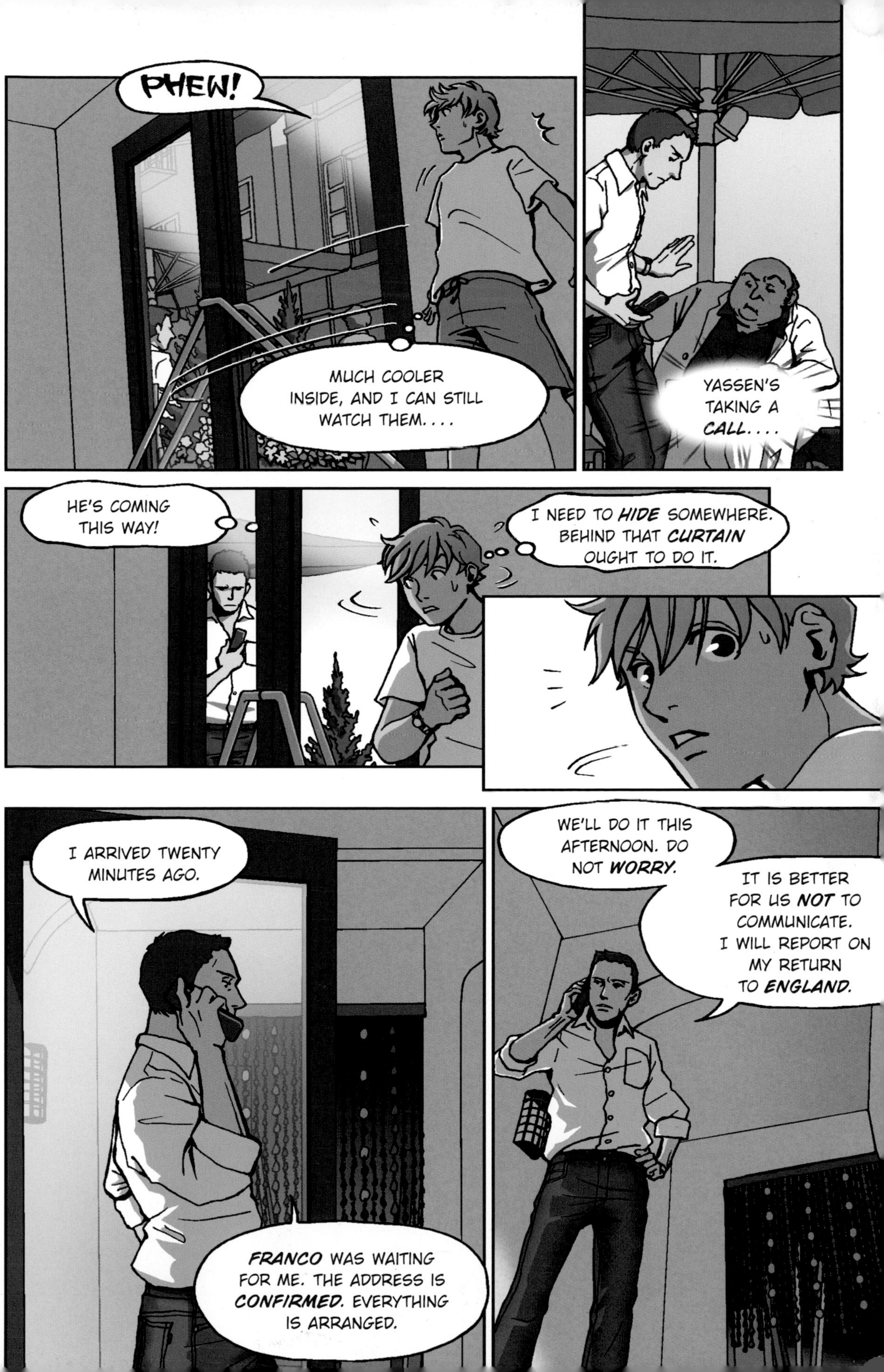
PHEW!
MUCH COOLER INSIDE, AND I CAN STILL WATCH THEM. . . .
YASSEN'S TAKING A *CALL*. . . .
HE'S COMING THIS WAY!
I NEED TO *HIDE* SOMEWHERE. BEHIND THAT *CURTAIN* OUGHT TO DO IT.
I ARRIVED TWENTY MINUTES AGO.
FRANCO WAS WAITING FOR ME. THE ADDRESS IS *CONFIRMED*. EVERYTHING IS ARRANGED.
WE'LL DO IT THIS AFTERNOON. DO NOT *WORRY*.
IT IS BETTER FOR US *NOT* TO COMMUNICATE. I WILL REPORT ON MY RETURN TO *ENGLAND*.

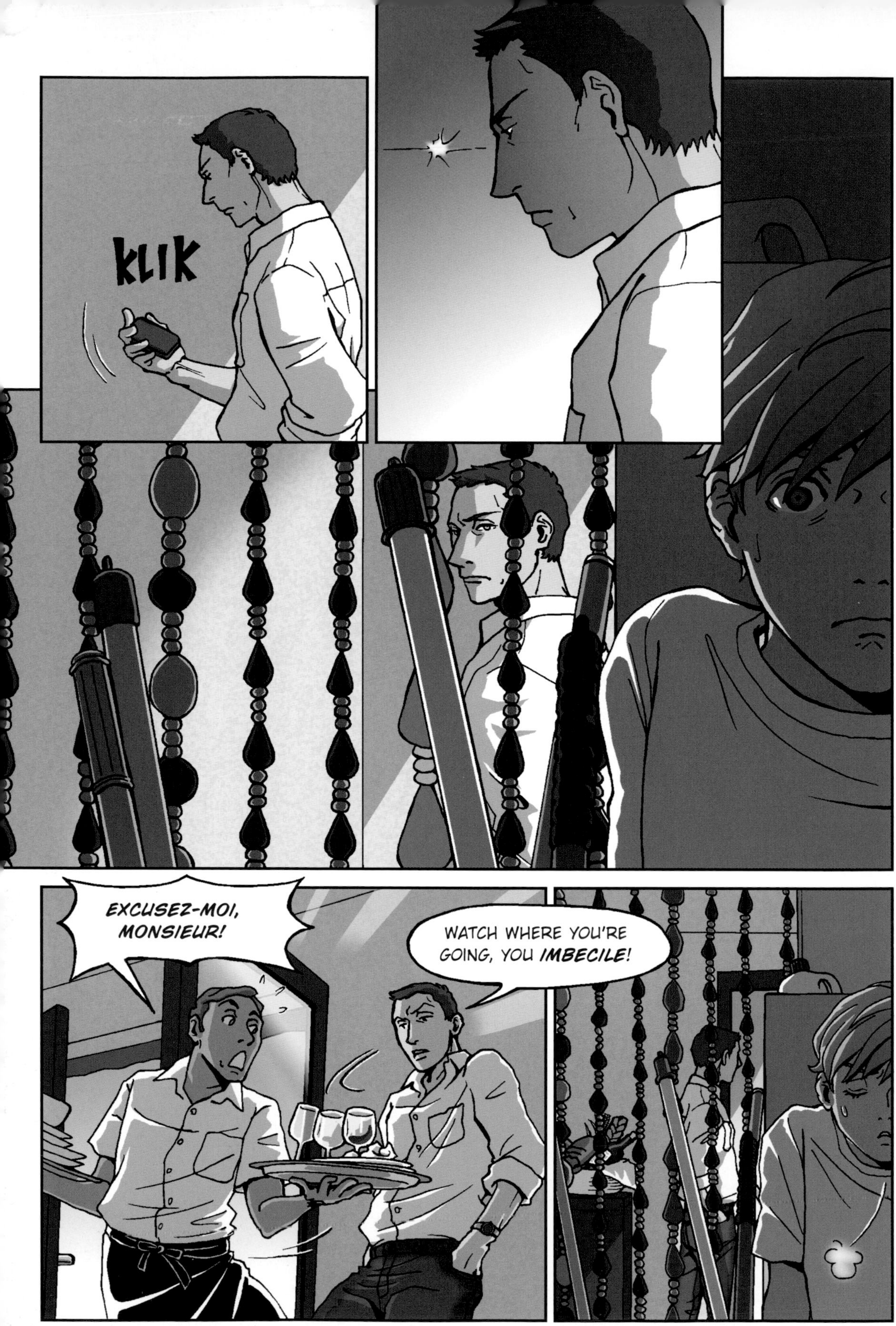
KLIK
EXCUSEZ-MOI, MONSIEUR!
WATCH WHERE YOU'RE GOING, YOU *IMBECILE*!

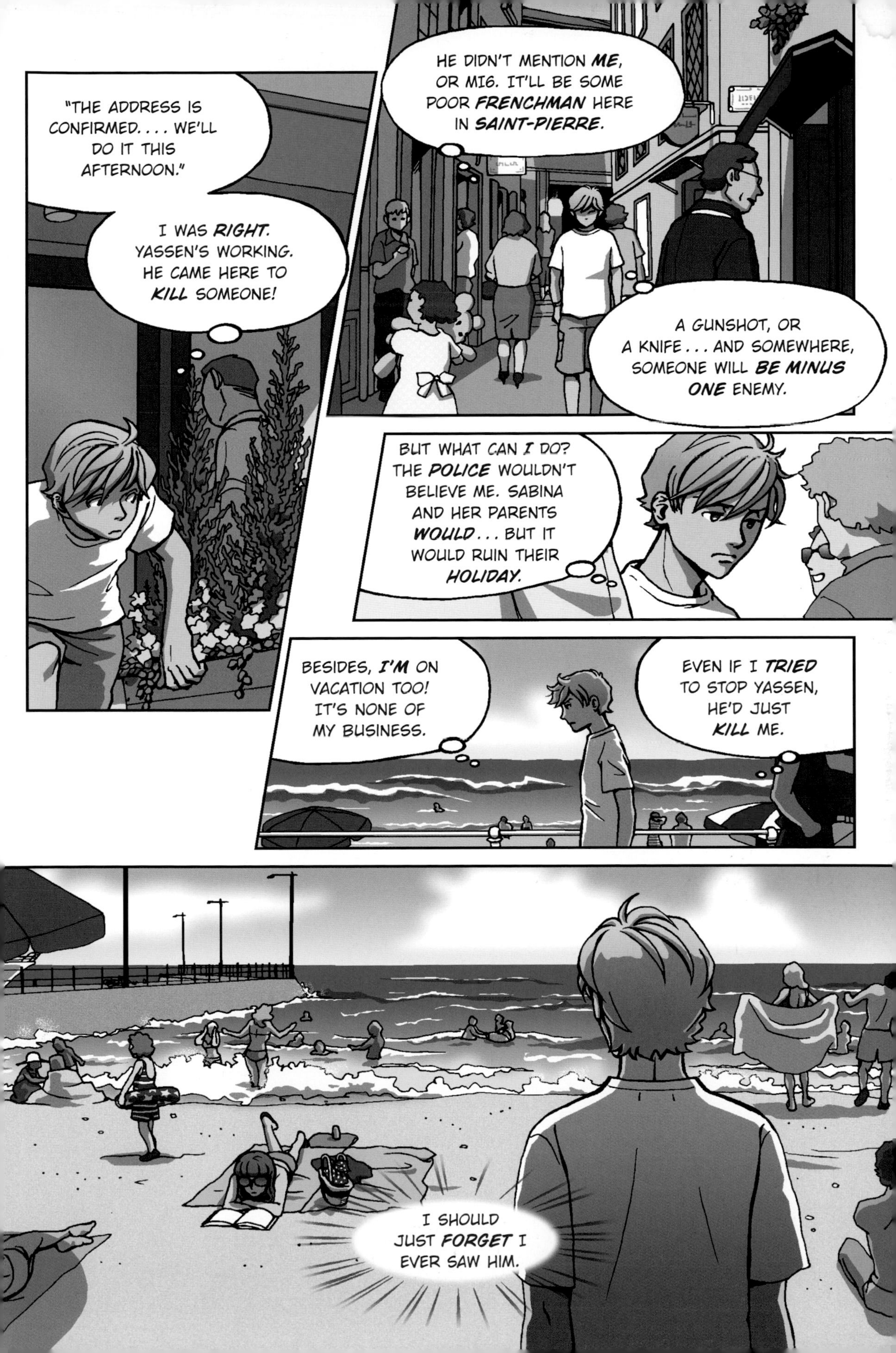

"THE ADDRESS IS CONFIRMED. . . . WE'LL DO IT THIS AFTERNOON."
I WAS RIGHT. YASSEN'S WORKING. HE CAME HERE TO KILL SOMEONE!
HE DIDN'T MENTION ME, OR MI6. IT'LL BE SOME POOR FRENCHMAN HERE IN SAINT-PIERRE.
A GUNSHOT, OR A KNIFE . . . AND SOMEWHERE, SOMEONE WILL BE MINUS ONE ENEMY.
BUT WHAT CAN I DO? THE POLICE WOULDN'T BELIEVE ME. SABINA AND HER PARENTS WOULD . . . BUT IT WOULD RUIN THEIR HOLIDAY.
BESIDES, I'M ON VACATION TOO! IT'S NONE OF MY BUSINESS.
EVEN IF I TRIED TO STOP YASSEN, HE'D JUST KILL ME.
I SHOULD JUST FORGET I EVER SAW HIM.

LATER
OH, GOD, LOOK AT THAT ONE!
FOUR OUT OF TWENTY, MAX.
THAT ONE'S SLIGHTLY BETTER.
MAYBE A SIX. AREN'T THERE ANY GOOD-LOOKING BOYS IN FRANCE?
PRESENT COMPANY EXCEPTED, OF COURSE, ALEX.
ALEX?
SORRY, I WAS MILES AWAY.
SO WHAT DO I SCORE ON YOUR FAMOUS BOY SCALE, THEN?
TWELVE AND A HALF. BUT DON'T WORRY. ANOTHER TEN YEARS AND YOU'LL BE PERFECT.
COME ON, LET'S GET OUT OF HERE.

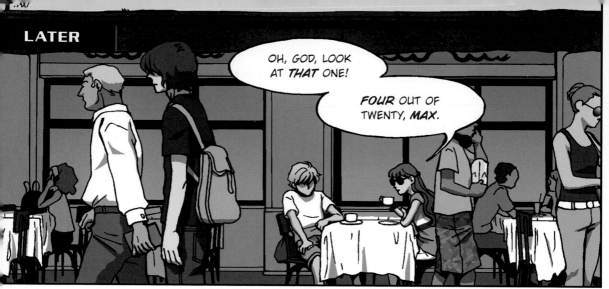

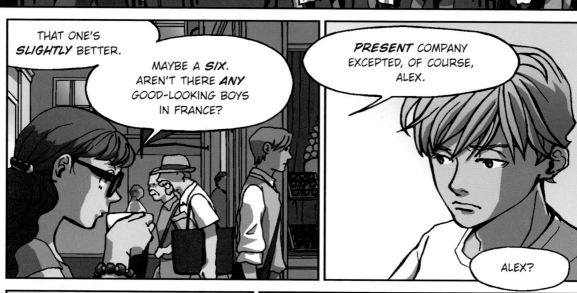

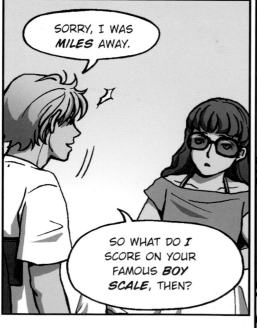

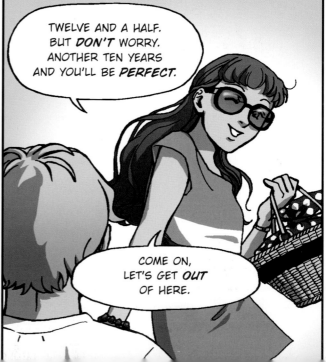

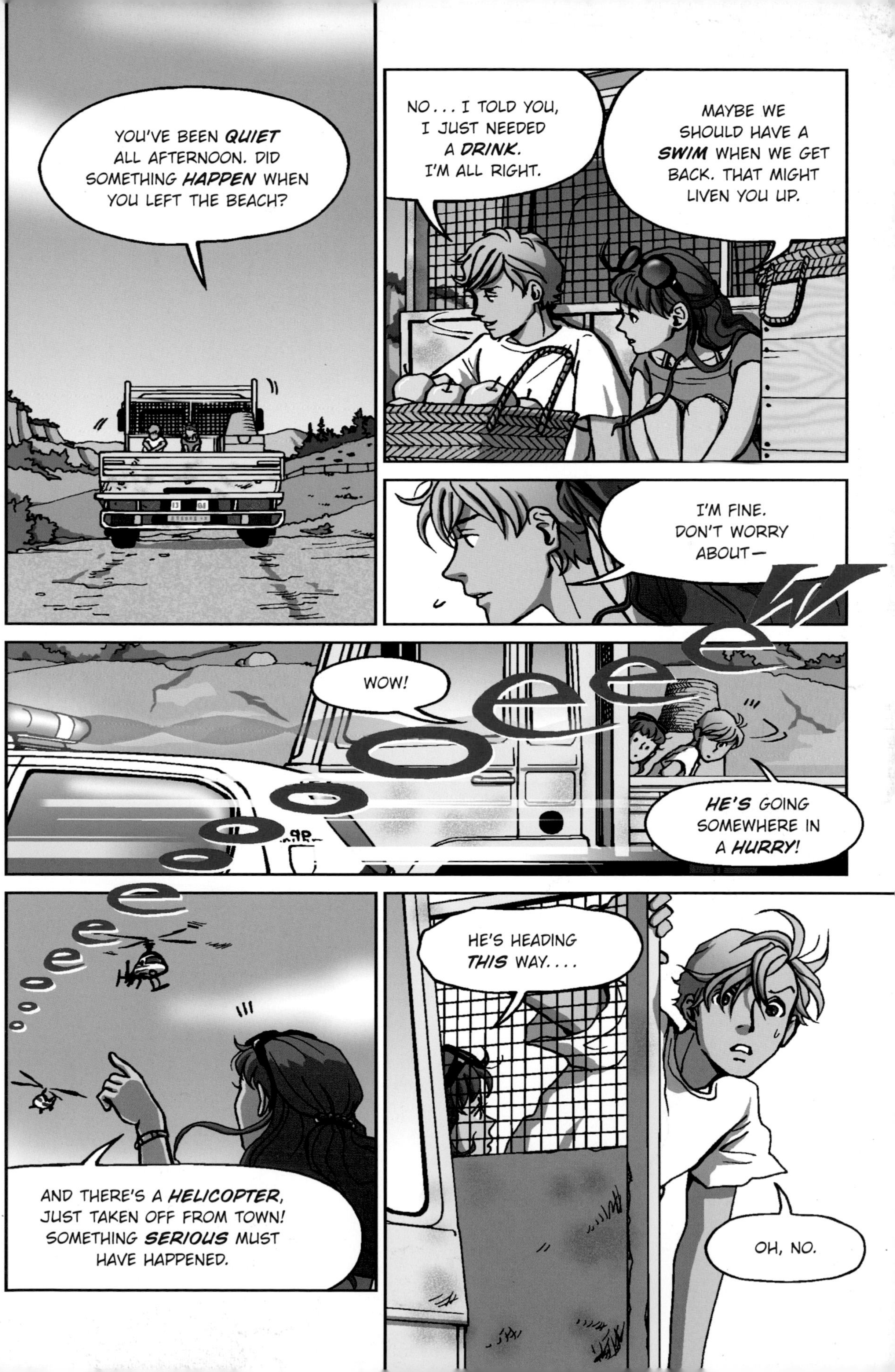
YOU'VE BEEN QUIET ALL AFTERNOON. DID SOMETHING HAPPEN WHEN YOU LEFT THE BEACH?
NO . . . I TOLD YOU, I JUST NEEDED A DRINK. I'M ALL RIGHT.
MAYBE WE SHOULD HAVE A SWIM WHEN WE GET BACK. THAT MIGHT LIVEN YOU UP.
I'M FINE. DON'T WORRY ABOUT—
WOW!
HE'S GOING SOMEWHERE IN A HURRY!
AND THERE'S A HELICOPTER, JUST TAKEN OFF FROM TOWN! SOMETHING SERIOUS MUST HAVE HAPPENED.
HE'S HEADING THIS WAY. . . .
OH, NO.

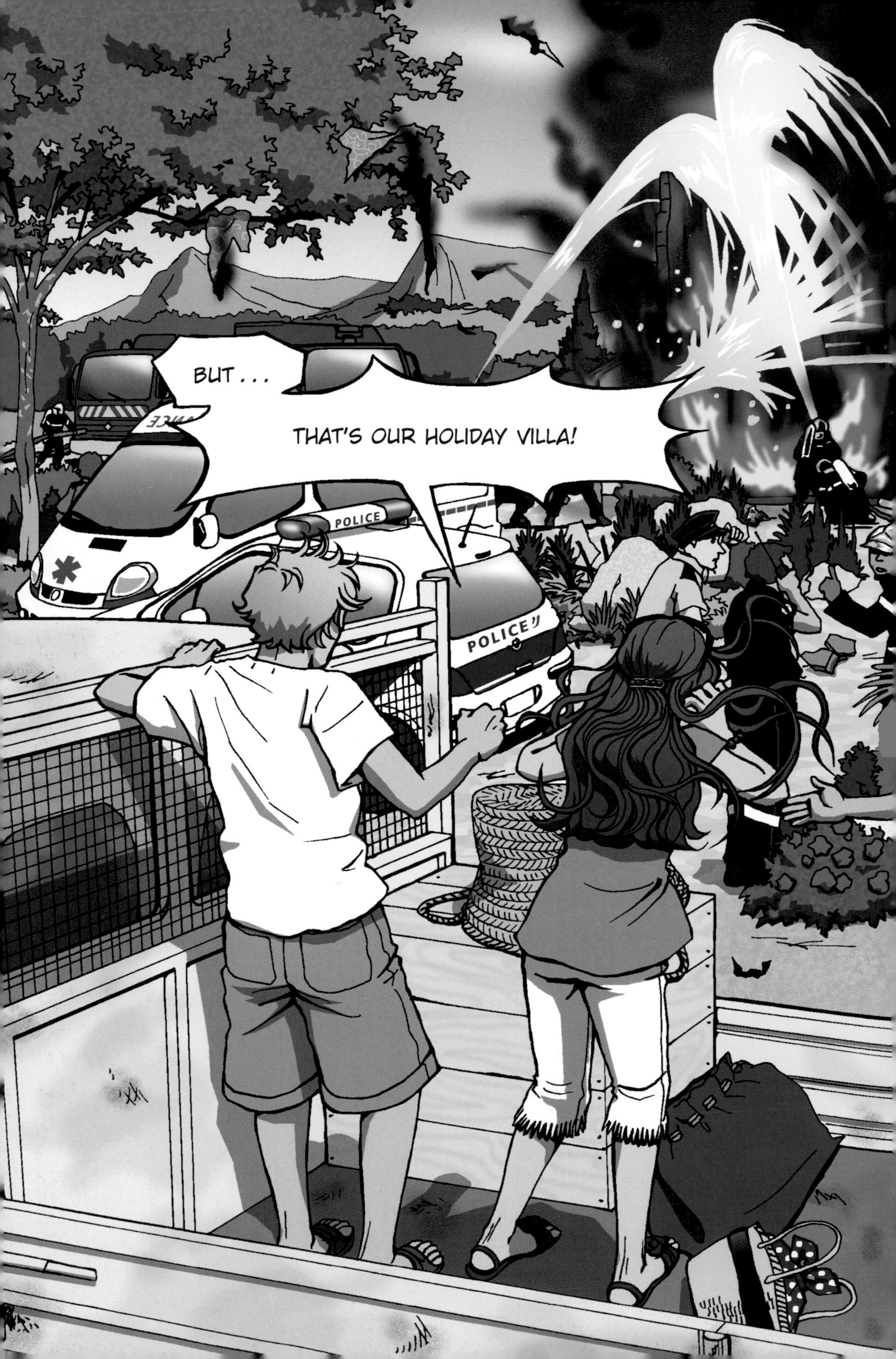
BUT . . .
THAT'S OUR HOLIDAY VILLA!
POLICE
POLICE

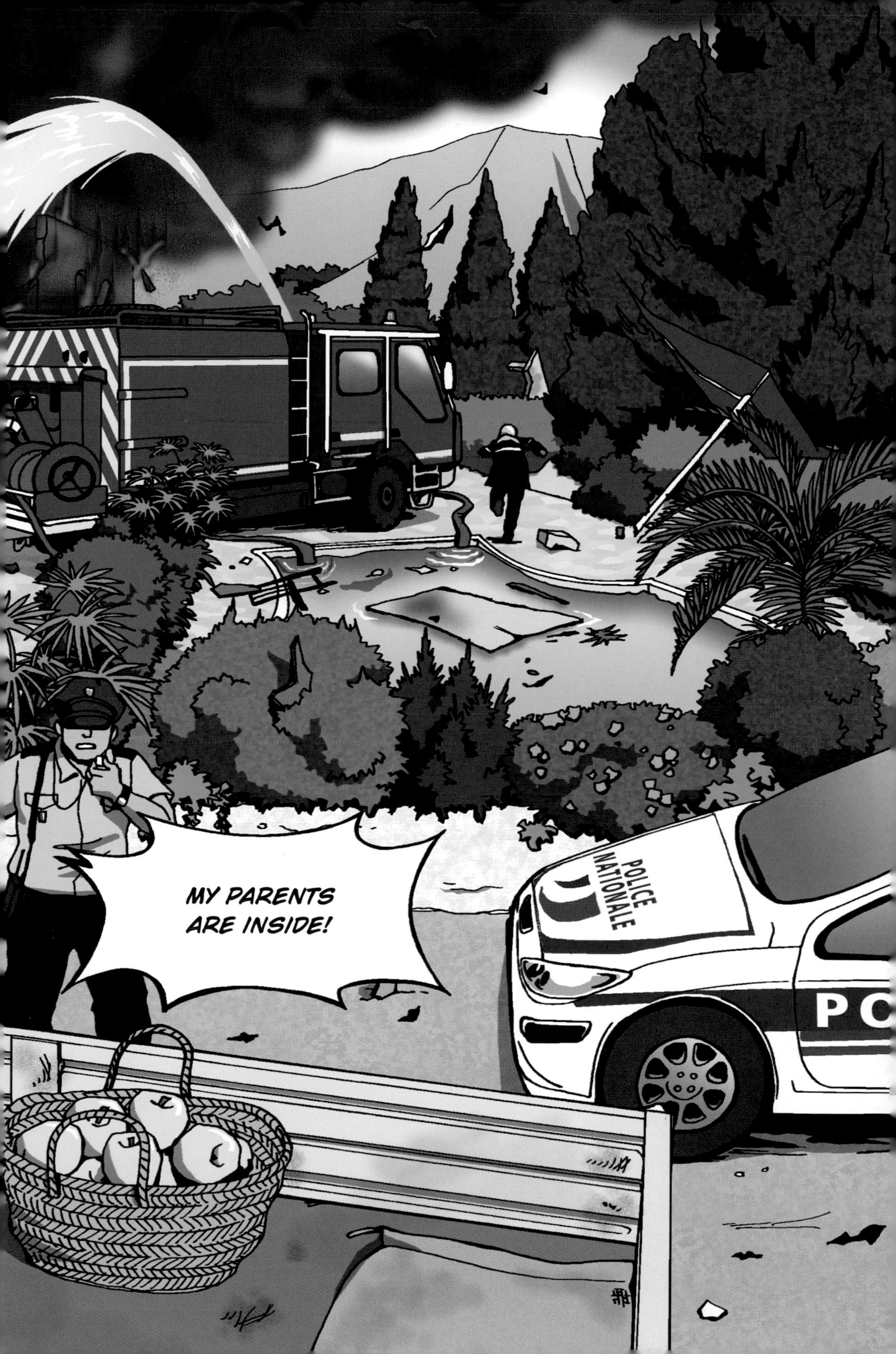
MY PARENTS ARE INSIDE!
POLICE NATIONALE
PO

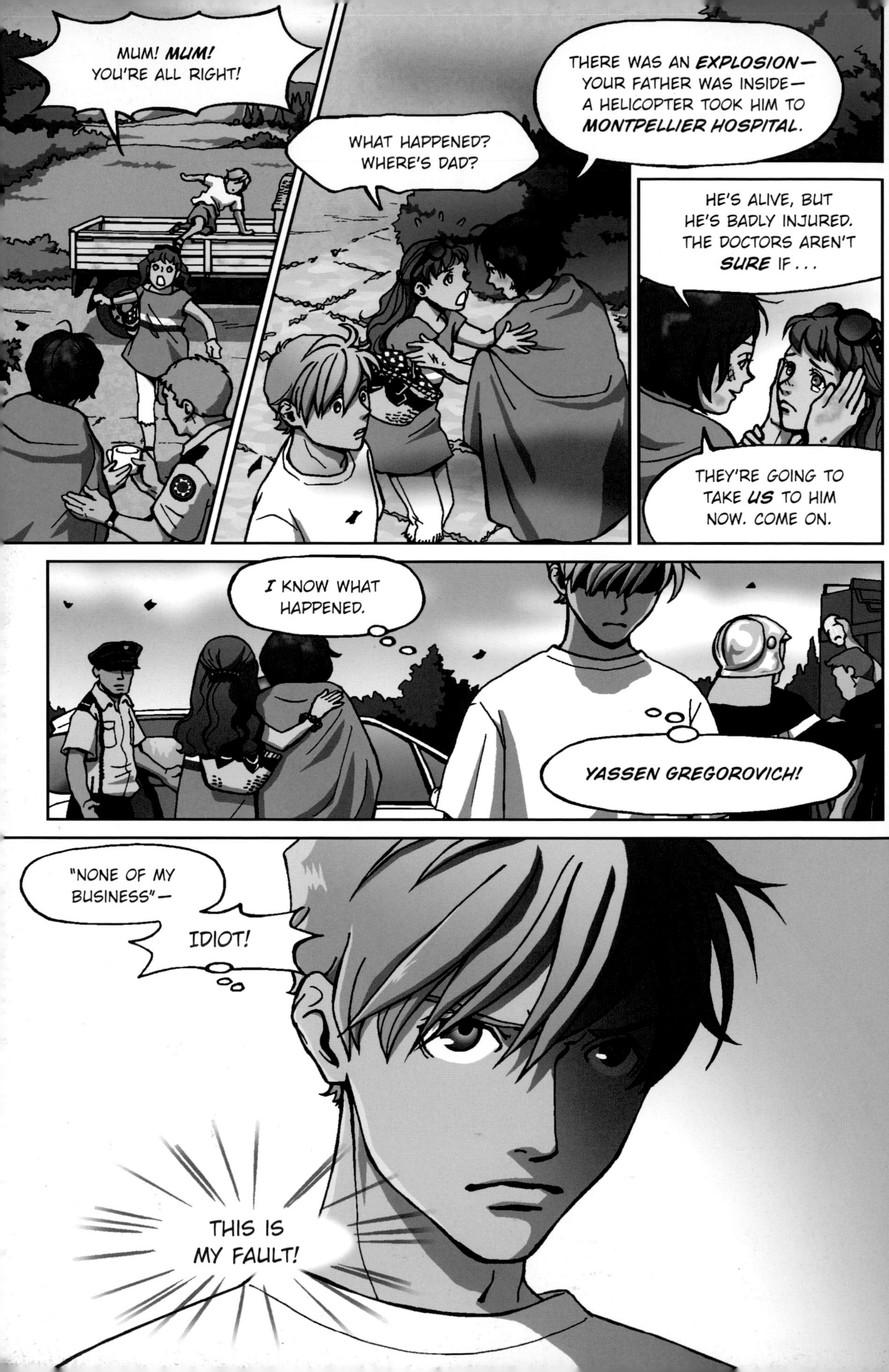
MUM! MUM! YOU'RE ALL RIGHT!
WHAT HAPPENED? WHERE'S DAD?
THERE WAS AN EXPLOSION— YOUR FATHER WAS INSIDE— A HELICOPTER TOOK HIM TO MONTPELLIER HOSPITAL.
HE'S ALIVE, BUT HE'S BADLY INJURED. THE DOCTORS AREN'T SURE IF . . .
THEY'RE GOING TO TAKE US TO HIM NOW. COME ON.
I KNOW WHAT HAPPENED.
YASSEN GREGOROVICH!
"NONE OF MY BUSINESS"—
IDIOT!
THIS IS MY FAULT!

Text and illustrations copyright © 2012 by Walker Books Ltd.
Based on the original novel *Eagle Strike,*
copyright © 2003 by Stormbreaker Productions Ltd.
Trademarks Alex Rider™, Boy with Torch Logo™,
AR Logo™ © 2003 Stormbreaker Productions Ltd.

Adapted by Antony Johnston
Inks by Yuzuru Takasaki
Colors by Kanako Damerum

First U.S. edition 2017

Library of Congress Catalog Card Number 2017947996
ISBN 978-0-7636-9256-8

20 21 22 APS 10 9 8 7 6 5 4 3

Printed in Humen, Dongguan, China

This book was typeset in WildWords and Serpentine Bold.

Candlewick Press
99 Dover Street
Somerville, Massachusetts 02144

visit us at www.candlewick.com

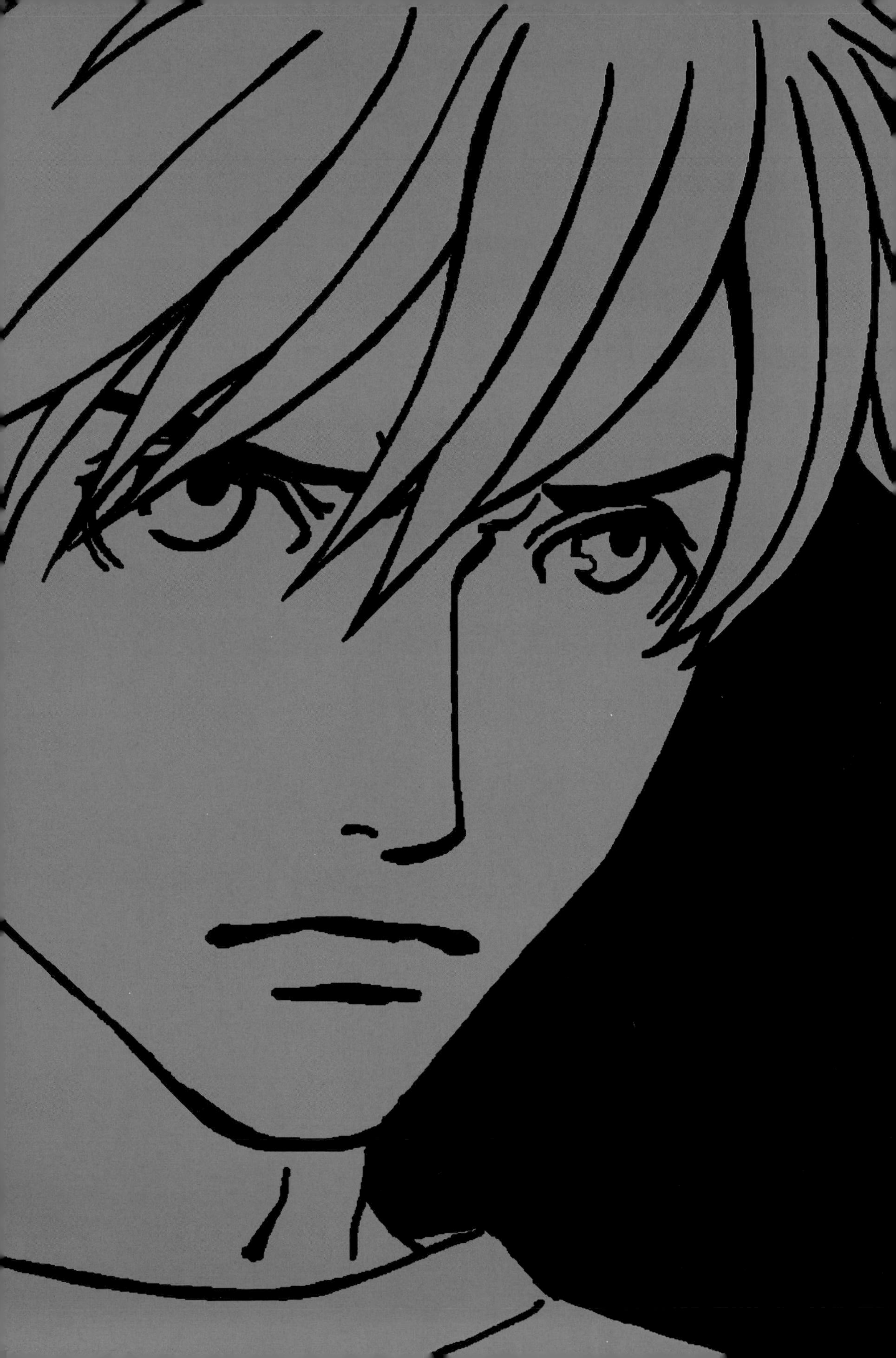

ALEX RIDER

ACTION
ADRENALINE
ADVENTURE

EAGLE STRIKE
THE GRAPHIC NOVEL

ANTHONY HOROWITZ

ANTONY JOHNSTON • KANAKO • YUZURU

CANDLEWICK PRESS

COMMENT?

THERE'S A BIG WHITE YACHT AT THE JETTY IN TOWN. YOU CAN'T MISS IT.

EXCUSEZ-MOI. I KNOW WHO DID THIS.

ON BOARD IS A MAN NAMED YASSEN GREGOROVICH. YOU MUST ARREST HIM BEFORE HE CAN ESCAPE.

AH...

WAIT HERE, PLEASE.

THEY HAVE TO BELIEVE ME. ALL THEY NEED TO DO IS CHECK OUT THE YACHT.

HELLO,

WHAT'S THAT?

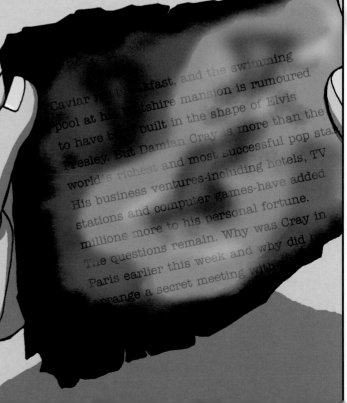

Caviar for breakfast, and the swimming pool at his Wiltshire mansion is rumoured to have been built in the shape of Elvis Presley. But Damian Cray is more than the world's richest and most successful pop star. His business ventures—including hotels, TV stations and computer games—have added millions more to his personal fortune. The questions remain. Why was Cray in Paris earlier this week and why did he arrange a secret meeting with

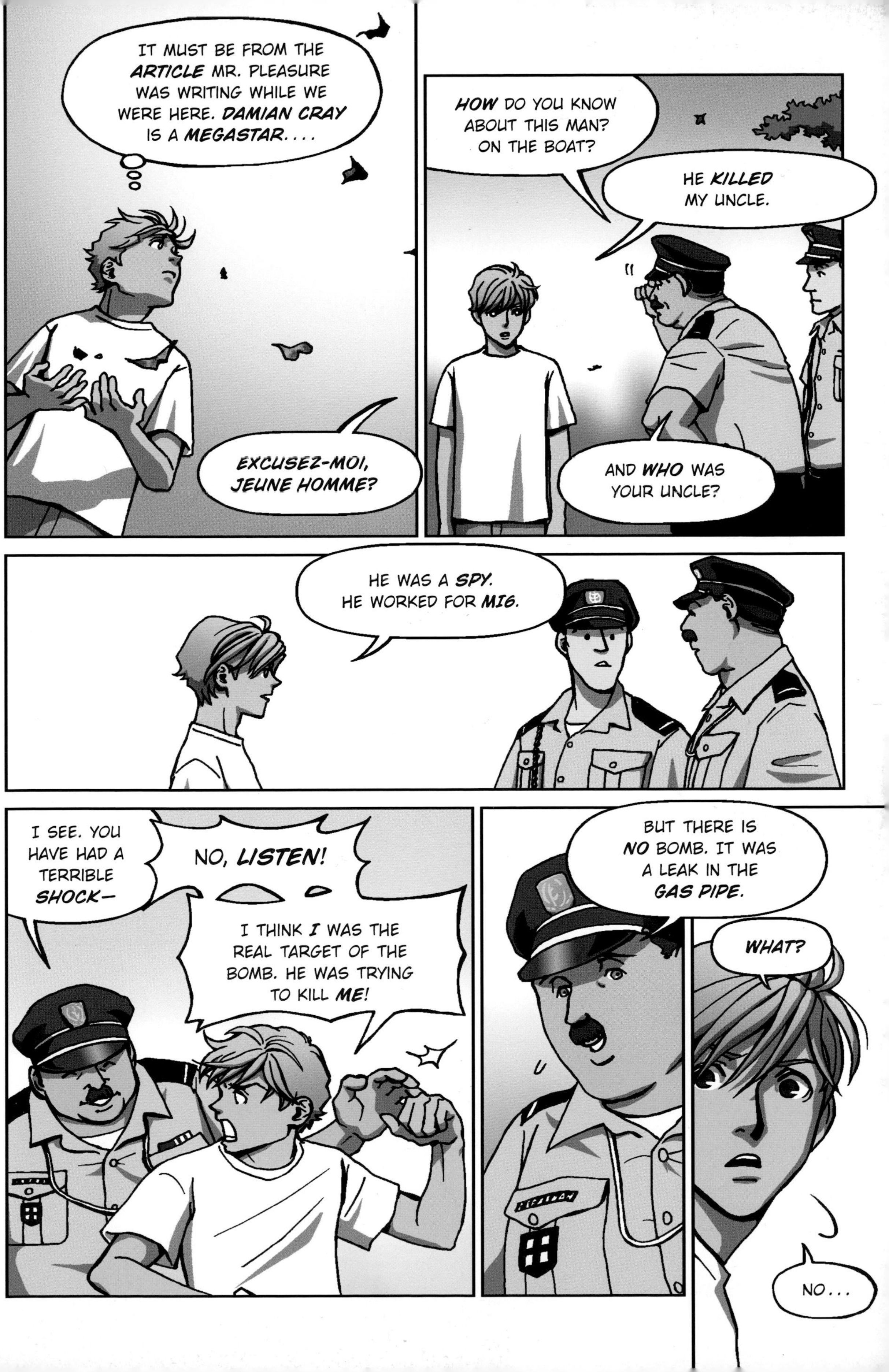
IT MUST BE FROM THE ARTICLE MR. PLEASURE WAS WRITING WHILE WE WERE HERE. DAMIAN CRAY IS A MEGASTAR. . . .
EXCUSEZ-MOI, JEUNE HOMME?
HOW DO YOU KNOW ABOUT THIS MAN? ON THE BOAT?
HE KILLED MY UNCLE.
AND WHO WAS YOUR UNCLE?
HE WAS A SPY. HE WORKED FOR MI6.
I SEE. YOU HAVE HAD A TERRIBLE SHOCK—
NO, LISTEN!
I THINK I WAS THE REAL TARGET OF THE BOMB. HE WAS TRYING TO KILL ME!
BUT THERE IS NO BOMB. IT WAS A LEAK IN THE GAS PIPE.
WHAT?
NO . . .

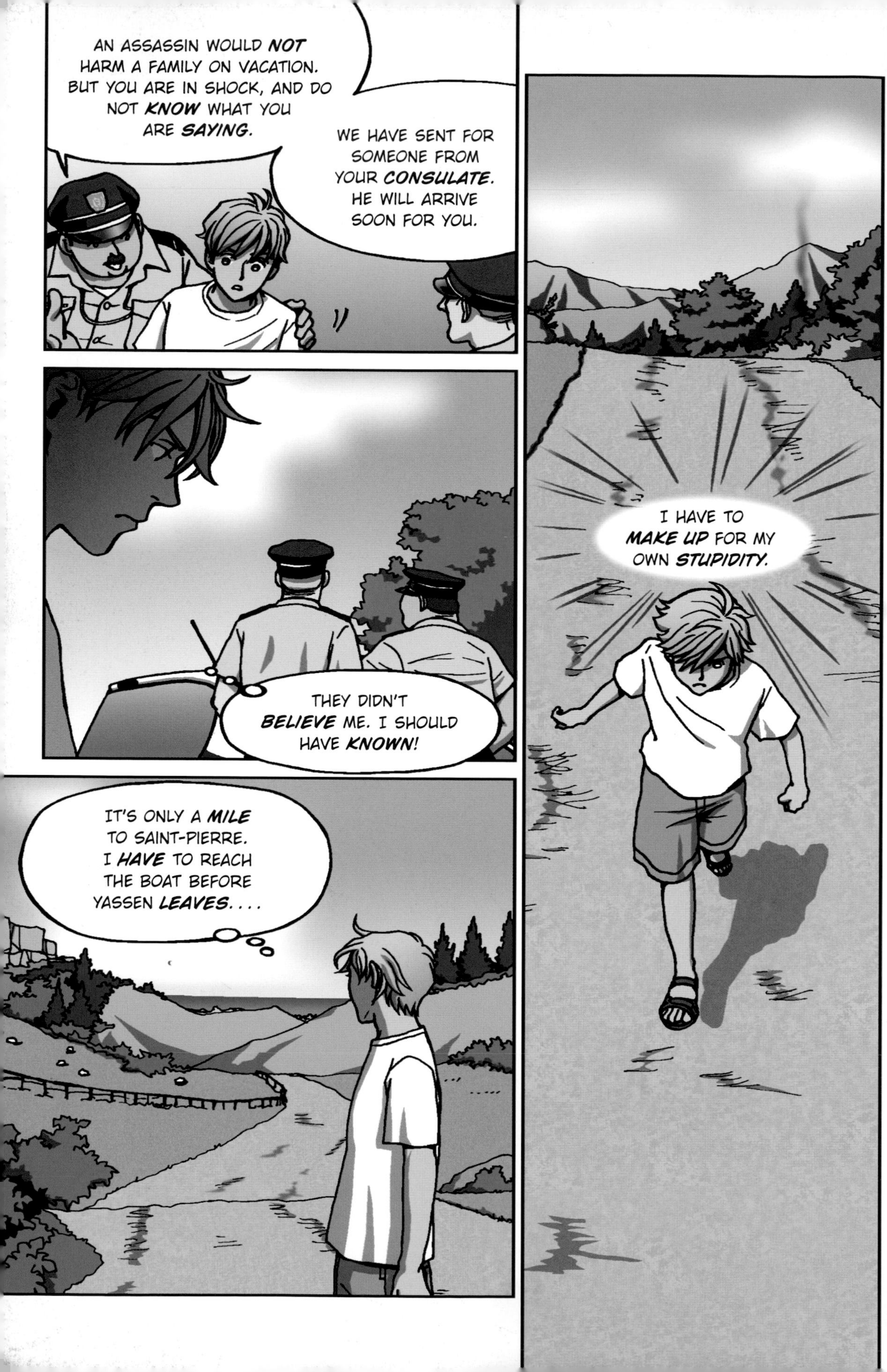
AN ASSASSIN WOULD NOT HARM A FAMILY ON VACATION. BUT YOU ARE IN SHOCK, AND DO NOT KNOW WHAT YOU ARE SAYING.
WE HAVE SENT FOR SOMEONE FROM YOUR CONSULATE. HE WILL ARRIVE SOON FOR YOU.
THEY DIDN'T BELIEVE ME. I SHOULD HAVE KNOWN!
IT'S ONLY A MILE TO SAINT-PIERRE. I HAVE TO REACH THE BOAT BEFORE YASSEN LEAVES. . . .
I HAVE TO MAKE UP FOR MY OWN STUPIDITY.

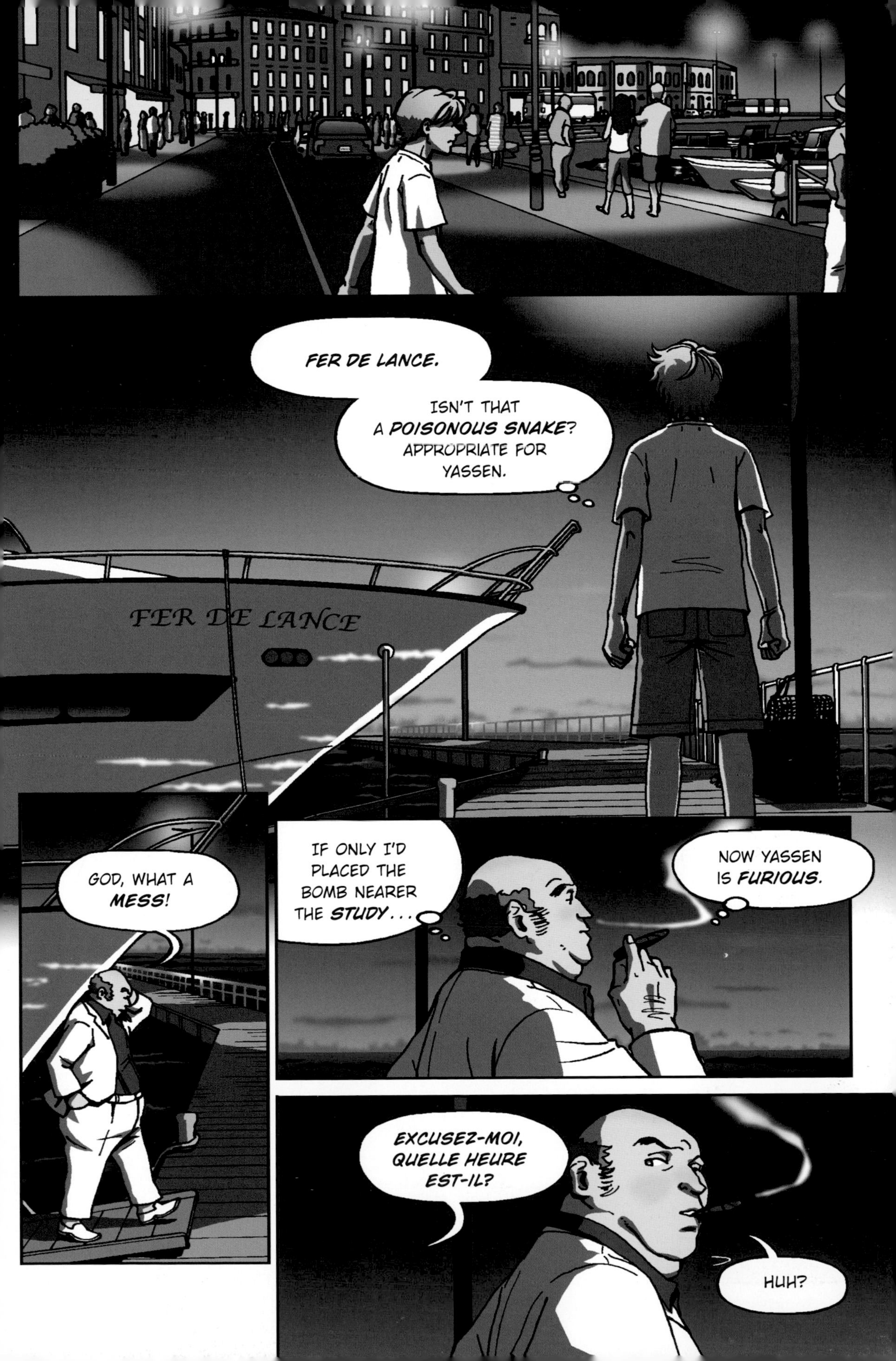
FER DE LANCE.
ISN'T THAT A POISONOUS SNAKE? APPROPRIATE FOR YASSEN.
FER DE LANCE
GOD, WHAT A MESS!
IF ONLY I'D PLACED THE BOMB NEARER THE STUDY . . .
NOW YASSEN IS FURIOUS.
EXCUSEZ-MOI, QUELLE HEURE EST-IL?
HUH?

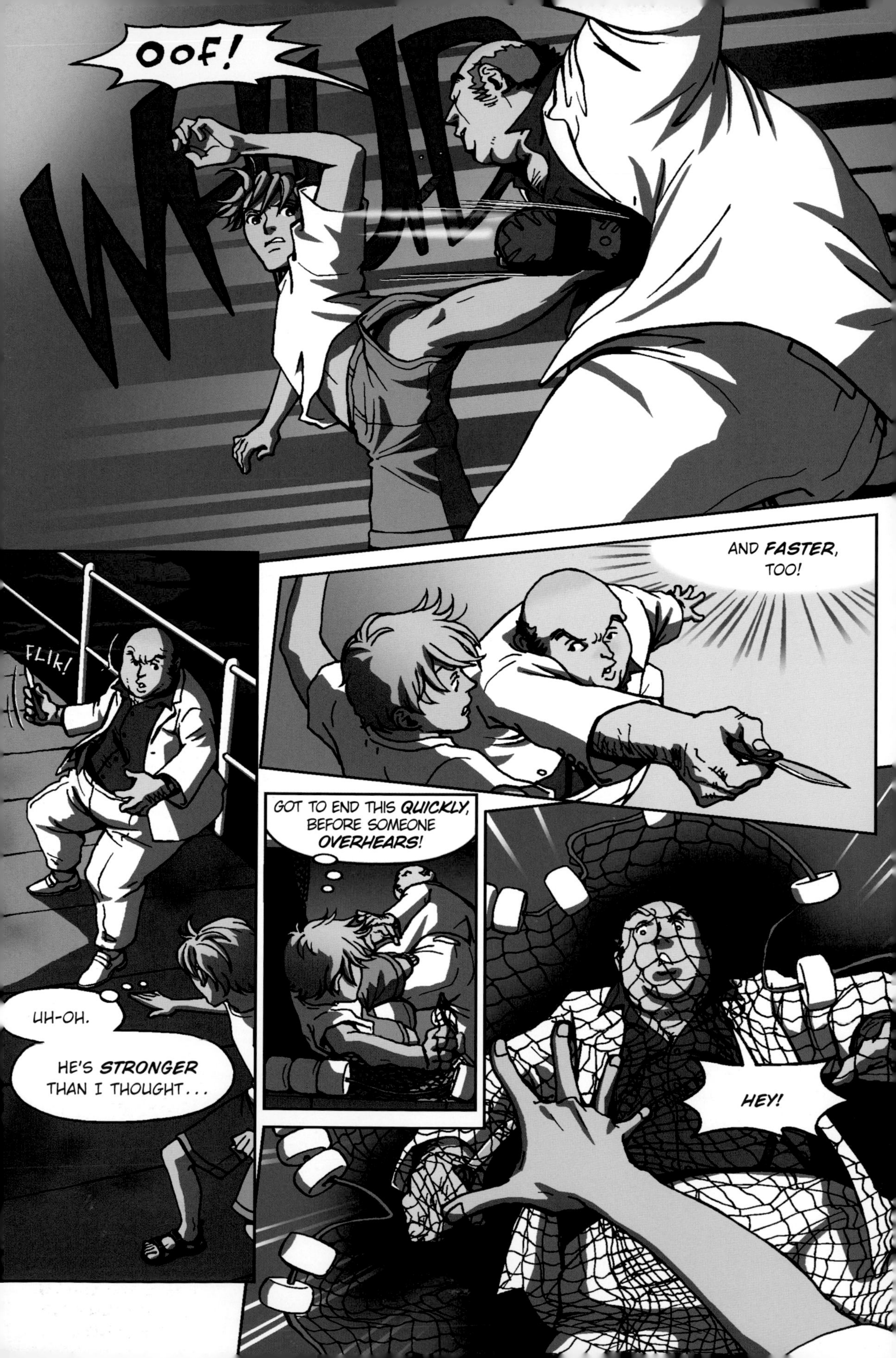
OOF!
WHUD
AND FASTER, TOO!
FLIK!
UH-OH.
HE'S STRONGER THAN I THOUGHT...
GOT TO END THIS QUICKLY, BEFORE SOMEONE OVERHEARS!
HEY!

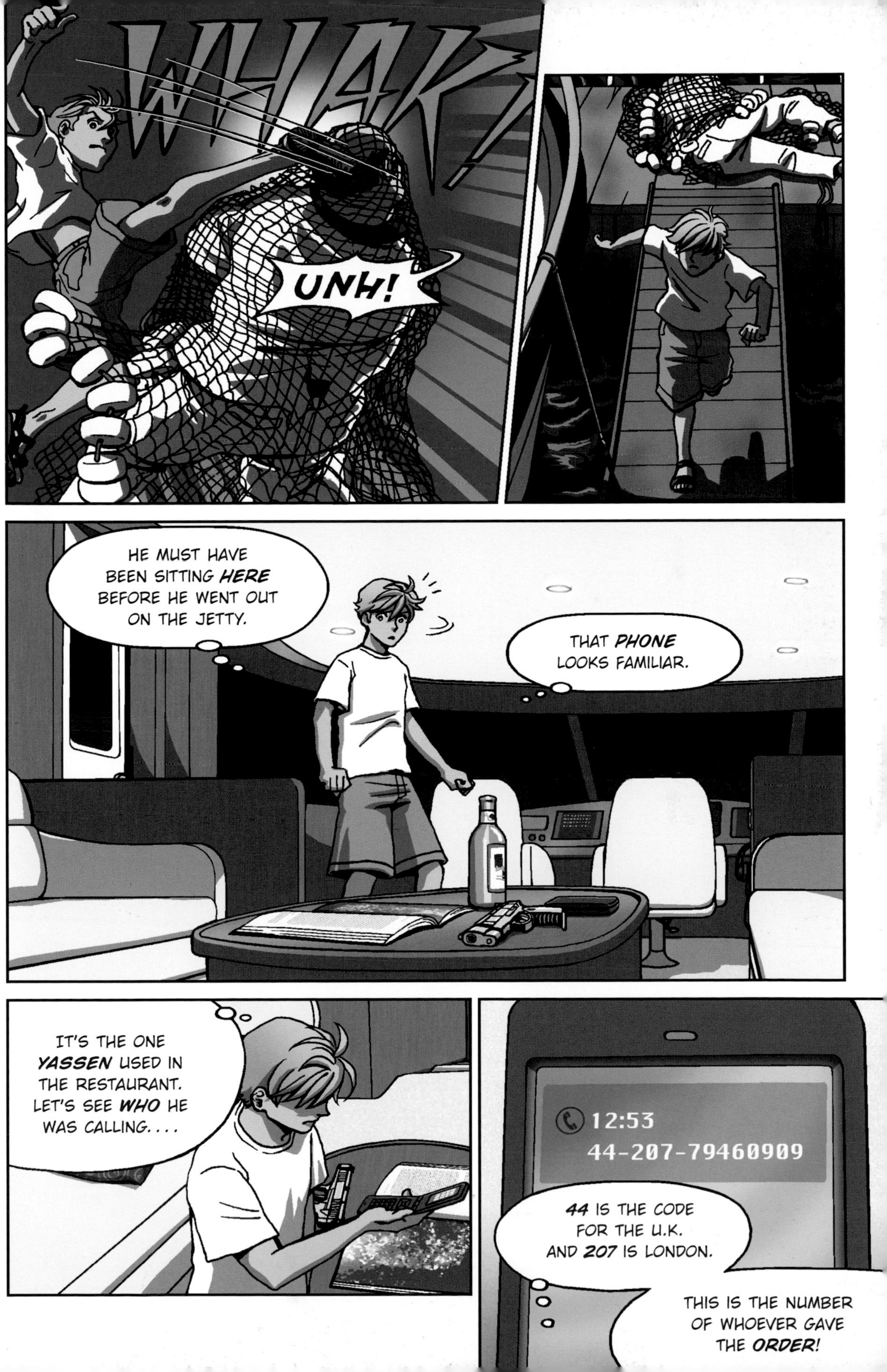
WHAK!
UNH!
HE MUST HAVE BEEN SITTING *HERE* BEFORE HE WENT OUT ON THE JETTY.
THAT *PHONE* LOOKS FAMILIAR.
IT'S THE ONE *YASSEN* USED IN THE RESTAURANT. LET'S SEE *WHO* HE WAS CALLING. . . .
12:53
44-207-79460909
44 IS THE CODE FOR THE U.K. AND *207* IS LONDON.
THIS IS THE NUMBER OF WHOEVER GAVE THE *ORDER!*

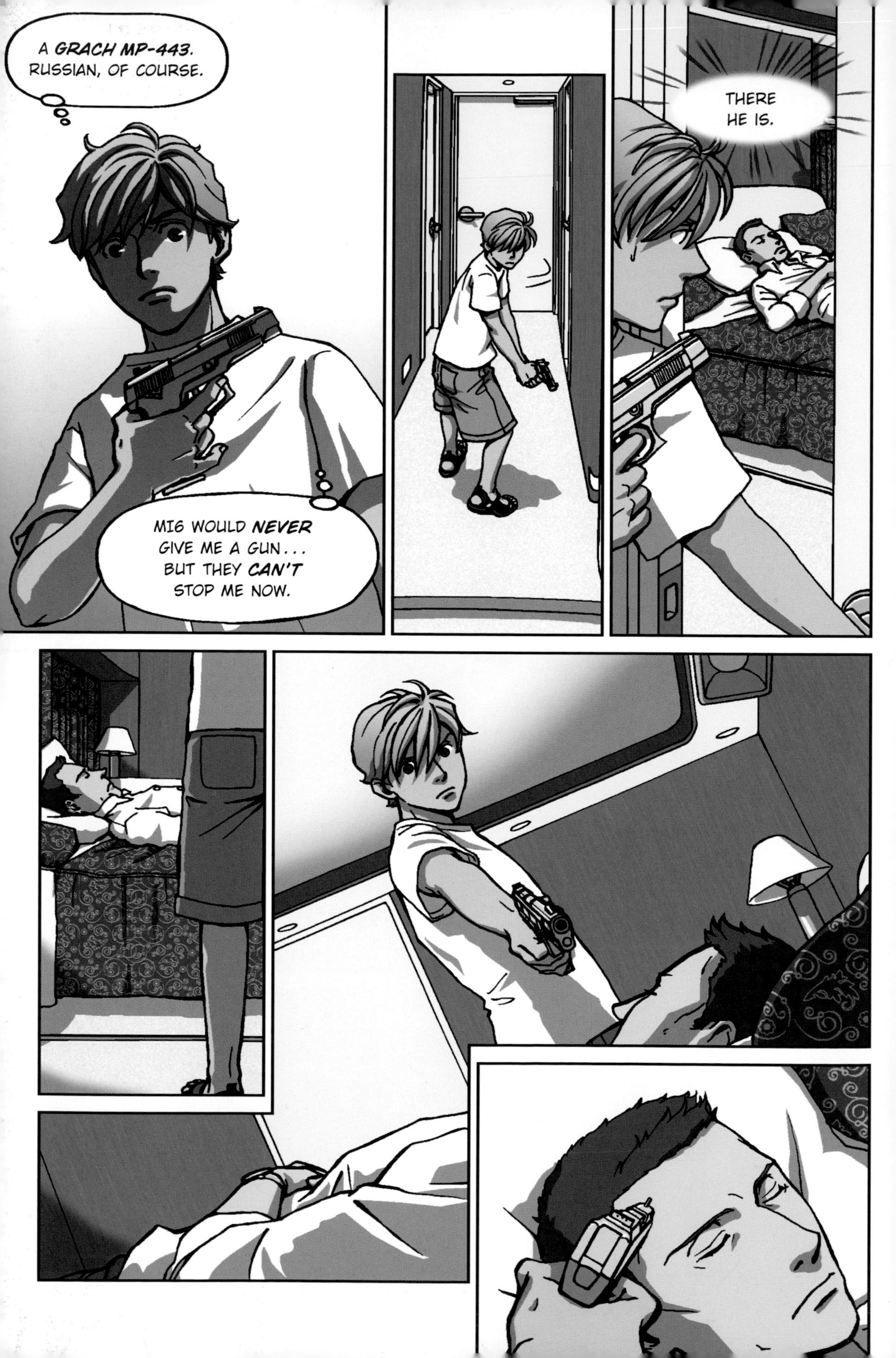
A GRACH MP-443.
RUSSIAN, OF COURSE.
MI6 WOULD NEVER GIVE ME A GUN . . . BUT THEY CAN'T STOP ME NOW.
THERE HE IS.

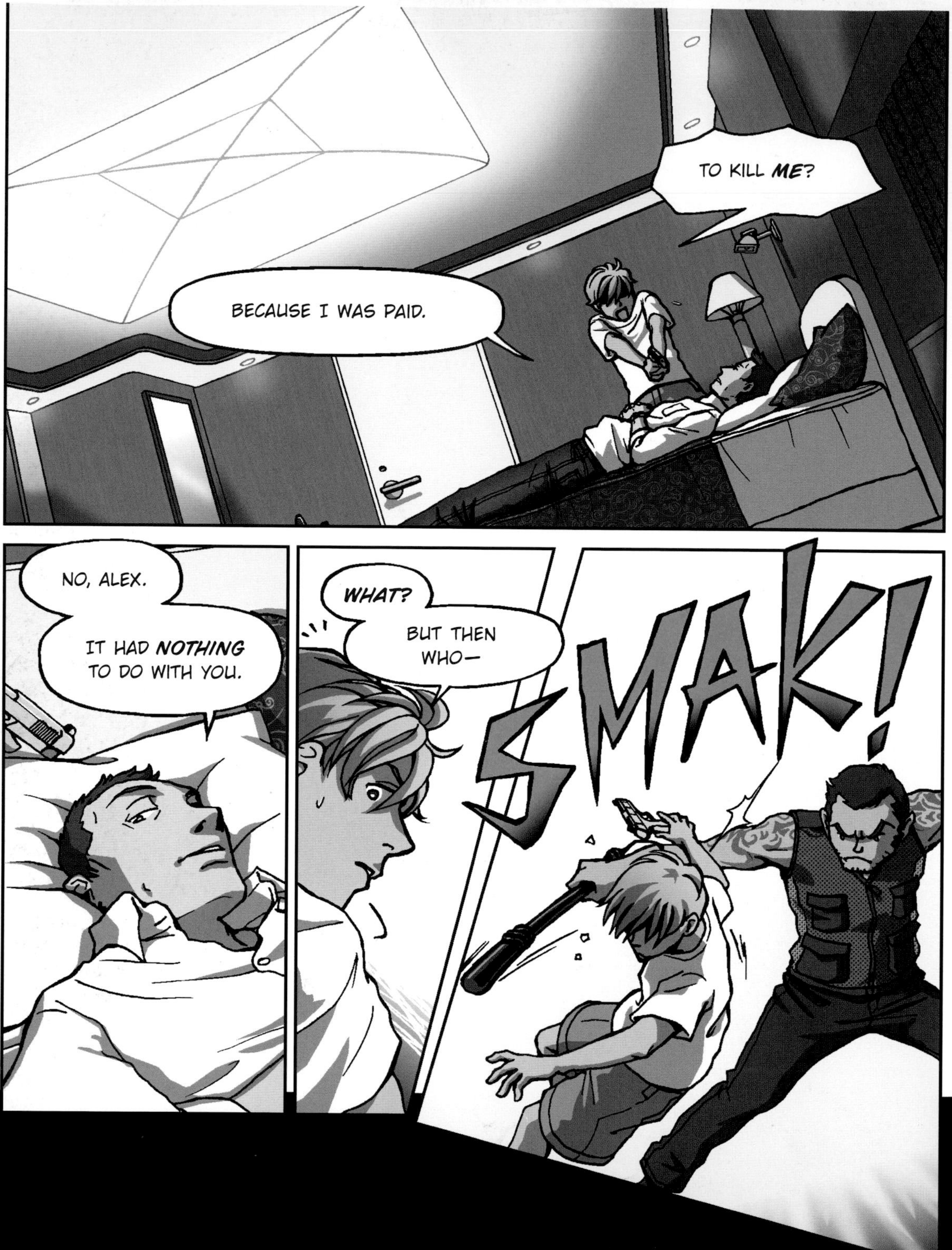
TO KILL ***ME***?
BECAUSE I WAS PAID.
NO, ALEX.
IT HAD ***NOTHING*** TO DO WITH YOU.
WHAT?
BUT THEN WHO—
SMAK!

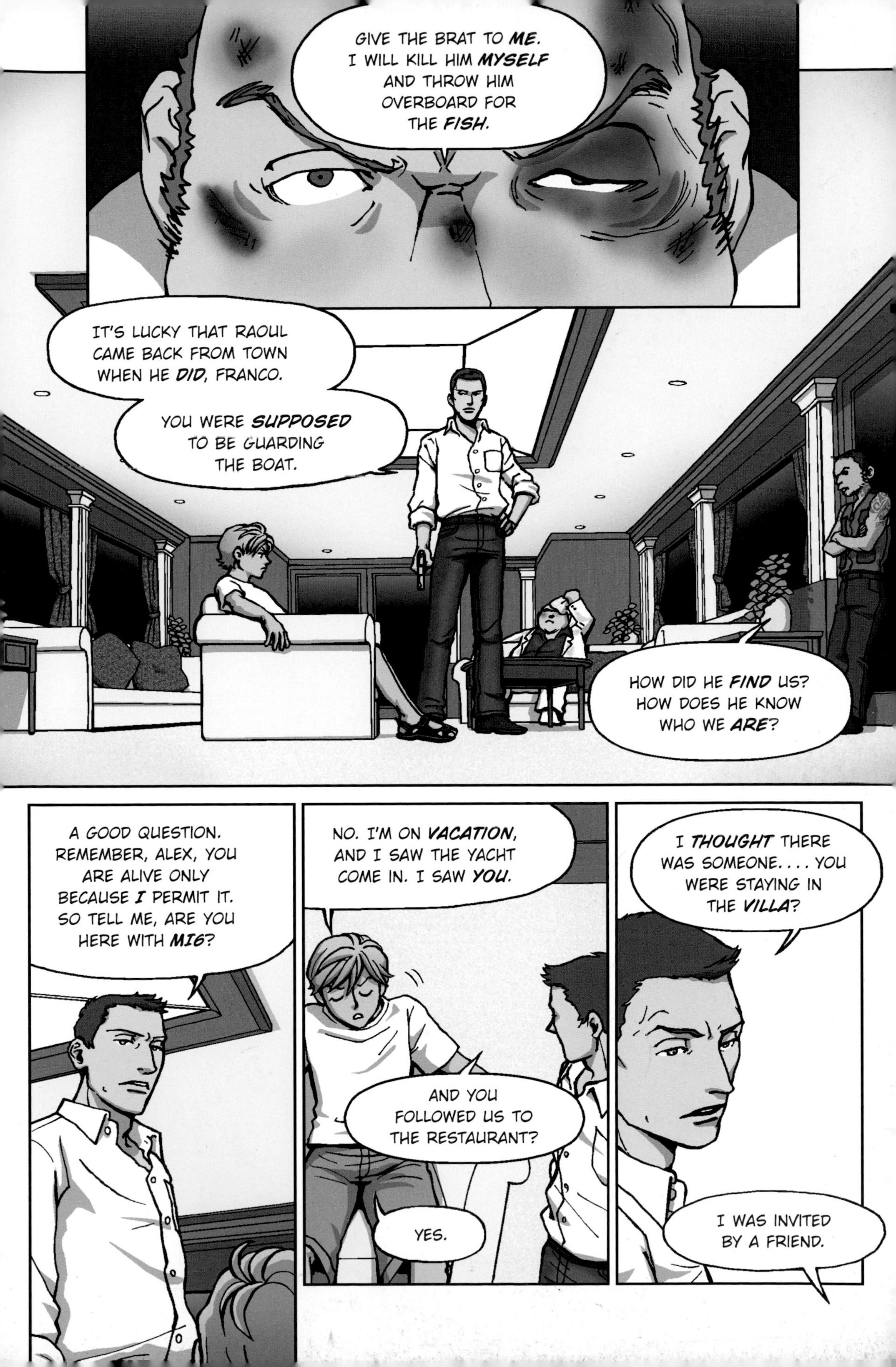
GIVE THE BRAT TO ME. I WILL KILL HIM MYSELF AND THROW HIM OVERBOARD FOR THE FISH.
IT'S LUCKY THAT RAOUL CAME BACK FROM TOWN WHEN HE DID, FRANCO.
YOU WERE SUPPOSED TO BE GUARDING THE BOAT.
HOW DID HE FIND US? HOW DOES HE KNOW WHO WE ARE?
A GOOD QUESTION. REMEMBER, ALEX, YOU ARE ALIVE ONLY BECAUSE I PERMIT IT. SO TELL ME, ARE YOU HERE WITH MI6?
NO. I'M ON VACATION, AND I SAW THE YACHT COME IN. I SAW YOU.
AND YOU FOLLOWED US TO THE RESTAURANT?
YES.
I THOUGHT THERE WAS SOMEONE. . . . YOU WERE STAYING IN THE VILLA?
I WAS INVITED BY A FRIEND.

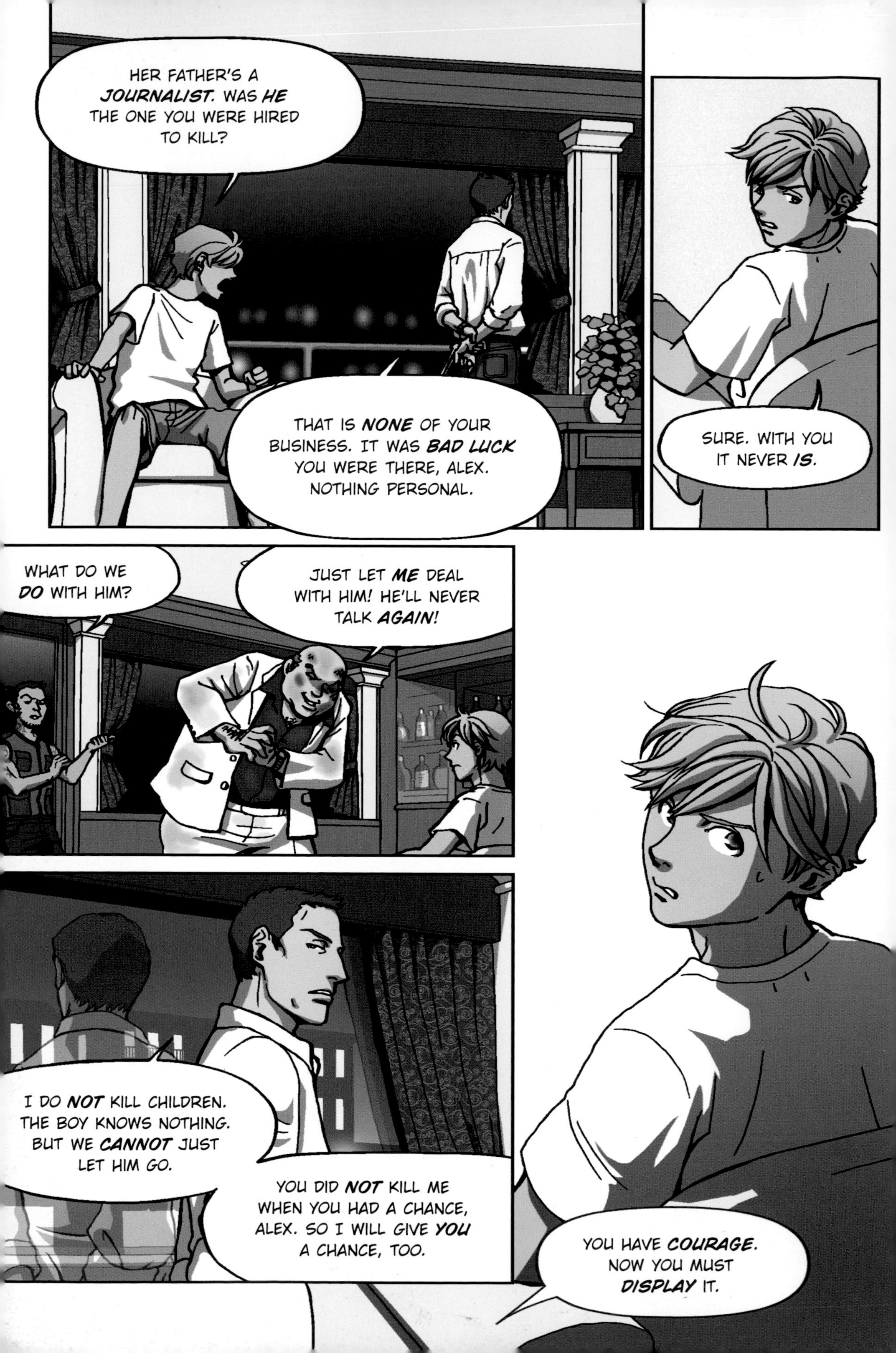
HER FATHER'S A JOURNALIST. WAS HE THE ONE YOU WERE HIRED TO KILL?
THAT IS NONE OF YOUR BUSINESS. IT WAS BAD LUCK YOU WERE THERE, ALEX. NOTHING PERSONAL.
SURE. WITH YOU IT NEVER IS.
WHAT DO WE DO WITH HIM?
JUST LET ME DEAL WITH HIM! HE'LL NEVER TALK AGAIN!
I DO NOT KILL CHILDREN. THE BOY KNOWS NOTHING. BUT WE CANNOT JUST LET HIM GO.
YOU DID NOT KILL ME WHEN YOU HAD A CHANCE, ALEX. SO I WILL GIVE YOU A CHANCE, TOO.
YOU HAVE COURAGE. NOW YOU MUST DISPLAY IT.

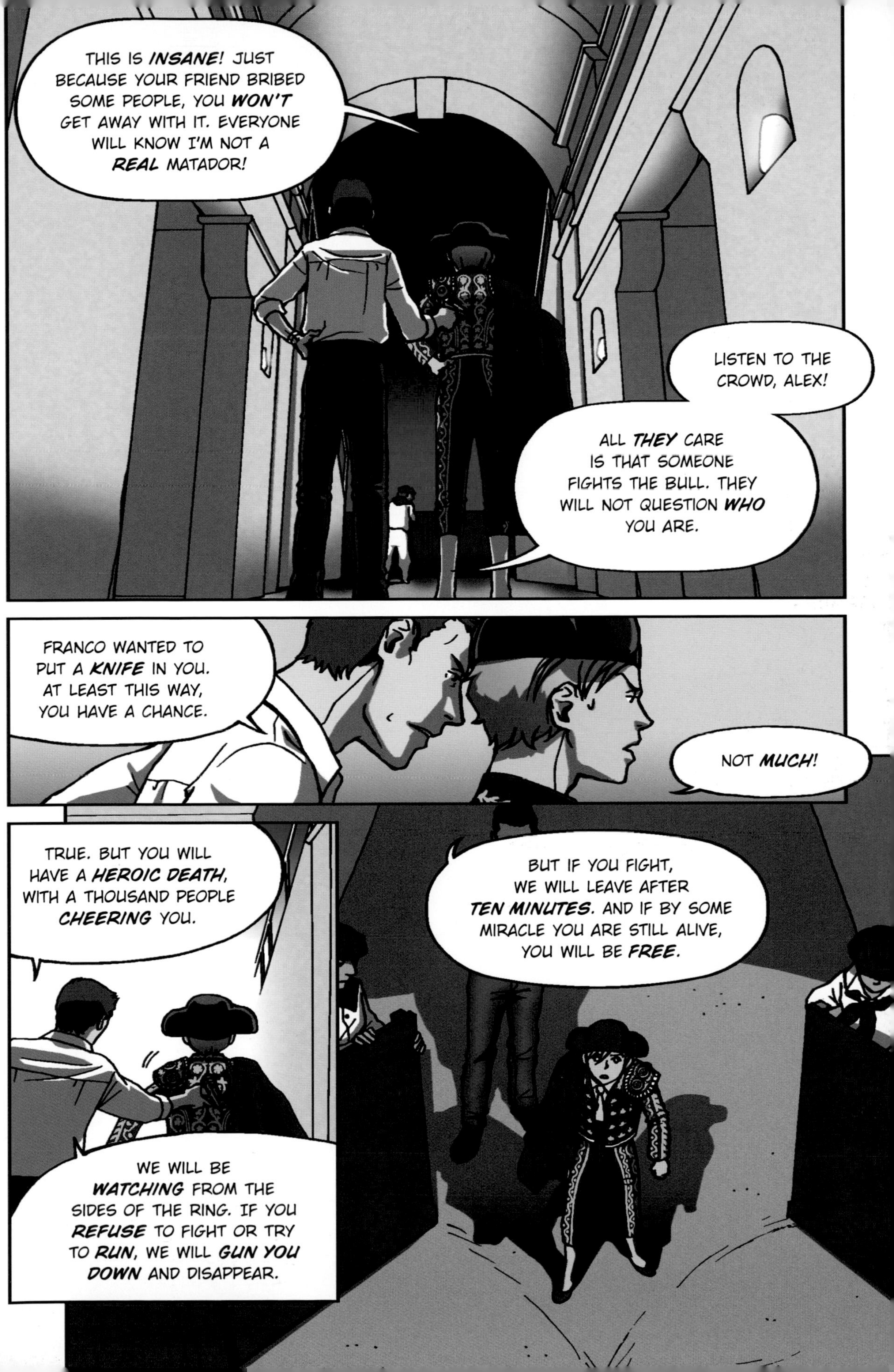
THIS IS *INSANE!* JUST BECAUSE YOUR FRIEND BRIBED SOME PEOPLE, YOU *WON'T* GET AWAY WITH IT. EVERYONE WILL KNOW I'M NOT A *REAL* MATADOR!
LISTEN TO THE CROWD, ALEX!
ALL *THEY* CARE IS THAT SOMEONE FIGHTS THE BULL. THEY WILL NOT QUESTION *WHO* YOU ARE.
FRANCO WANTED TO PUT A *KNIFE* IN YOU. AT LEAST THIS WAY, YOU HAVE A CHANCE.
NOT *MUCH!*
TRUE. BUT YOU WILL HAVE A *HEROIC DEATH*, WITH A THOUSAND PEOPLE *CHEERING* YOU.
WE WILL BE *WATCHING* FROM THE SIDES OF THE RING. IF YOU *REFUSE* TO FIGHT OR TRY TO *RUN*, WE WILL *GUN YOU DOWN* AND DISAPPEAR.
BUT IF YOU FIGHT, WE WILL LEAVE AFTER *TEN MINUTES.* AND IF BY SOME MIRACLE YOU ARE STILL ALIVE, YOU WILL BE *FREE*.

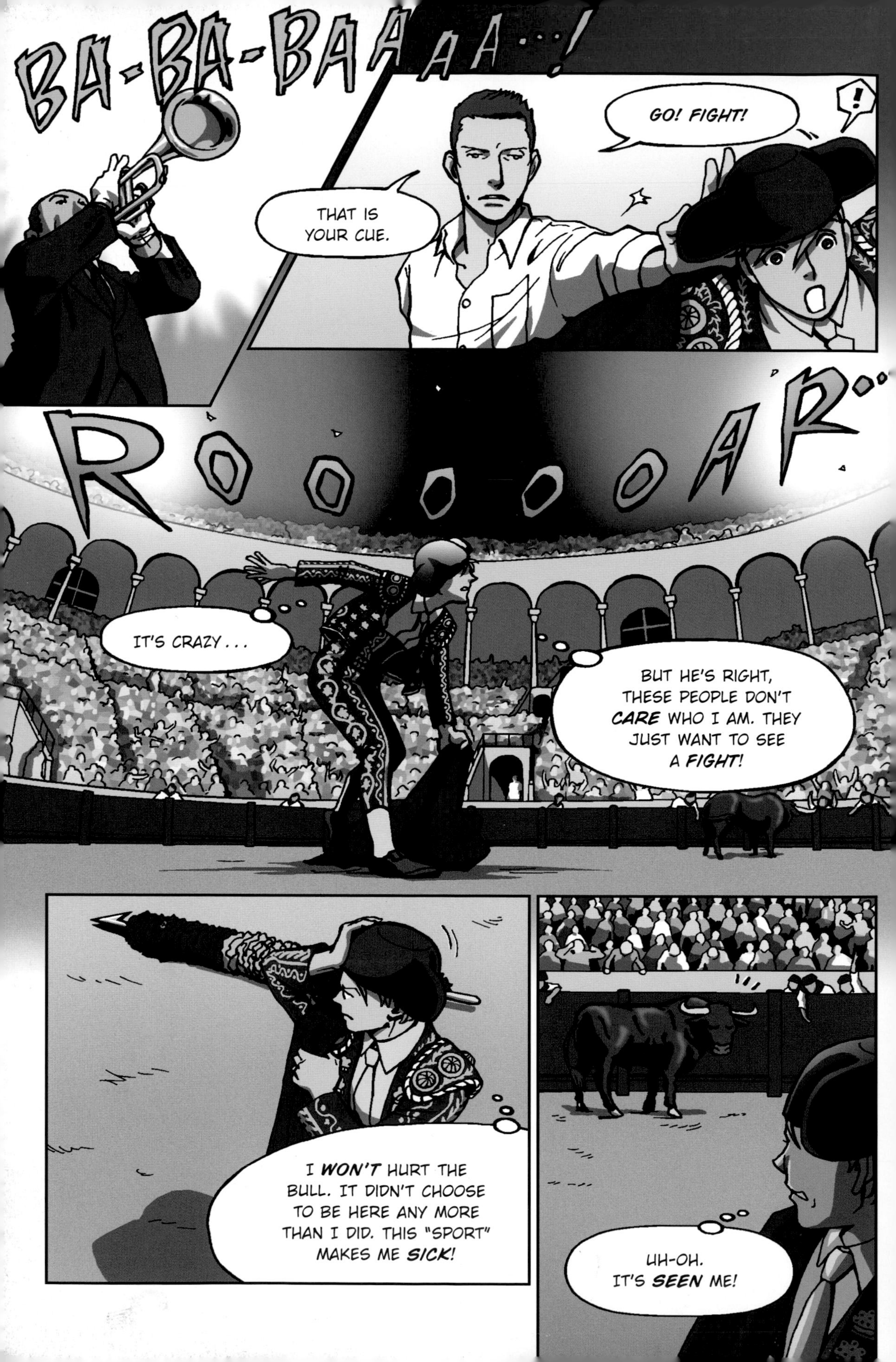
BA-BA-BAAAAA...!
THAT IS YOUR CUE.
GO! FIGHT!
!
ROOOOOAR..
IT'S CRAZY . . .
BUT HE'S RIGHT, THESE PEOPLE DON'T CARE WHO I AM. THEY JUST WANT TO SEE A FIGHT!
I WON'T HURT THE BULL. IT DIDN'T CHOOSE TO BE HERE ANY MORE THAN I DID. THIS "SPORT" MAKES ME SICK!
UH-OH. IT'S SEEN ME!

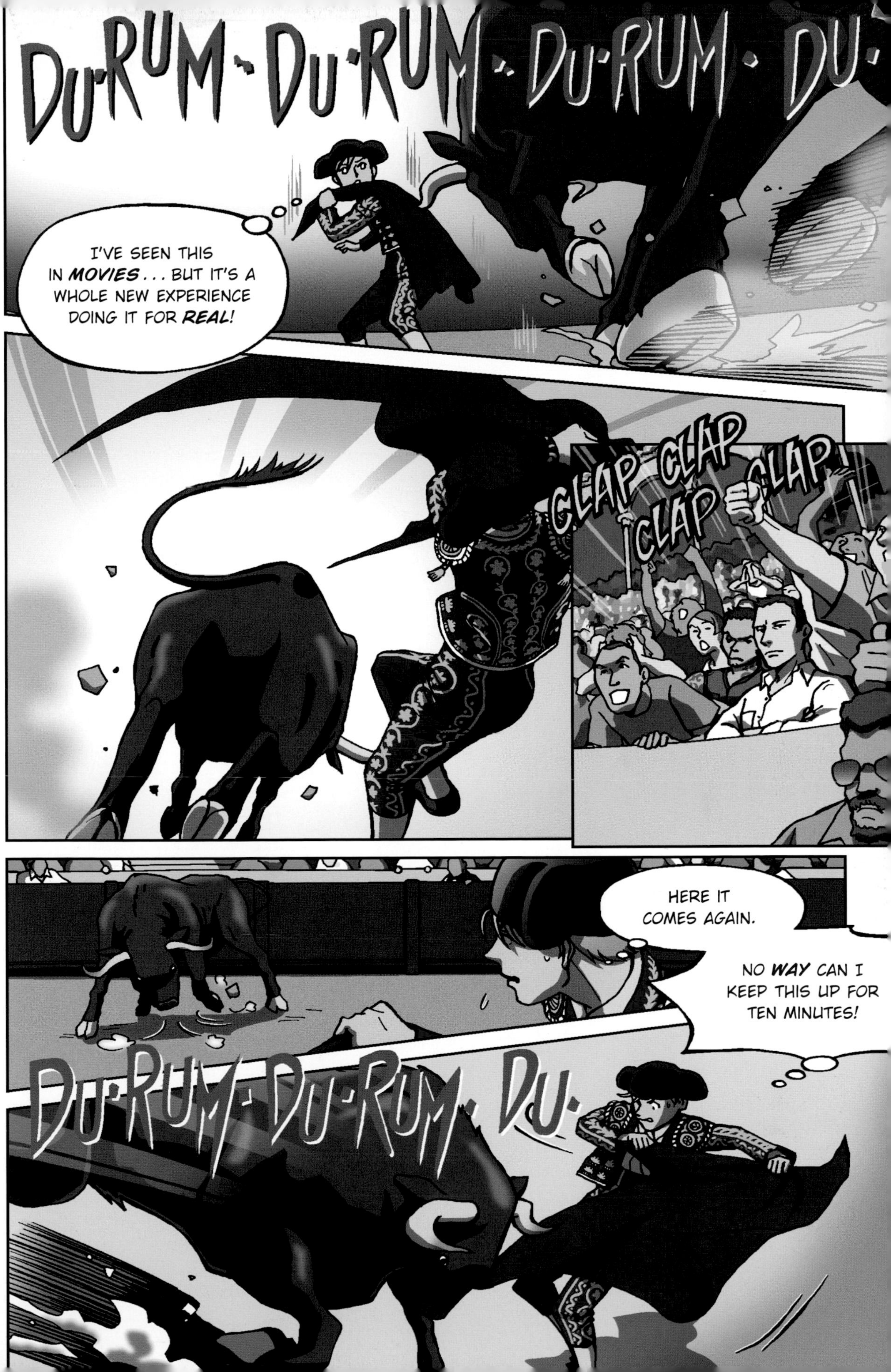
DU-RUM-DU-RUM-DU-RUM-DU-
I'VE SEEN THIS IN MOVIES . . . BUT IT'S A WHOLE NEW EXPERIENCE DOING IT FOR REAL!
CLAP CLAP CLAP CLAP
HERE IT COMES AGAIN.
NO WAY CAN I KEEP THIS UP FOR TEN MINUTES!
DU-RUM-DU-RUM-DU-

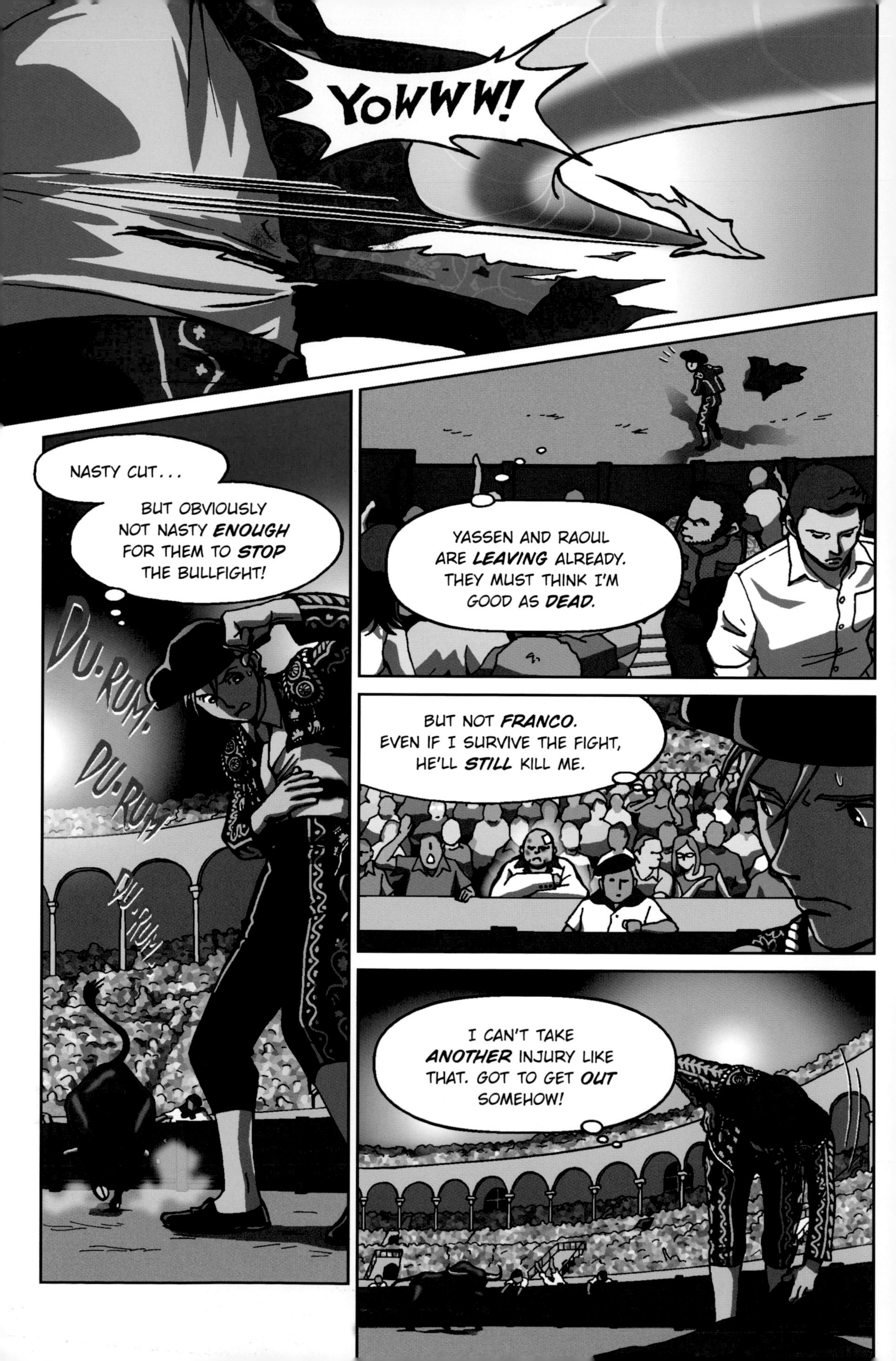
YOWWW!
NASTY CUT . . .
BUT OBVIOUSLY NOT NASTY ENOUGH FOR THEM TO STOP THE BULLFIGHT!
DU-RUM DU-RUM DU-RUM
YASSEN AND RAOUL ARE LEAVING ALREADY. THEY MUST THINK I'M GOOD AS DEAD.
BUT NOT FRANCO. EVEN IF I SURVIVE THE FIGHT, HE'LL STILL KILL ME.
I CAN'T TAKE ANOTHER INJURY LIKE THAT. GOT TO GET OUT SOMEHOW!

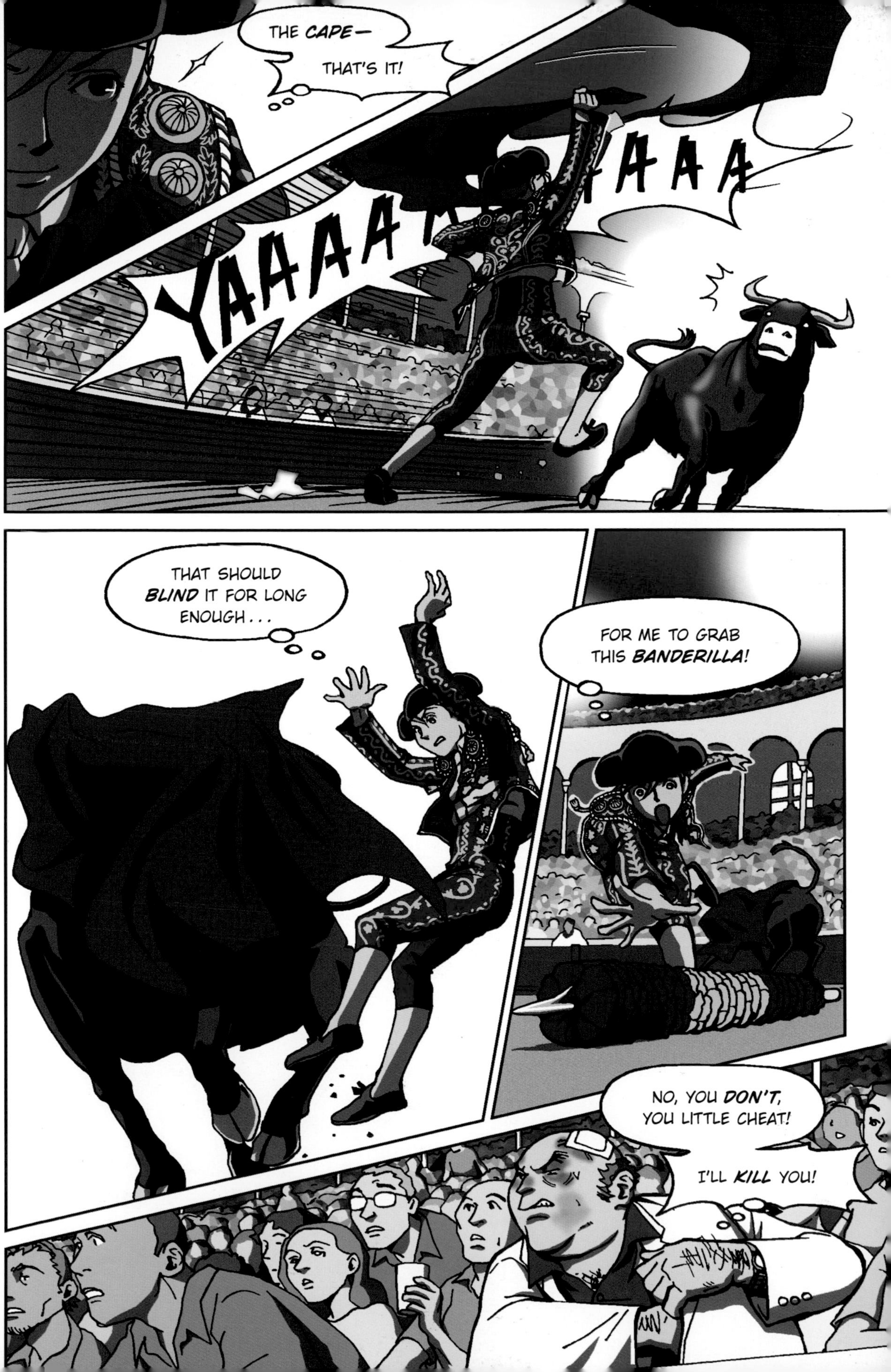
THE CAPE—
THAT'S IT!
YAAAAAAAAA
THAT SHOULD BLIND IT FOR LONG ENOUGH . . .
FOR ME TO GRAB THIS BANDERILLA!
NO, YOU DON'T, YOU LITTLE CHEAT!
I'LL KILL YOU!

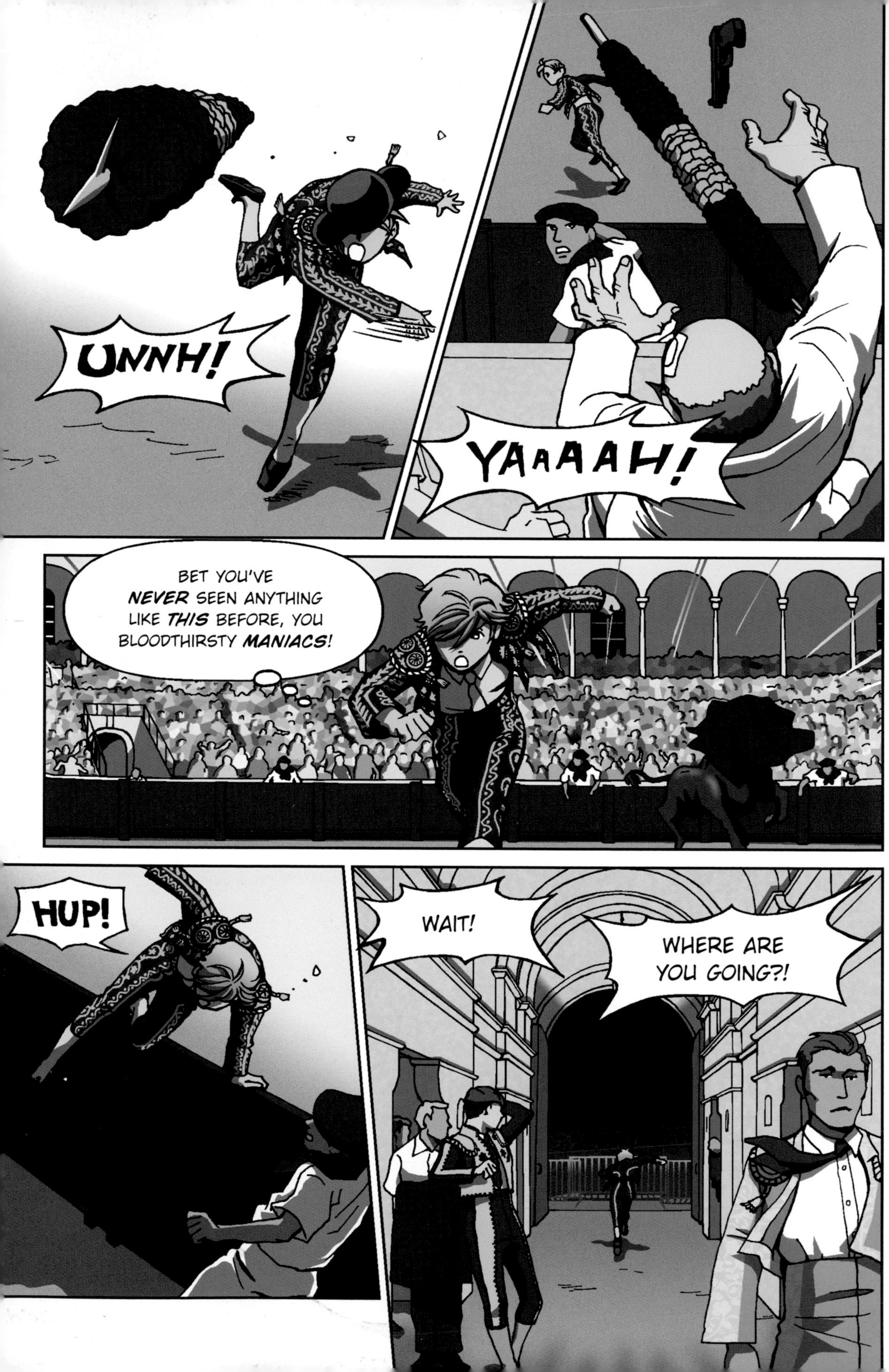
UNNH!
YAAAAH!
BET YOU'VE NEVER SEEN ANYTHING LIKE THIS BEFORE, YOU BLOODTHIRSTY MANIACS!
HUP!
WAIT!
WHERE ARE YOU GOING?!

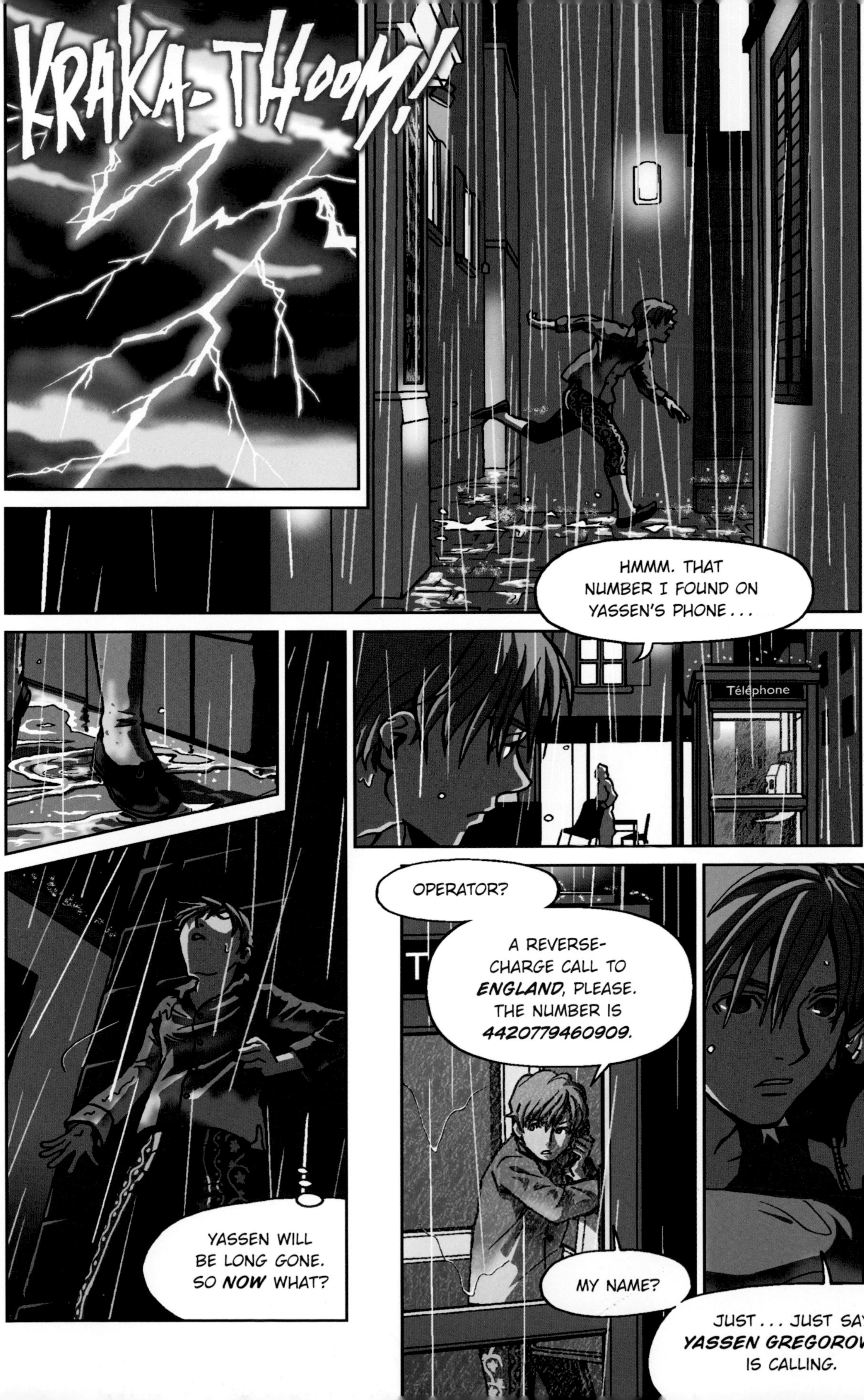
KRAKA-THOOM!!
HMMM. THAT NUMBER I FOUND ON YASSEN'S PHONE . . .
Téléphone
YASSEN WILL BE LONG GONE. SO NOW WHAT?
OPERATOR?
A REVERSE-CHARGE CALL TO ENGLAND, PLEASE. THE NUMBER IS 4420779460909.
MY NAME?
JUST . . . JUST SAY YASSEN GREGOROVICH IS CALLING.

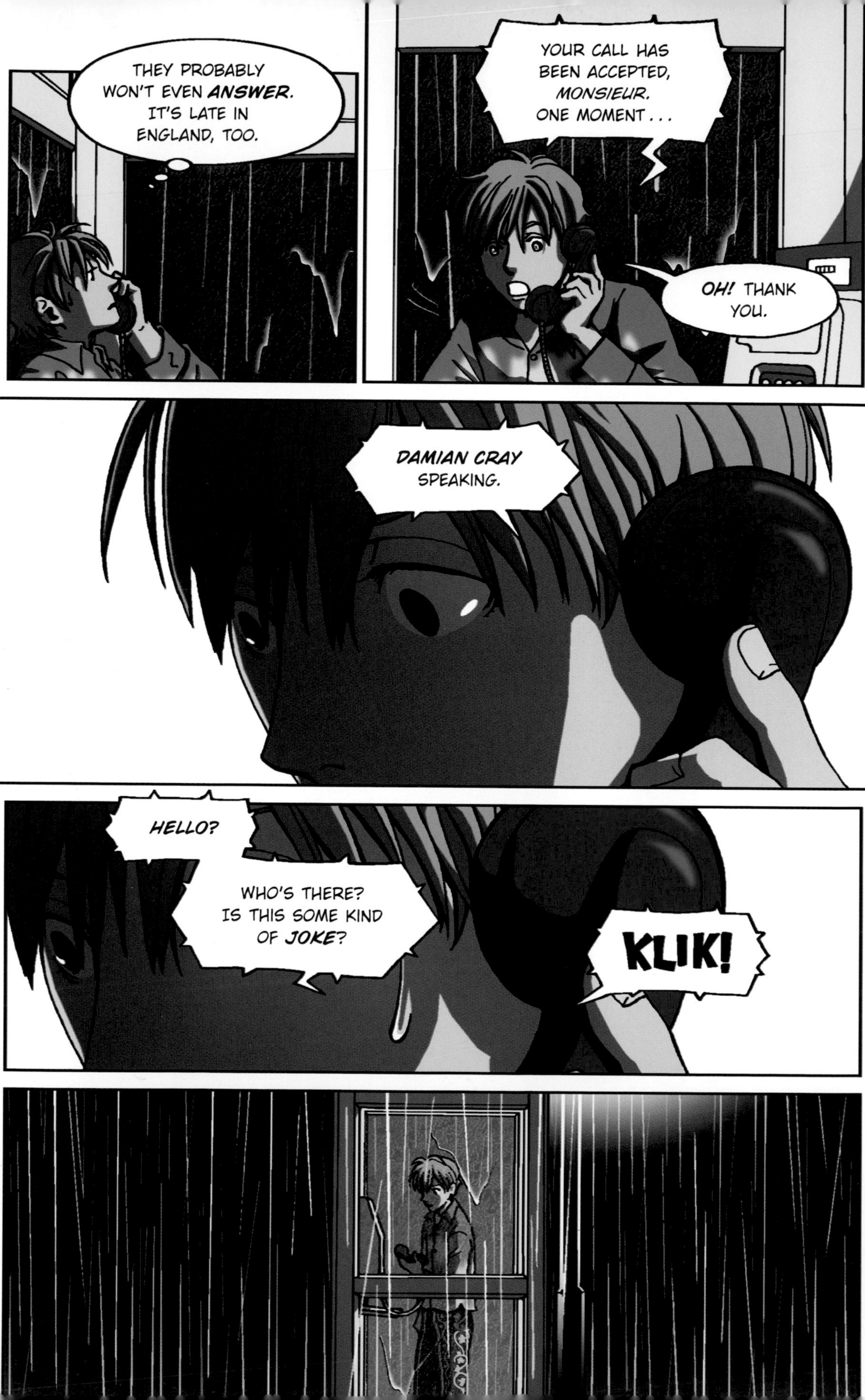
THEY PROBABLY WON'T EVEN ANSWER. IT'S LATE IN ENGLAND, TOO.
YOUR CALL HAS BEEN ACCEPTED, MONSIEUR. ONE MOMENT . . .
OH! THANK YOU.
DAMIAN CRAY SPEAKING.
HELLO?
WHO'S THERE? IS THIS SOME KIND OF JOKE?
KLIK!

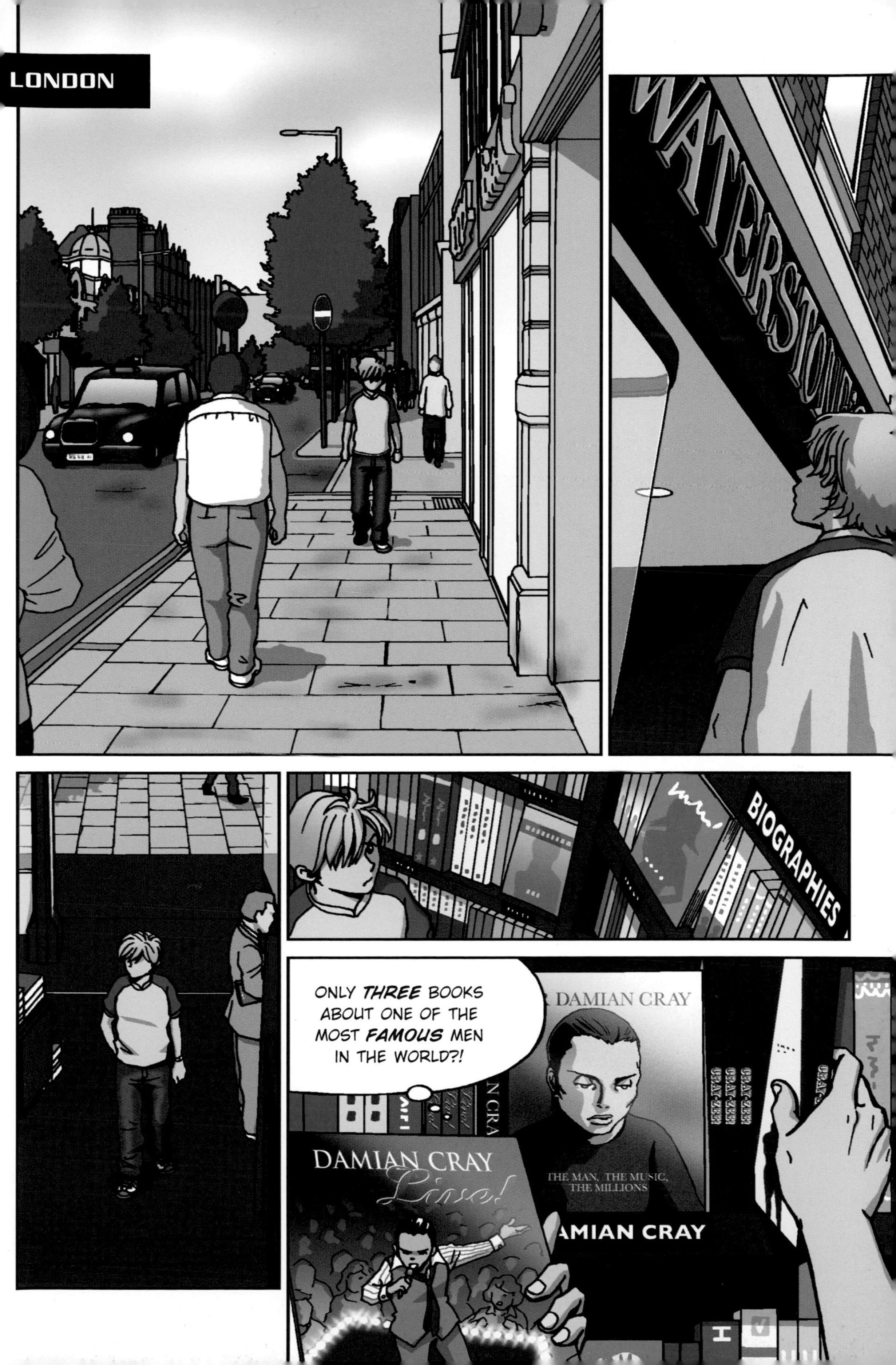
LONDON
WATERSTONE'S
BIOGRAPHIES
ONLY THREE BOOKS ABOUT ONE OF THE MOST FAMOUS MEN IN THE WORLD?!
DAMIAN CRAY
THE MAN, THE MUSIC, THE MILLIONS
DAMIAN CRAY
Live!
AMIAN CRAY

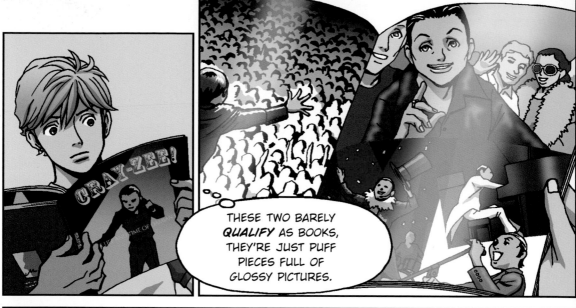

THESE TWO BARELY *QUALIFY* AS BOOKS, THEY'RE JUST PUFF PIECES FULL OF GLOSSY PICTURES.

AND THIS ONE LOOKS LIKE IT WAS WRITTEN BY SOMEONE WHO READS THE *FINANCIAL TIMES* FOR *LAUGHS*.

SIR DAMIAN C

THE MAN, THE MUSIC, THE MILLIONS

NONE OF THEM WILL TELL ME ANYTHING *NEW.* WHAT I NEED TO KNOW IS WHY DAMIAN CRAY'S NUMBER WAS ON *YASSEN'S* PHONE!

OH, WELL. HOME, I GUESS.

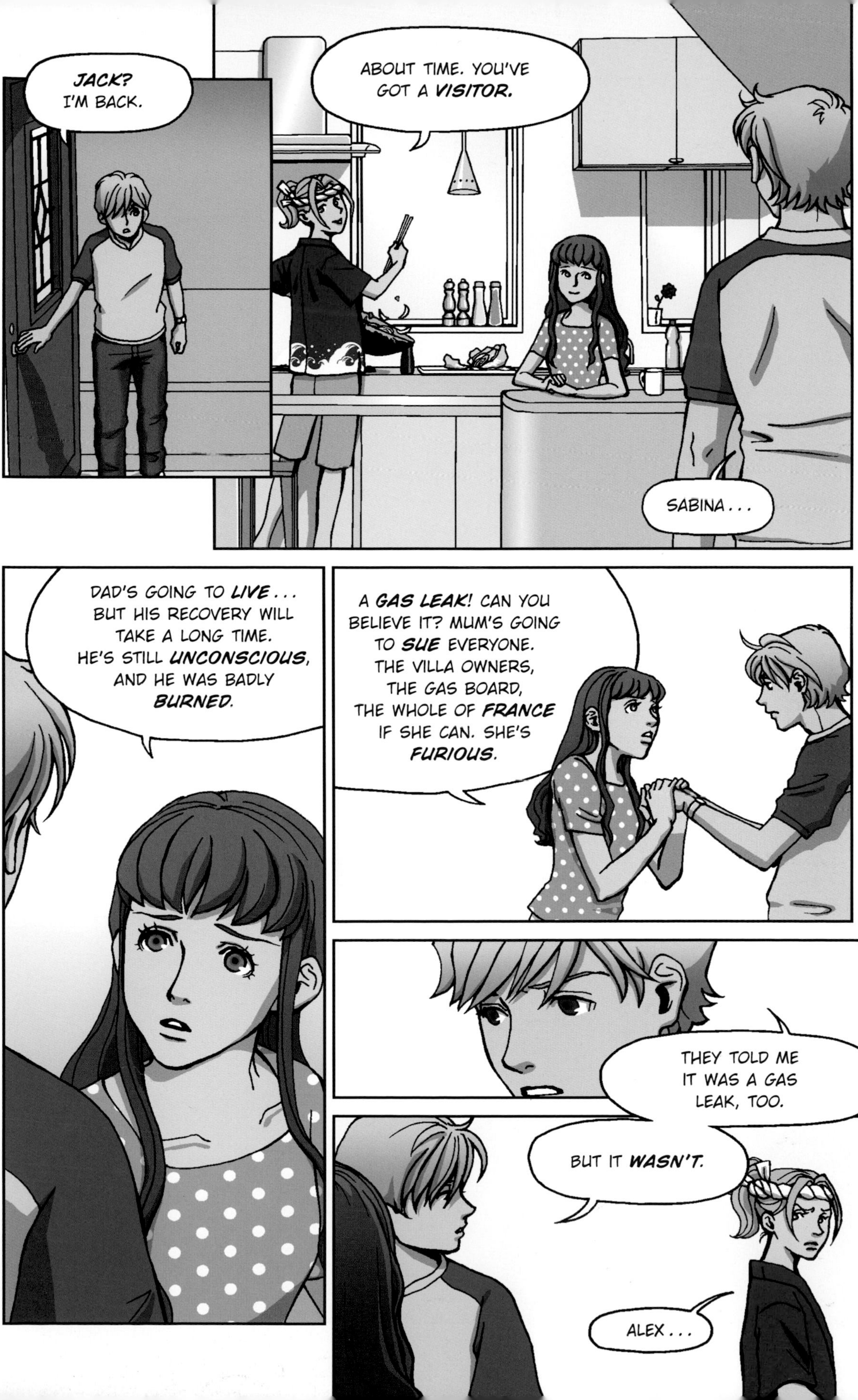
JACK? I'M BACK.
ABOUT TIME. YOU'VE GOT A VISITOR.
SABINA . . .
DAD'S GOING TO LIVE . . . BUT HIS RECOVERY WILL TAKE A LONG TIME. HE'S STILL UNCONSCIOUS, AND HE WAS BADLY BURNED.
A GAS LEAK! CAN YOU BELIEVE IT? MUM'S GOING TO SUE EVERYONE. THE VILLA OWNERS, THE GAS BOARD, THE WHOLE OF FRANCE IF SHE CAN. SHE'S FURIOUS.
THEY TOLD ME IT WAS A GAS LEAK, TOO.
BUT IT WASN'T.
ALEX . . .

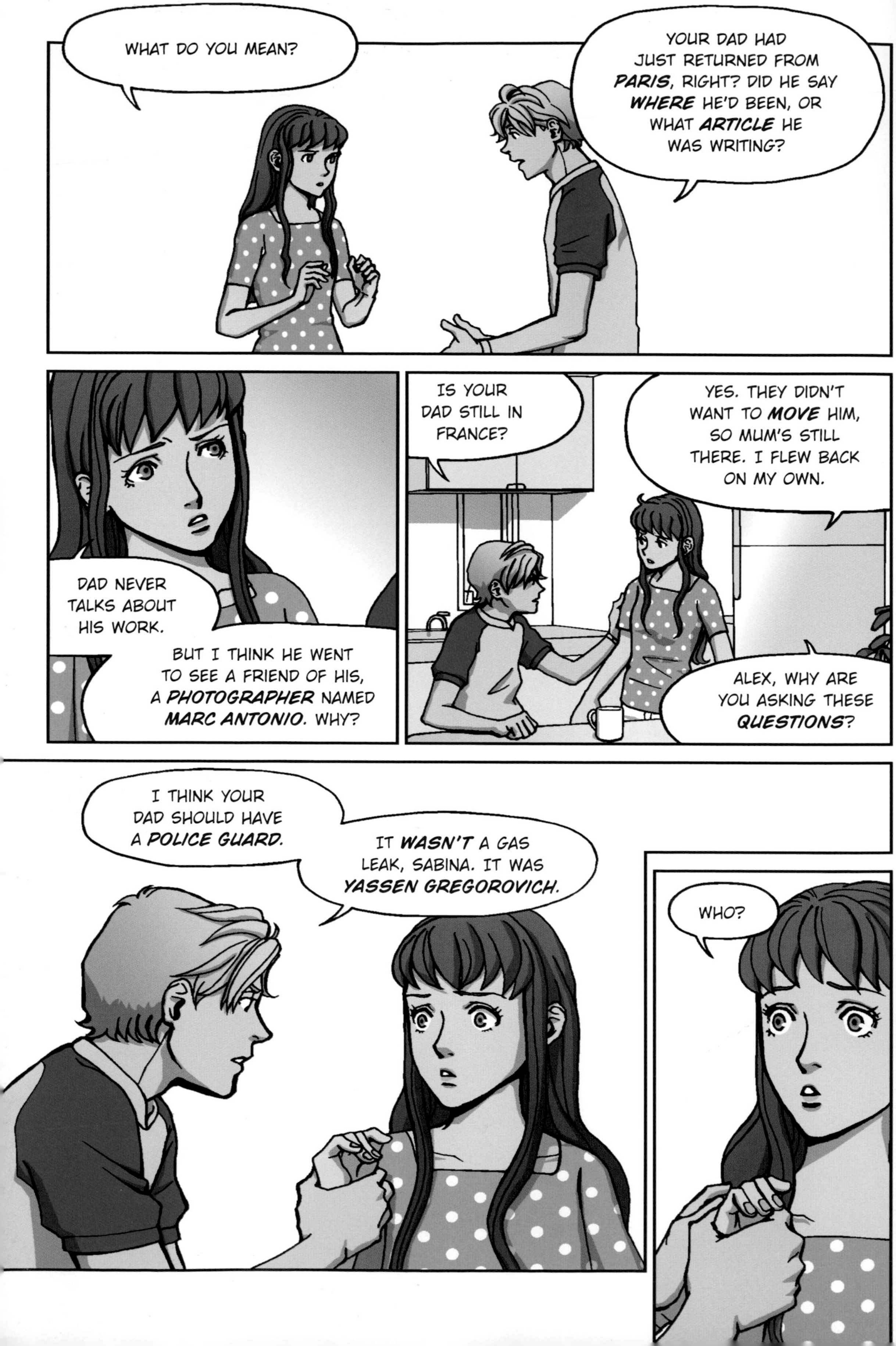
WHAT DO YOU MEAN?
YOUR DAD HAD JUST RETURNED FROM PARIS, RIGHT? DID HE SAY WHERE HE'D BEEN, OR WHAT ARTICLE HE WAS WRITING?
DAD NEVER TALKS ABOUT HIS WORK.
BUT I THINK HE WENT TO SEE A FRIEND OF HIS, A PHOTOGRAPHER NAMED MARC ANTONIO. WHY?
IS YOUR DAD STILL IN FRANCE?
YES. THEY DIDN'T WANT TO MOVE HIM, SO MUM'S STILL THERE. I FLEW BACK ON MY OWN.
ALEX, WHY ARE YOU ASKING THESE QUESTIONS?
I THINK YOUR DAD SHOULD HAVE A POLICE GUARD.
IT WASN'T A GAS LEAK, SABINA. IT WAS YASSEN GREGOROVICH.
WHO?

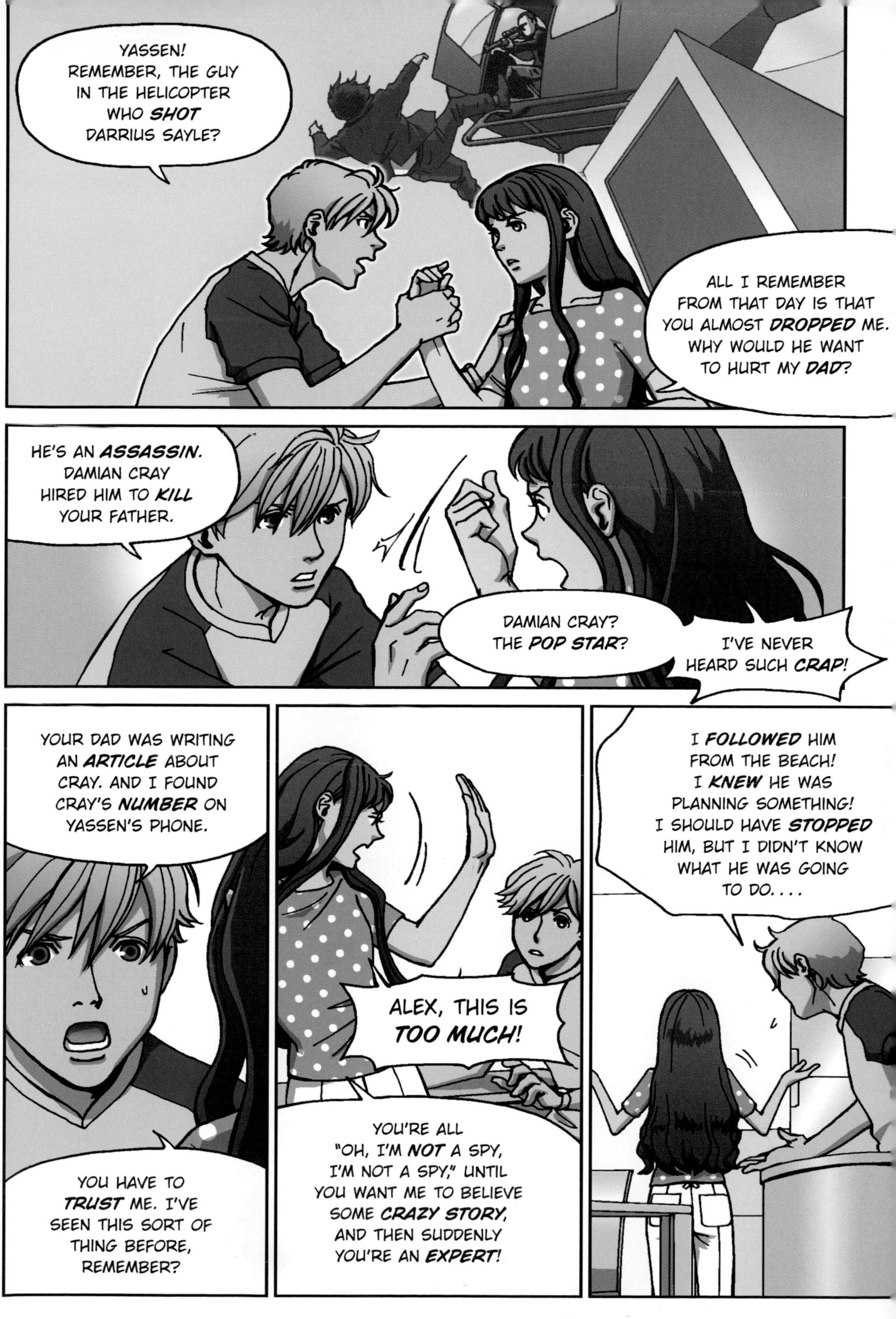
YASSEN! REMEMBER, THE GUY IN THE HELICOPTER WHO SHOT DARRIUS SAYLE?
ALL I REMEMBER FROM THAT DAY IS THAT YOU ALMOST DROPPED ME. WHY WOULD HE WANT TO HURT MY DAD?
HE'S AN ASSASSIN. DAMIAN CRAY HIRED HIM TO KILL YOUR FATHER.
DAMIAN CRAY? THE POP STAR?
I'VE NEVER HEARD SUCH CRAP!
YOUR DAD WAS WRITING AN ARTICLE ABOUT CRAY. AND I FOUND CRAY'S NUMBER ON YASSEN'S PHONE.
YOU HAVE TO TRUST ME. I'VE SEEN THIS SORT OF THING BEFORE, REMEMBER?
ALEX, THIS IS TOO MUCH!
YOU'RE ALL "OH, I'M NOT A SPY, I'M NOT A SPY," UNTIL YOU WANT ME TO BELIEVE SOME CRAZY STORY, AND THEN SUDDENLY YOU'RE AN EXPERT!
I FOLLOWED HIM FROM THE BEACH! I KNEW HE WAS PLANNING SOMETHING! I SHOULD HAVE STOPPED HIM, BUT I DIDN'T KNOW WHAT HE WAS GOING TO DO. . . .

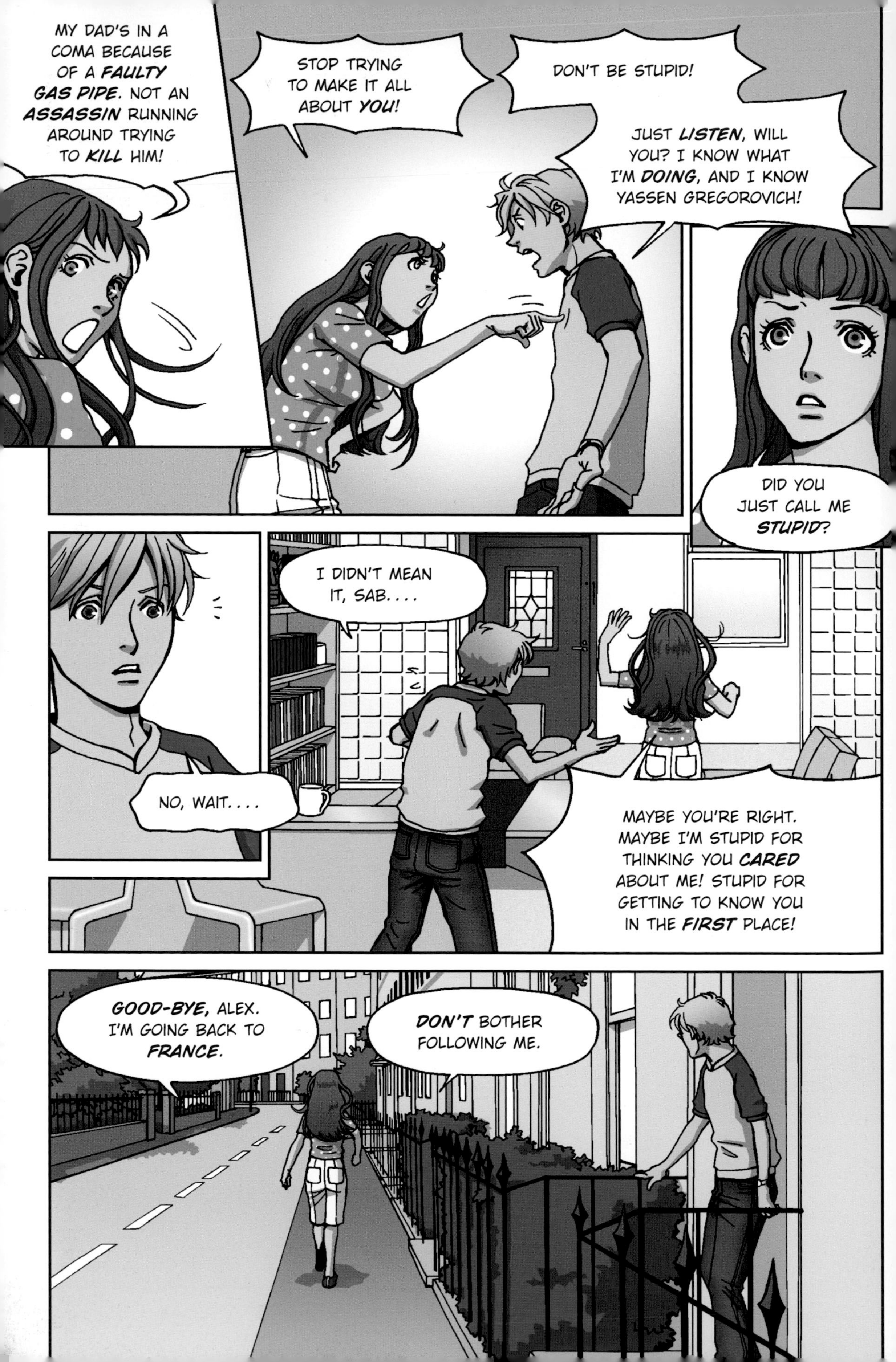

MY DAD'S IN A COMA BECAUSE OF A FAULTY GAS PIPE. NOT AN ASSASSIN RUNNING AROUND TRYING TO KILL HIM!
STOP TRYING TO MAKE IT ALL ABOUT YOU!
DON'T BE STUPID!
JUST LISTEN, WILL YOU? I KNOW WHAT I'M DOING, AND I KNOW YASSEN GREGOROVICH!
DID YOU JUST CALL ME STUPID?
NO, WAIT. . . .
I DIDN'T MEAN IT, SAB. . . .
MAYBE YOU'RE RIGHT. MAYBE I'M STUPID FOR THINKING YOU CARED ABOUT ME! STUPID FOR GETTING TO KNOW YOU IN THE FIRST PLACE!
GOOD-BYE, ALEX. I'M GOING BACK TO FRANCE.
DON'T BOTHER FOLLOWING ME.

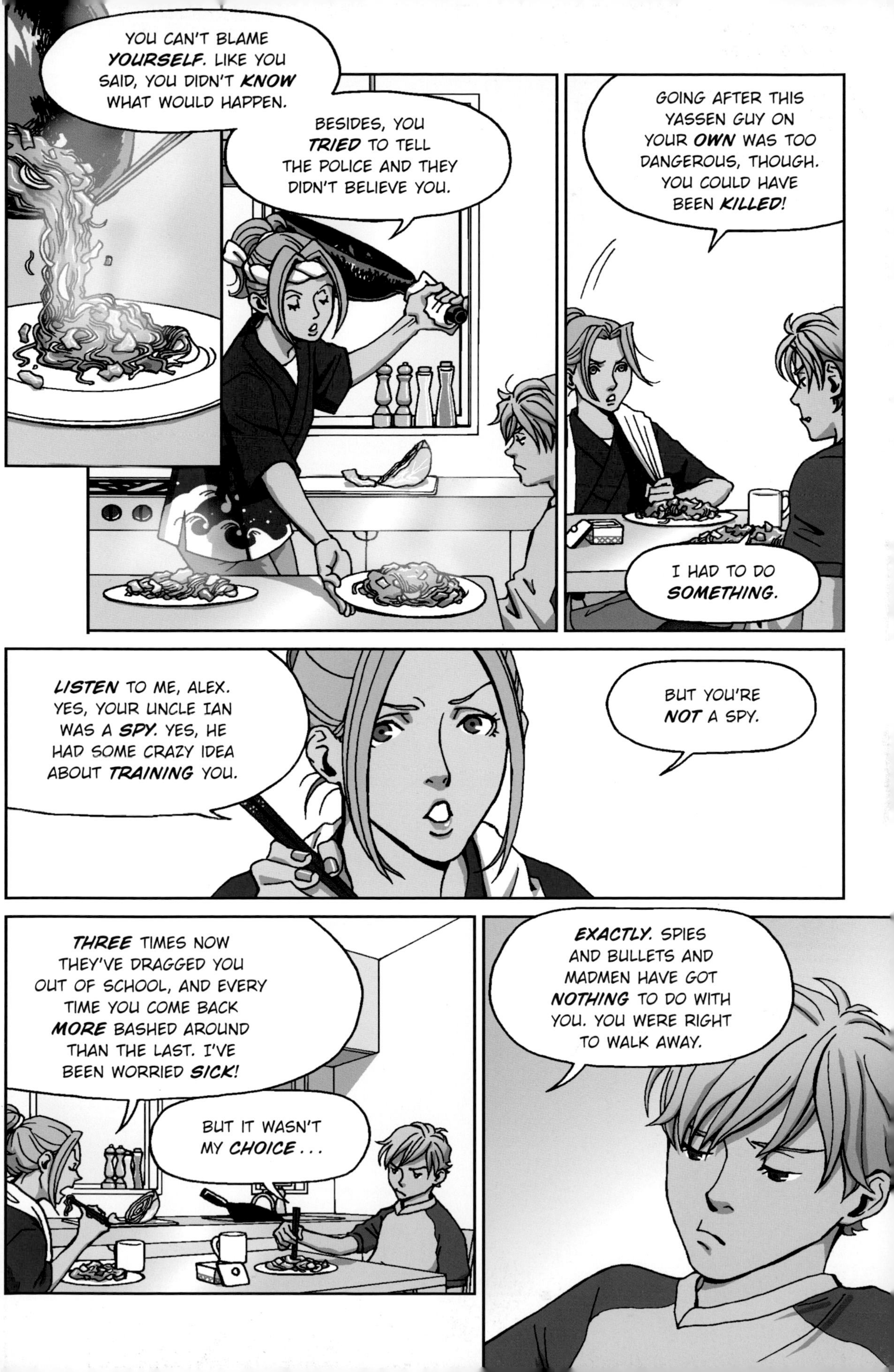
YOU CAN'T BLAME **YOURSELF**. LIKE YOU SAID, YOU DIDN'T **KNOW** WHAT WOULD HAPPEN.
BESIDES, YOU **TRIED** TO TELL THE POLICE AND THEY DIDN'T BELIEVE YOU.
GOING AFTER THIS YASSEN GUY ON YOUR **OWN** WAS TOO DANGEROUS, THOUGH. YOU COULD HAVE BEEN **KILLED**!
I HAD TO DO **SOMETHING**.
LISTEN TO ME, ALEX. YES, YOUR UNCLE IAN WAS A **SPY**. YES, HE HAD SOME CRAZY IDEA ABOUT **TRAINING** YOU.
BUT YOU'RE **NOT** A SPY.
THREE TIMES NOW THEY'VE DRAGGED YOU OUT OF SCHOOL, AND EVERY TIME YOU COME BACK **MORE** BASHED AROUND THAN THE LAST. I'VE BEEN WORRIED **SICK**!
BUT IT WASN'T MY **CHOICE** . . .
EXACTLY. SPIES AND BULLETS AND MADMEN HAVE GOT **NOTHING** TO DO WITH YOU. YOU WERE RIGHT TO WALK AWAY.

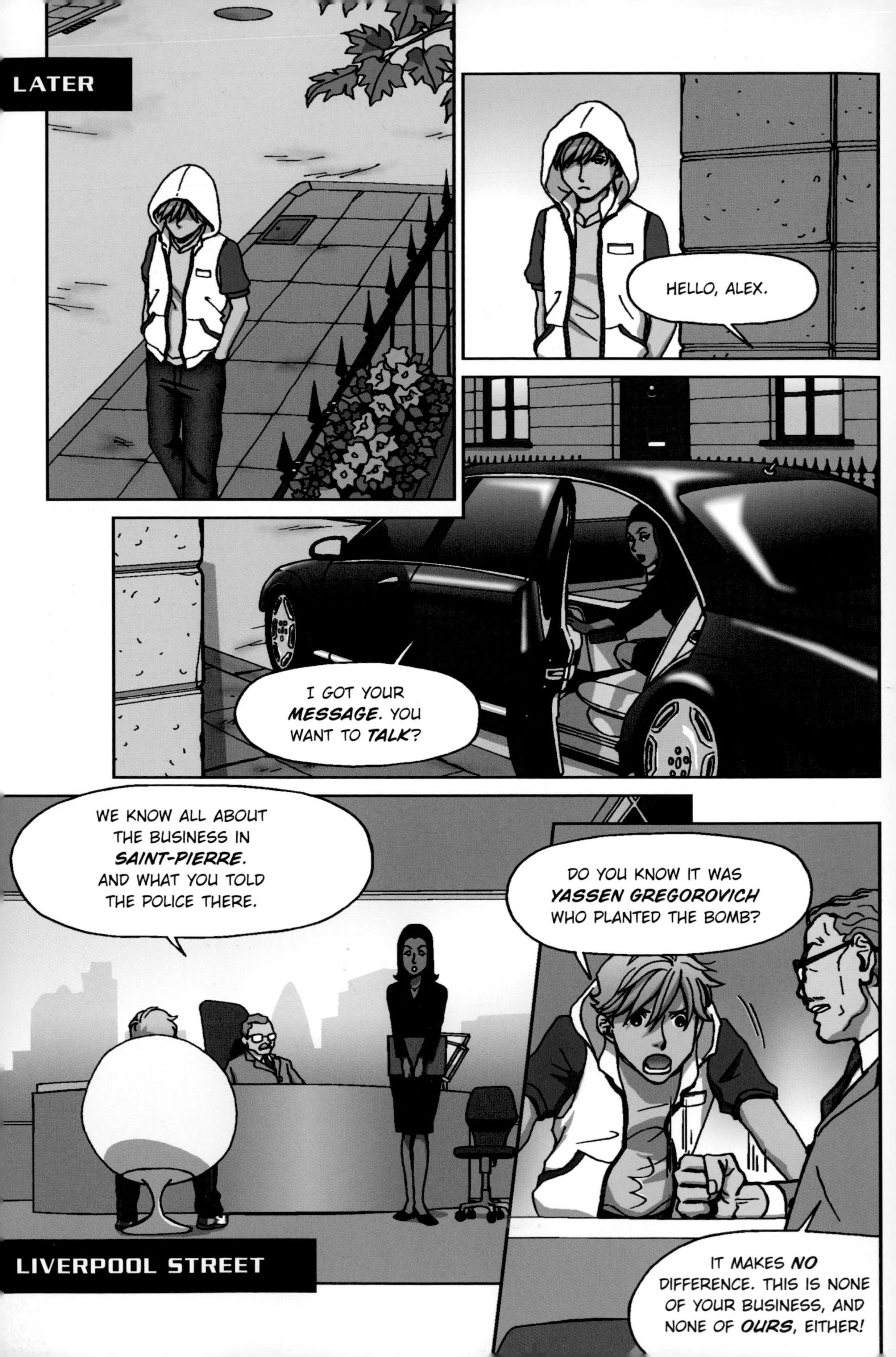

LATER
HELLO, ALEX.
I GOT YOUR MESSAGE. YOU WANT TO TALK?
WE KNOW ALL ABOUT THE BUSINESS IN SAINT-PIERRE. AND WHAT YOU TOLD THE POLICE THERE.
LIVERPOOL STREET
DO YOU KNOW IT WAS YASSEN GREGOROVICH WHO PLANTED THE BOMB?
IT MAKES NO DIFFERENCE. THIS IS NONE OF YOUR BUSINESS, AND NONE OF OURS, EITHER!

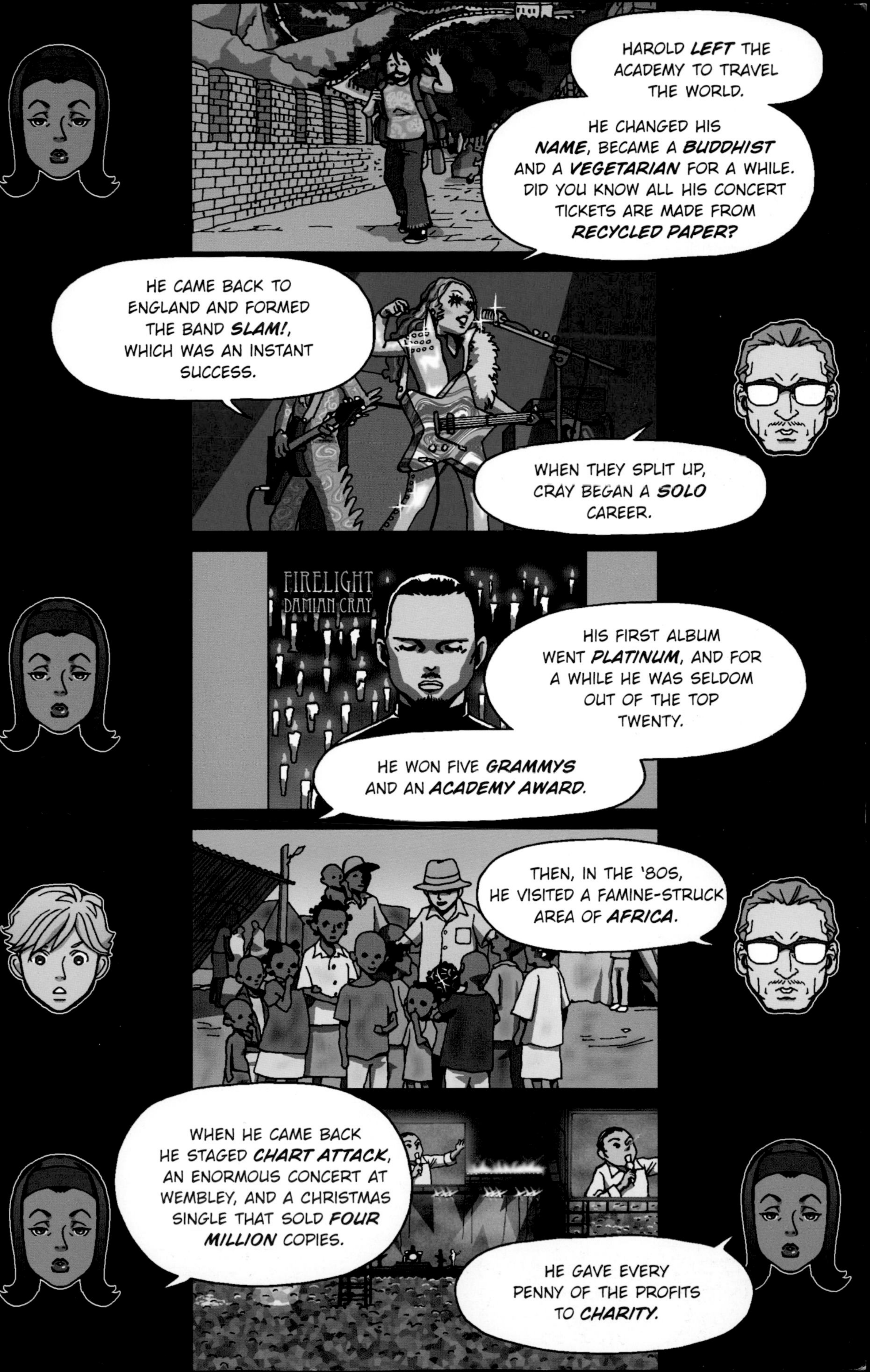

HAROLD LEFT THE ACADEMY TO TRAVEL THE WORLD.
HE CHANGED HIS NAME, BECAME A BUDDHIST AND A VEGETARIAN FOR A WHILE. DID YOU KNOW ALL HIS CONCERT TICKETS ARE MADE FROM RECYCLED PAPER?
HE CAME BACK TO ENGLAND AND FORMED THE BAND SLAM!, WHICH WAS AN INSTANT SUCCESS.
WHEN THEY SPLIT UP, CRAY BEGAN A SOLO CAREER.
FIRELIGHT
DAMIAN CRAY
HIS FIRST ALBUM WENT PLATINUM, AND FOR A WHILE HE WAS SELDOM OUT OF THE TOP TWENTY.
HE WON FIVE GRAMMYS AND AN ACADEMY AWARD.
THEN, IN THE '80S, HE VISITED A FAMINE-STRUCK AREA OF AFRICA.
WHEN HE CAME BACK HE STAGED CHART ATTACK, AN ENORMOUS CONCERT AT WEMBLEY, AND A CHRISTMAS SINGLE THAT SOLD FOUR MILLION COPIES.
HE GAVE EVERY PENNY OF THE PROFITS TO CHARITY.

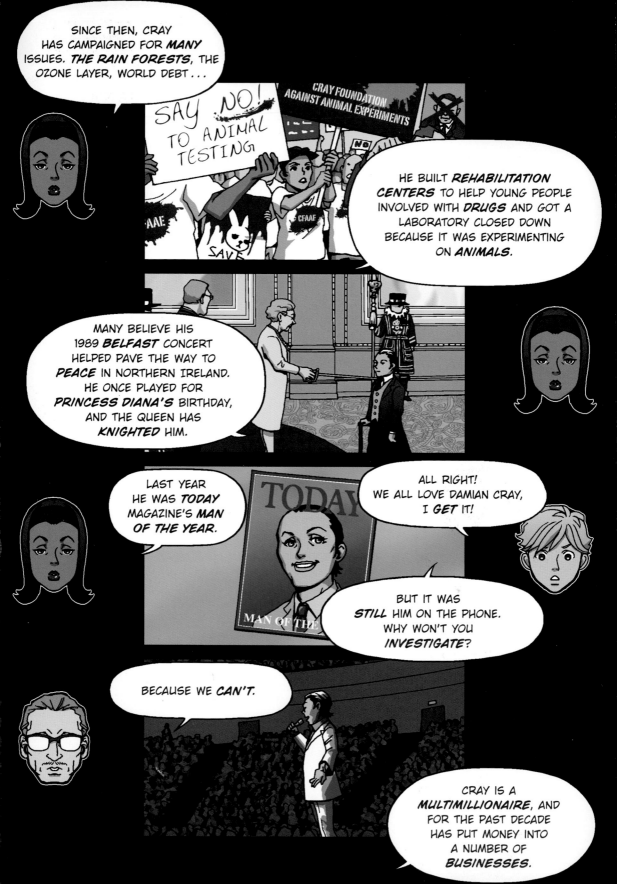

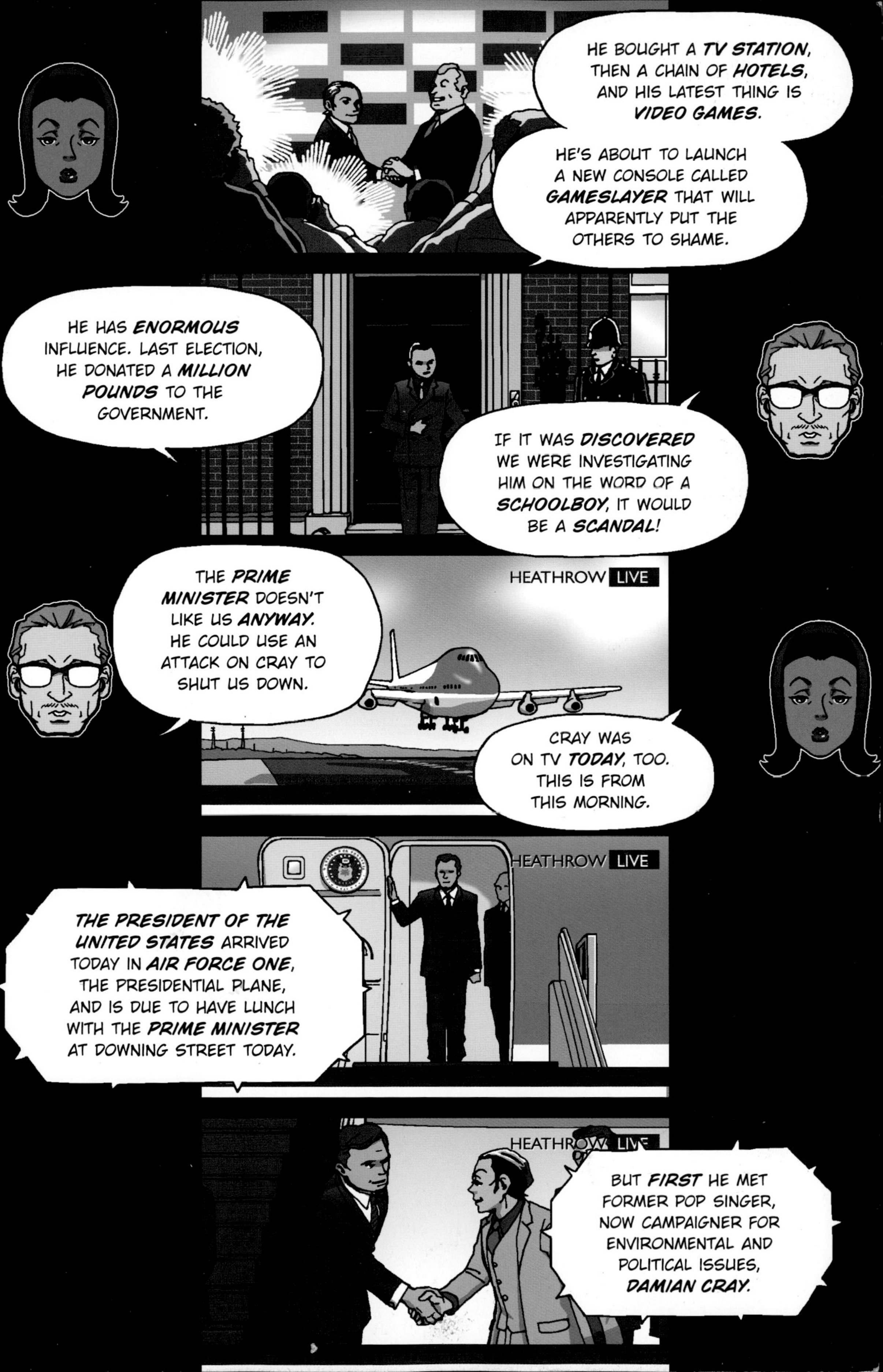
HE BOUGHT A TV STATION, THEN A CHAIN OF HOTELS, AND HIS LATEST THING IS VIDEO GAMES.
HE'S ABOUT TO LAUNCH A NEW CONSOLE CALLED GAMESLAYER THAT WILL APPARENTLY PUT THE OTHERS TO SHAME.
HE HAS ENORMOUS INFLUENCE. LAST ELECTION, HE DONATED A MILLION POUNDS TO THE GOVERNMENT.
IF IT WAS DISCOVERED WE WERE INVESTIGATING HIM ON THE WORD OF A SCHOOLBOY, IT WOULD BE A SCANDAL!
HEATHROW LIVE
THE PRIME MINISTER DOESN'T LIKE US ANYWAY. HE COULD USE AN ATTACK ON CRAY TO SHUT US DOWN.
CRAY WAS ON TV TODAY, TOO. THIS IS FROM THIS MORNING.
HEATHROW LIVE
THE PRESIDENT OF THE UNITED STATES ARRIVED TODAY IN AIR FORCE ONE, THE PRESIDENTIAL PLANE, AND IS DUE TO HAVE LUNCH WITH THE PRIME MINISTER AT DOWNING STREET TODAY.
BUT FIRST HE MET FORMER POP SINGER, NOW CAMPAIGNER FOR ENVIRONMENTAL AND POLITICAL ISSUES, DAMIAN CRAY.

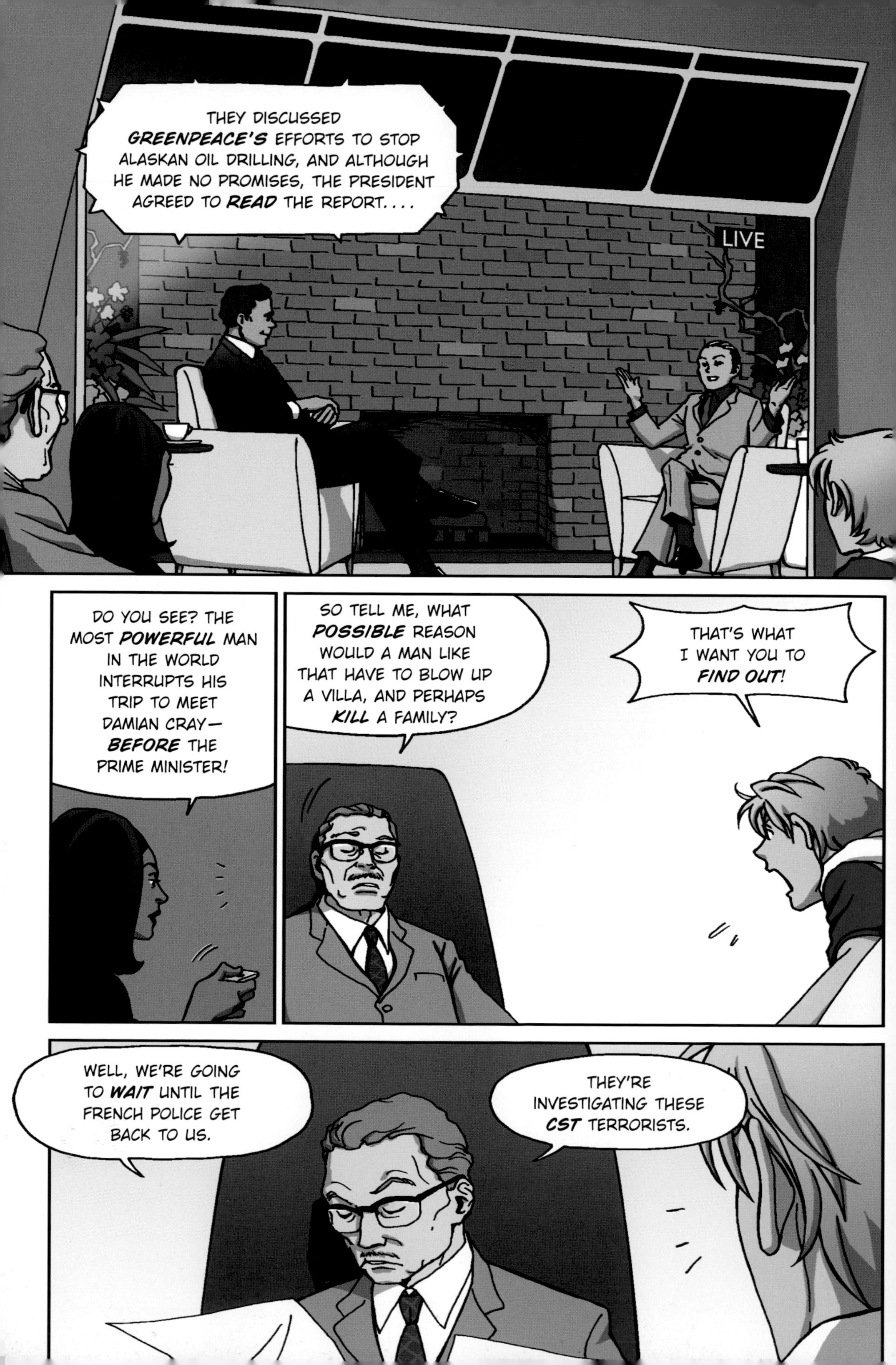
THEY DISCUSSED GREENPEACE'S EFFORTS TO STOP ALASKAN OIL DRILLING, AND ALTHOUGH HE MADE NO PROMISES, THE PRESIDENT AGREED TO READ THE REPORT. . . .
LIVE
DO YOU SEE? THE MOST POWERFUL MAN IN THE WORLD INTERRUPTS HIS TRIP TO MEET DAMIAN CRAY—BEFORE THE PRIME MINISTER!
SO TELL ME, WHAT POSSIBLE REASON WOULD A MAN LIKE THAT HAVE TO BLOW UP A VILLA, AND PERHAPS KILL A FAMILY?
THAT'S WHAT I WANT YOU TO FIND OUT!
WELL, WE'RE GOING TO WAIT UNTIL THE FRENCH POLICE GET BACK TO US.
THEY'RE INVESTIGATING THESE CST TERRORISTS.

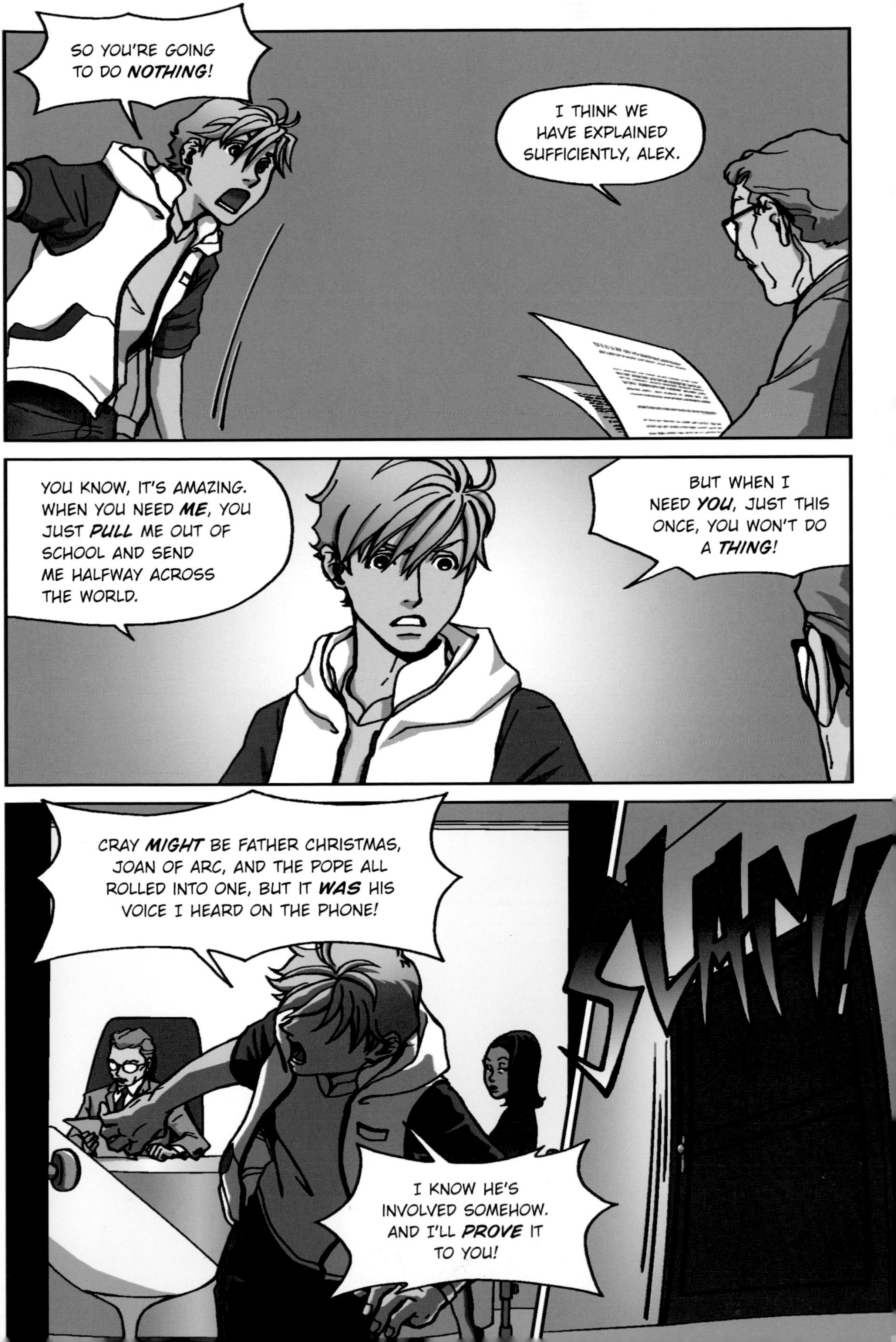
SO YOU'RE GOING TO DO ***NOTHING***!
I THINK WE HAVE EXPLAINED SUFFICIENTLY, ALEX.
YOU KNOW, IT'S AMAZING. WHEN YOU NEED ***ME***, YOU JUST ***PULL*** ME OUT OF SCHOOL AND SEND ME HALFWAY ACROSS THE WORLD.
BUT WHEN I NEED ***YOU***, JUST THIS ONCE, YOU WON'T DO A ***THING***!
CRAY ***MIGHT*** BE FATHER CHRISTMAS, JOAN OF ARC, AND THE POPE ALL ROLLED INTO ONE, BUT IT ***WAS*** HIS VOICE I HEARD ON THE PHONE!
SLAM!
I KNOW HE'S INVOLVED SOMEHOW. AND I'LL ***PROVE*** IT TO YOU!

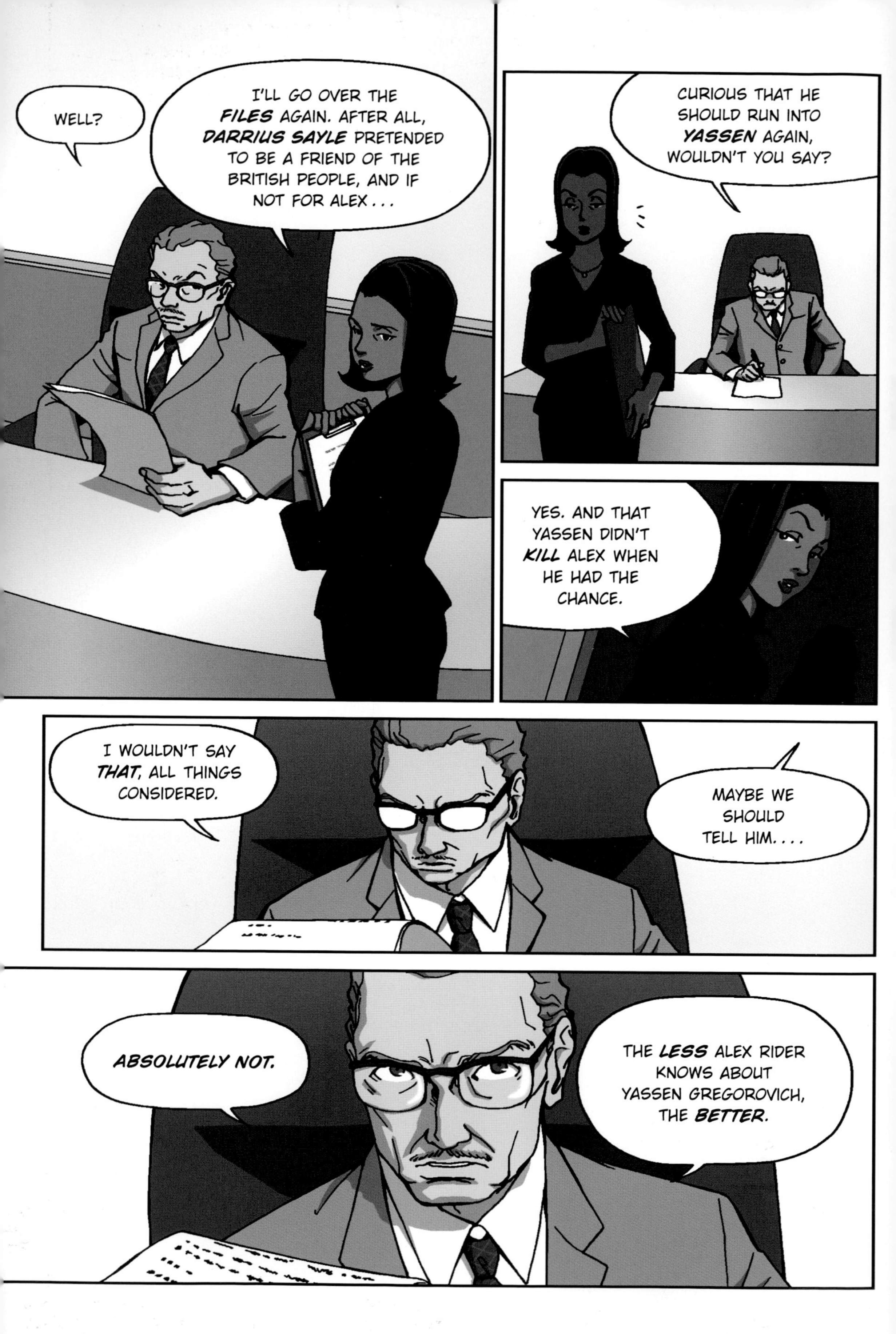
WELL?
I'LL GO OVER THE FILES AGAIN. AFTER ALL, DARRIUS SAYLE PRETENDED TO BE A FRIEND OF THE BRITISH PEOPLE, AND IF NOT FOR ALEX . . .
CURIOUS THAT HE SHOULD RUN INTO YASSEN AGAIN, WOULDN'T YOU SAY?
YES. AND THAT YASSEN DIDN'T KILL ALEX WHEN HE HAD THE CHANCE.
I WOULDN'T SAY THAT, ALL THINGS CONSIDERED.
MAYBE WE SHOULD TELL HIM. . . .
ABSOLUTELY NOT.
THE LESS ALEX RIDER KNOWS ABOUT YASSEN GREGOROVICH, THE BETTER.

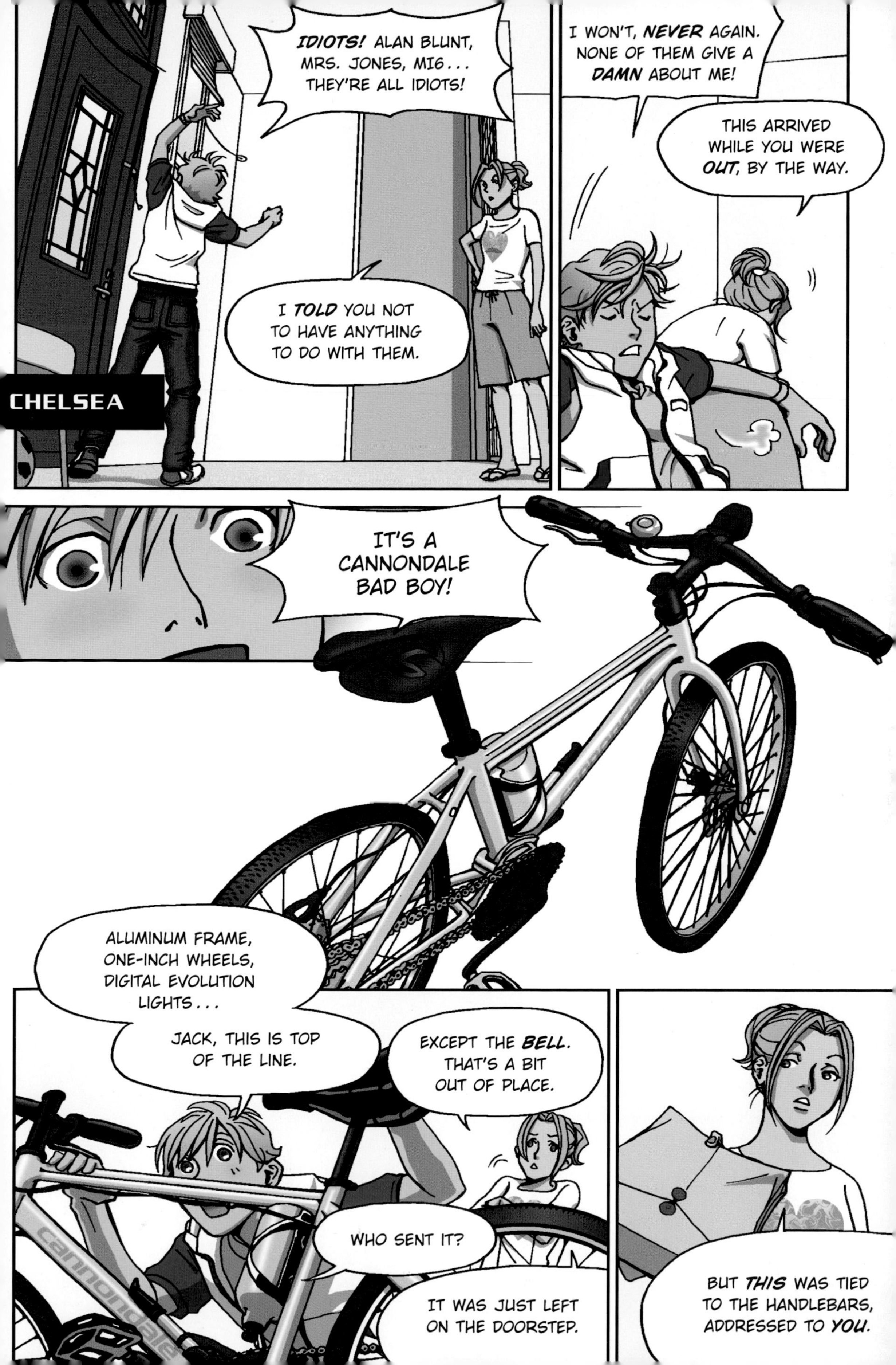
IDIOTS! ALAN BLUNT, MRS. JONES, MI6 . . . THEY'RE ALL IDIOTS!
CHELSEA
I TOLD YOU NOT TO HAVE ANYTHING TO DO WITH THEM.
I WON'T, NEVER AGAIN. NONE OF THEM GIVE A DAMN ABOUT ME!
THIS ARRIVED WHILE YOU WERE OUT, BY THE WAY.
IT'S A CANNONDALE BAD BOY!
ALUMINUM FRAME, ONE-INCH WHEELS, DIGITAL EVOLUTION LIGHTS . . .
JACK, THIS IS TOP OF THE LINE.
EXCEPT THE BELL. THAT'S A BIT OUT OF PLACE.
WHO SENT IT?
IT WAS JUST LEFT ON THE DOORSTEP.
BUT THIS WAS TIED TO THE HANDLEBARS, ADDRESSED TO YOU.

Dear Alex,
I'll get a roasting for this, but I don't
like you taking off without backup.
Been working on this for you.

Look after yourself!

Derek Smithers

P.S. This letter will self-destruct
in ten seconds.

YAAA!

I'D BETTER CHECK OUT THE INSTRUCTION BOOK.

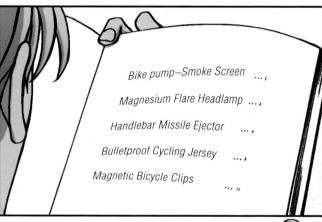

Bike pump—Smoke Screen ...,

Magnesium Flare Headlamp ...,

Handlebar Missile Ejector ...,

Bulletproof Cycling Jersey ...,

Magnetic Bicycle Clips ...,,

WHO'S SMITHERS?

I THOUGHT I HAD NO **FRIENDS** AT MI6.

BUT I WAS **WRONG**. I HAVE ONE, AT LEAST.

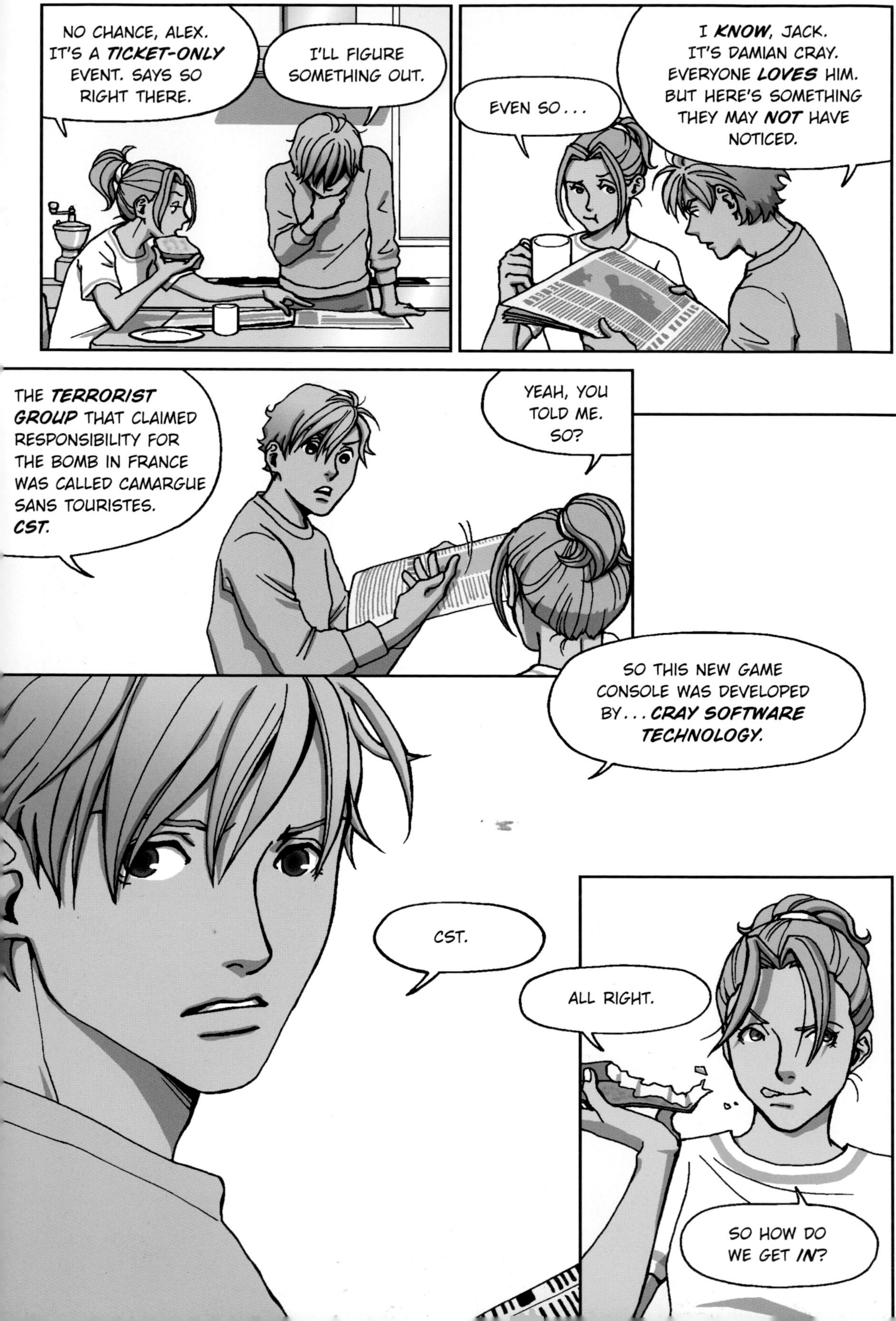
NO CHANCE, ALEX. IT'S A TICKET-ONLY EVENT. SAYS SO RIGHT THERE.
I'LL FIGURE SOMETHING OUT.
EVEN SO . . .
I KNOW, JACK. IT'S DAMIAN CRAY. EVERYONE LOVES HIM. BUT HERE'S SOMETHING THEY MAY NOT HAVE NOTICED.
THE TERRORIST GROUP THAT CLAIMED RESPONSIBILITY FOR THE BOMB IN FRANCE WAS CALLED CAMARGUE SANS TOURISTES. CST.
YEAH, YOU TOLD ME. SO?
SO THIS NEW GAME CONSOLE WAS DEVELOPED BY . . . CRAY SOFTWARE TECHNOLOGY.
CST.
ALL RIGHT.
SO HOW DO WE GET IN?

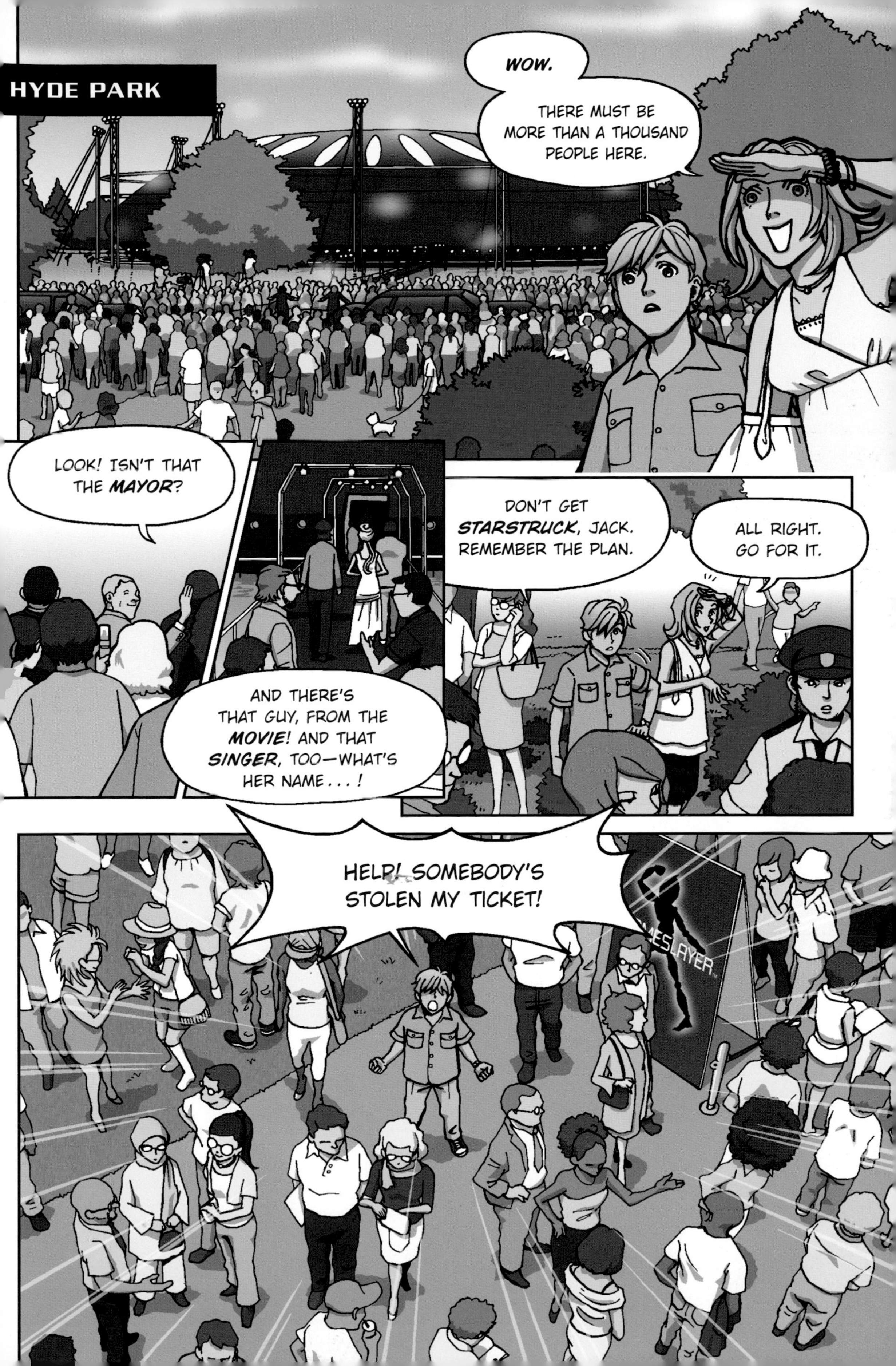
HYDE PARK
WOW.
THERE MUST BE MORE THAN A THOUSAND PEOPLE HERE.
LOOK! ISN'T THAT THE MAYOR?
AND THERE'S THAT GUY, FROM THE MOVIE! AND THAT SINGER, TOO—WHAT'S HER NAME . . . !
DON'T GET STARSTRUCK, JACK. REMEMBER THE PLAN.
ALL RIGHT. GO FOR IT.
HELP! SOMEBODY'S STOLEN MY TICKET!

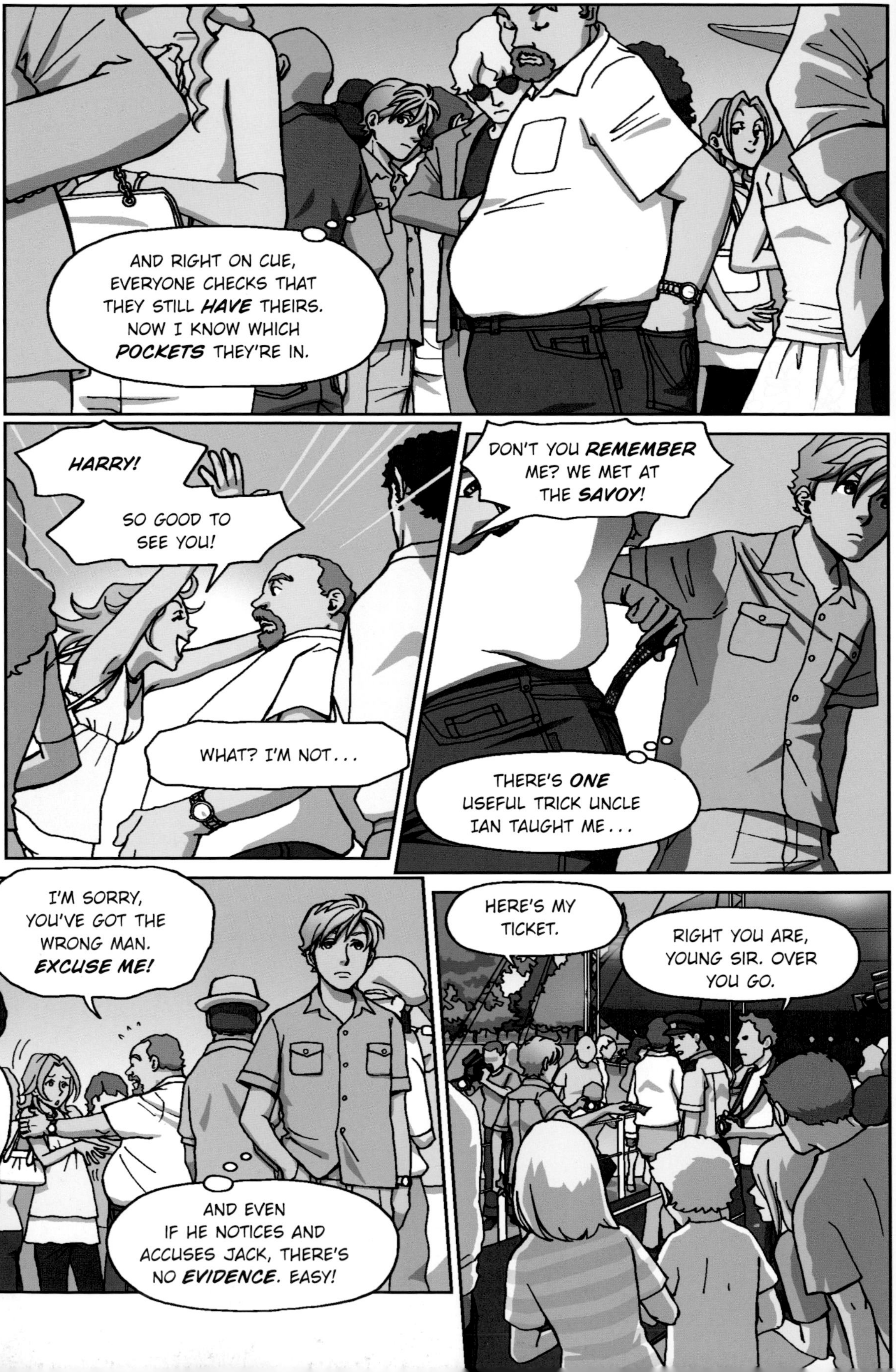
AND RIGHT ON CUE, EVERYONE CHECKS THAT THEY STILL HAVE THEIRS. NOW I KNOW WHICH POCKETS THEY'RE IN.
HARRY!
SO GOOD TO SEE YOU!
WHAT? I'M NOT . . .
DON'T YOU REMEMBER ME? WE MET AT THE SAVOY!
THERE'S ONE USEFUL TRICK UNCLE IAN TAUGHT ME . . .
I'M SORRY, YOU'VE GOT THE WRONG MAN. EXCUSE ME!
AND EVEN IF HE NOTICES AND ACCUSES JACK, THERE'S NO EVIDENCE. EASY!
HERE'S MY TICKET.
RIGHT YOU ARE, YOUNG SIR. OVER YOU GO.

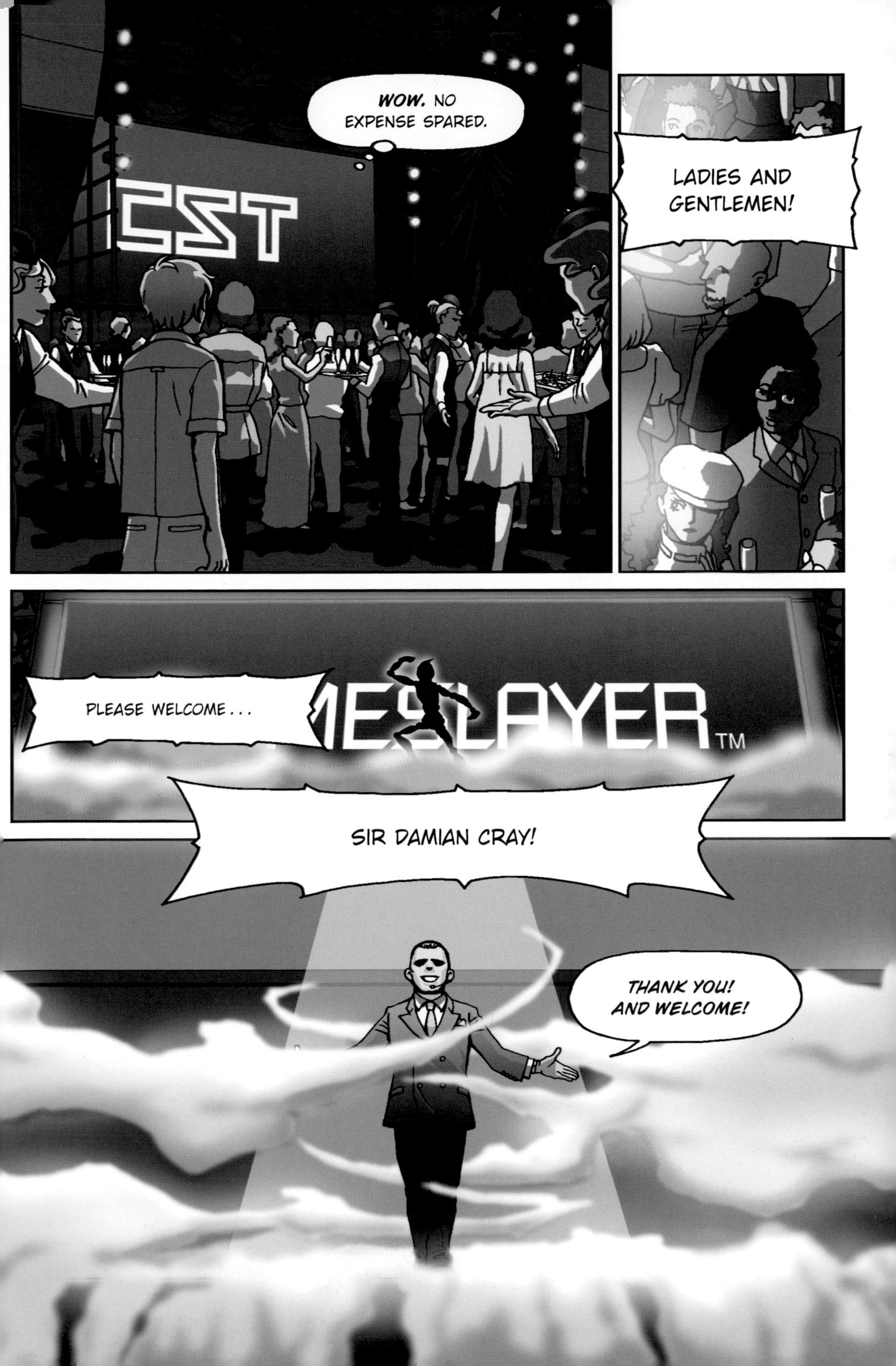
WOW. NO EXPENSE SPARED.
CST
LADIES AND GENTLEMEN!
PLEASE WELCOME . . .
MESLAYER™
SIR DAMIAN CRAY!
THANK YOU! AND WELCOME!

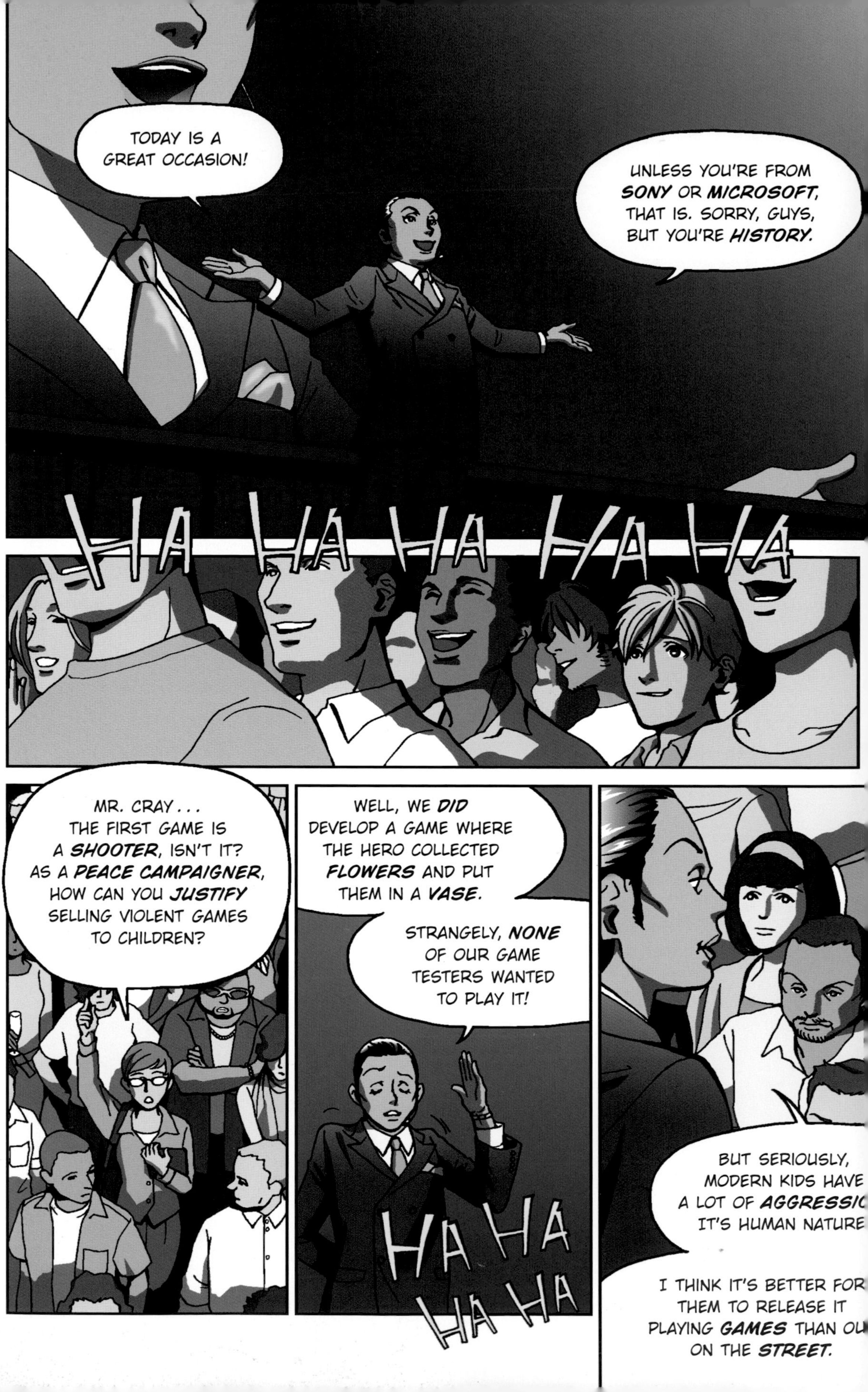
TODAY IS A GREAT OCCASION!
UNLESS YOU'RE FROM SONY OR MICROSOFT, THAT IS. SORRY, GUYS, BUT YOU'RE HISTORY.
HA HA HA HA HA
MR. CRAY . . . THE FIRST GAME IS A SHOOTER, ISN'T IT? AS A PEACE CAMPAIGNER, HOW CAN YOU JUSTIFY SELLING VIOLENT GAMES TO CHILDREN?
WELL, WE DID DEVELOP A GAME WHERE THE HERO COLLECTED FLOWERS AND PUT THEM IN A VASE.
STRANGELY, NONE OF OUR GAME TESTERS WANTED TO PLAY IT!
HA HA HA HA HA
BUT SERIOUSLY, MODERN KIDS HAVE A LOT OF AGGRESSIO
IT'S HUMAN NATURE
I THINK IT'S BETTER FOR THEM TO RELEASE IT PLAYING GAMES THAN OU ON THE STREET.

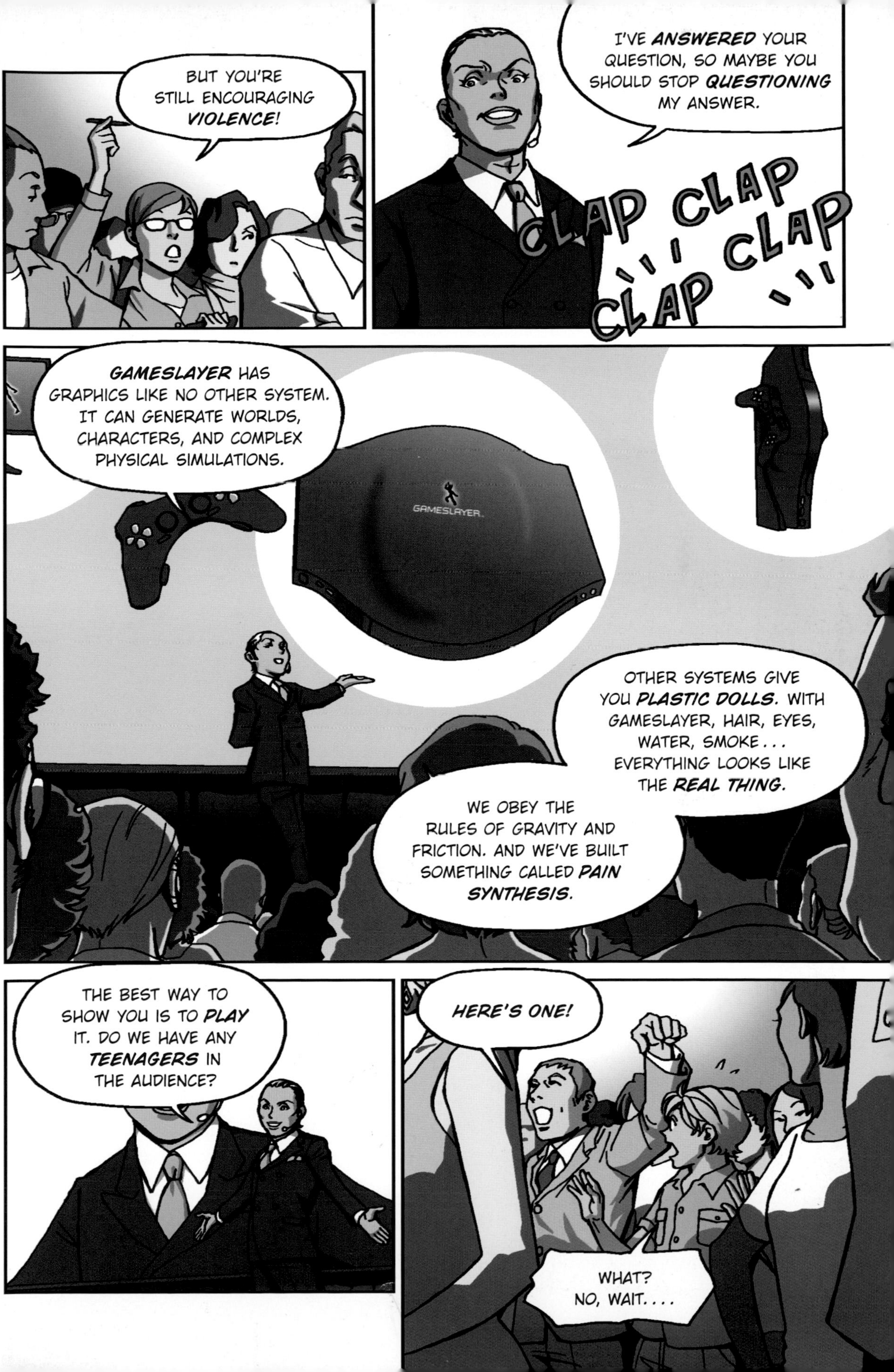
BUT YOU'RE STILL ENCOURAGING *VIOLENCE!*
I'VE *ANSWERED* YOUR QUESTION, SO MAYBE YOU SHOULD STOP *QUESTIONING* MY ANSWER.
CLAP CLAP CLAP CLAP
GAMESLAYER HAS GRAPHICS LIKE NO OTHER SYSTEM. IT CAN GENERATE WORLDS, CHARACTERS, AND COMPLEX PHYSICAL SIMULATIONS.
GAMESLAYER
OTHER SYSTEMS GIVE YOU *PLASTIC DOLLS.* WITH GAMESLAYER, HAIR, EYES, WATER, SMOKE . . . EVERYTHING LOOKS LIKE THE *REAL THING.*
WE OBEY THE RULES OF GRAVITY AND FRICTION. AND WE'VE BUILT SOMETHING CALLED *PAIN SYNTHESIS.*
THE BEST WAY TO SHOW YOU IS TO *PLAY* IT. DO WE HAVE ANY *TEENAGERS* IN THE AUDIENCE?
HERE'S ONE!
WHAT? NO, WAIT. . . .

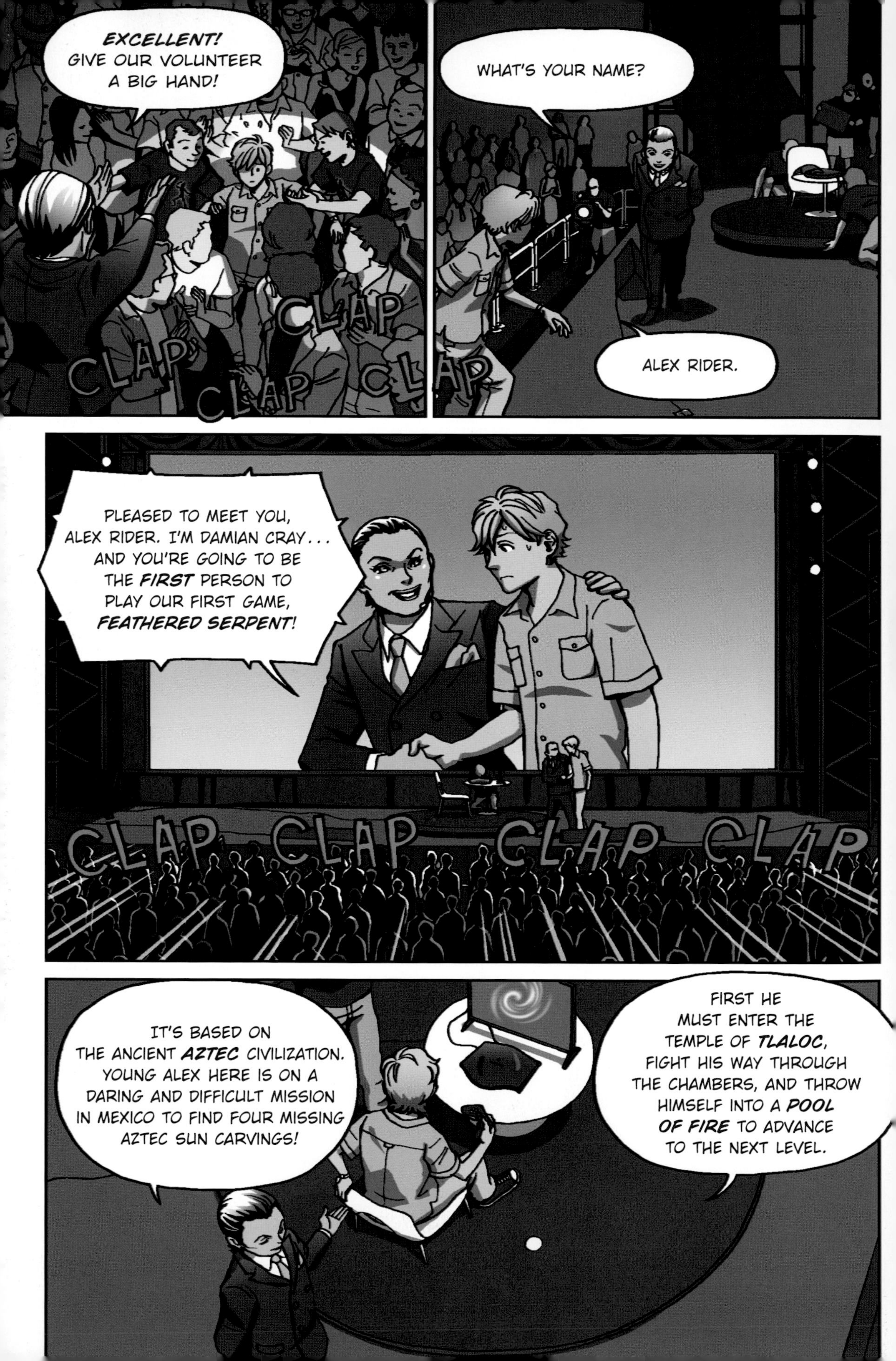
EXCELLENT! GIVE OUR VOLUNTEER A BIG HAND!
CLAP CLAP CLAP CLAP
WHAT'S YOUR NAME?
ALEX RIDER.
PLEASED TO MEET YOU, ALEX RIDER. I'M DAMIAN CRAY... AND YOU'RE GOING TO BE THE FIRST PERSON TO PLAY OUR FIRST GAME, FEATHERED SERPENT!
CLAP CLAP CLAP CLAP
IT'S BASED ON THE ANCIENT AZTEC CIVILIZATION. YOUNG ALEX HERE IS ON A DARING AND DIFFICULT MISSION IN MEXICO TO FIND FOUR MISSING AZTEC SUN CARVINGS!
FIRST HE MUST ENTER THE TEMPLE OF TLALOC, FIGHT HIS WAY THROUGH THE CHAMBERS, AND THROW HIMSELF INTO A POOL OF FIRE TO ADVANCE TO THE NEXT LEVEL.

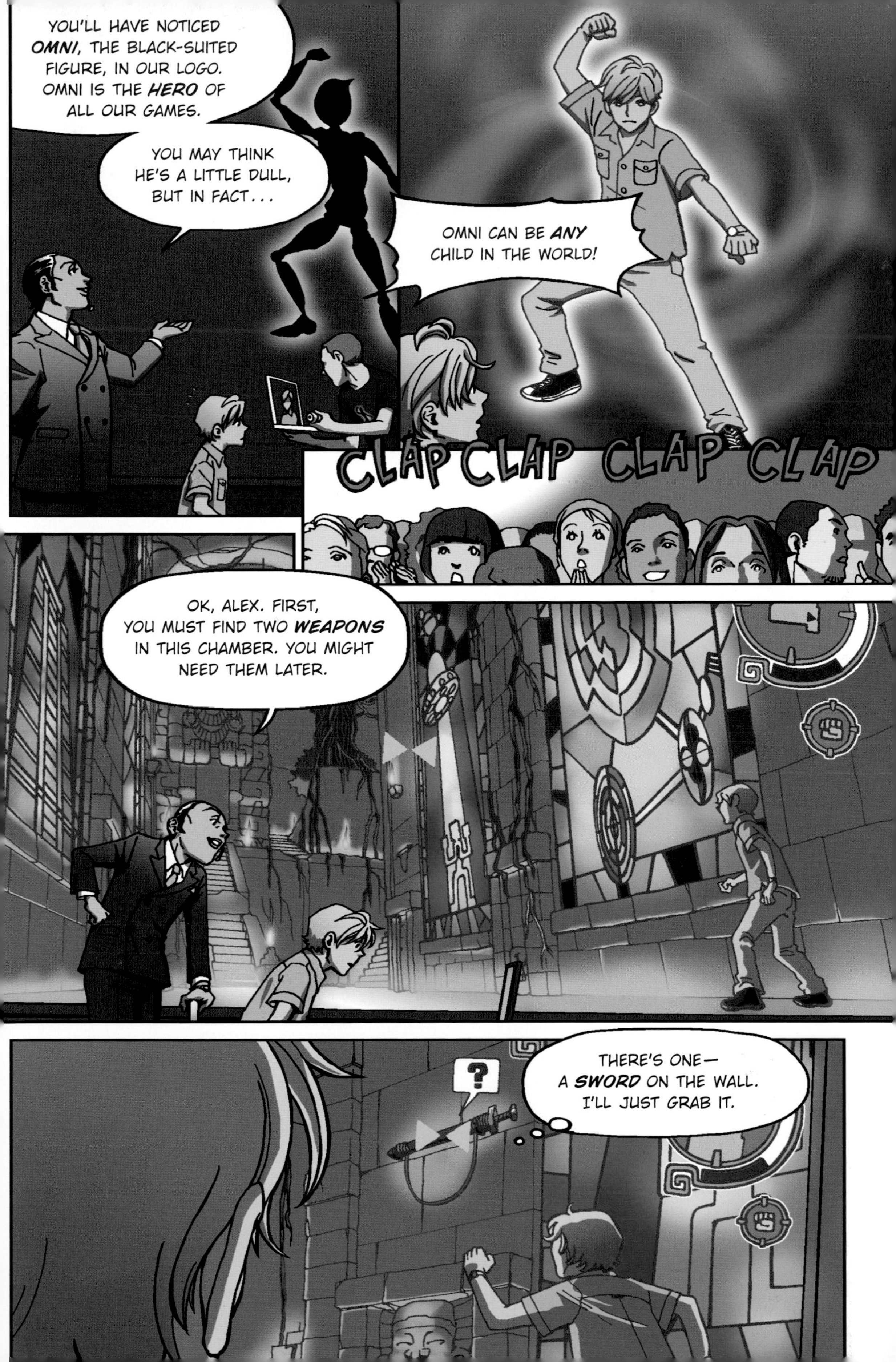
YOU'LL HAVE NOTICED OMNI, THE BLACK-SUITED FIGURE, IN OUR LOGO. OMNI IS THE HERO OF ALL OUR GAMES.
YOU MAY THINK HE'S A LITTLE DULL, BUT IN FACT . . .
OMNI CAN BE ANY CHILD IN THE WORLD!
CLAP CLAP CLAP CLAP
OK, ALEX. FIRST, YOU MUST FIND TWO WEAPONS IN THIS CHAMBER. YOU MIGHT NEED THEM LATER.
?
THERE'S ONE— A SWORD ON THE WALL. I'LL JUST GRAB IT.

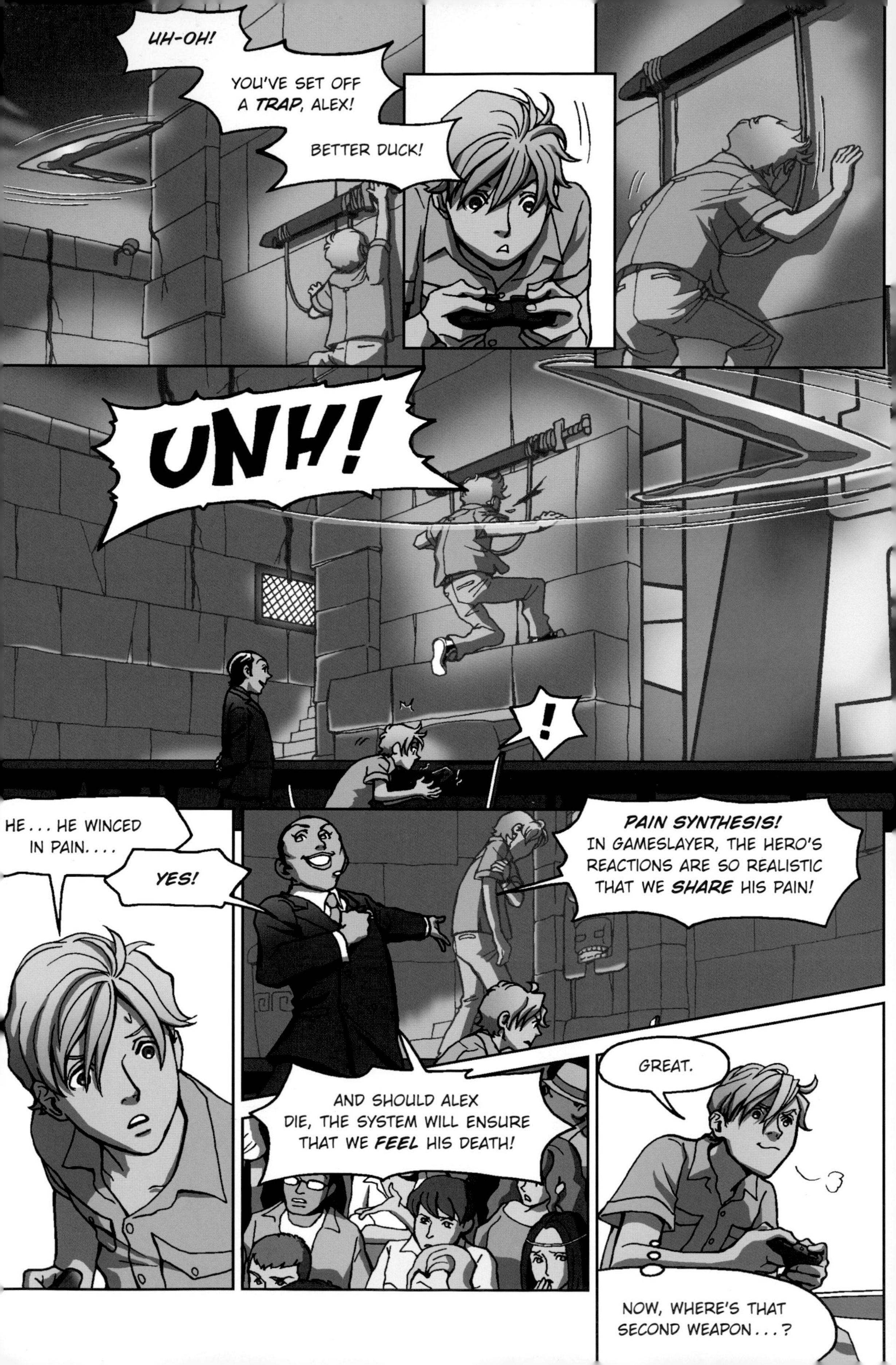
UH-OH!
YOU'VE SET OFF A TRAP, ALEX!
BETTER DUCK!
UNH!
!
HE . . . HE WINCED IN PAIN. . . .
YES!
PAIN SYNTHESIS! IN GAMESLAYER, THE HERO'S REACTIONS ARE SO REALISTIC THAT WE SHARE HIS PAIN!
AND SHOULD ALEX DIE, THE SYSTEM WILL ENSURE THAT WE FEEL HIS DEATH!
GREAT.
NOW, WHERE'S THAT SECOND WEAPON . . . ?

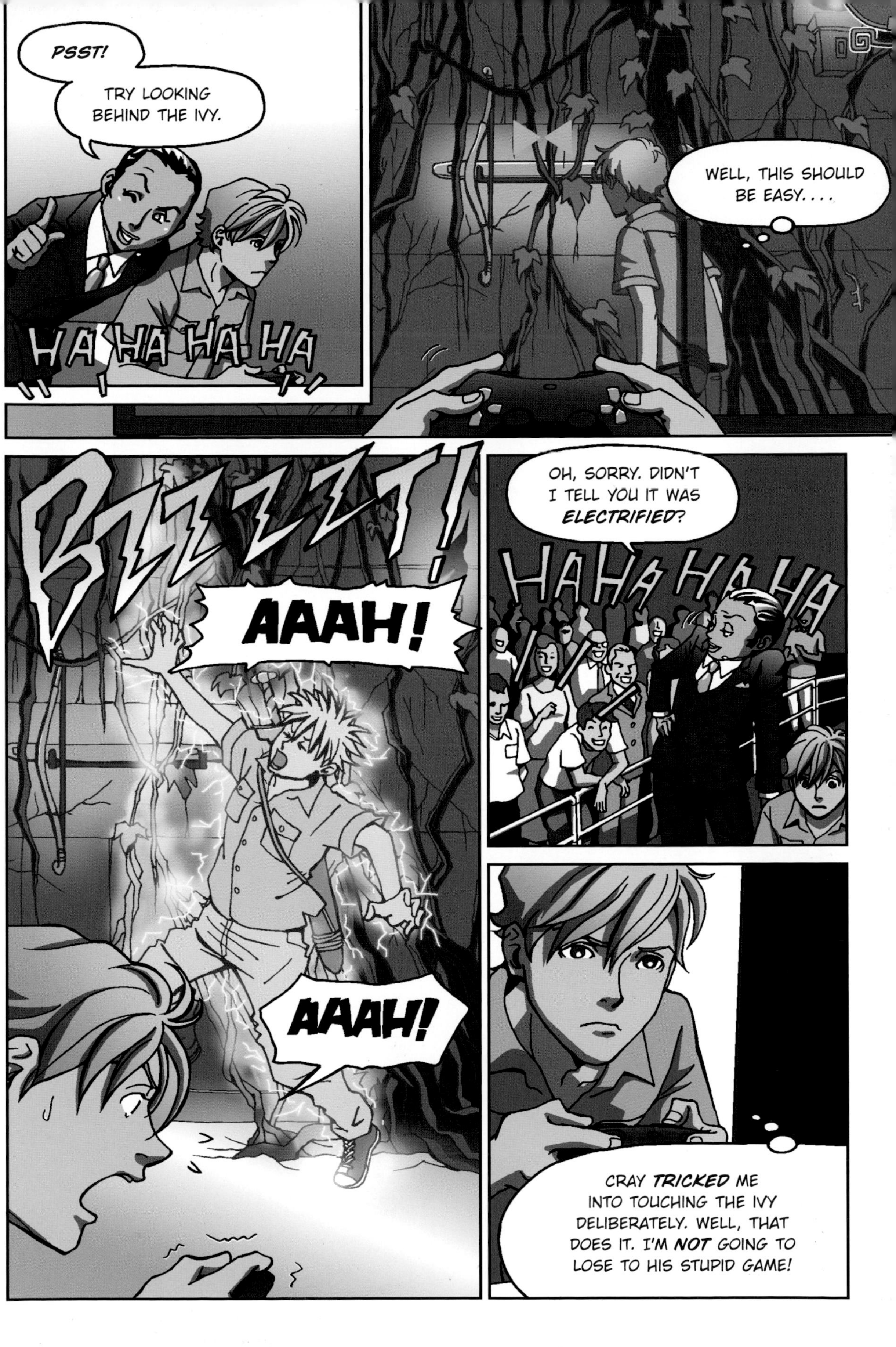
PSST!
TRY LOOKING BEHIND THE IVY.
HA HA HA HA
WELL, THIS SHOULD BE EASY. . . .
BZZZZT!
AAAH!
AAAH!
OH, SORRY. DIDN'T I TELL YOU IT WAS ELECTRIFIED?
HAHA HAHA
CRAY TRICKED ME INTO TOUCHING THE IVY DELIBERATELY. WELL, THAT DOES IT. I'M NOT GOING TO LOSE TO HIS STUPID GAME!

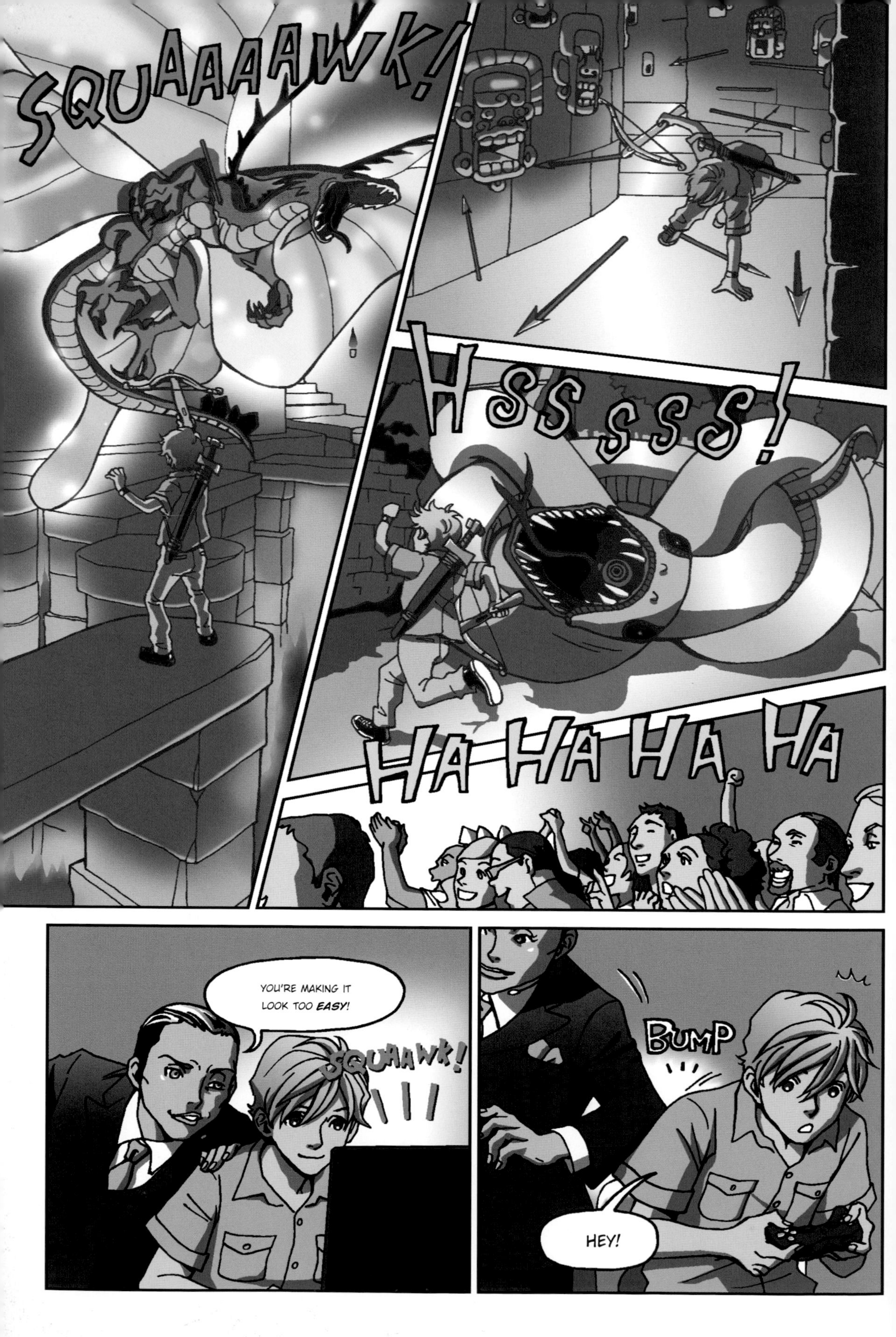
SQUAAAAAWK!
HSSSSS!
HA HA HA HA
YOU'RE MAKING IT LOOK TOO *EASY*!
SQUAAWK!
BUMP
HEY!

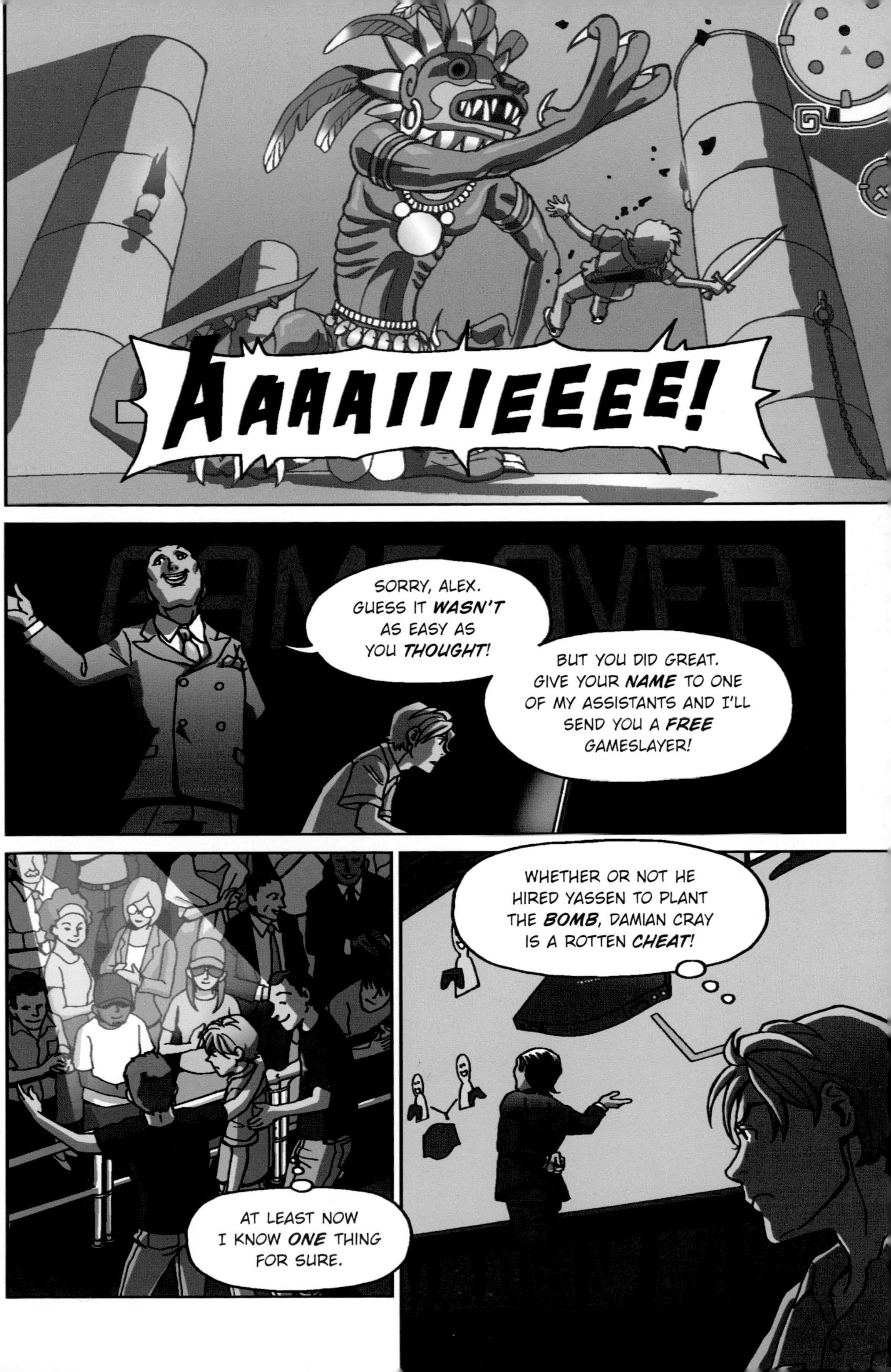
AAAAIIIEEEE!
SORRY, ALEX. GUESS IT WASN'T AS EASY AS YOU THOUGHT!
BUT YOU DID GREAT. GIVE YOUR NAME TO ONE OF MY ASSISTANTS AND I'LL SEND YOU A FREE GAMESLAYER!
AT LEAST NOW I KNOW ONE THING FOR SURE.
WHETHER OR NOT HE HIRED YASSEN TO PLANT THE BOMB, DAMIAN CRAY IS A ROTTEN CHEAT!

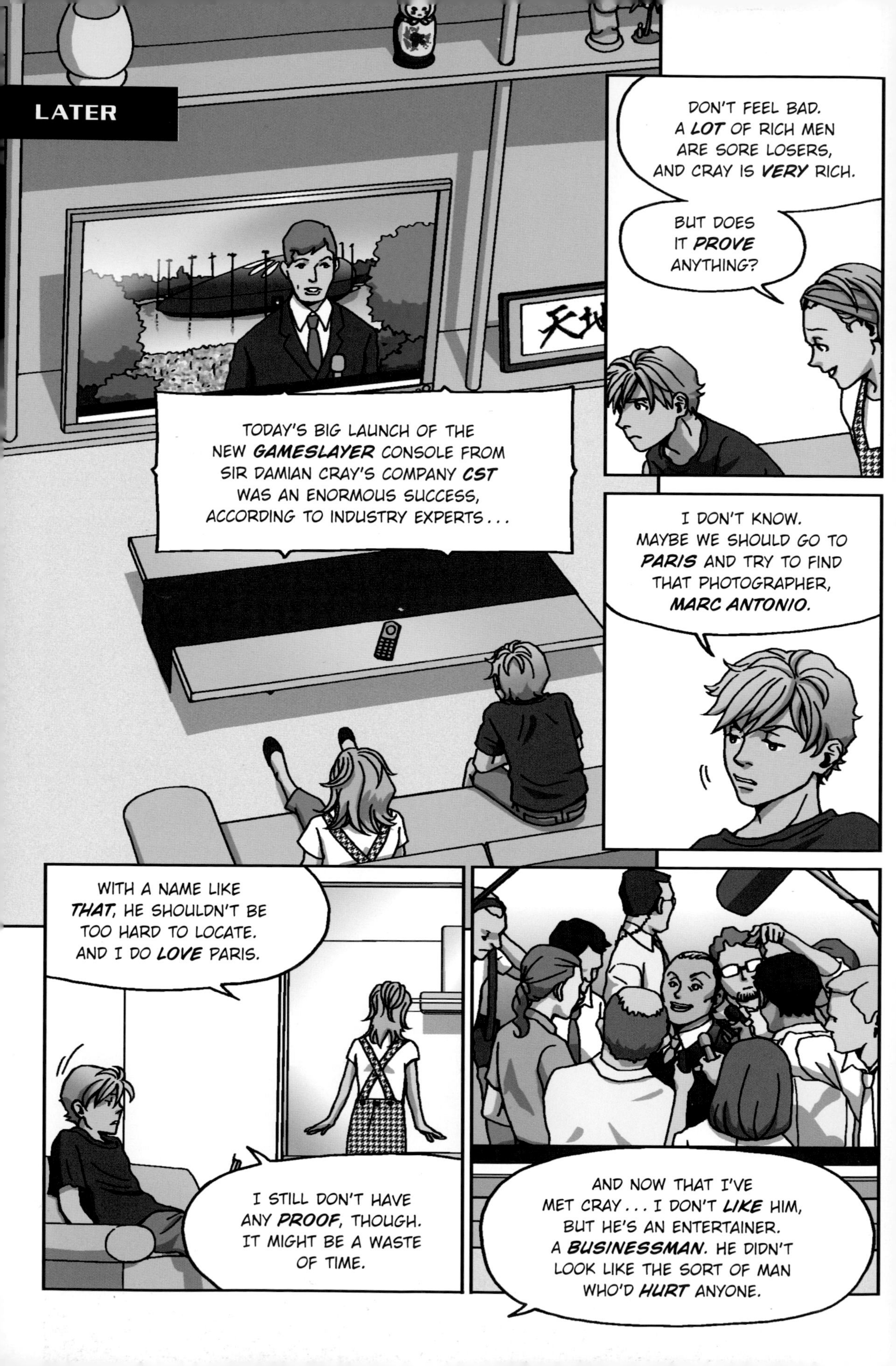
LATER
TODAY'S BIG LAUNCH OF THE NEW GAMESLAYER CONSOLE FROM SIR DAMIAN CRAY'S COMPANY CST WAS AN ENORMOUS SUCCESS, ACCORDING TO INDUSTRY EXPERTS . . .
DON'T FEEL BAD. A LOT OF RICH MEN ARE SORE LOSERS, AND CRAY IS VERY RICH.
BUT DOES IT PROVE ANYTHING?
I DON'T KNOW. MAYBE WE SHOULD GO TO PARIS AND TRY TO FIND THAT PHOTOGRAPHER, MARC ANTONIO.
WITH A NAME LIKE THAT, HE SHOULDN'T BE TOO HARD TO LOCATE. AND I DO LOVE PARIS.
I STILL DON'T HAVE ANY PROOF, THOUGH. IT MIGHT BE A WASTE OF TIME.
AND NOW THAT I'VE MET CRAY . . . I DON'T LIKE HIM, BUT HE'S AN ENTERTAINER. A BUSINESSMAN. HE DIDN'T LOOK LIKE THE SORT OF MAN WHO'D HURT ANYONE.

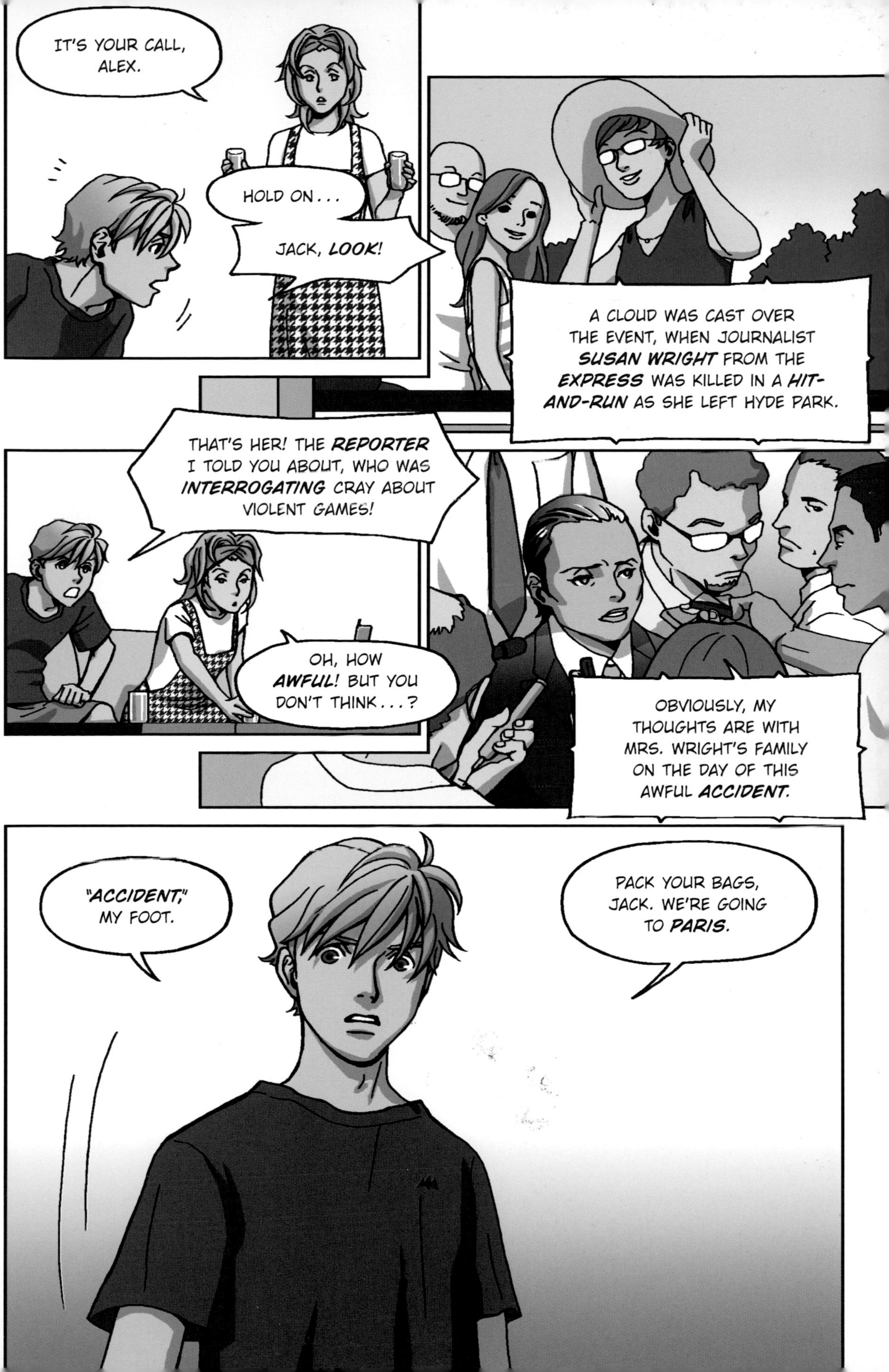
IT'S YOUR CALL, ALEX.
HOLD ON . . .
JACK, LOOK!
A CLOUD WAS CAST OVER THE EVENT, WHEN JOURNALIST SUSAN WRIGHT FROM THE EXPRESS WAS KILLED IN A HIT-AND-RUN AS SHE LEFT HYDE PARK.
THAT'S HER! THE REPORTER I TOLD YOU ABOUT, WHO WAS INTERROGATING CRAY ABOUT VIOLENT GAMES!
OH, HOW AWFUL! BUT YOU DON'T THINK . . .?
OBVIOUSLY, MY THOUGHTS ARE WITH MRS. WRIGHT'S FAMILY ON THE DAY OF THIS AWFUL ACCIDENT.
"ACCIDENT," MY FOOT.
PACK YOUR BAGS, JACK. WE'RE GOING TO PARIS.

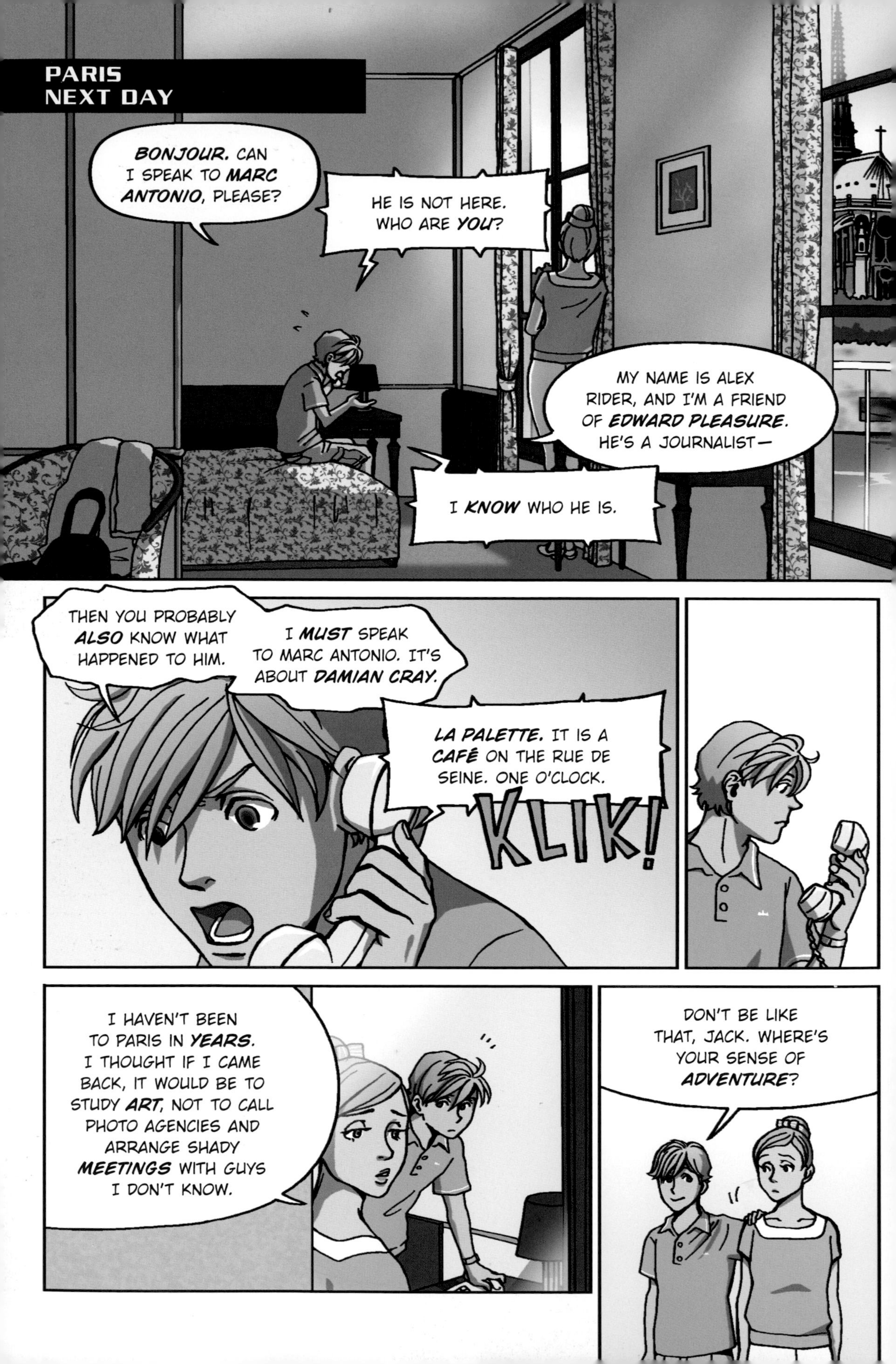
PARIS
NEXT DAY
BONJOUR. CAN I SPEAK TO MARC ANTONIO, PLEASE?
HE IS NOT HERE. WHO ARE YOU?
MY NAME IS ALEX RIDER, AND I'M A FRIEND OF EDWARD PLEASURE. HE'S A JOURNALIST—
I KNOW WHO HE IS.
THEN YOU PROBABLY ALSO KNOW WHAT HAPPENED TO HIM.
I MUST SPEAK TO MARC ANTONIO. IT'S ABOUT DAMIAN CRAY.
LA PALETTE. IT IS A CAFÉ ON THE RUE DE SEINE. ONE O'CLOCK.
KLIK!
I HAVEN'T BEEN TO PARIS IN YEARS. I THOUGHT IF I CAME BACK, IT WOULD BE TO STUDY ART, NOT TO CALL PHOTO AGENCIES AND ARRANGE SHADY MEETINGS WITH GUYS I DON'T KNOW.
DON'T BE LIKE THAT, JACK. WHERE'S YOUR SENSE OF ADVENTURE?

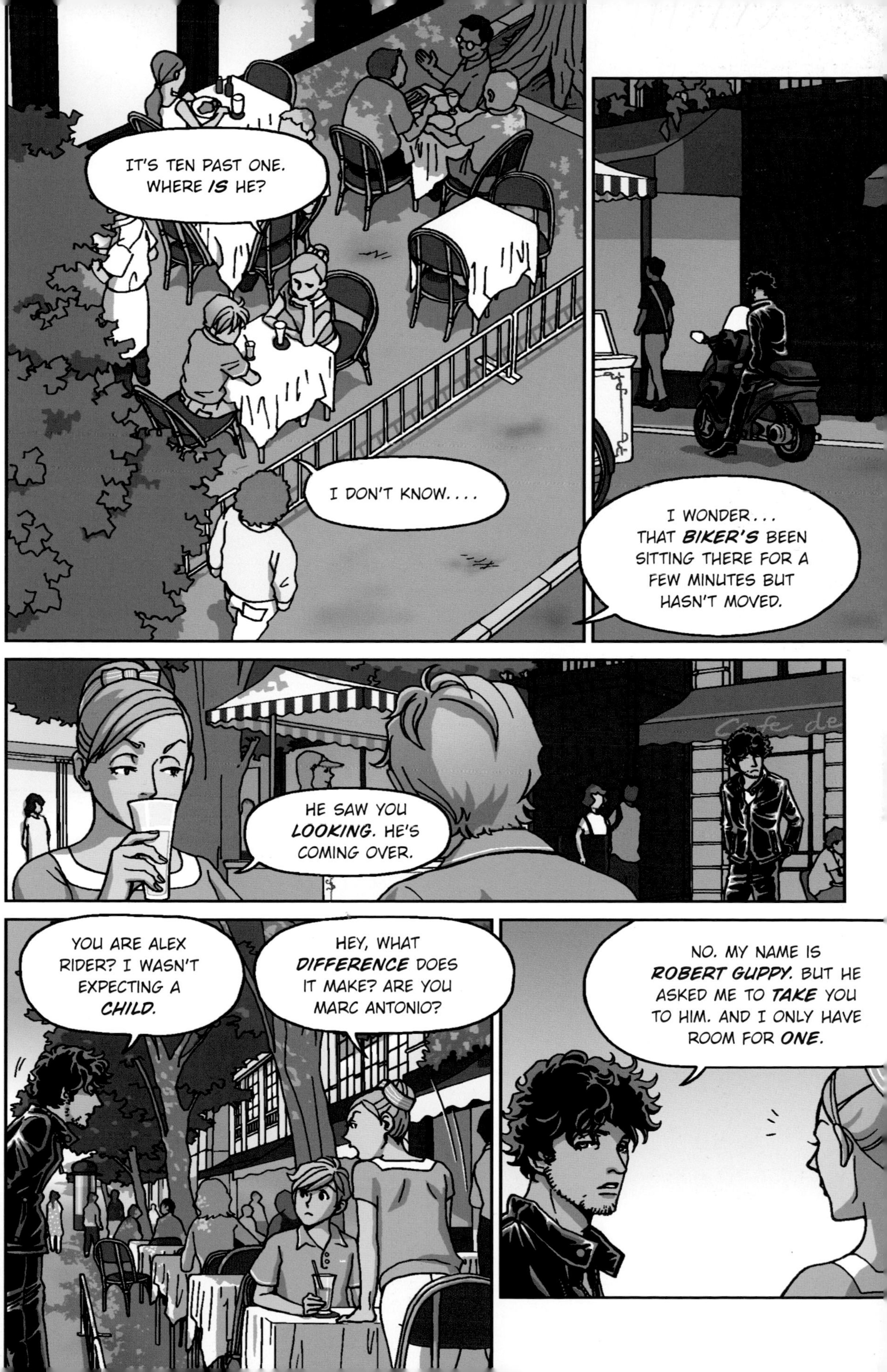
IT'S TEN PAST ONE. WHERE IS HE?
I DON'T KNOW. . . .
I WONDER . . . THAT BIKER'S BEEN SITTING THERE FOR A FEW MINUTES BUT HASN'T MOVED.
HE SAW YOU LOOKING. HE'S COMING OVER.
YOU ARE ALEX RIDER? I WASN'T EXPECTING A CHILD.
HEY, WHAT DIFFERENCE DOES IT MAKE? ARE YOU MARC ANTONIO?
NO. MY NAME IS ROBERT GUPPY. BUT HE ASKED ME TO TAKE YOU TO HIM. AND I ONLY HAVE ROOM FOR ONE.

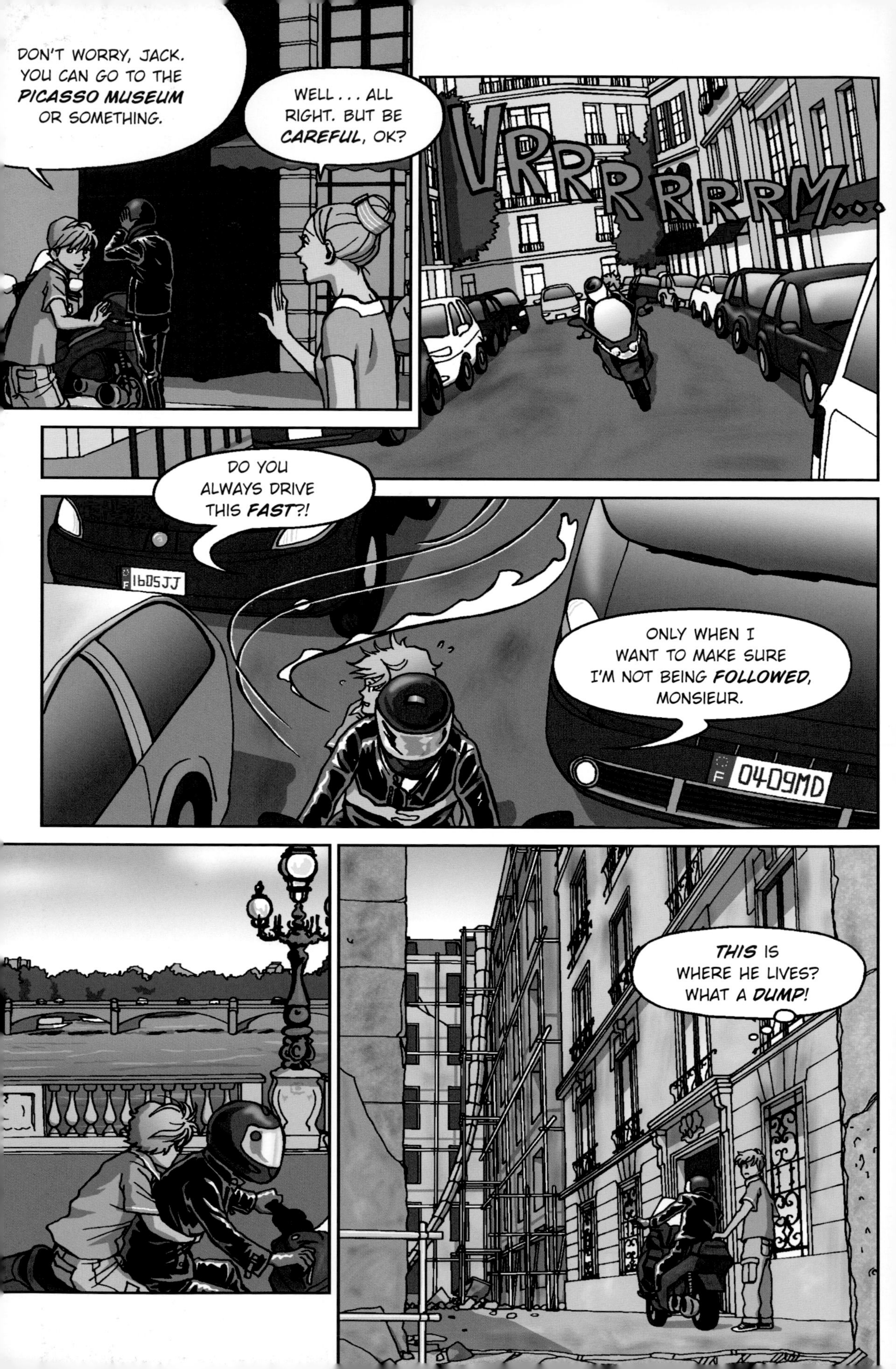

DON'T WORRY, JACK. YOU CAN GO TO THE *PICASSO MUSEUM* OR SOMETHING.
WELL . . . ALL RIGHT. BUT BE *CAREFUL*, OK?
VRRRRRRRM...
DO YOU ALWAYS DRIVE THIS *FAST*?!
16O5JJ
ONLY WHEN I WANT TO MAKE SURE I'M NOT BEING *FOLLOWED*, MONSIEUR.
F
O4O9MD
THIS IS WHERE HE LIVES? WHAT A *DUMP*!

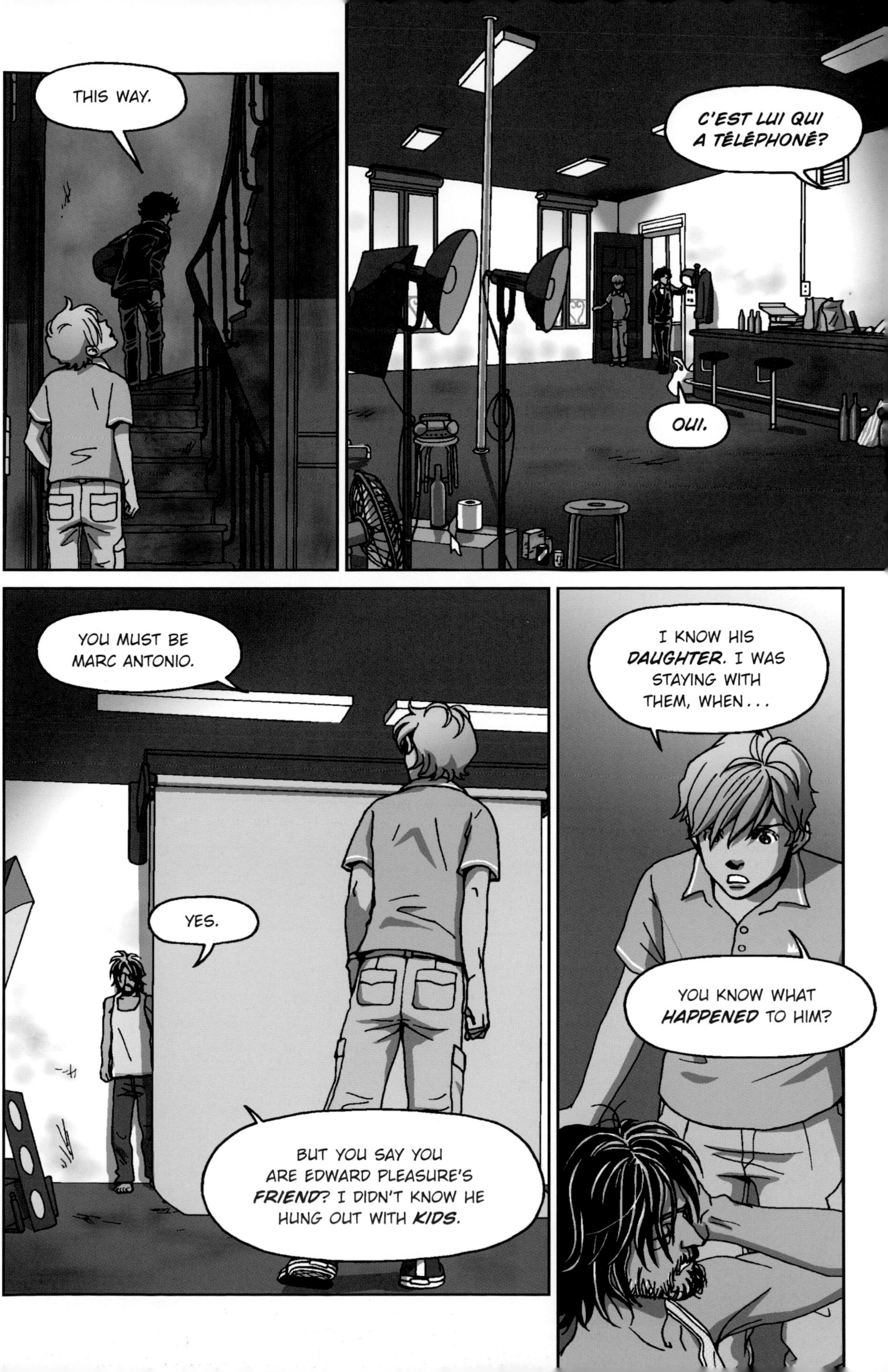
THIS WAY.
C'EST LUI QUI A TÉLÉPHONÉ?
OUI.
YOU MUST BE MARC ANTONIO.
YES.
BUT YOU SAY YOU ARE EDWARD PLEASURE'S *FRIEND*? I DIDN'T KNOW HE HUNG OUT WITH *KIDS*.
I KNOW HIS *DAUGHTER*. I WAS STAYING WITH THEM, WHEN . . .
YOU KNOW WHAT *HAPPENED* TO HIM?

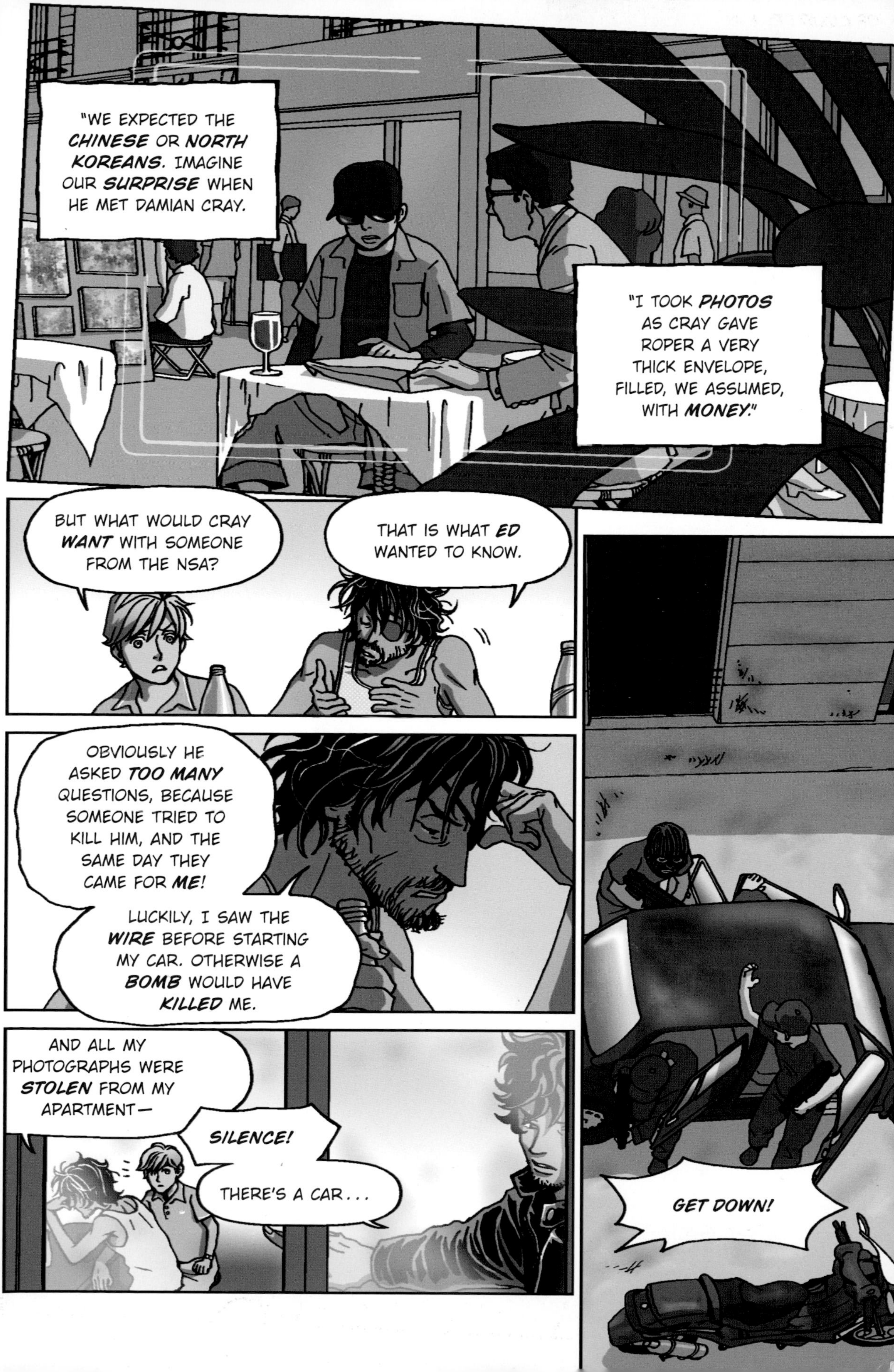
"WE EXPECTED THE CHINESE OR NORTH KOREANS. IMAGINE OUR SURPRISE WHEN HE MET DAMIAN CRAY.
"I TOOK PHOTOS AS CRAY GAVE ROPER A VERY THICK ENVELOPE, FILLED, WE ASSUMED, WITH MONEY."
BUT WHAT WOULD CRAY WANT WITH SOMEONE FROM THE NSA?
THAT IS WHAT ED WANTED TO KNOW.
OBVIOUSLY HE ASKED TOO MANY QUESTIONS, BECAUSE SOMEONE TRIED TO KILL HIM, AND THE SAME DAY THEY CAME FOR ME!
LUCKILY, I SAW THE WIRE BEFORE STARTING MY CAR. OTHERWISE A BOMB WOULD HAVE KILLED ME.
AND ALL MY PHOTOGRAPHS WERE STOLEN FROM MY APARTMENT—
SILENCE!
THERE'S A CAR . . .
GET DOWN!

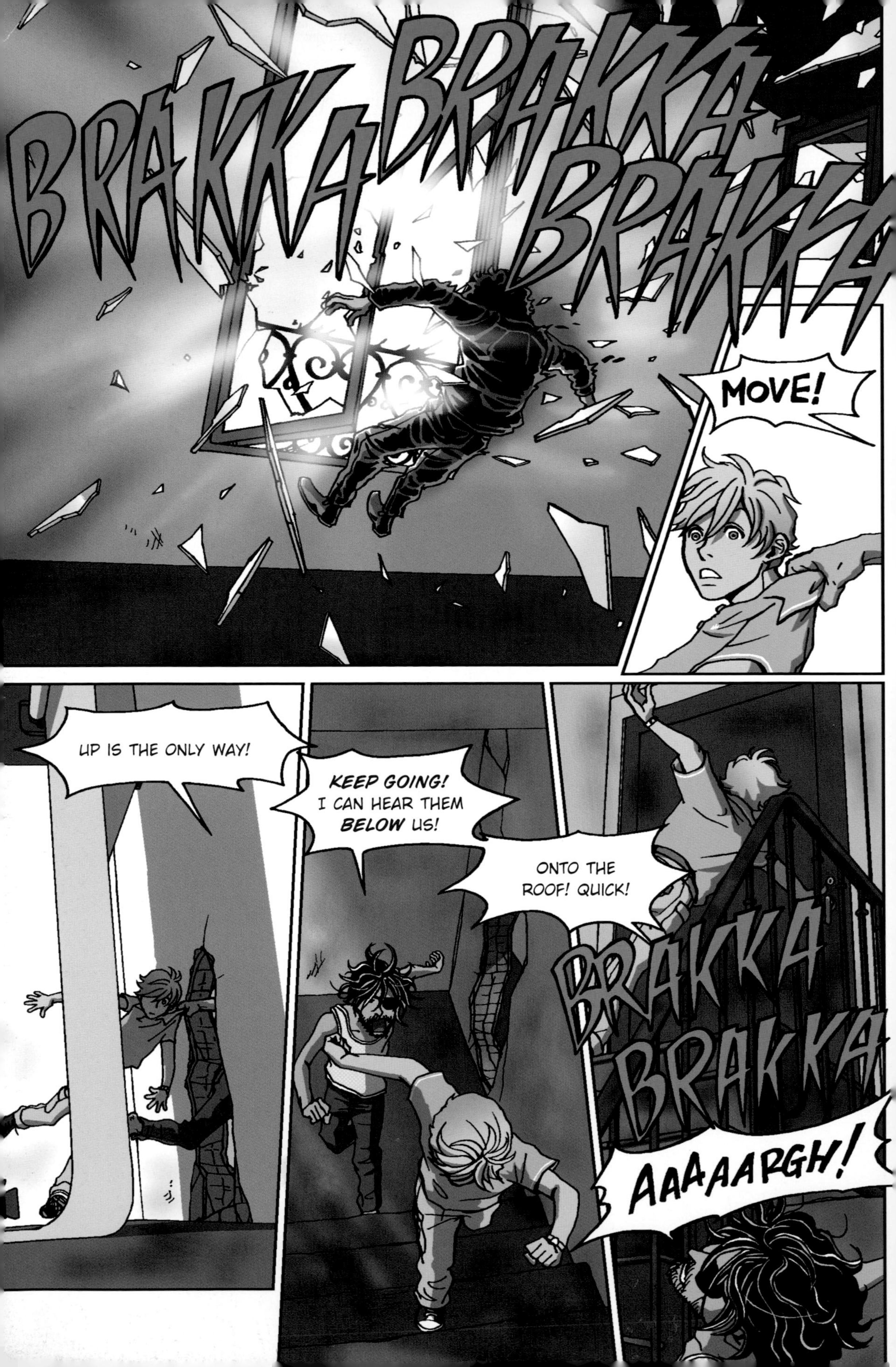
BRAKKA BRAKKA BRAKKA
MOVE!
UP IS THE ONLY WAY!
KEEP GOING! I CAN HEAR THEM BELOW US!
ONTO THE ROOF! QUICK!
BRAKKA BRAKKA
AAAAARGH!

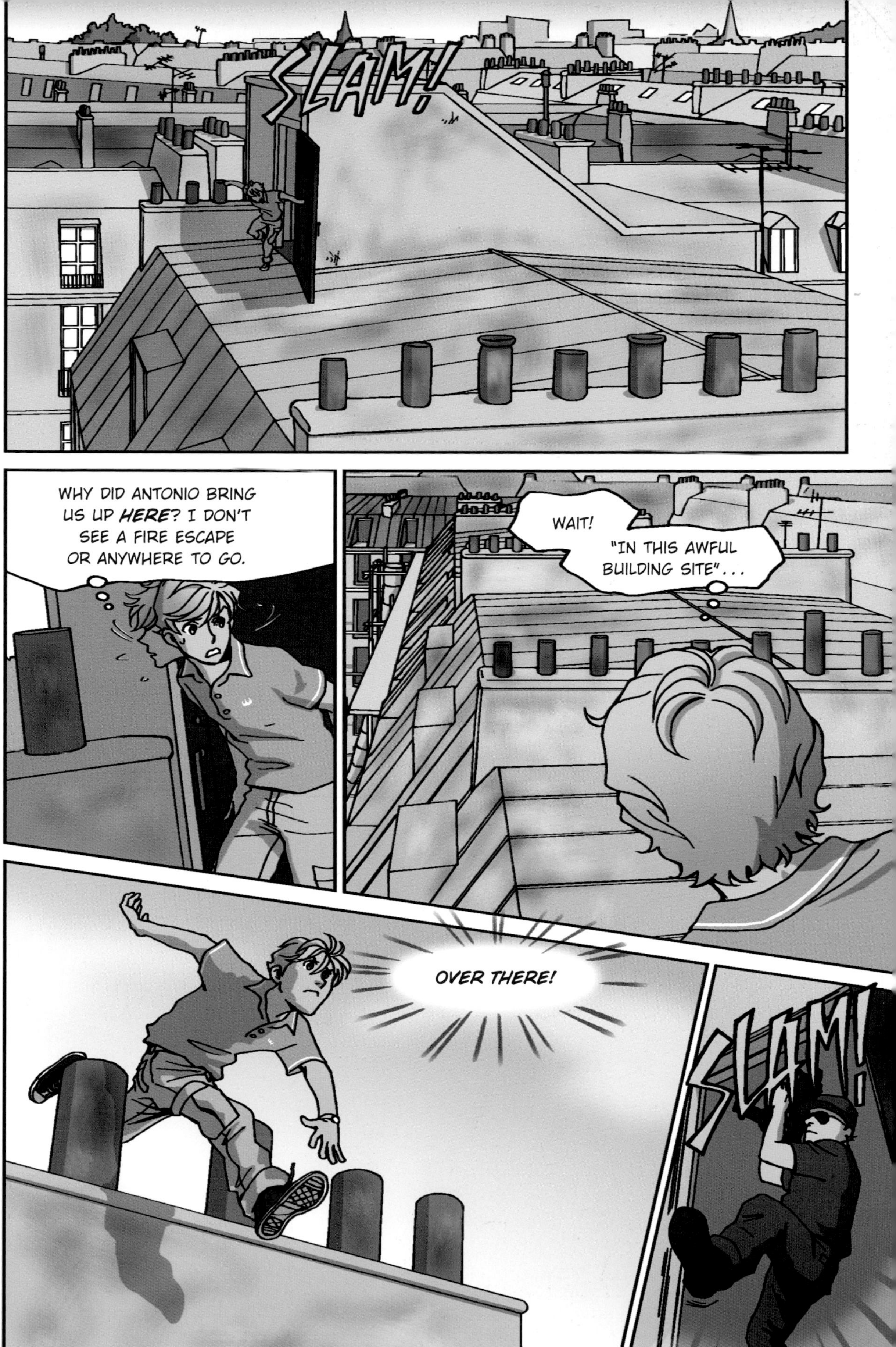
SLAM!
WHY DID ANTONIO BRING US UP *HERE*? I DON'T SEE A FIRE ESCAPE OR ANYWHERE TO GO.
WAIT!
"IN THIS AWFUL BUILDING SITE". . .
OVER THERE!
SLAM!

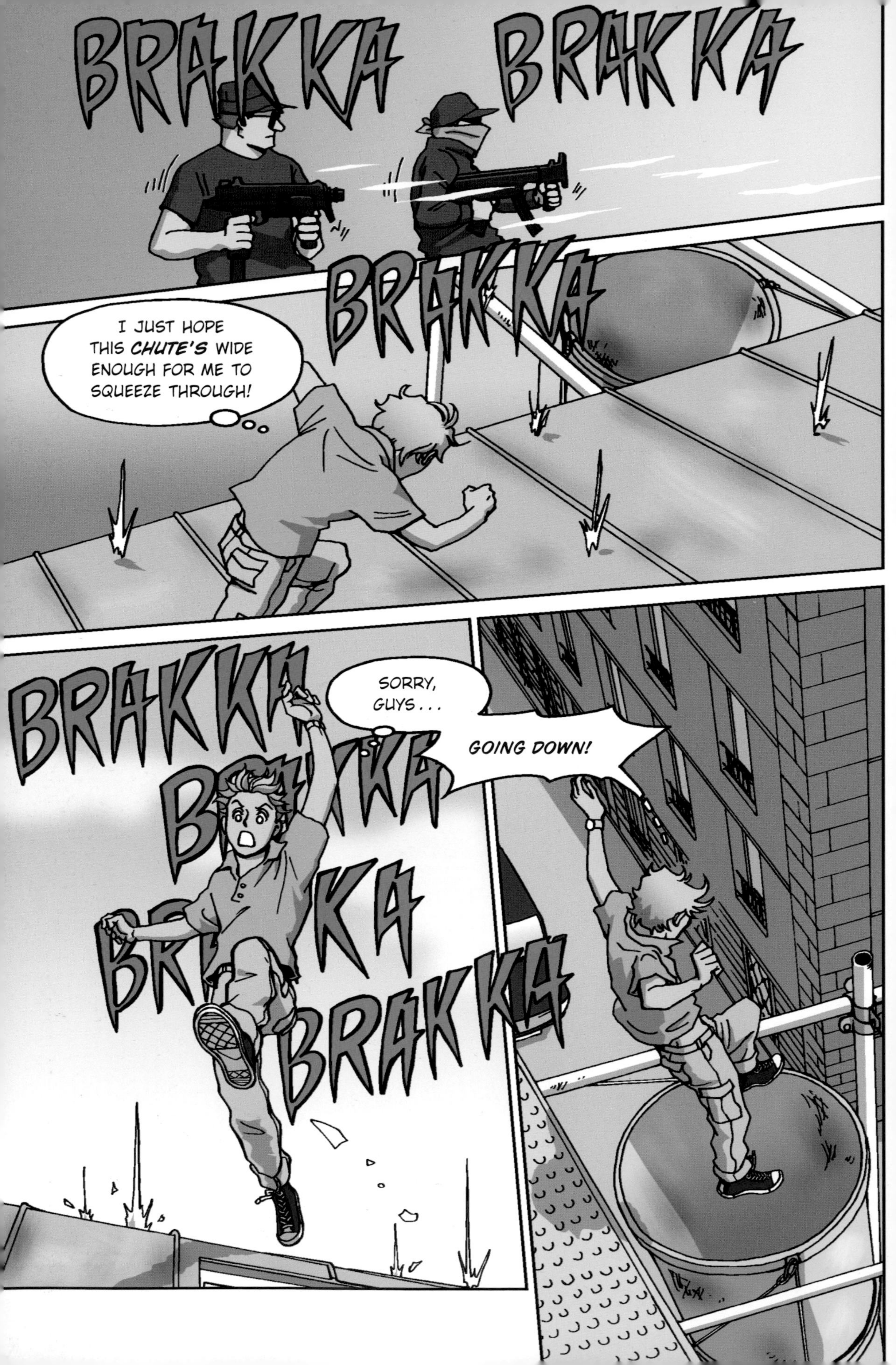
BRAKKA BRAKKA
BRAKKA
I JUST HOPE THIS CHUTE'S WIDE ENOUGH FOR ME TO SQUEEZE THROUGH!
BRAKKA
SORRY, GUYS . . .
GOING DOWN!
BRAKKA
BRAKKA

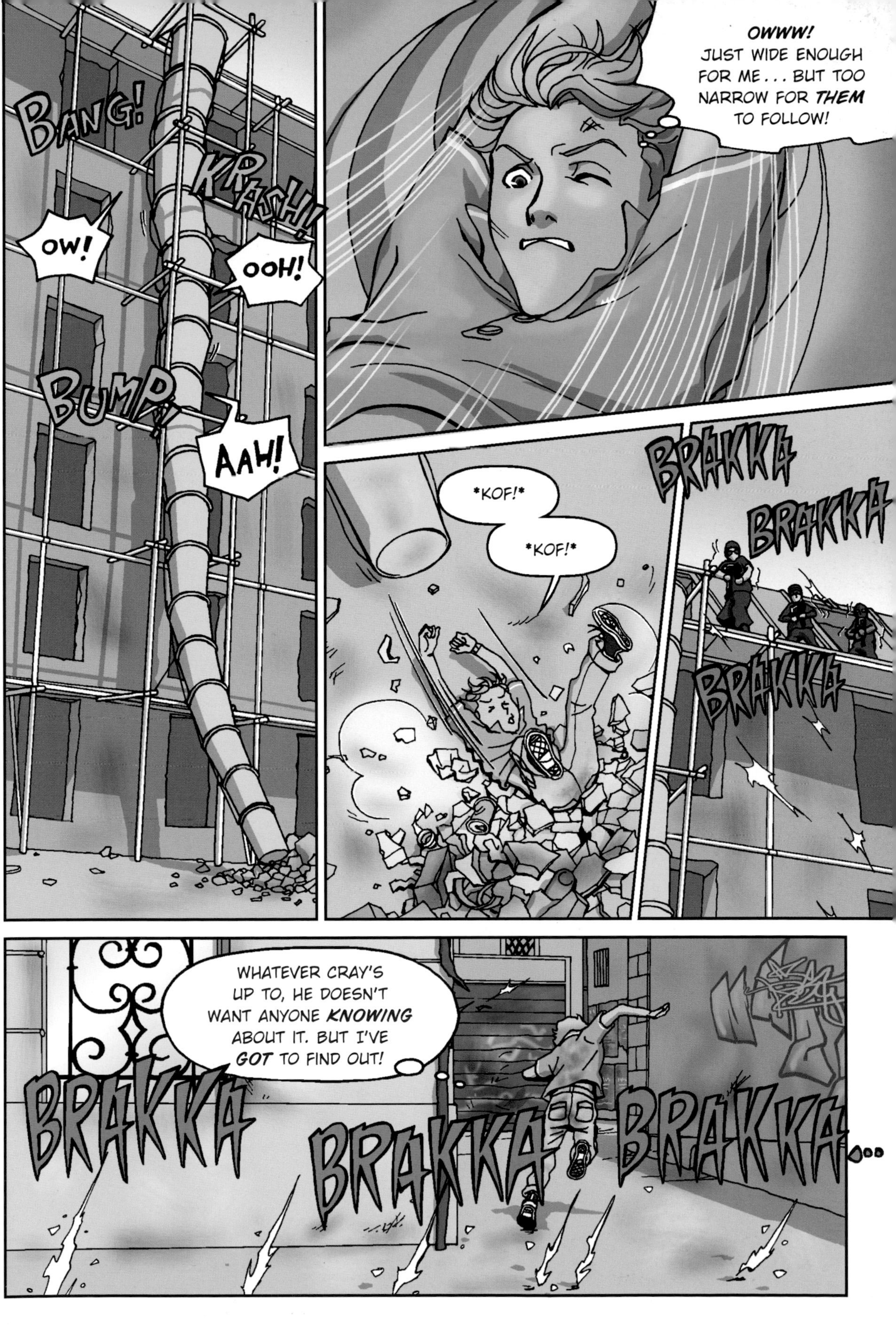
BANG!
KRASH!!
OW!
OOH!
BUMP!!
AAH!
OWWW!
JUST WIDE ENOUGH FOR ME . . . BUT TOO NARROW FOR THEM TO FOLLOW!
KOF!
KOF!
BRAKKA
BRAKKA
BRAKKA
WHATEVER CRAY'S UP TO, HE DOESN'T WANT ANYONE KNOWING ABOUT IT. BUT I'VE GOT TO FIND OUT!
BRAKKA
BRAKKA
BRAKKA...

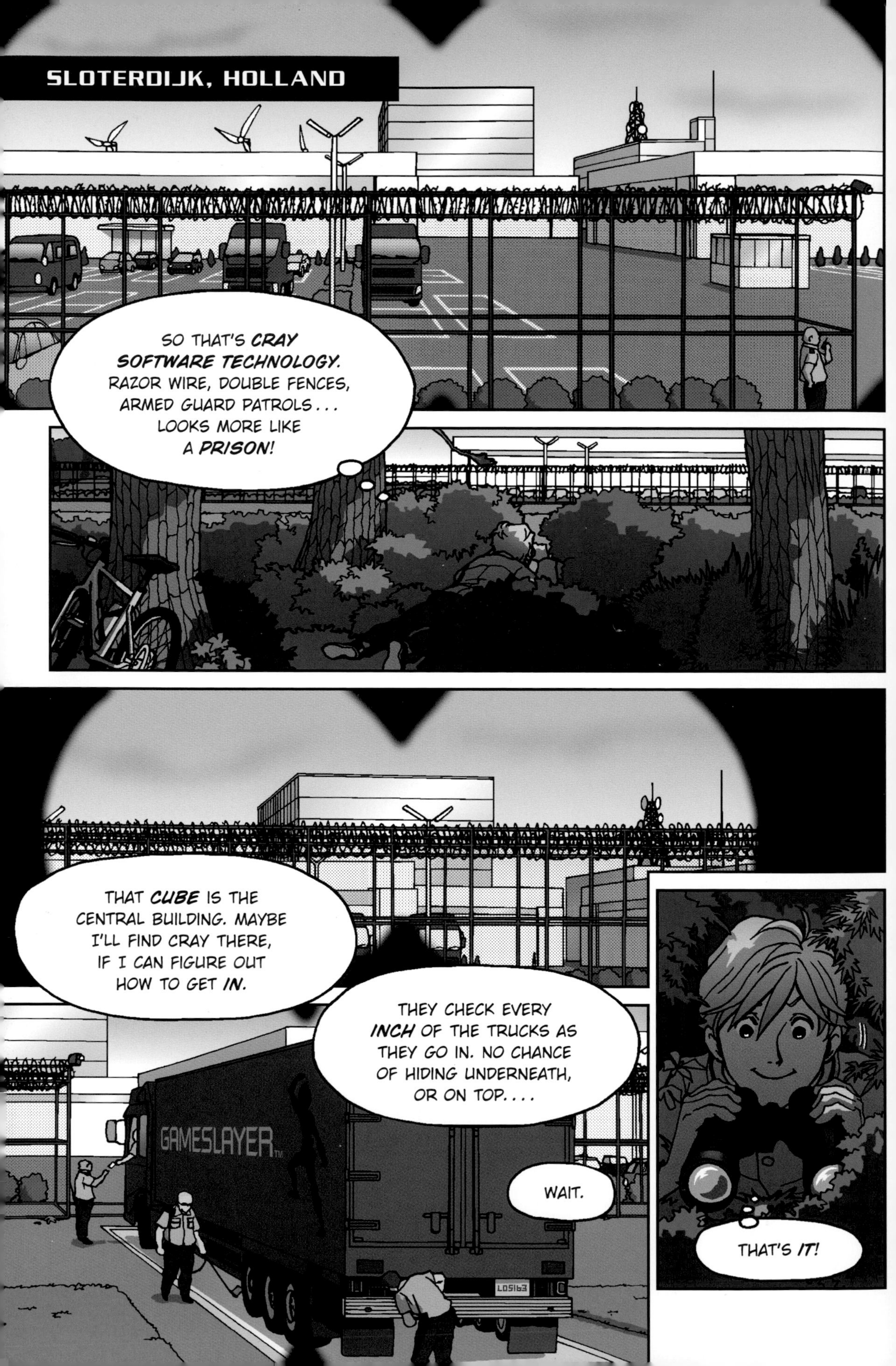
SLOTERDIJK, HOLLAND
SO THAT'S CRAY SOFTWARE TECHNOLOGY. RAZOR WIRE, DOUBLE FENCES, ARMED GUARD PATROLS . . . LOOKS MORE LIKE A PRISON!
THAT CUBE IS THE CENTRAL BUILDING. MAYBE I'LL FIND CRAY THERE, IF I CAN FIGURE OUT HOW TO GET IN.
THEY CHECK EVERY INCH OF THE TRUCKS AS THEY GO IN. NO CHANCE OF HIDING UNDERNEATH, OR ON TOP. . . .
GAMESLAYER™
WAIT.
THAT'S IT!

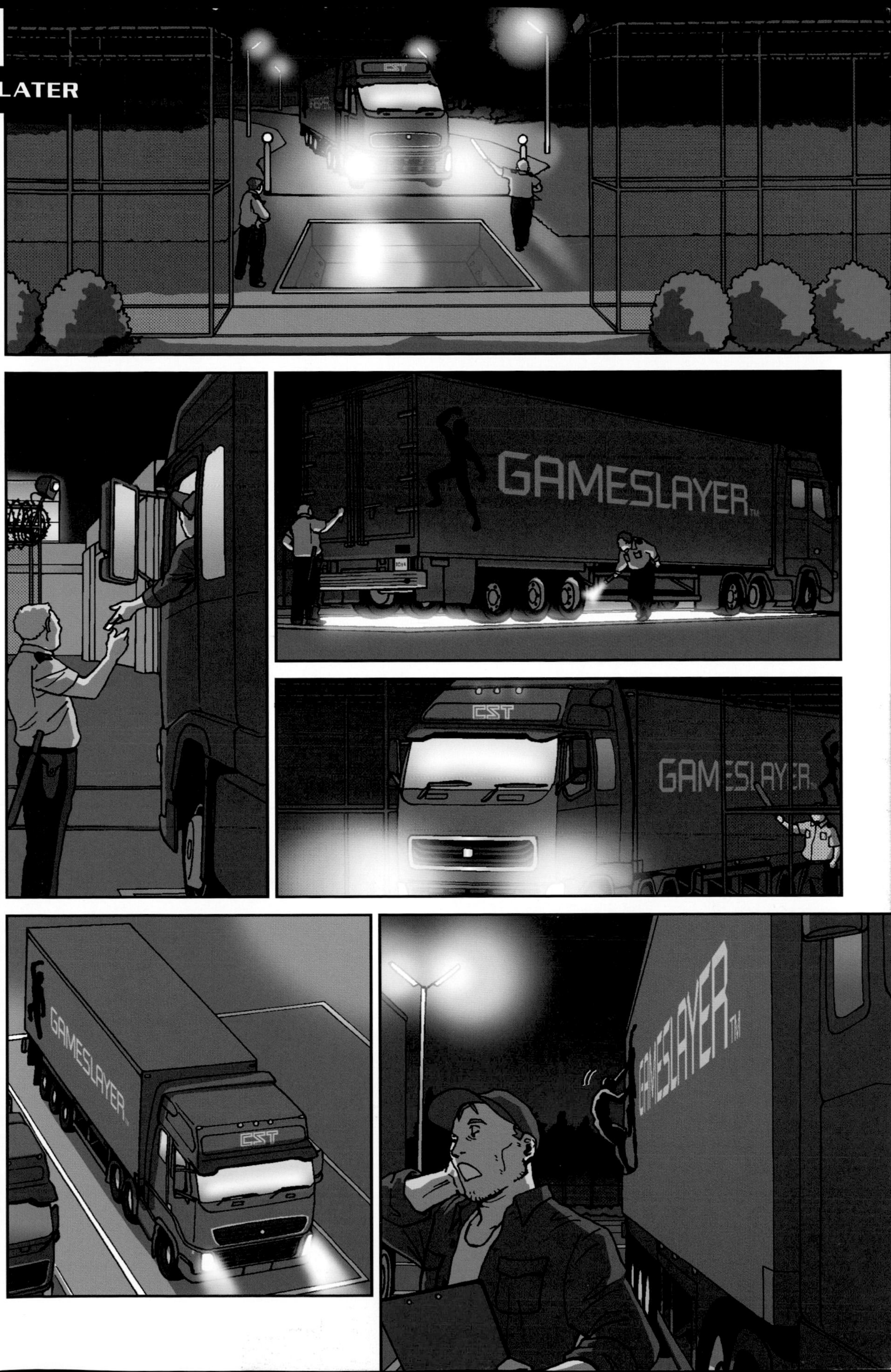
LATER
CST
GAMESLAYER™
CST
GAMESLAYER
GAMESLAYER
CST
GAMESLAYER™

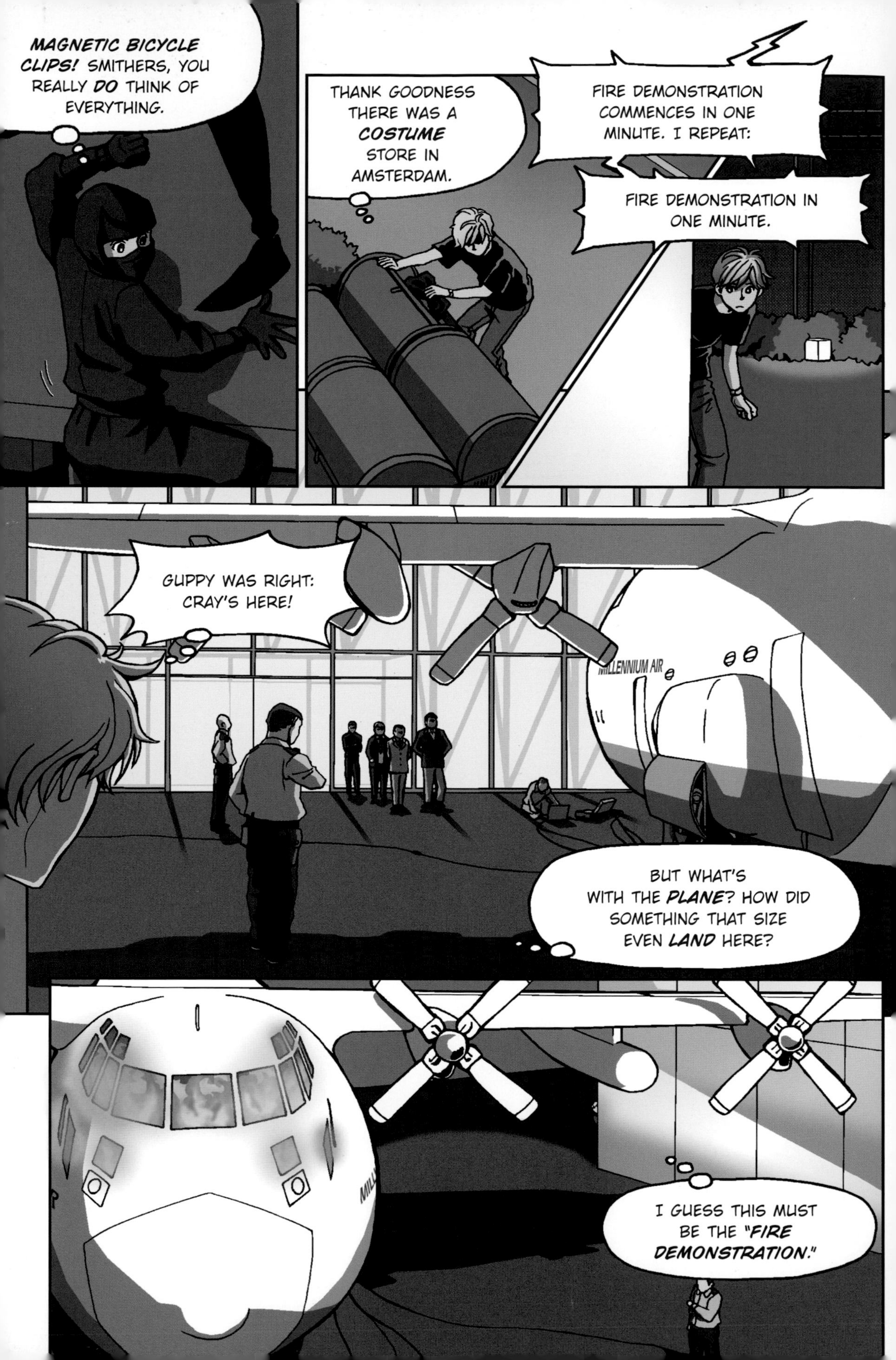
MAGNETIC BICYCLE CLIPS! SMITHERS, YOU REALLY DO THINK OF EVERYTHING.
THANK GOODNESS THERE WAS A COSTUME STORE IN AMSTERDAM.
FIRE DEMONSTRATION COMMENCES IN ONE MINUTE. I REPEAT:
FIRE DEMONSTRATION IN ONE MINUTE.
GUPPY WAS RIGHT: CRAY'S HERE!
MILLENNIUM AIR
BUT WHAT'S WITH THE PLANE? HOW DID SOMETHING THAT SIZE EVEN LAND HERE?
I GUESS THIS MUST BE THE "FIRE DEMONSTRATION."

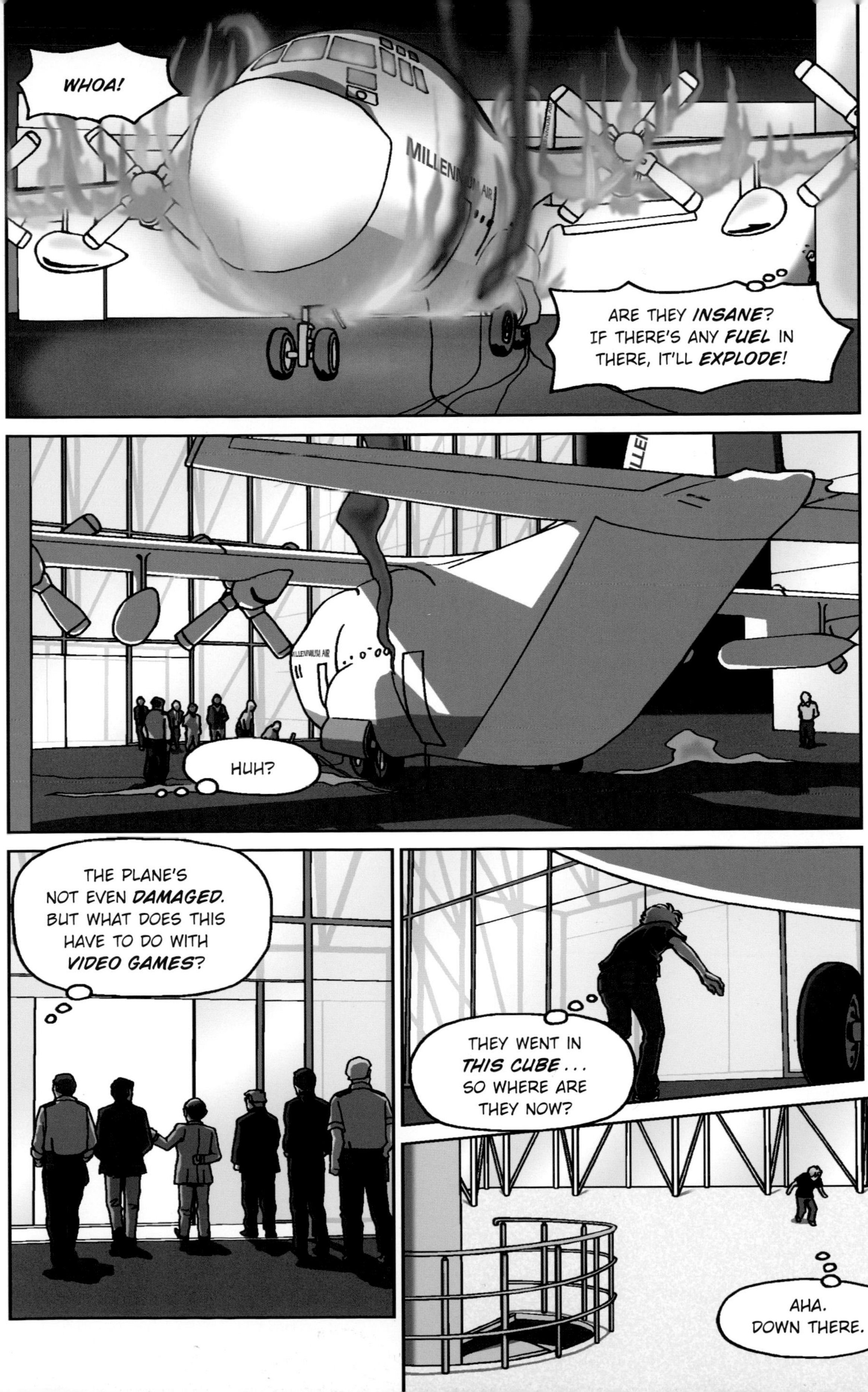

WHOA!
MILLENNIUM AIR
ARE THEY INSANE? IF THERE'S ANY FUEL IN THERE, IT'LL EXPLODE!
MILLENNIUM AIR
HUH?
THE PLANE'S NOT EVEN DAMAGED. BUT WHAT DOES THIS HAVE TO DO WITH VIDEO GAMES?
THEY WENT IN THIS CUBE . . . SO WHERE ARE THEY NOW?
AHA. DOWN THERE.

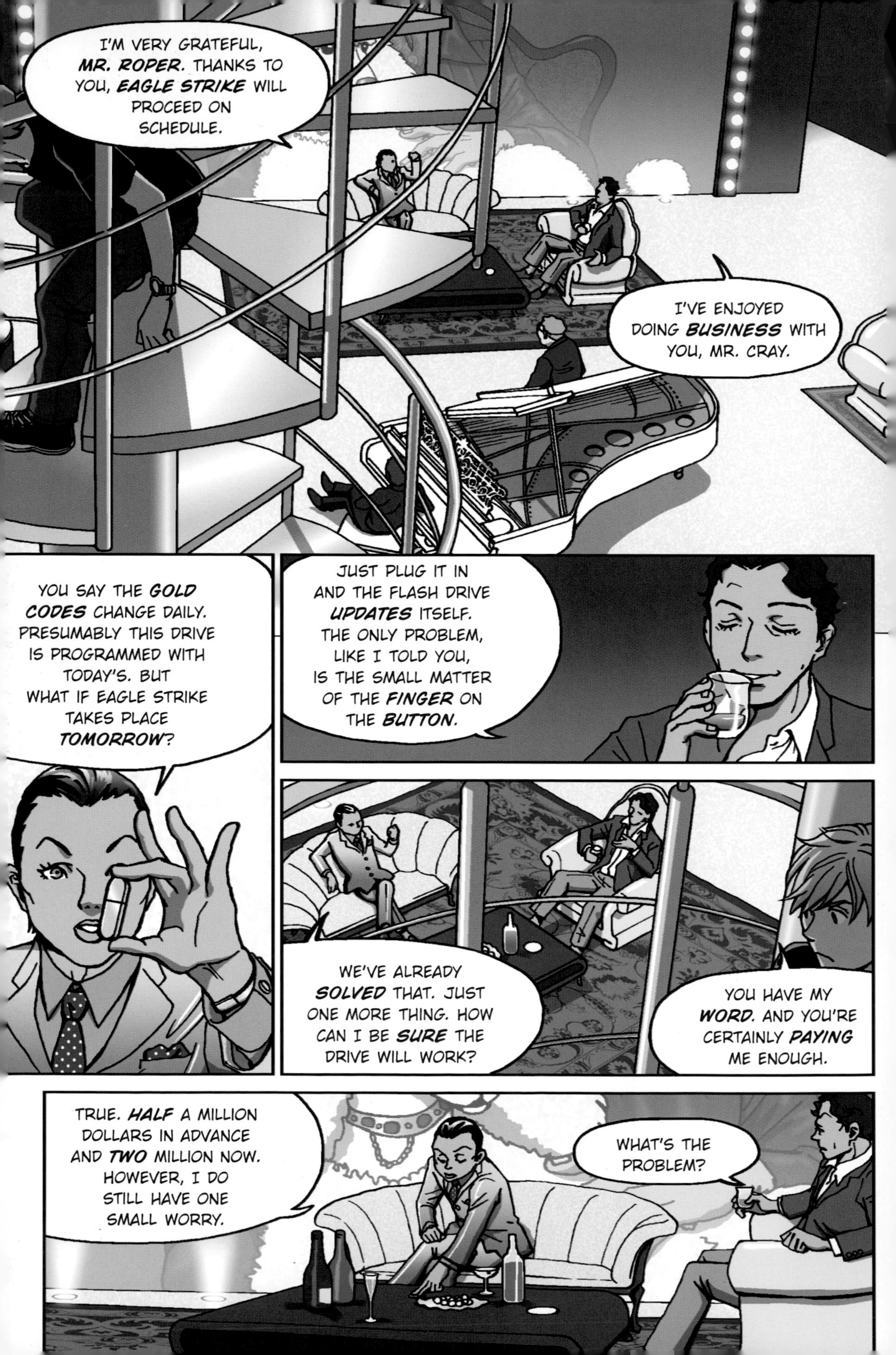
I'M VERY GRATEFUL, MR. ROPER. THANKS TO YOU, EAGLE STRIKE WILL PROCEED ON SCHEDULE.
I'VE ENJOYED DOING BUSINESS WITH YOU, MR. CRAY.
YOU SAY THE GOLD CODES CHANGE DAILY. PRESUMABLY THIS DRIVE IS PROGRAMMED WITH TODAY'S. BUT WHAT IF EAGLE STRIKE TAKES PLACE TOMORROW?
JUST PLUG IT IN AND THE FLASH DRIVE UPDATES ITSELF. THE ONLY PROBLEM, LIKE I TOLD YOU, IS THE SMALL MATTER OF THE FINGER ON THE BUTTON.
WE'VE ALREADY SOLVED THAT. JUST ONE MORE THING. HOW CAN I BE SURE THE DRIVE WILL WORK?
YOU HAVE MY WORD. AND YOU'RE CERTAINLY PAYING ME ENOUGH.
TRUE. HALF A MILLION DOLLARS IN ADVANCE AND TWO MILLION NOW. HOWEVER, I DO STILL HAVE ONE SMALL WORRY.
WHAT'S THE PROBLEM?

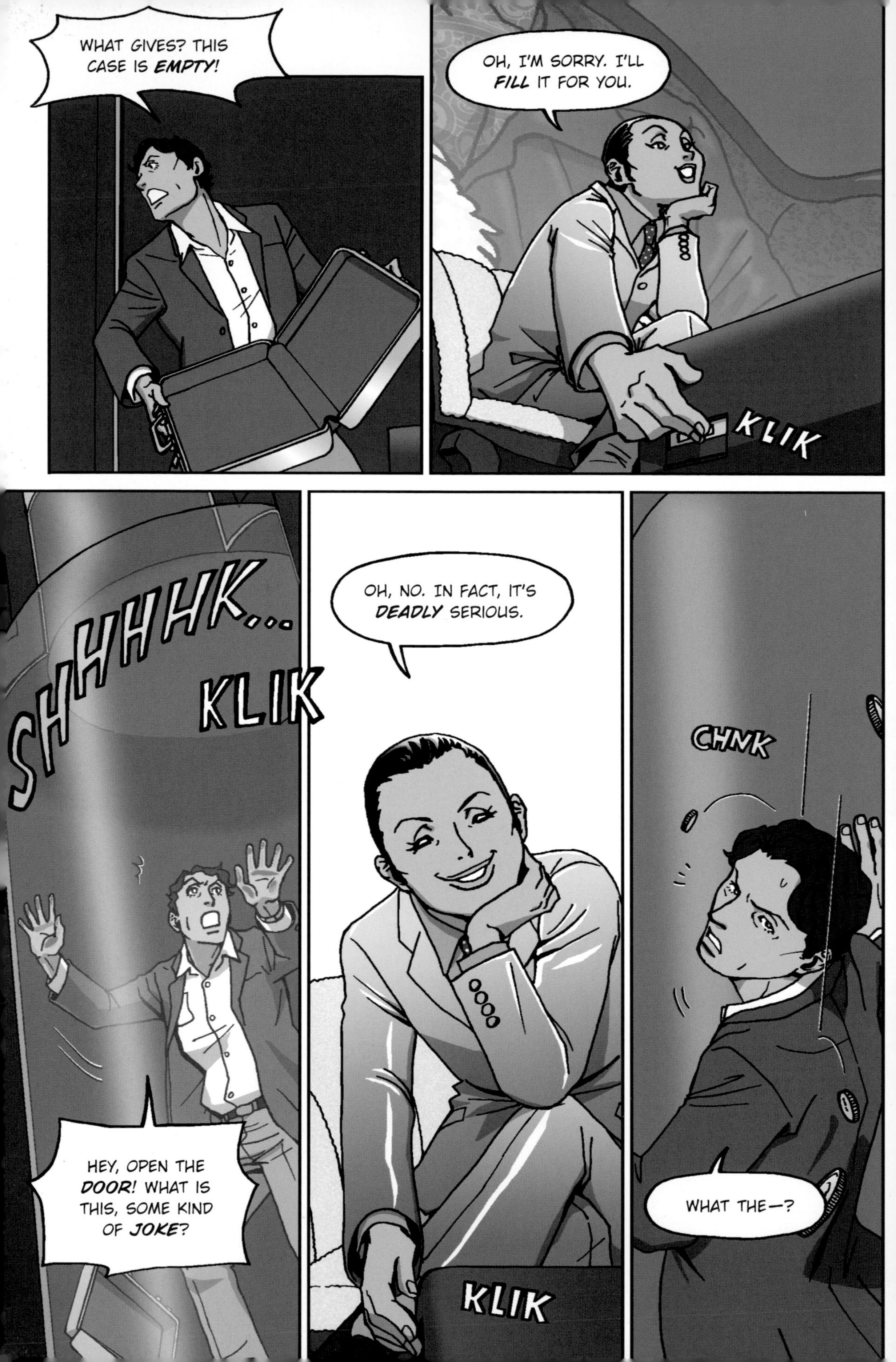
WHAT GIVES? THIS CASE IS *EMPTY*!
OH, I'M SORRY. I'LL *FILL* IT FOR YOU.
KLIK
SHHHHK...
KLIK
HEY, OPEN THE *DOOR*! WHAT IS THIS, SOME KIND OF *JOKE*?
OH, NO. IN FACT, IT'S *DEADLY* SERIOUS.
KLIK
CHNK
WHAT THE—?

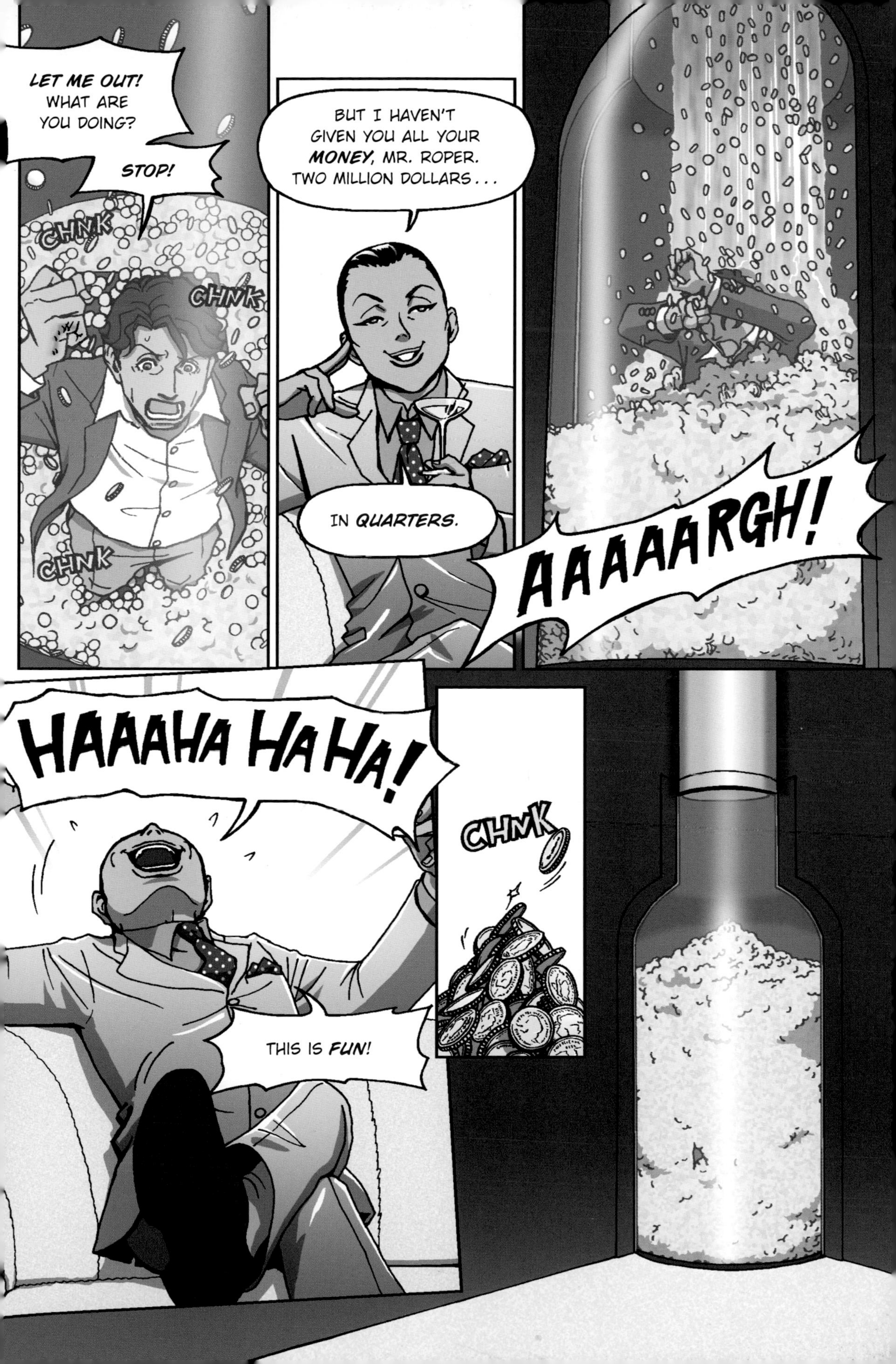

LET ME OUT! WHAT ARE YOU DOING?
STOP!
CHNK
CHNK
CHNK
BUT I HAVEN'T GIVEN YOU ALL YOUR *MONEY*, MR. ROPER. TWO MILLION DOLLARS . . .
IN *QUARTERS*.
AAAAARGH!
HAAAHA HAHA!
THIS IS *FUN*!
CHNK

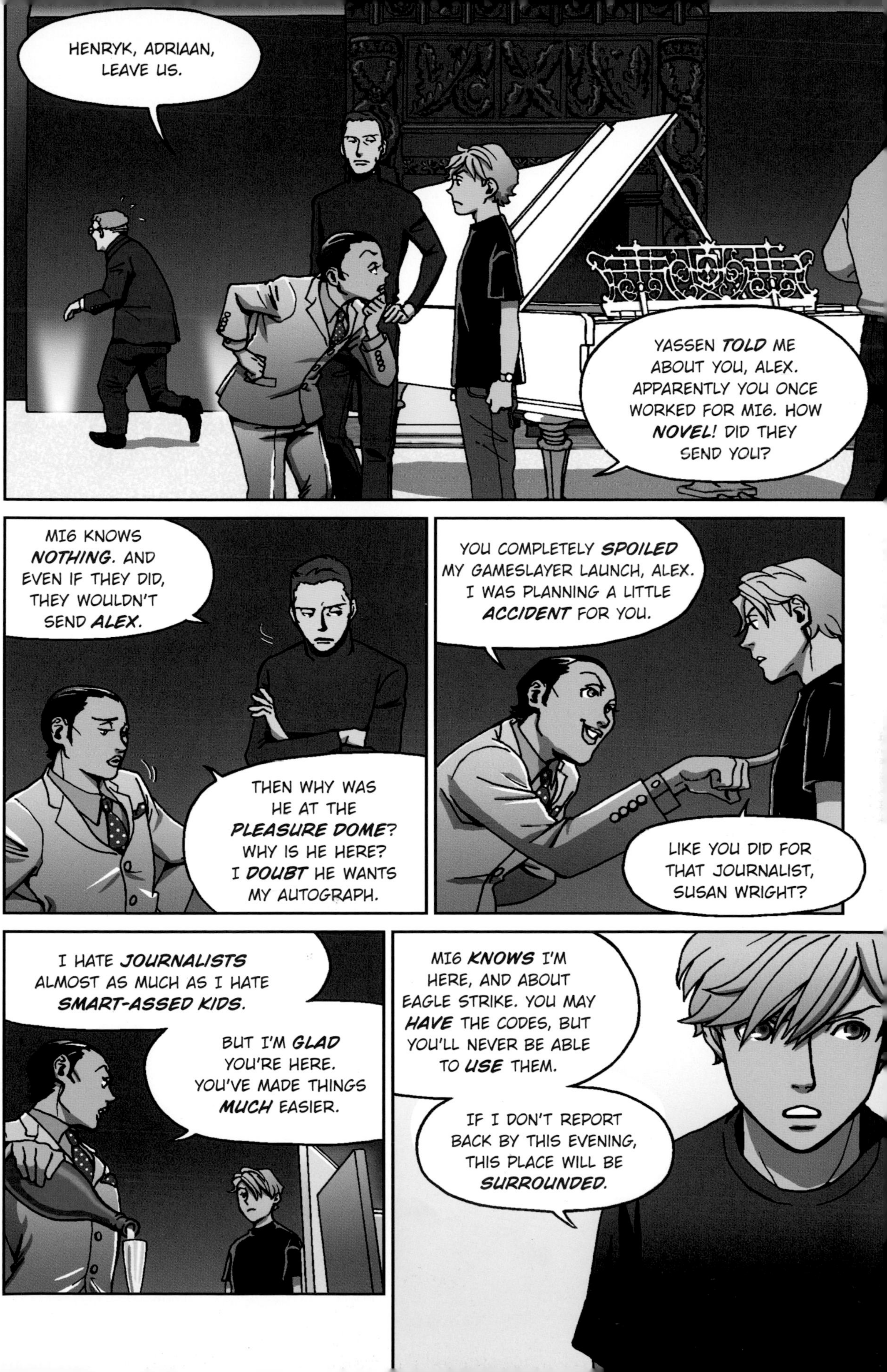
HENRYK, ADRIAAN, LEAVE US.
YASSEN TOLD ME ABOUT YOU, ALEX. APPARENTLY YOU ONCE WORKED FOR MI6. HOW NOVEL! DID THEY SEND YOU?
MI6 KNOWS NOTHING. AND EVEN IF THEY DID, THEY WOULDN'T SEND ALEX.
THEN WHY WAS HE AT THE PLEASURE DOME? WHY IS HE HERE? I DOUBT HE WANTS MY AUTOGRAPH.
YOU COMPLETELY SPOILED MY GAMESLAYER LAUNCH, ALEX. I WAS PLANNING A LITTLE ACCIDENT FOR YOU.
LIKE YOU DID FOR THAT JOURNALIST, SUSAN WRIGHT?
I HATE JOURNALISTS ALMOST AS MUCH AS I HATE SMART-ASSED KIDS.
BUT I'M GLAD YOU'RE HERE. YOU'VE MADE THINGS MUCH EASIER.
MI6 KNOWS I'M HERE, AND ABOUT EAGLE STRIKE. YOU MAY HAVE THE CODES, BUT YOU'LL NEVER BE ABLE TO USE THEM.
IF I DON'T REPORT BACK BY THIS EVENING, THIS PLACE WILL BE SURROUNDED.

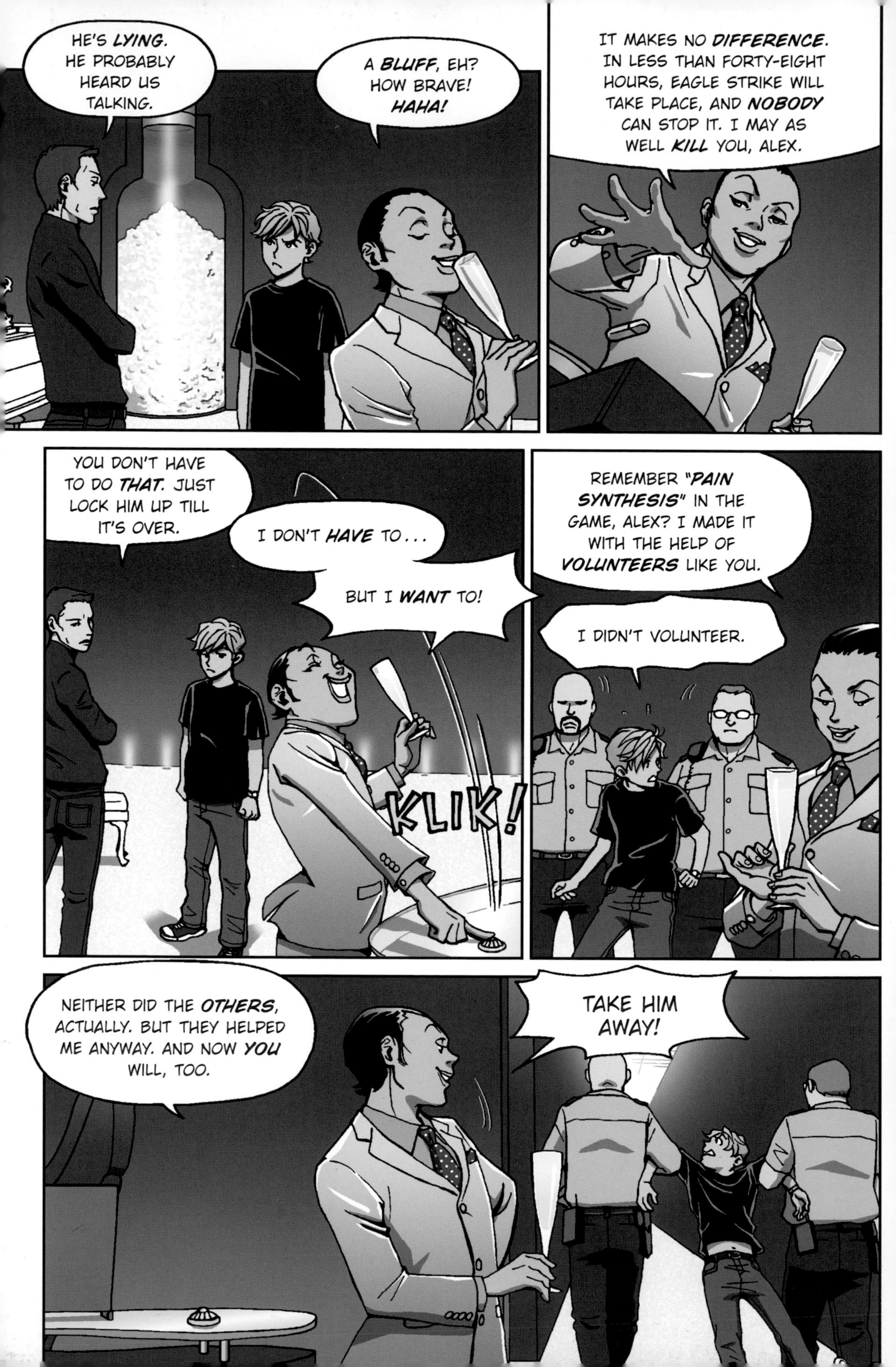
HE'S LYING. HE PROBABLY HEARD US TALKING.
A BLUFF, EH? HOW BRAVE! HAHA!
IT MAKES NO DIFFERENCE. IN LESS THAN FORTY-EIGHT HOURS, EAGLE STRIKE WILL TAKE PLACE, AND NOBODY CAN STOP IT. I MAY AS WELL KILL YOU, ALEX.
YOU DON'T HAVE TO DO THAT. JUST LOCK HIM UP TILL IT'S OVER.
I DON'T HAVE TO . . .
BUT I WANT TO!
KLIK!
REMEMBER "PAIN SYNTHESIS" IN THE GAME, ALEX? I MADE IT WITH THE HELP OF VOLUNTEERS LIKE YOU.
I DIDN'T VOLUNTEER.
NEITHER DID THE OTHERS, ACTUALLY. BUT THEY HELPED ME ANYWAY. AND NOW YOU WILL, TOO.
TAKE HIM AWAY!

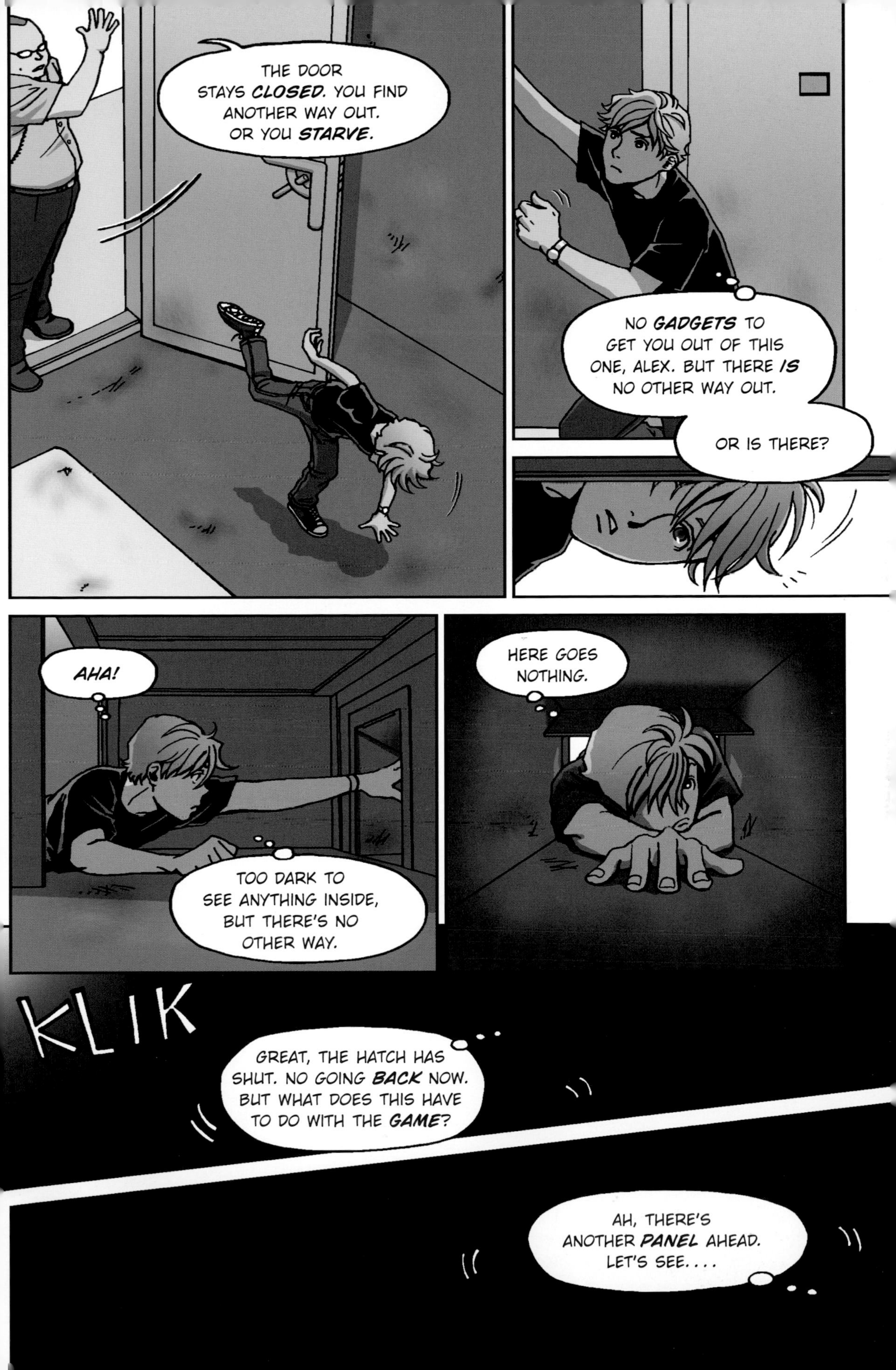
THE DOOR STAYS CLOSED. YOU FIND ANOTHER WAY OUT. OR YOU STARVE.
NO GADGETS TO GET YOU OUT OF THIS ONE, ALEX. BUT THERE IS NO OTHER WAY OUT.
OR IS THERE?
AHA!
TOO DARK TO SEE ANYTHING INSIDE, BUT THERE'S NO OTHER WAY.
HERE GOES NOTHING.
KLIK
GREAT, THE HATCH HAS SHUT. NO GOING BACK NOW. BUT WHAT DOES THIS HAVE TO DO WITH THE GAME?
AH, THERE'S ANOTHER PANEL AHEAD. LET'S SEE. . . .

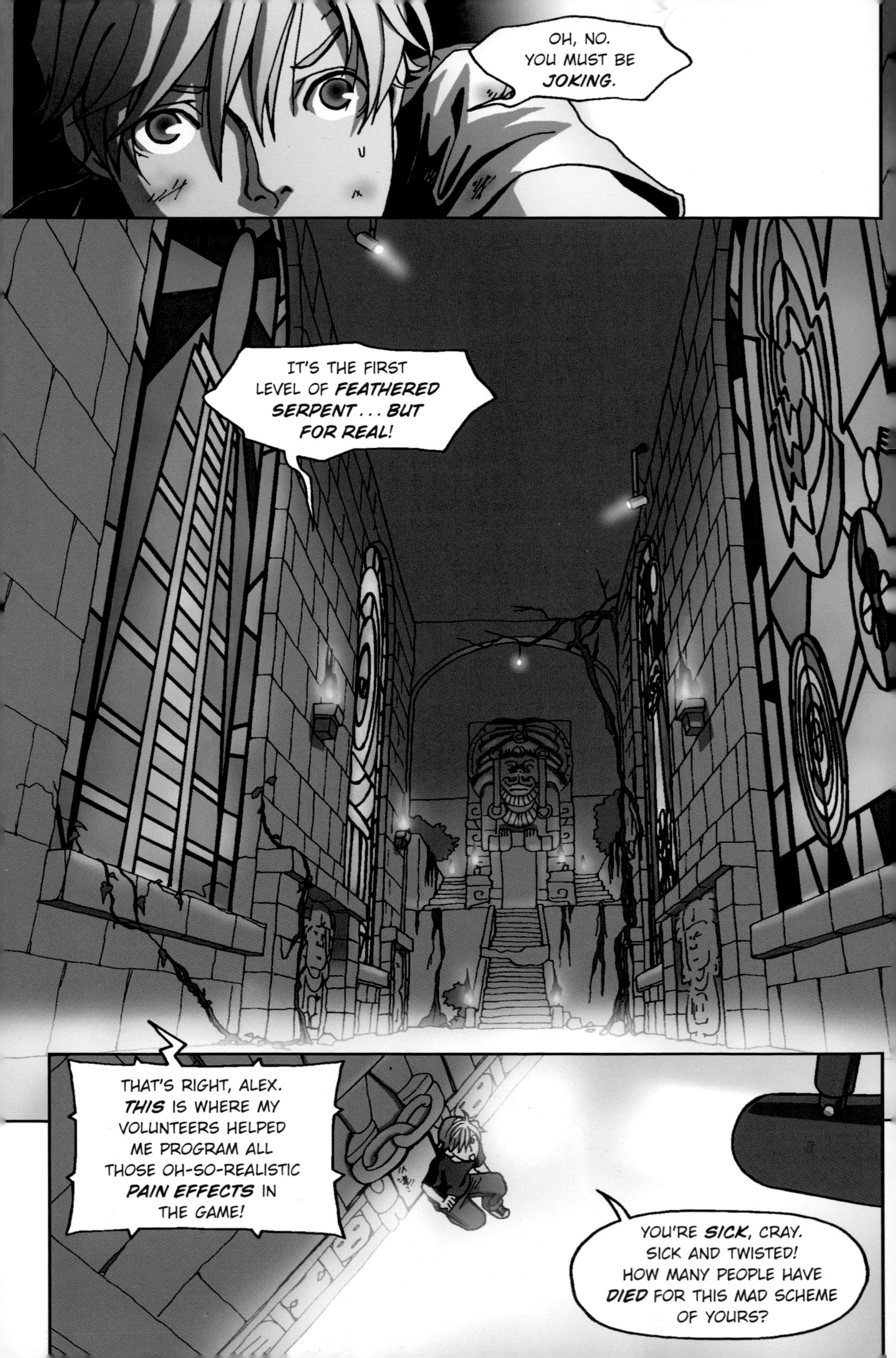
OH, NO. YOU MUST BE JOKING.
IT'S THE FIRST LEVEL OF FEATHERED SERPENT . . . BUT FOR REAL!
THAT'S RIGHT, ALEX. THIS IS WHERE MY VOLUNTEERS HELPED ME PROGRAM ALL THOSE OH-SO-REALISTIC PAIN EFFECTS IN THE GAME!
YOU'RE SICK, CRAY. SICK AND TWISTED! HOW MANY PEOPLE HAVE DIED FOR THIS MAD SCHEME OF YOURS?

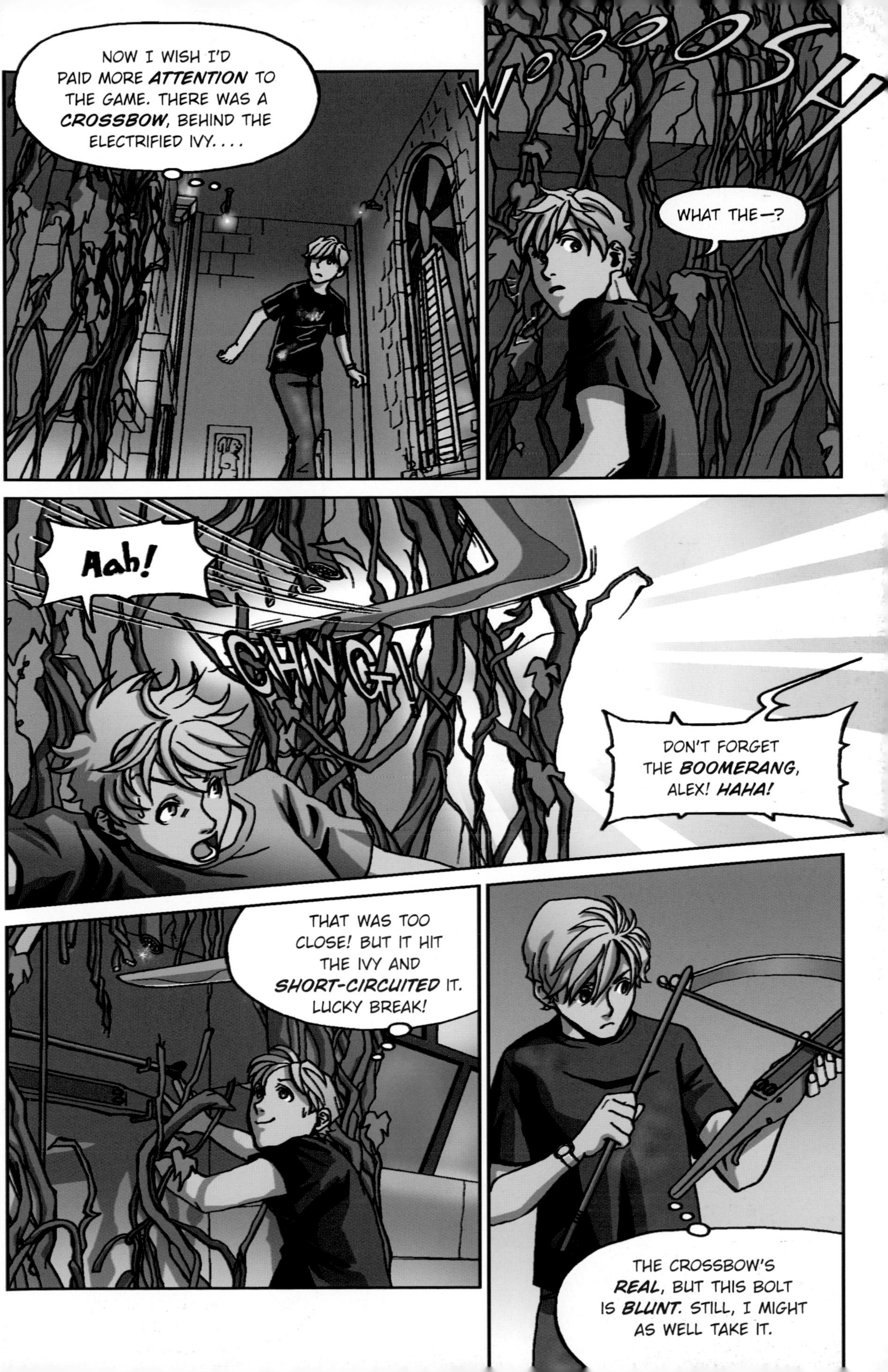

NOW I WISH I'D PAID MORE ATTENTION TO THE GAME. THERE WAS A CROSSBOW, BEHIND THE ELECTRIFIED IVY. . . .
WOOOOSH
WHAT THE—?
Aah!
CHNG!
DON'T FORGET THE BOOMERANG, ALEX! HAHA!
THAT WAS TOO CLOSE! BUT IT HIT THE IVY AND SHORT-CIRCUITED IT. LUCKY BREAK!
THE CROSSBOW'S REAL, BUT THIS BOLT IS BLUNT. STILL, I MIGHT AS WELL TAKE IT.

NOW FOR THE SWORD... NO, *WAIT!*

THERE WAS ANOTHER *BOOMERANG.*

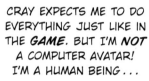

CRAY EXPECTS ME TO DO EVERYTHING JUST LIKE IN THE *GAME.* BUT I'M *NOT* A COMPUTER AVATAR! I'M A HUMAN BEING...

AND I CAN *CHEAT!*

THIS IS THE CHAMBER WHERE THE *FLYING CREATURE* ATTACKED.

THERE, A *MODEL* UP IN THE RAFTERS! AND IT'S ON A *WIRE,* WAITING TILL I'M HALFWAY ACROSS.

WELL, NOT FOR LONG.

SNAP!

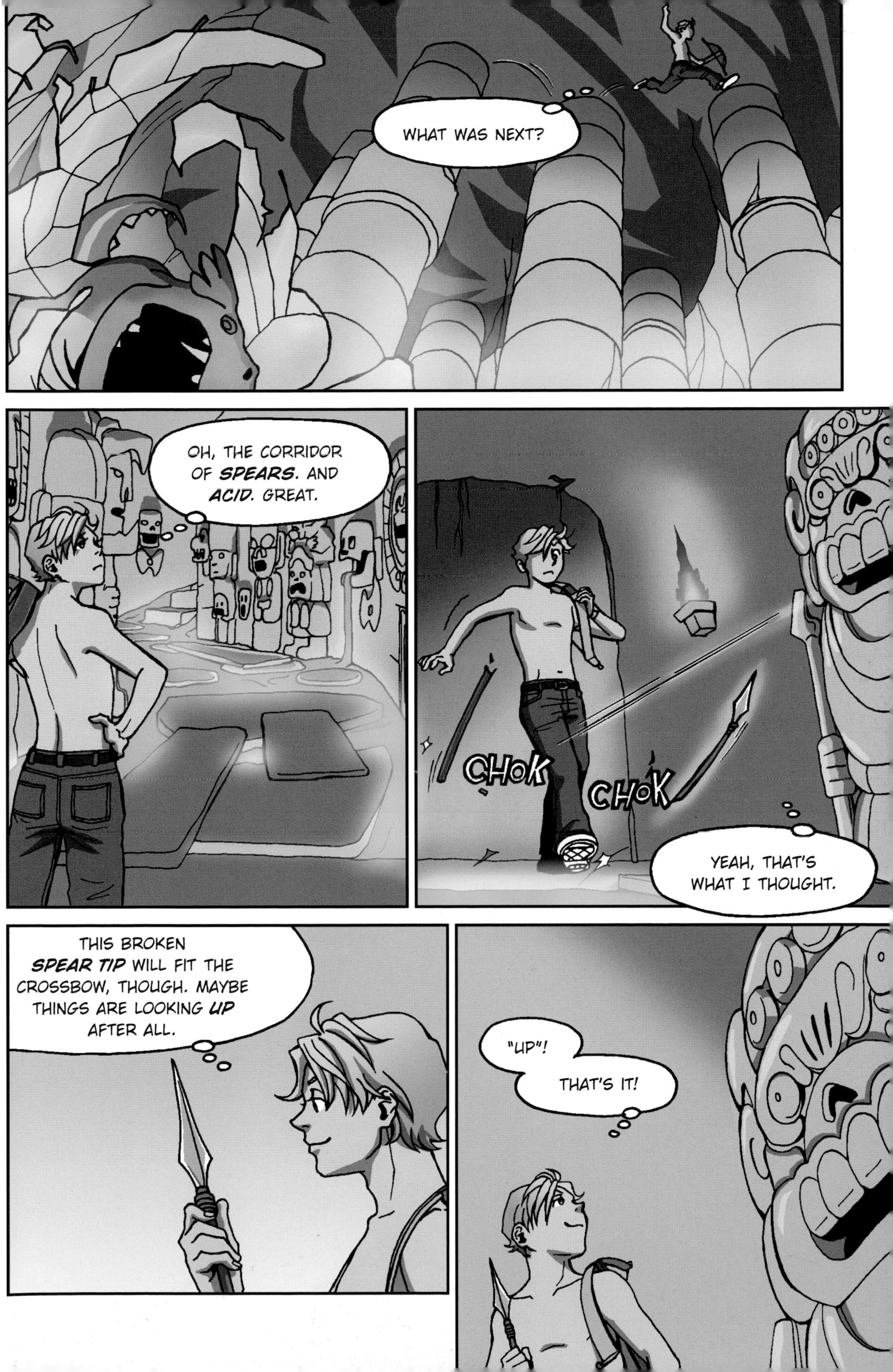

WHAT WAS NEXT?
OH, THE CORRIDOR OF SPEARS. AND ACID. GREAT.
CHOK
CHOK
YEAH, THAT'S WHAT I THOUGHT.
THIS BROKEN SPEAR TIP WILL FIT THE CROSSBOW, THOUGH. MAYBE THINGS ARE LOOKING UP AFTER ALL.
"UP"!
THAT'S IT!

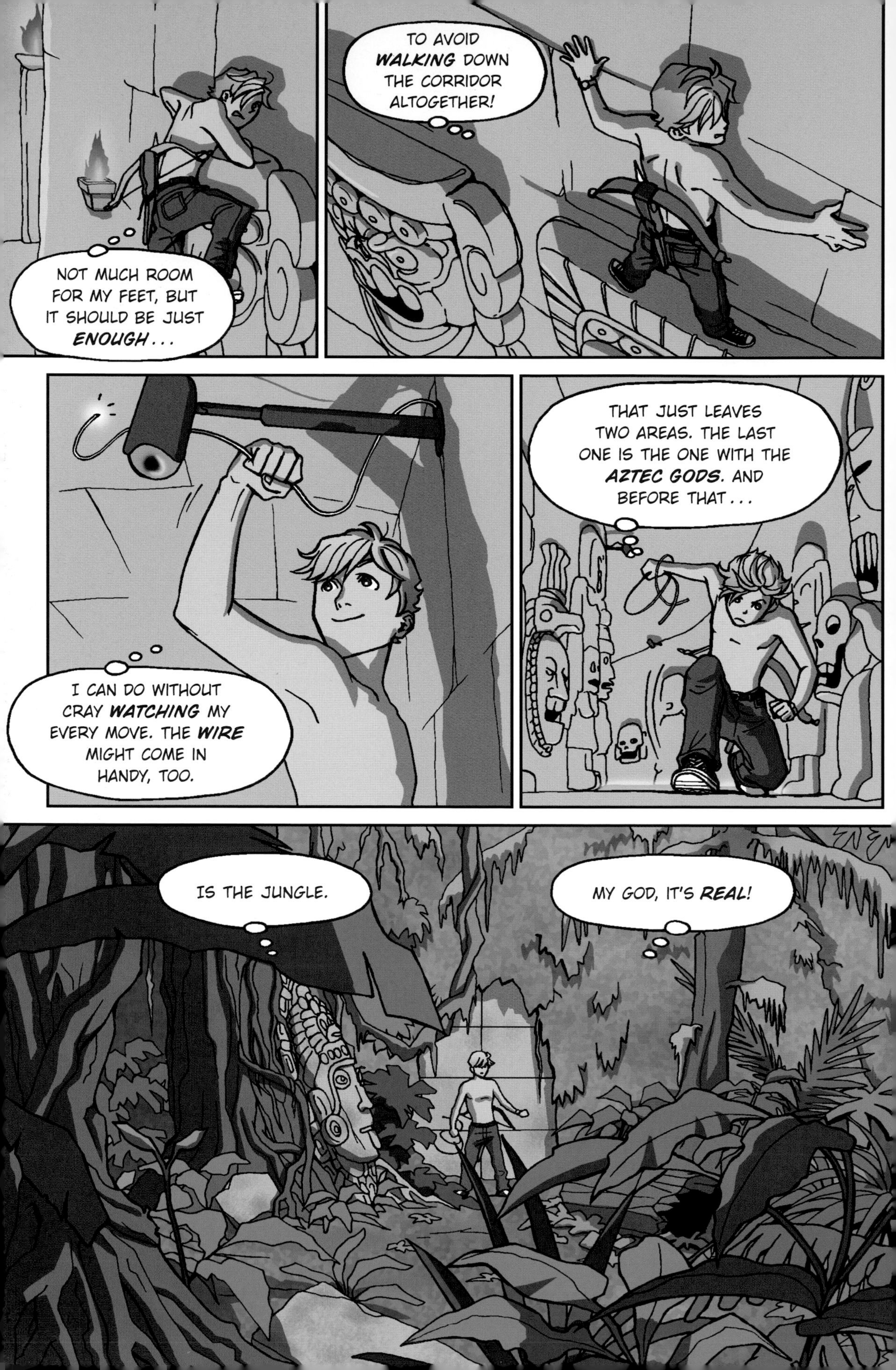
NOT MUCH ROOM FOR MY FEET, BUT IT SHOULD BE JUST ENOUGH . . .
TO AVOID WALKING DOWN THE CORRIDOR ALTOGETHER!
I CAN DO WITHOUT CRAY WATCHING MY EVERY MOVE. THE WIRE MIGHT COME IN HANDY, TOO.
THAT JUST LEAVES TWO AREAS. THE LAST ONE IS THE ONE WITH THE AZTEC GODS. AND BEFORE THAT . . .
IS THE JUNGLE.
MY GOD, IT'S REAL!

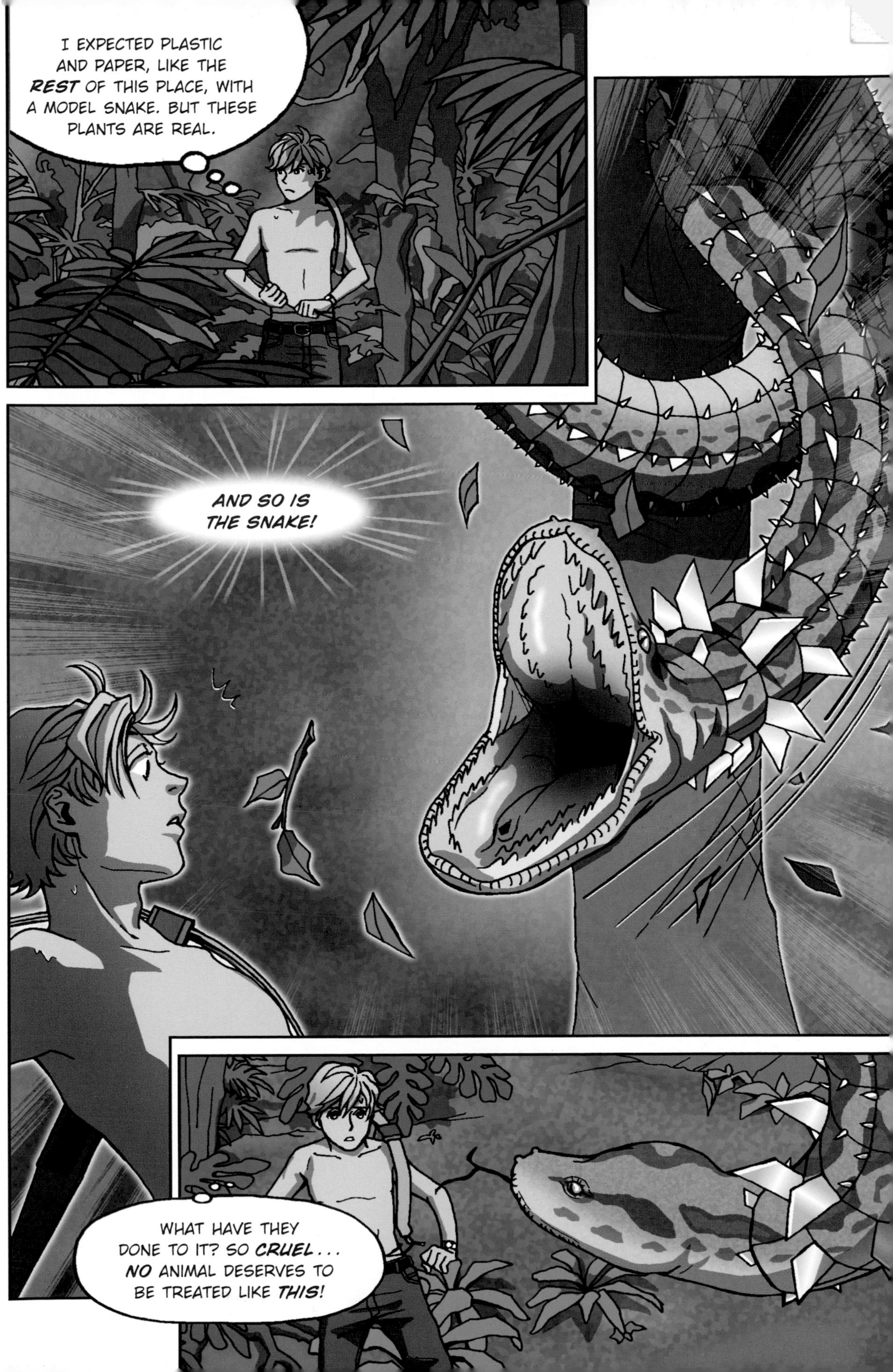
I EXPECTED PLASTIC AND PAPER, LIKE THE ***REST*** OF THIS PLACE, WITH A MODEL SNAKE. BUT THESE PLANTS ARE REAL.
AND SO IS THE SNAKE!
WHAT HAVE THEY DONE TO IT? SO ***CRUEL*** . . . ***NO*** ANIMAL DESERVES TO BE TREATED LIKE ***THIS!***

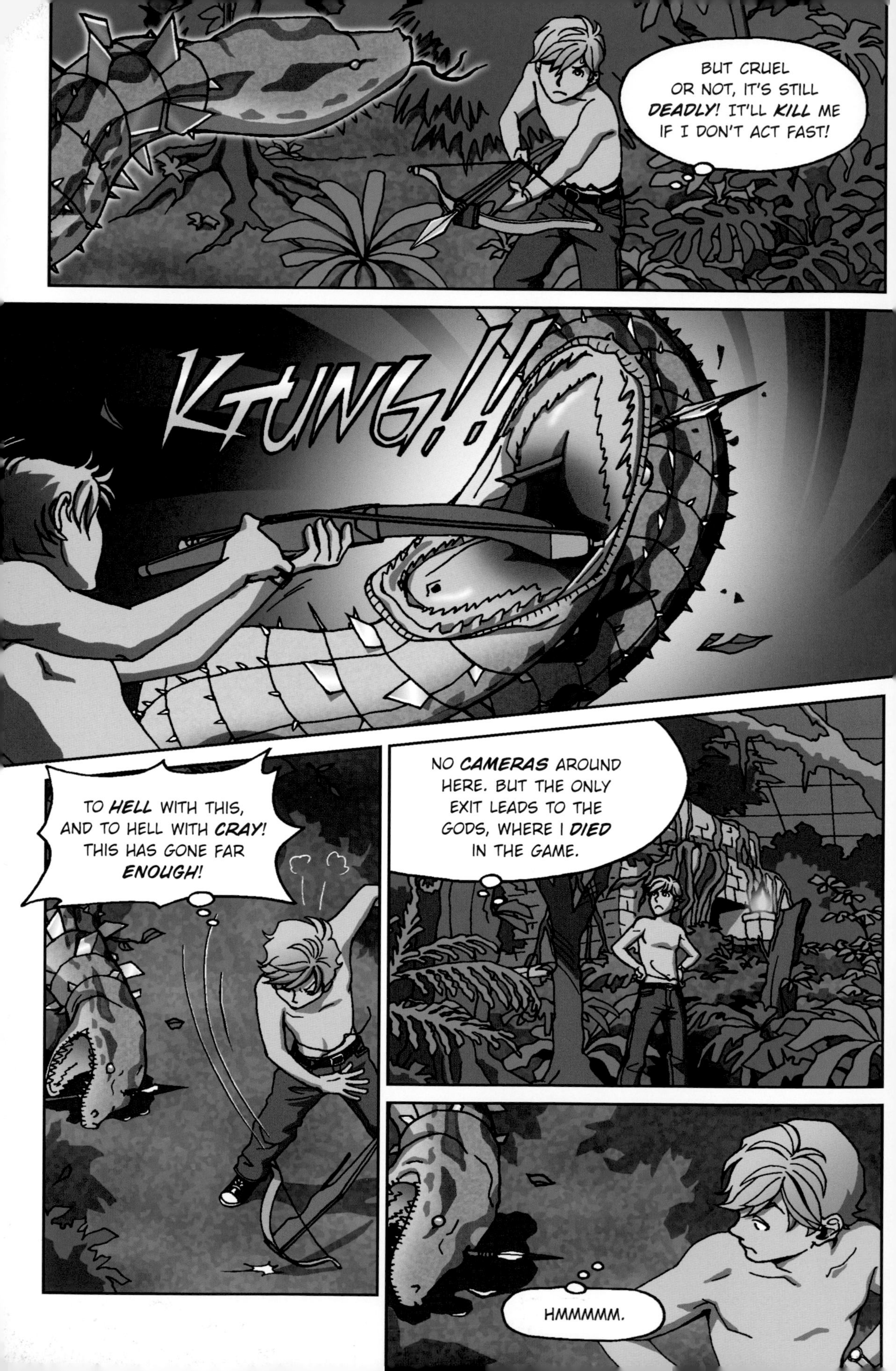
BUT CRUEL OR NOT, IT'S STILL DEADLY! IT'LL KILL ME IF I DON'T ACT FAST!
KTUNG!!
TO HELL WITH THIS, AND TO HELL WITH CRAY! THIS HAS GONE FAR ENOUGH!
NO CAMERAS AROUND HERE. BUT THE ONLY EXIT LEADS TO THE GODS, WHERE I DIED IN THE GAME.
HMMMMM.

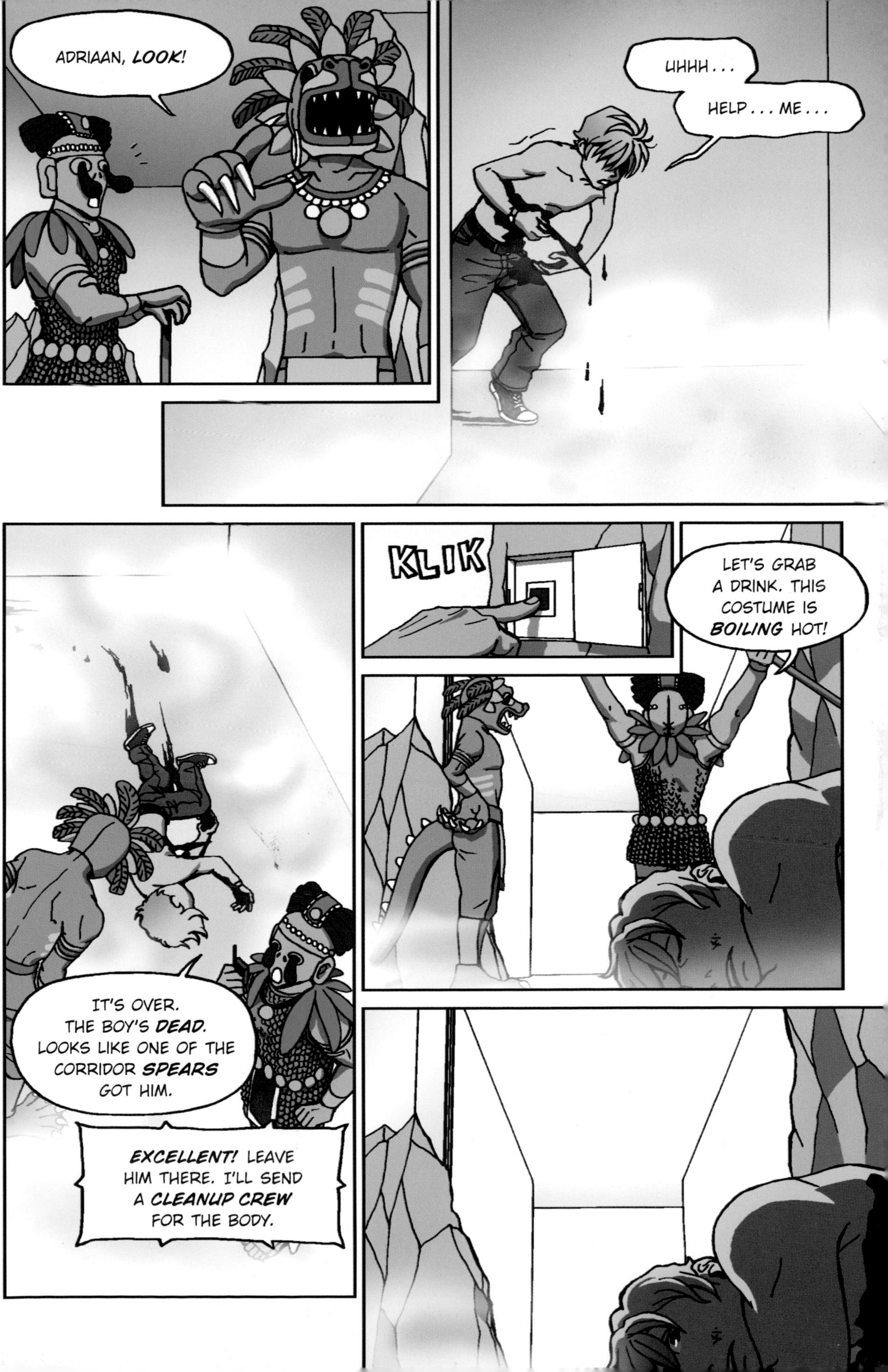
ADRIAAN, LOOK!
UHHH . . .
HELP . . . ME . . .
IT'S OVER. THE BOY'S DEAD. LOOKS LIKE ONE OF THE CORRIDOR SPEARS GOT HIM.
EXCELLENT! LEAVE HIM THERE. I'LL SEND A CLEANUP CREW FOR THE BODY.
KLIK
LET'S GRAB A DRINK. THIS COSTUME IS BOILING HOT!

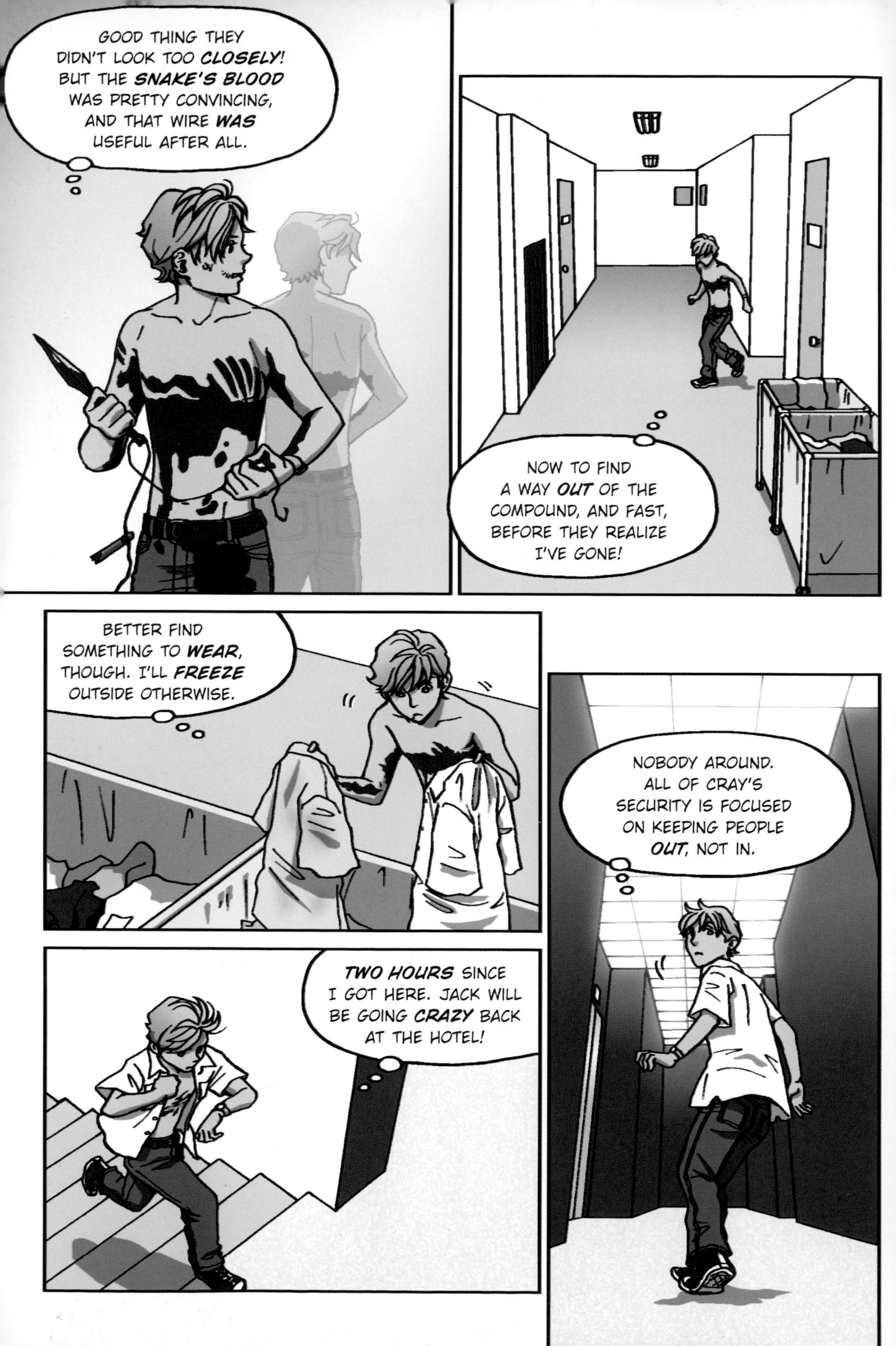
GOOD THING THEY DIDN'T LOOK TOO CLOSELY! BUT THE SNAKE'S BLOOD WAS PRETTY CONVINCING, AND THAT WIRE WAS USEFUL AFTER ALL.
NOW TO FIND A WAY OUT OF THE COMPOUND, AND FAST, BEFORE THEY REALIZE I'VE GONE!
BETTER FIND SOMETHING TO WEAR, THOUGH. I'LL FREEZE OUTSIDE OTHERWISE.
TWO HOURS SINCE I GOT HERE. JACK WILL BE GOING CRAZY BACK AT THE HOTEL!
NOBODY AROUND. ALL OF CRAY'S SECURITY IS FOCUSED ON KEEPING PEOPLE OUT, NOT IN.

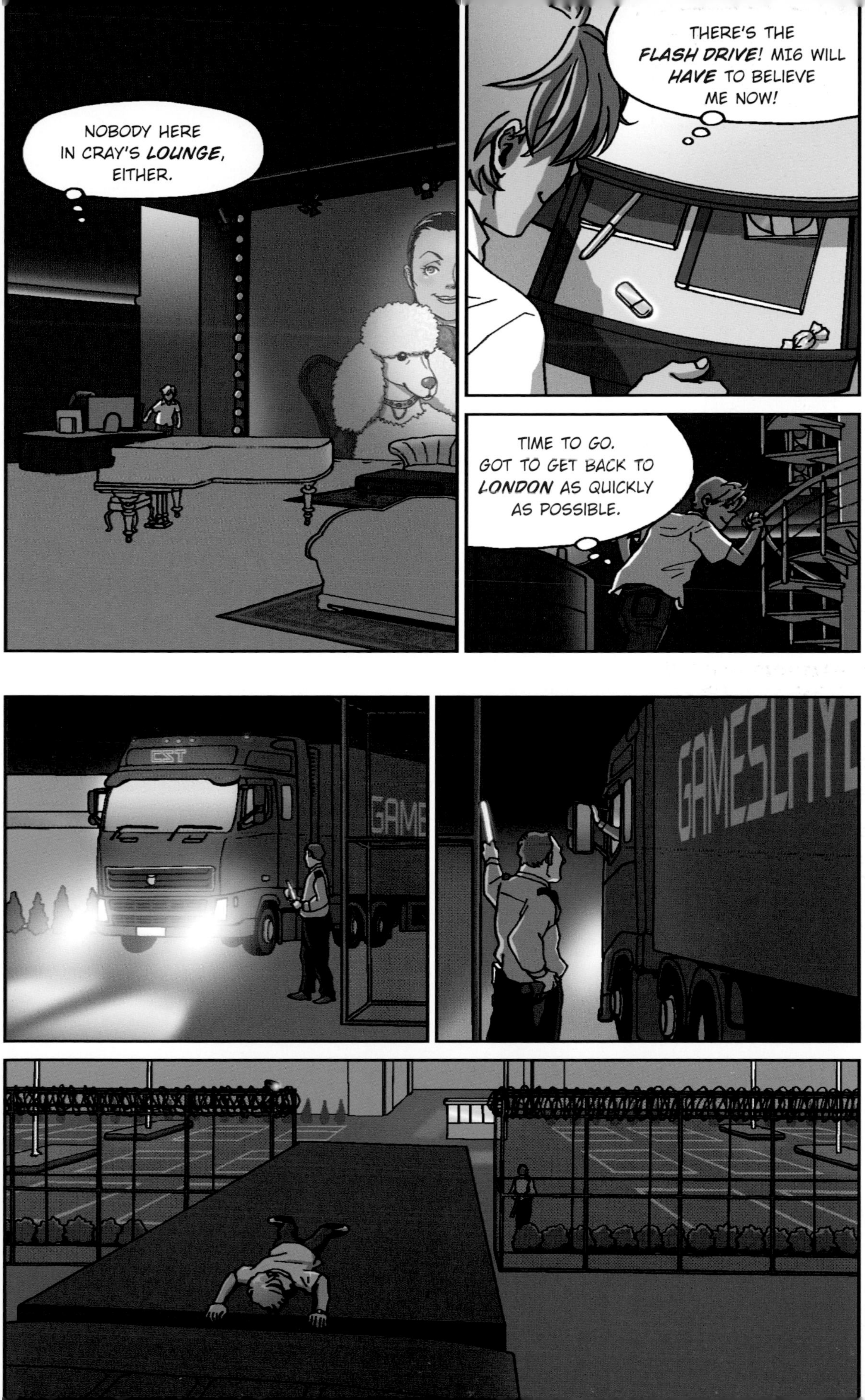
NOBODY HERE IN CRAY'S LOUNGE, EITHER.
THERE'S THE FLASH DRIVE! MI6 WILL HAVE TO BELIEVE ME NOW!
TIME TO GO. GOT TO GET BACK TO LONDON AS QUICKLY AS POSSIBLE.
CST
GAME
GAMESLAYE

THEY TOLD ME HE WAS **DEAD!** AND NOW HE'S **STOLEN** THE FLASH DRIVE!

YOU **KNEW** HE'D COME IN HERE!

I SUSPECTED IT. HE IS **ALEX,** AFTER ALL.

WHO **IS** THIS BOY? **TELL** ME ABOUT HIM!

THERE IS NO OTHER BOY **LIKE** HIM. CONSIDER: TONIGHT YOU TRIED TO **KILL** HIM, IN A MANNER THAT SHOULD HAVE **TERRIFIED** HIM.

AND WHEN MOST BOYS—MOST **MEN,** EVEN—WOULD HAVE RUN STRAIGHT FOR THE STAIRS, HE DID **NOT.**

BUT NOT ONLY DID HE **SURVIVE,** HE ALSO **ESCAPED.**

HE STOPPED AND SEARCHED. HE CARRIED OUT HIS **OBJECTIVE.**

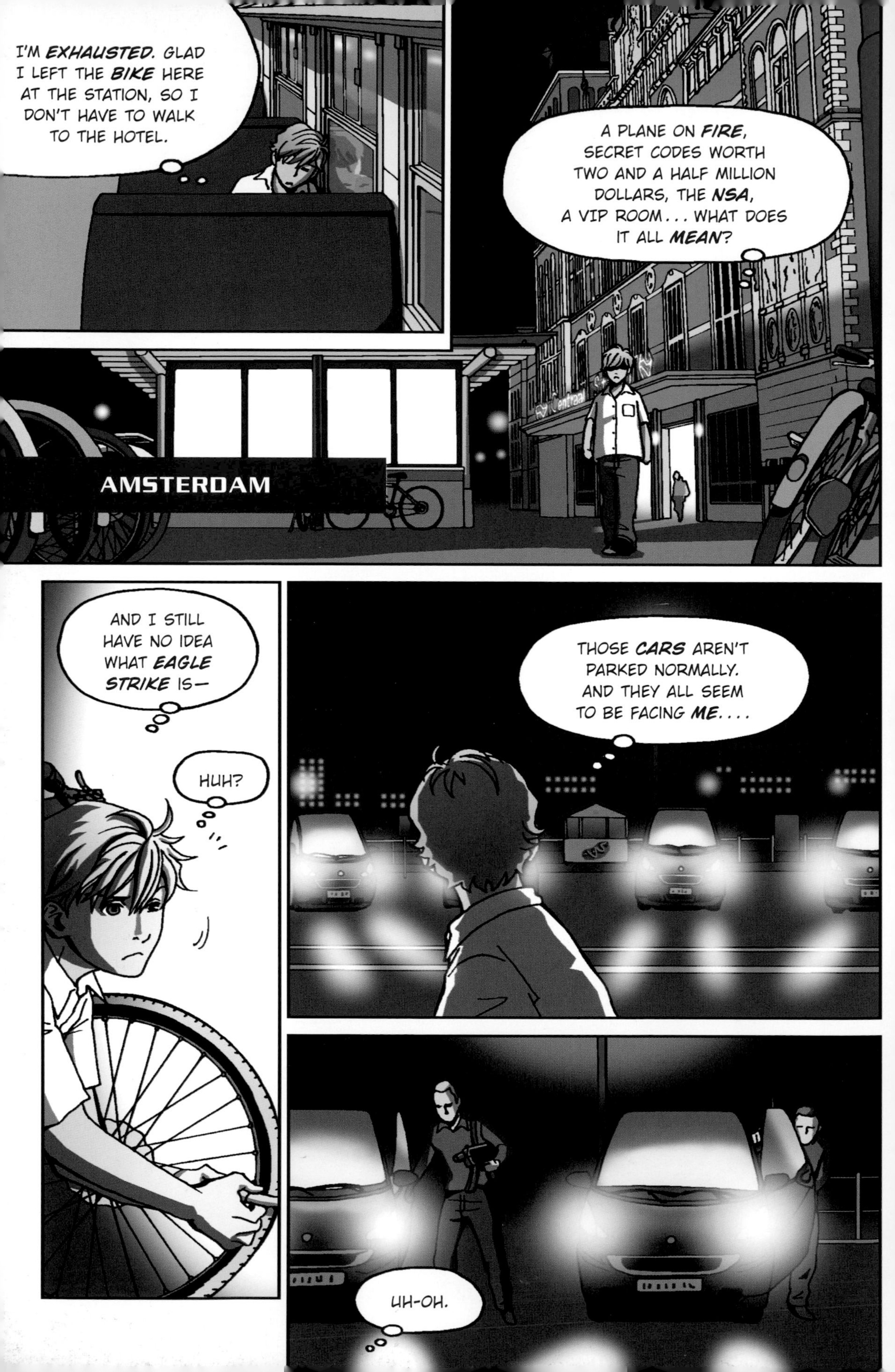
I'M EXHAUSTED. GLAD I LEFT THE BIKE HERE AT THE STATION, SO I DON'T HAVE TO WALK TO THE HOTEL.
A PLANE ON FIRE, SECRET CODES WORTH TWO AND A HALF MILLION DOLLARS, THE NSA, A VIP ROOM . . . WHAT DOES IT ALL MEAN?
AMSTERDAM
AND I STILL HAVE NO IDEA WHAT EAGLE STRIKE IS—
HUH?
THOSE CARS AREN'T PARKED NORMALLY. AND THEY ALL SEEM TO BE FACING ME. . . .
UH-OH.

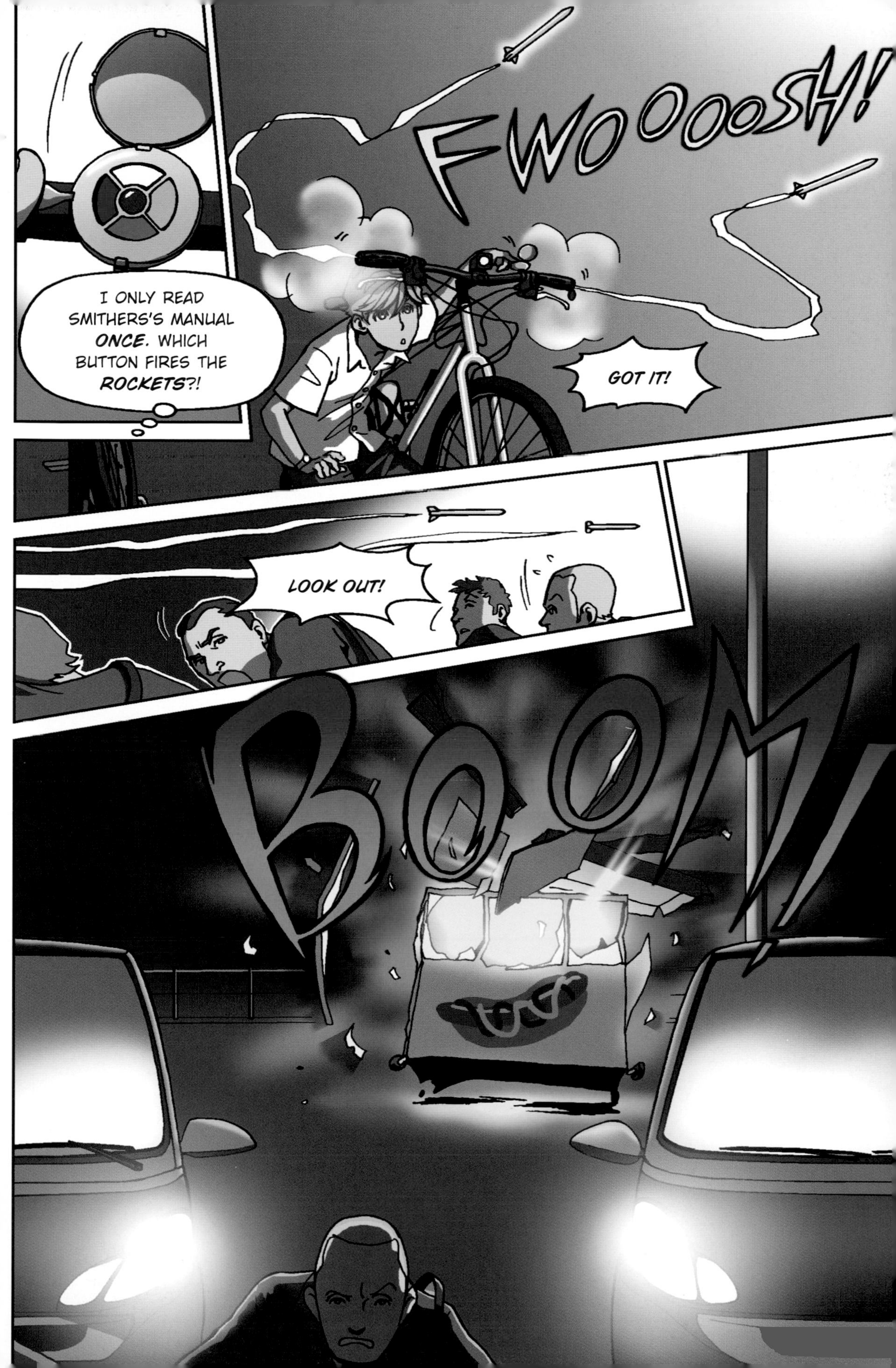
FWOOOOOSH!
I ONLY READ SMITHERS'S MANUAL ONCE. WHICH BUTTON FIRES THE ROCKETS?!
GOT IT!
LOOK OUT!
BOOOM!

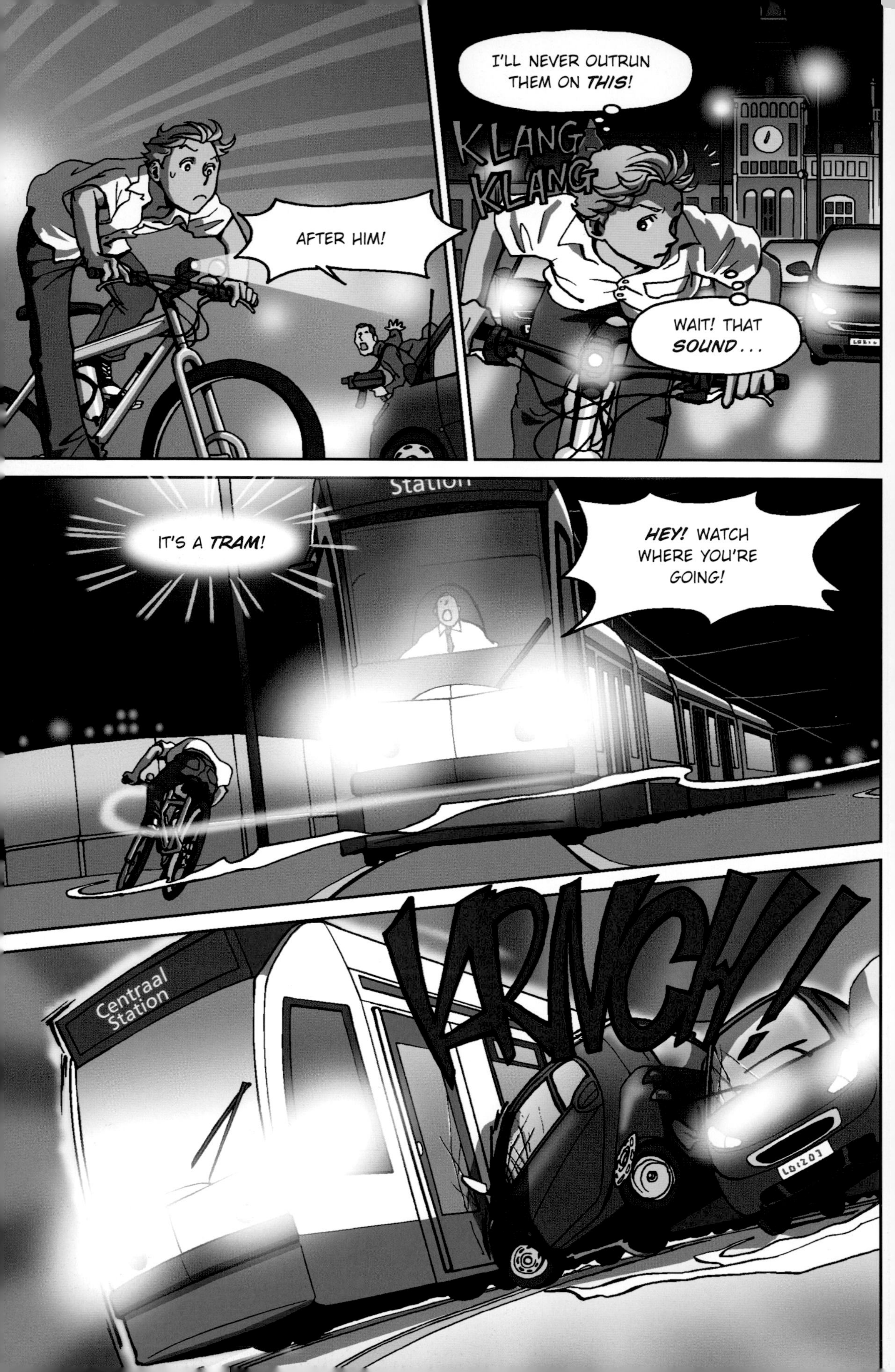
AFTER HIM!
I'LL NEVER OUTRUN THEM ON *THIS*!
KLANG KLANG
WAIT! THAT **SOUND** . . .
Station
IT'S A ***TRAM***!
HEY! WATCH WHERE YOU'RE GOING!
Centraal Station
KRUNCH!

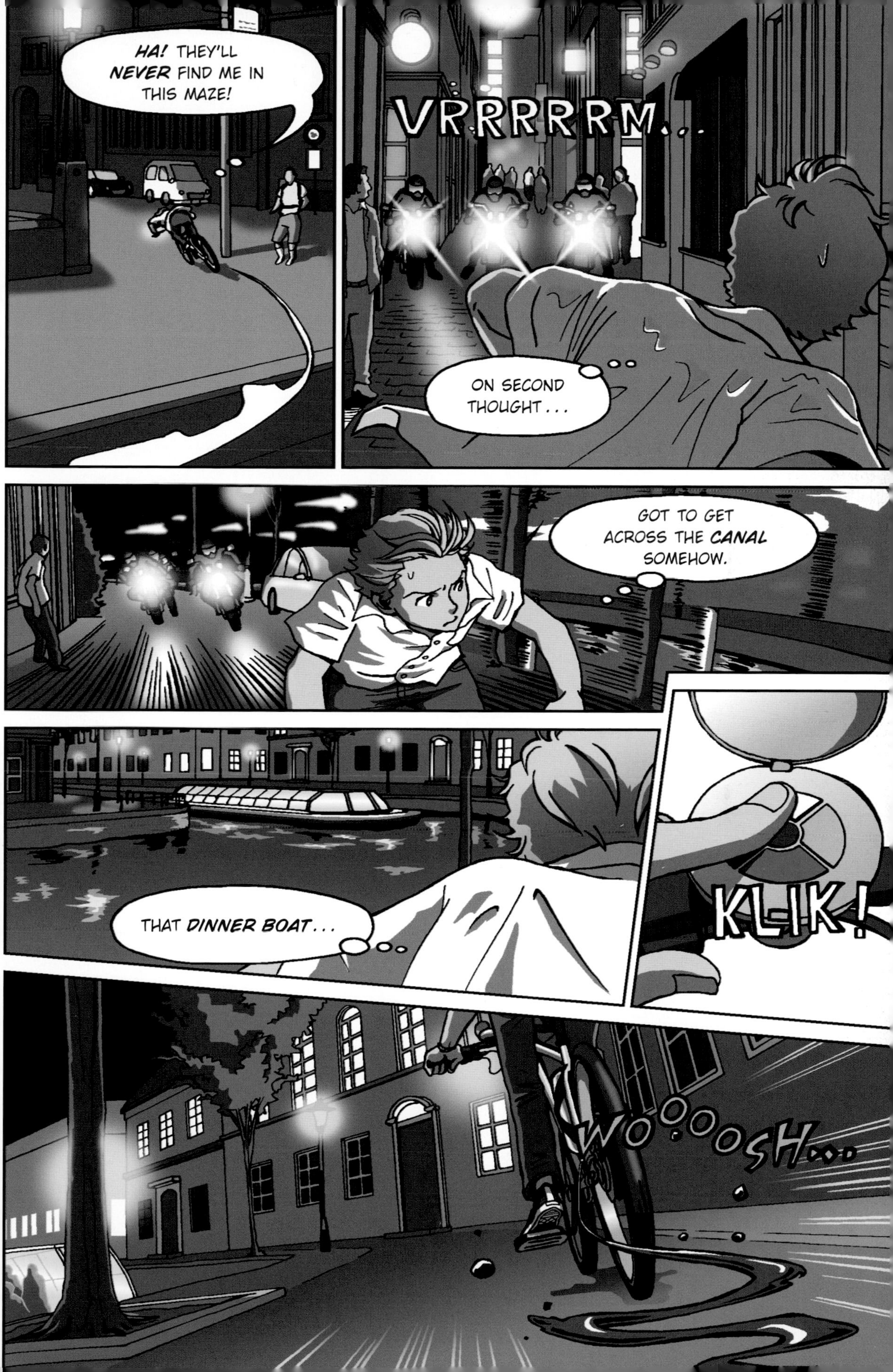
HA! THEY'LL NEVER FIND ME IN THIS MAZE!
VRRRRRRM...
ON SECOND THOUGHT . . .
GOT TO GET ACROSS THE CANAL SOMEHOW.
THAT DINNER BOAT . . .
KLIK!
WOOOOSH...

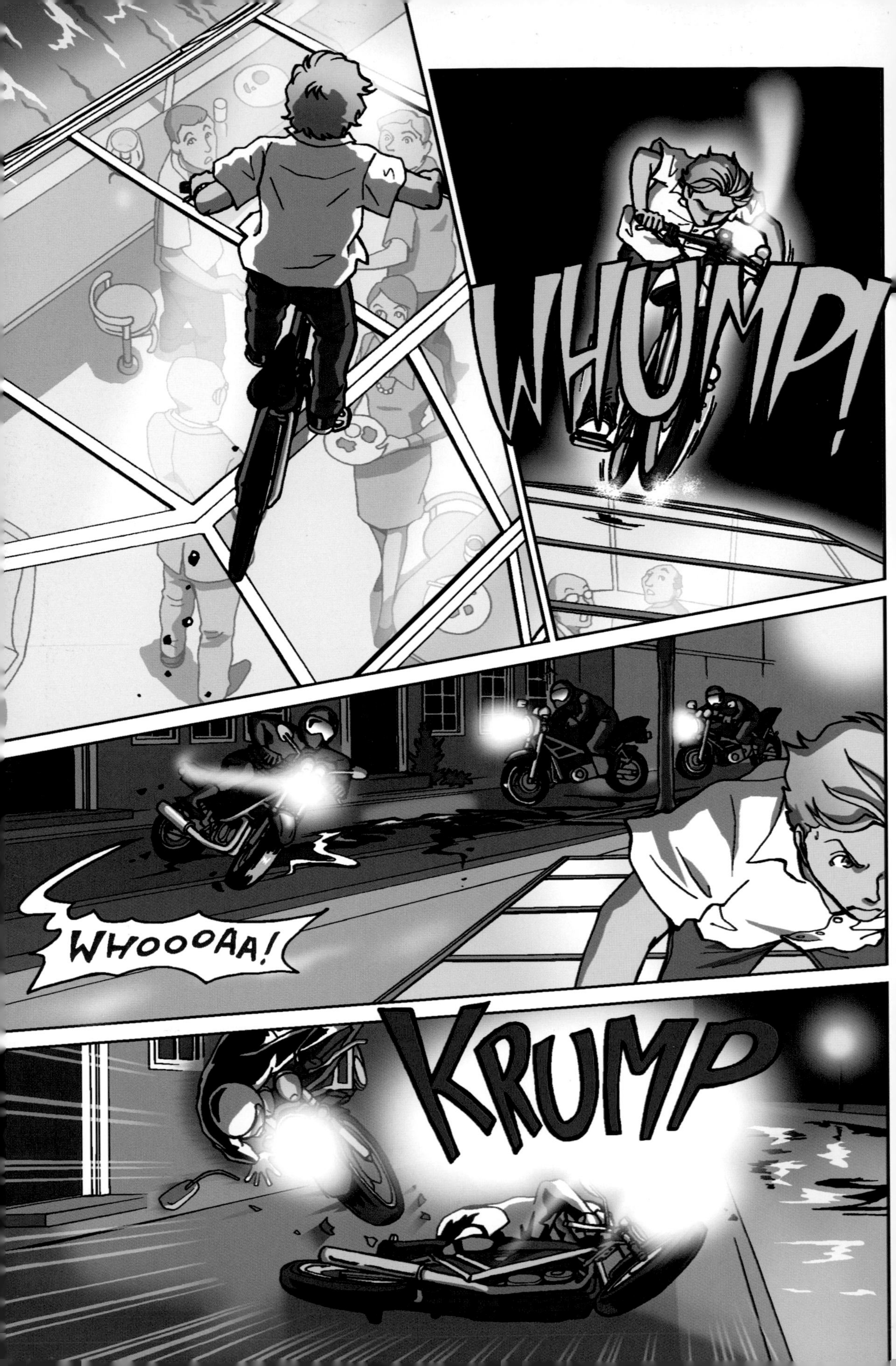
WHUMP!
WHOOOAA!
KRUMP

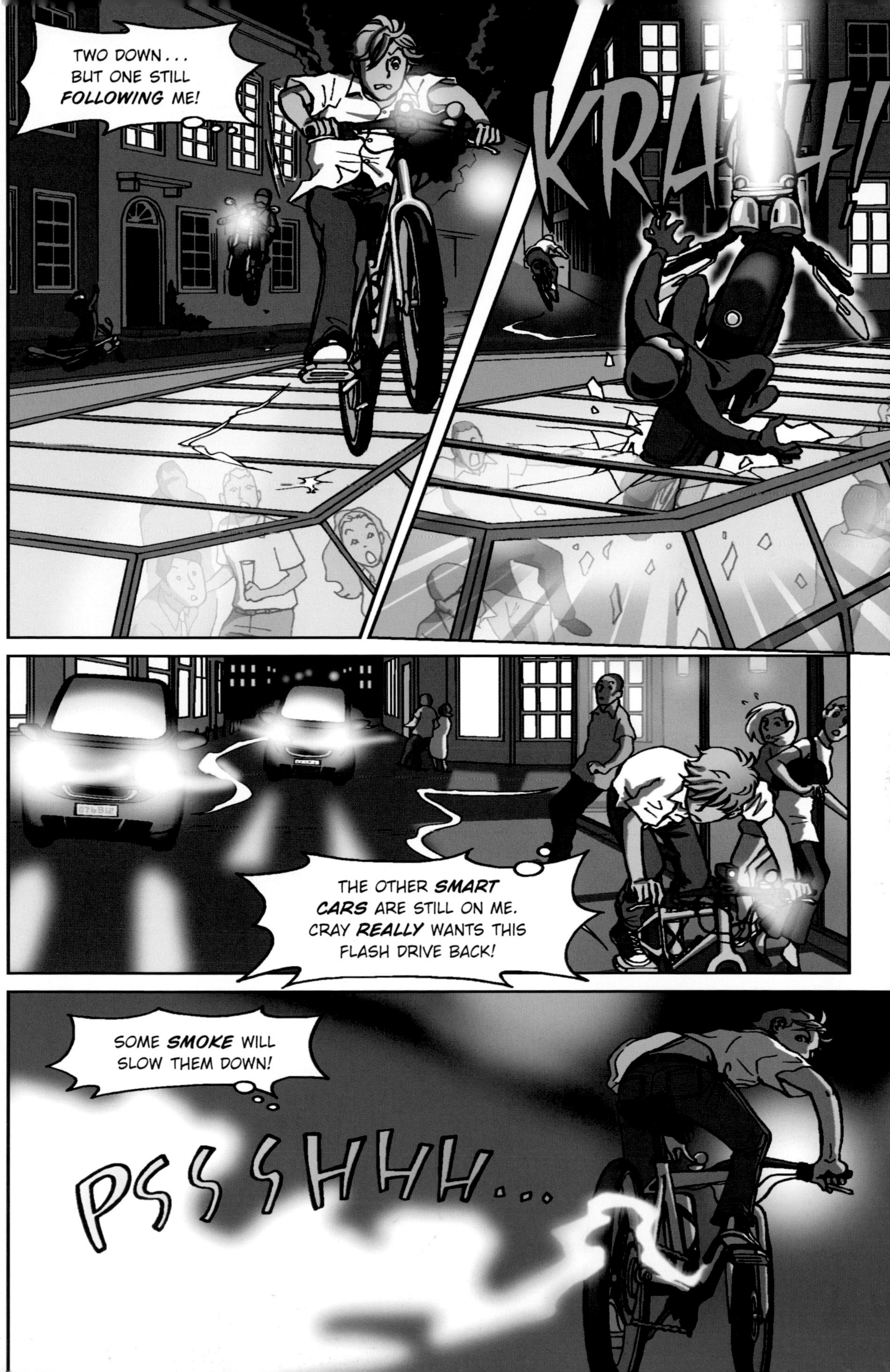

TWO DOWN . . . BUT ONE STILL FOLLOWING ME!
KRAAH!
THE OTHER SMART CARS ARE STILL ON ME. CRAY REALLY WANTS THIS FLASH DRIVE BACK!
SOME SMOKE WILL SLOW THEM DOWN!
PSSSHHH. . .

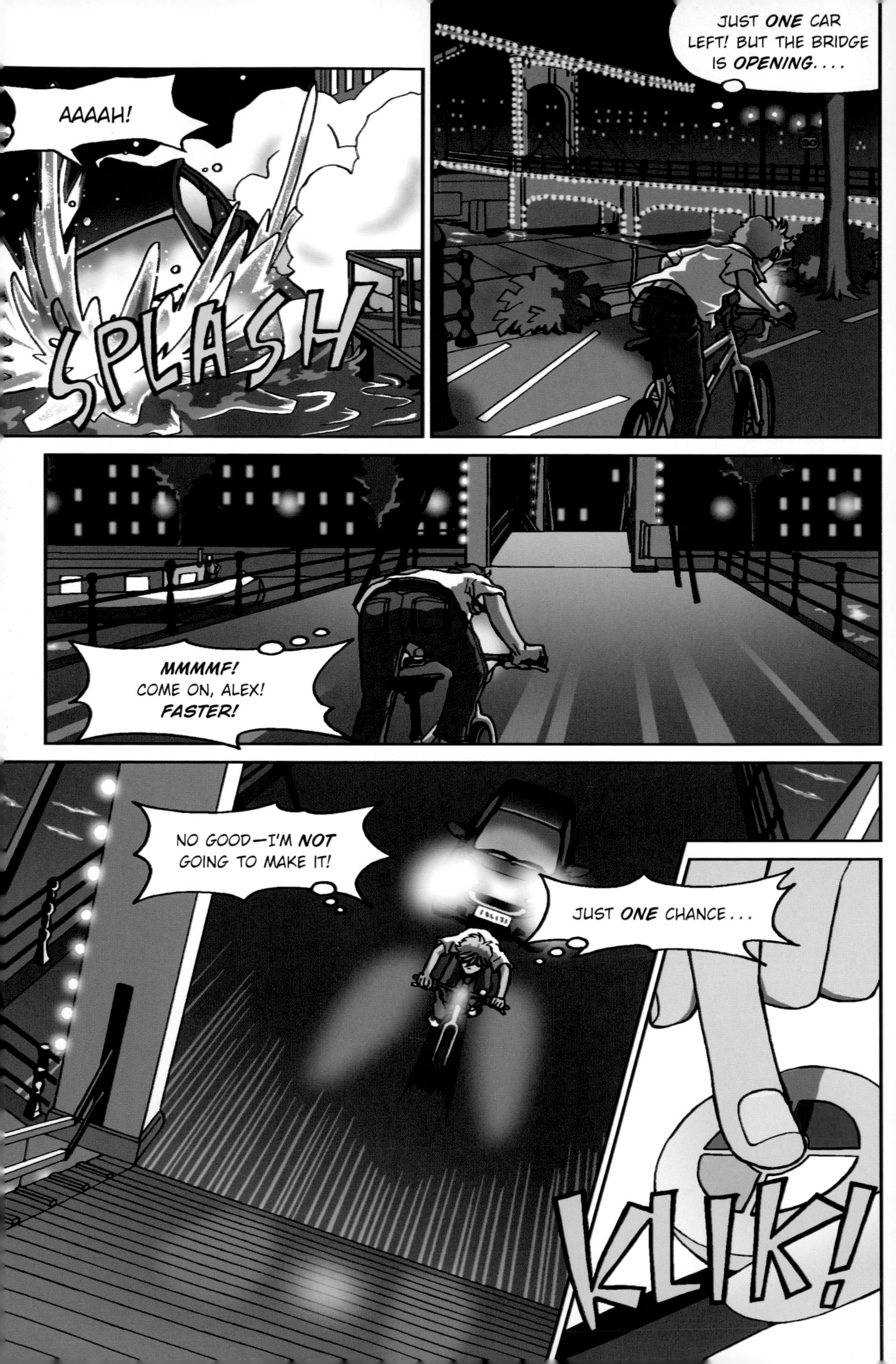
AAAAH!
SPLASH
JUST ONE CAR LEFT! BUT THE BRIDGE IS OPENING. . . .
MMMMF! COME ON, ALEX! FASTER!
NO GOOD—I'M NOT GOING TO MAKE IT!
JUST ONE CHANCE . . .
KLIK!

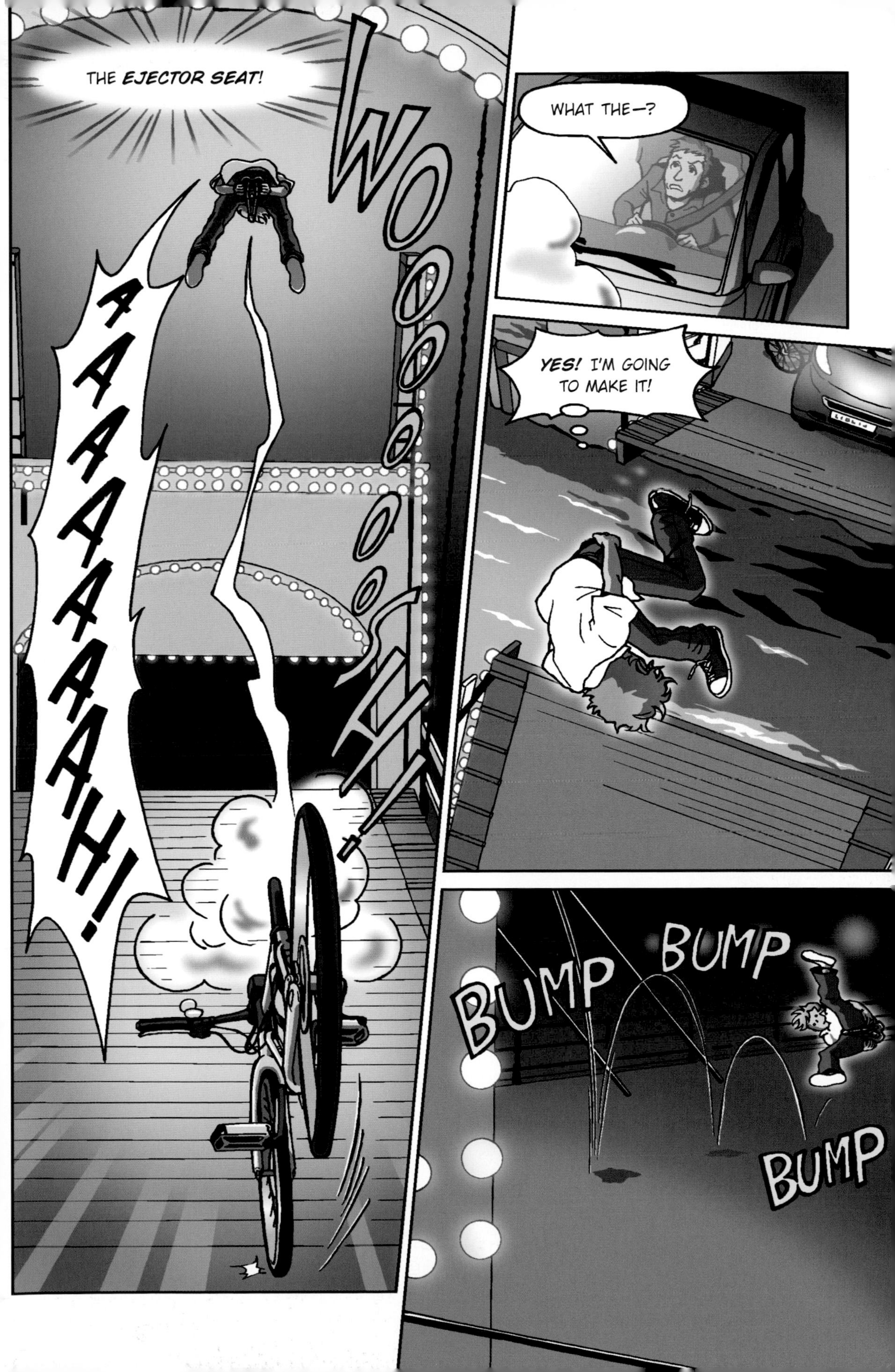
THE EJECTOR SEAT!
WOOOOOOOSH!
AAAAAAAAH!
WHAT THE—?
YES! I'M GOING TO MAKE IT!
BUMP
BUMP
BUMP

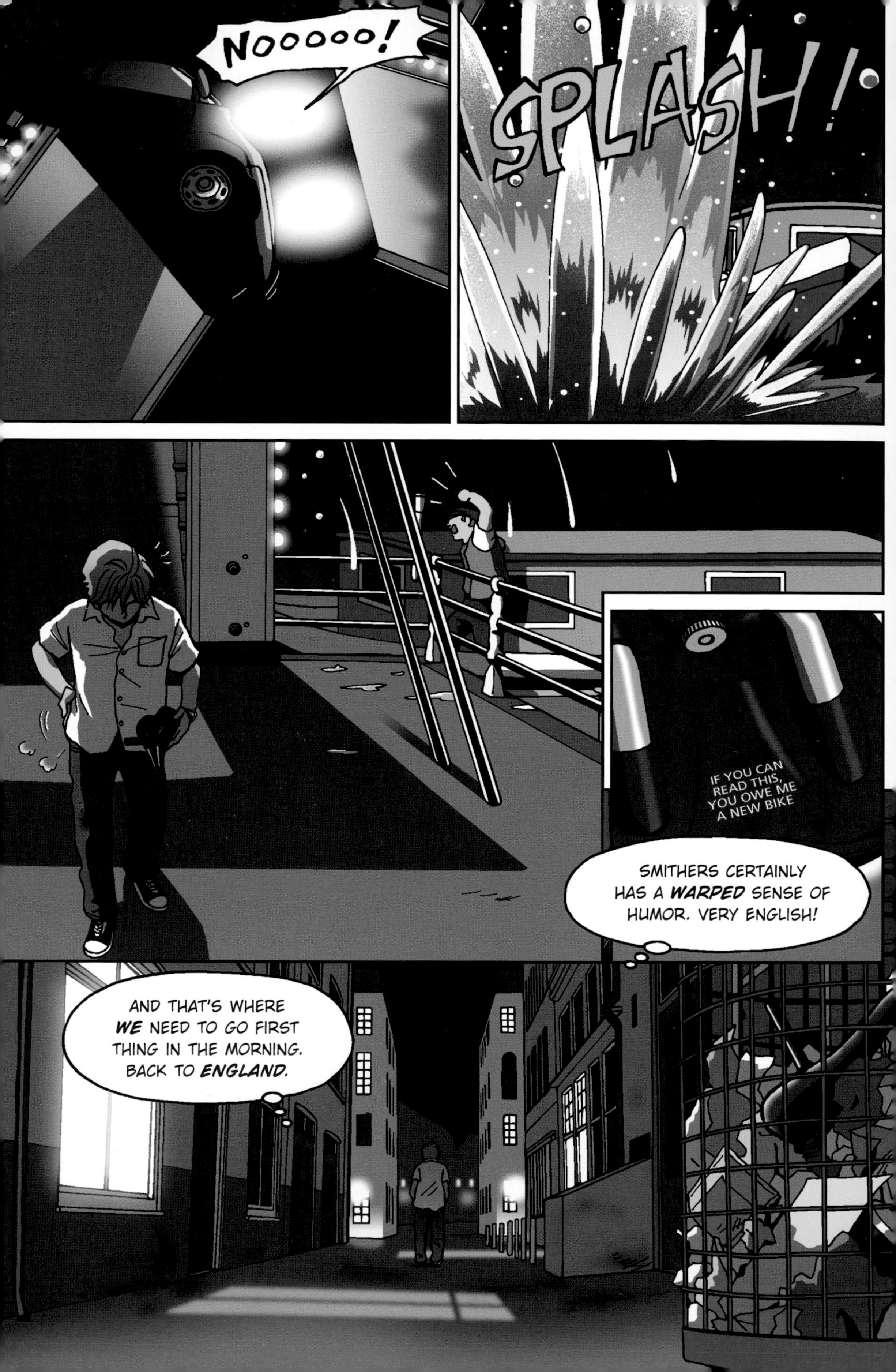
NOOOOO!
SPLASH!
IF YOU CAN READ THIS, YOU OWE ME A NEW BIKE
SMITHERS CERTAINLY HAS A WARPED SENSE OF HUMOR. VERY ENGLISH!
AND THAT'S WHERE WE NEED TO GO FIRST THING IN THE MORNING. BACK TO ENGLAND.

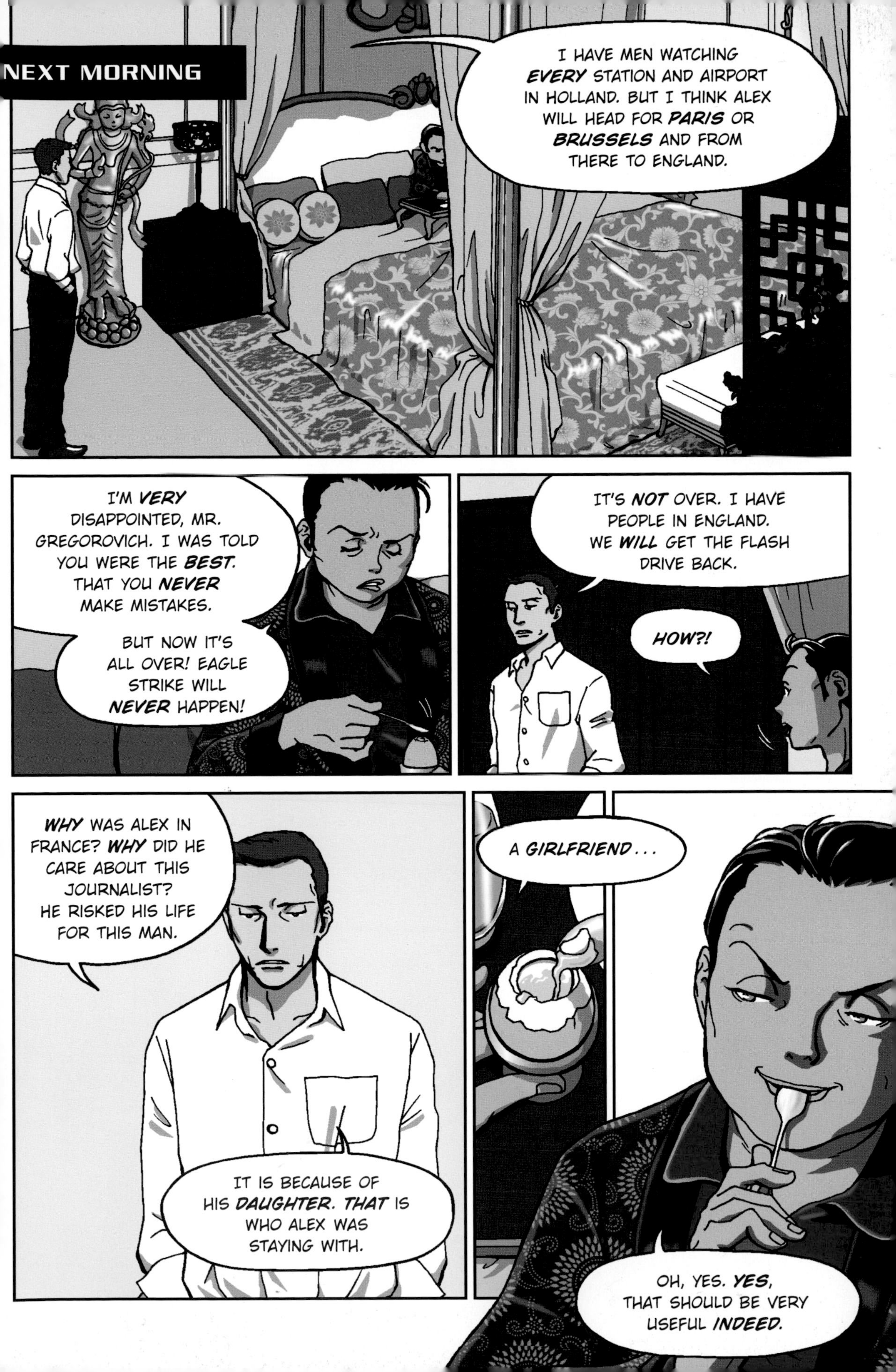
NEXT MORNING
I HAVE MEN WATCHING EVERY STATION AND AIRPORT IN HOLLAND. BUT I THINK ALEX WILL HEAD FOR PARIS OR BRUSSELS AND FROM THERE TO ENGLAND.
I'M VERY DISAPPOINTED, MR. GREGOROVICH. I WAS TOLD YOU WERE THE BEST. THAT YOU NEVER MAKE MISTAKES.
BUT NOW IT'S ALL OVER! EAGLE STRIKE WILL NEVER HAPPEN!
IT'S NOT OVER. I HAVE PEOPLE IN ENGLAND. WE WILL GET THE FLASH DRIVE BACK.
HOW?!
WHY WAS ALEX IN FRANCE? WHY DID HE CARE ABOUT THIS JOURNALIST? HE RISKED HIS LIFE FOR THIS MAN.
IT IS BECAUSE OF HIS DAUGHTER. THAT IS WHO ALEX WAS STAYING WITH.
A GIRLFRIEND . . .
OH, YES. YES, THAT SHOULD BE VERY USEFUL INDEED.

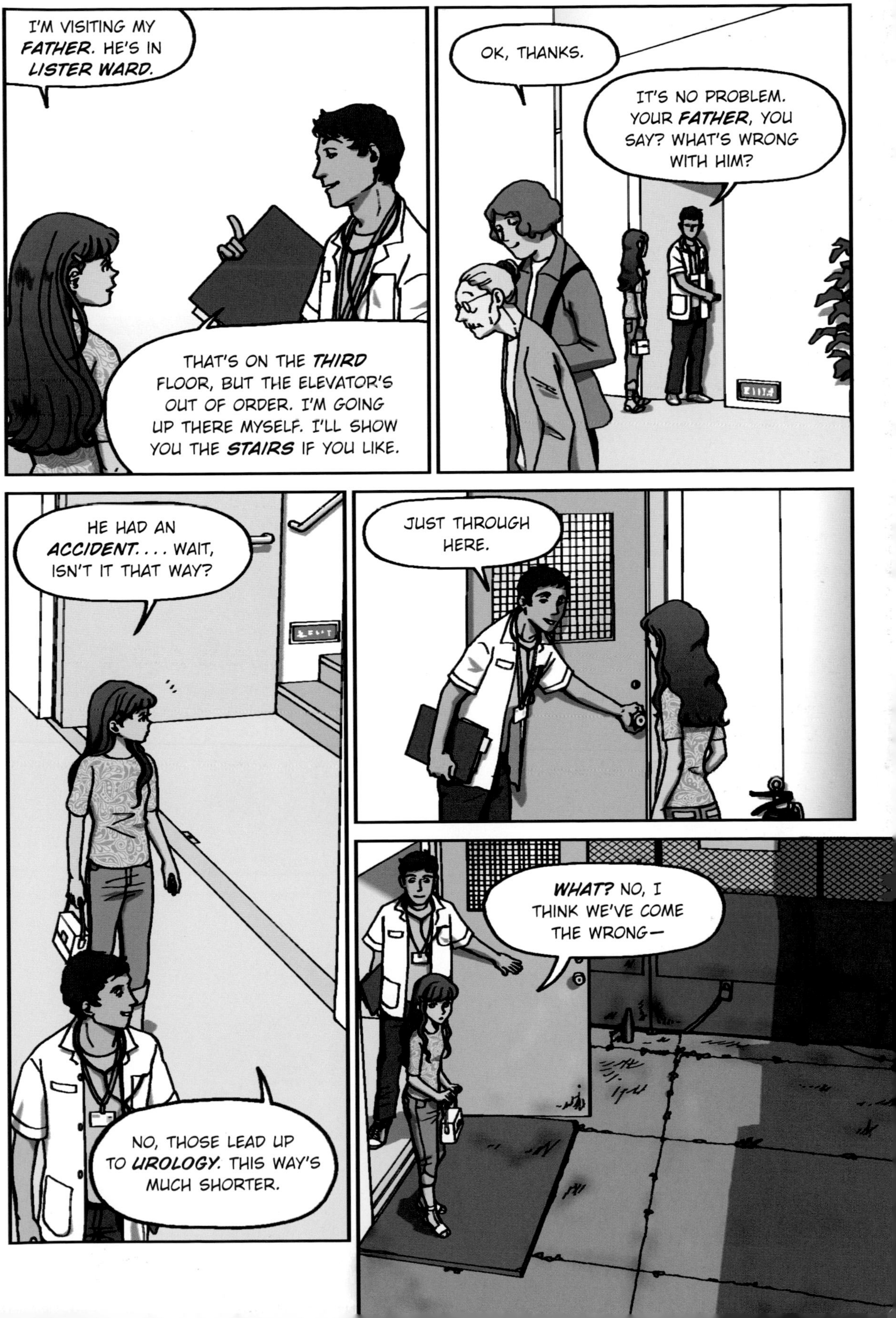
I'M VISITING MY FATHER. HE'S IN LISTER WARD.
THAT'S ON THE THIRD FLOOR, BUT THE ELEVATOR'S OUT OF ORDER. I'M GOING UP THERE MYSELF. I'LL SHOW YOU THE STAIRS IF YOU LIKE.
OK, THANKS.
IT'S NO PROBLEM. YOUR FATHER, YOU SAY? WHAT'S WRONG WITH HIM?
HE HAD AN ACCIDENT. . . . WAIT, ISN'T IT THAT WAY?
NO, THOSE LEAD UP TO UROLOGY. THIS WAY'S MUCH SHORTER.
JUST THROUGH HERE.
WHAT? NO, I THINK WE'VE COME THE WRONG—

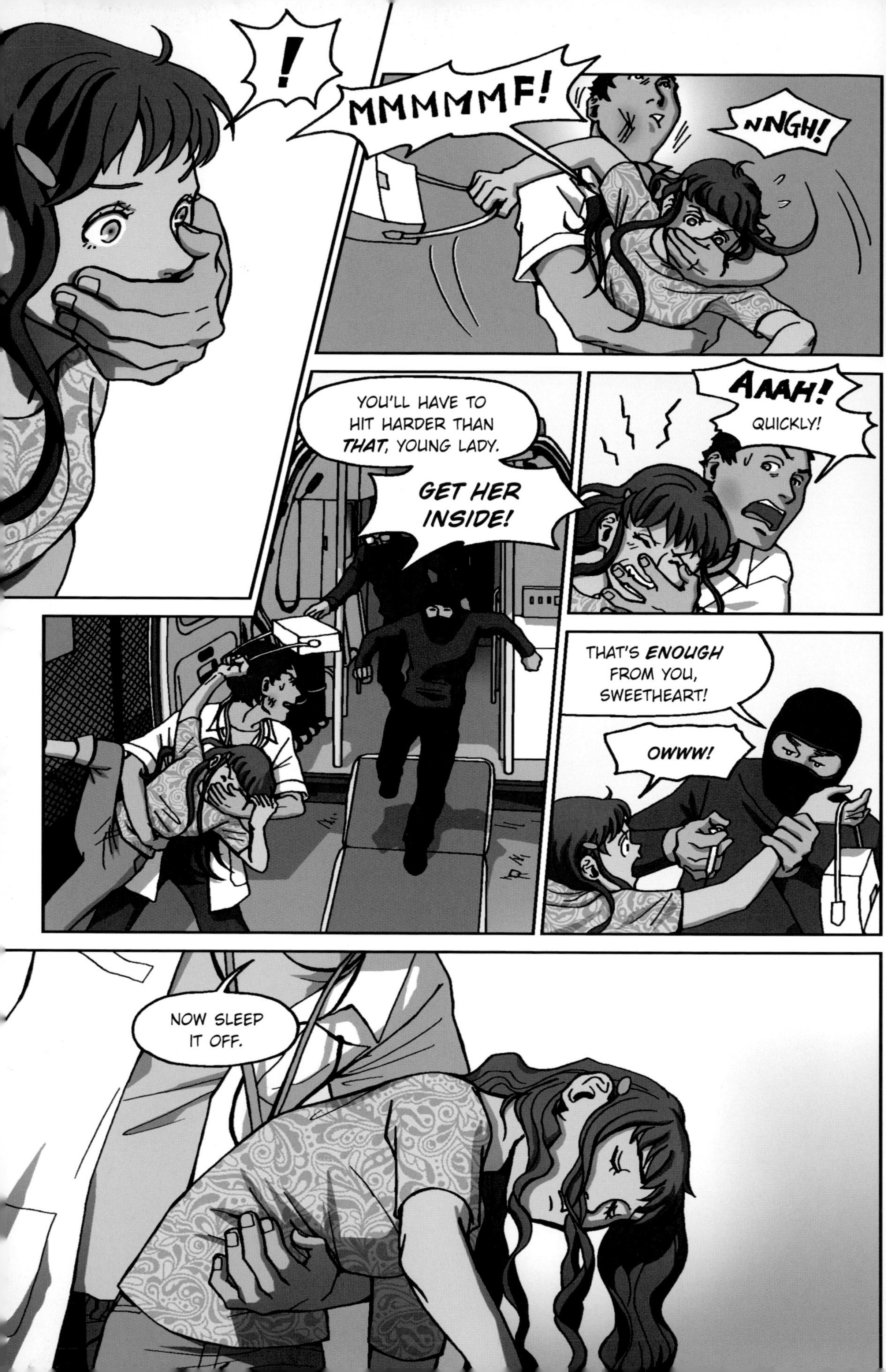
!
MMMMMF!
NNGH!
YOU'LL HAVE TO HIT HARDER THAN *THAT*, YOUNG LADY.
GET HER INSIDE!
AAAH!
QUICKLY!
THAT'S *ENOUGH* FROM YOU, SWEETHEART!
OWWW!
NOW SLEEP IT OFF.

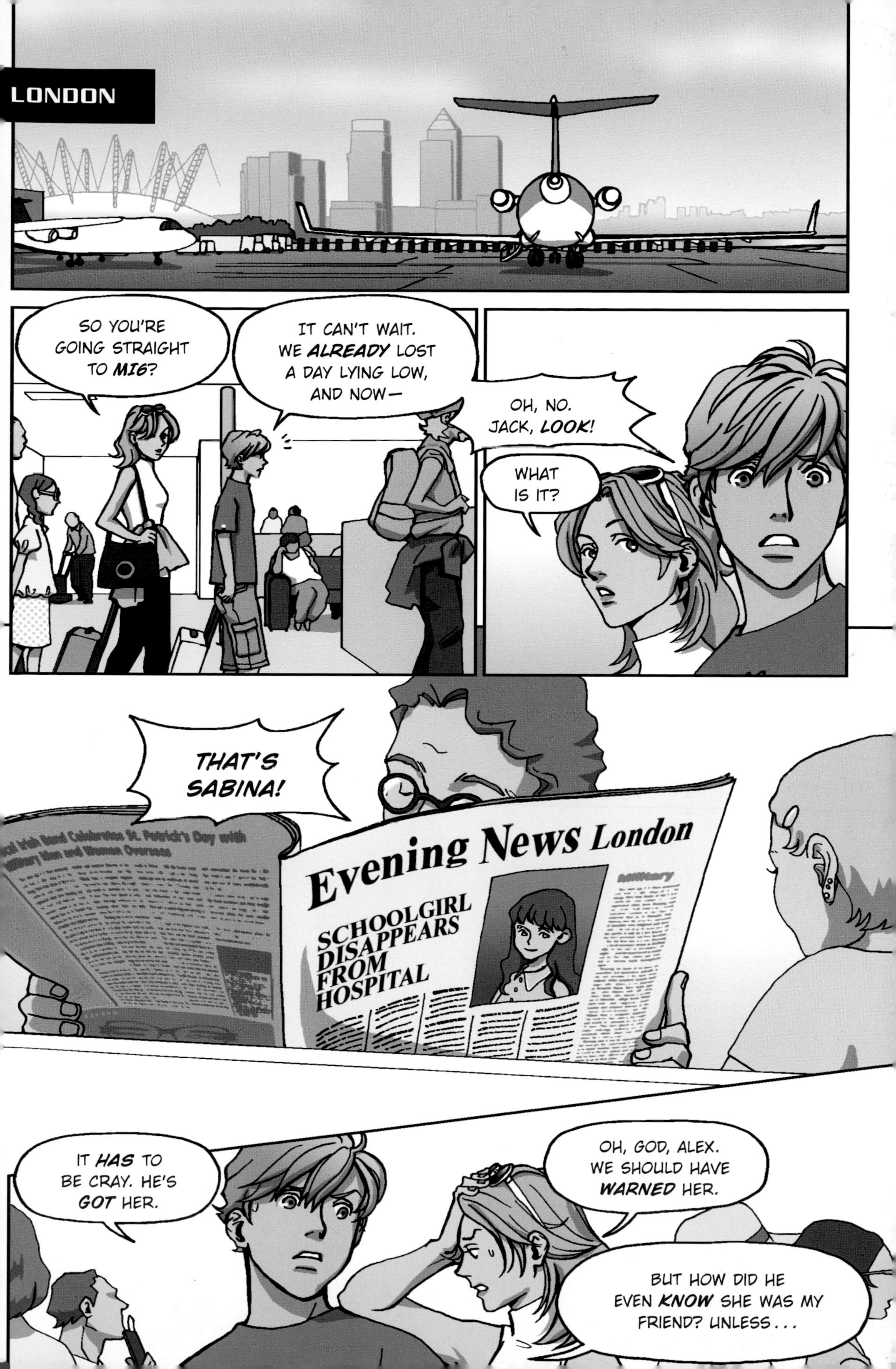
LONDON
SO YOU'RE GOING STRAIGHT TO MI6?
IT CAN'T WAIT. WE ALREADY LOST A DAY LYING LOW, AND NOW—
OH, NO. JACK, LOOK!
WHAT IS IT?
THAT'S SABINA!
Evening News London
SCHOOLGIRL DISAPPEARS FROM HOSPITAL
IT HAS TO BE CRAY. HE'S GOT HER.
OH, GOD, ALEX. WE SHOULD HAVE WARNED HER.
BUT HOW DID HE EVEN KNOW SHE WAS MY FRIEND? UNLESS . . .

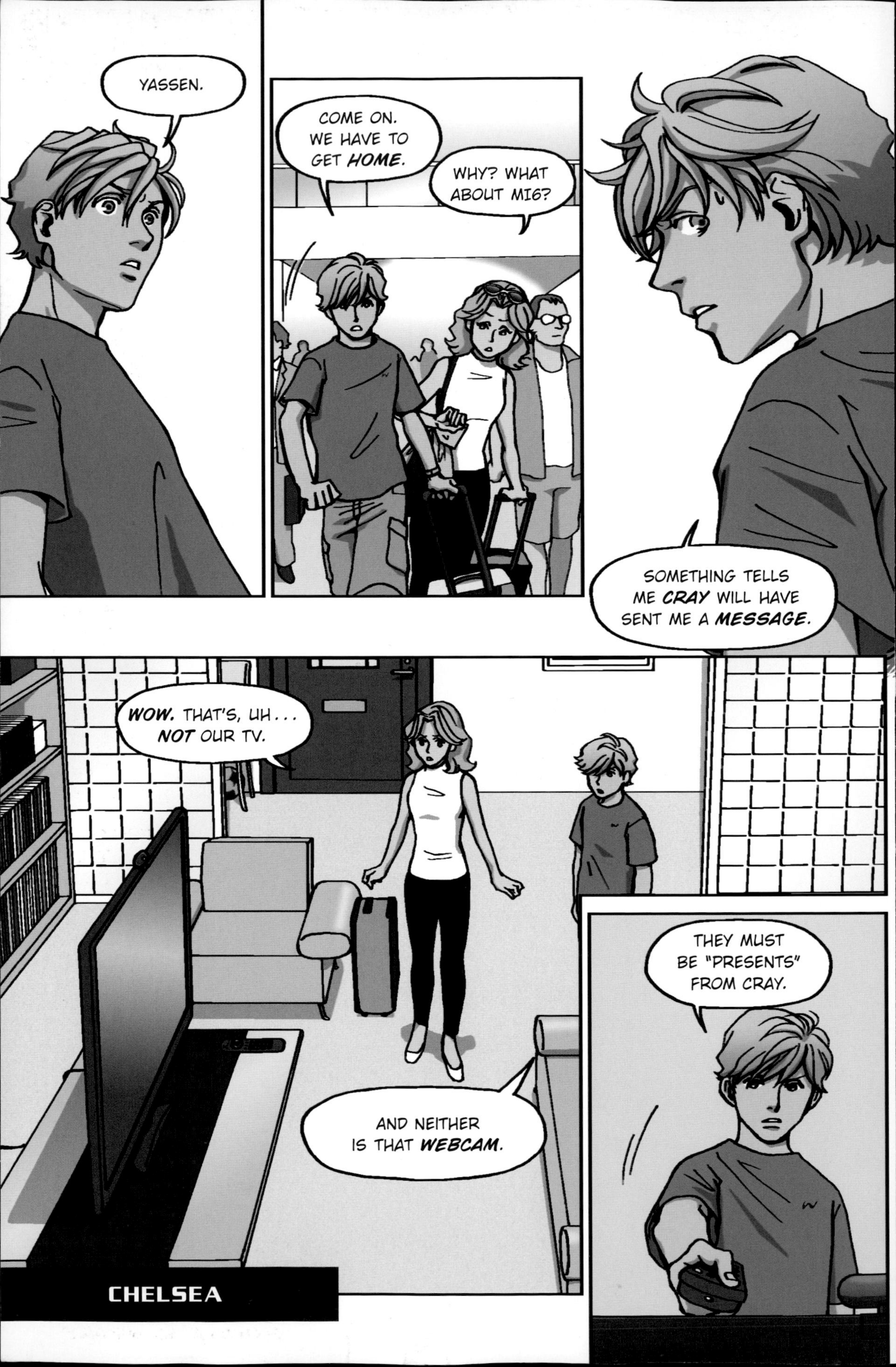
YASSEN.
COME ON. WE HAVE TO GET HOME.
WHY? WHAT ABOUT MI6?
SOMETHING TELLS ME CRAY WILL HAVE SENT ME A MESSAGE.
CHELSEA
WOW. THAT'S, UH . . . NOT OUR TV.
AND NEITHER IS THAT WEBCAM.
THEY MUST BE "PRESENTS" FROM CRAY.

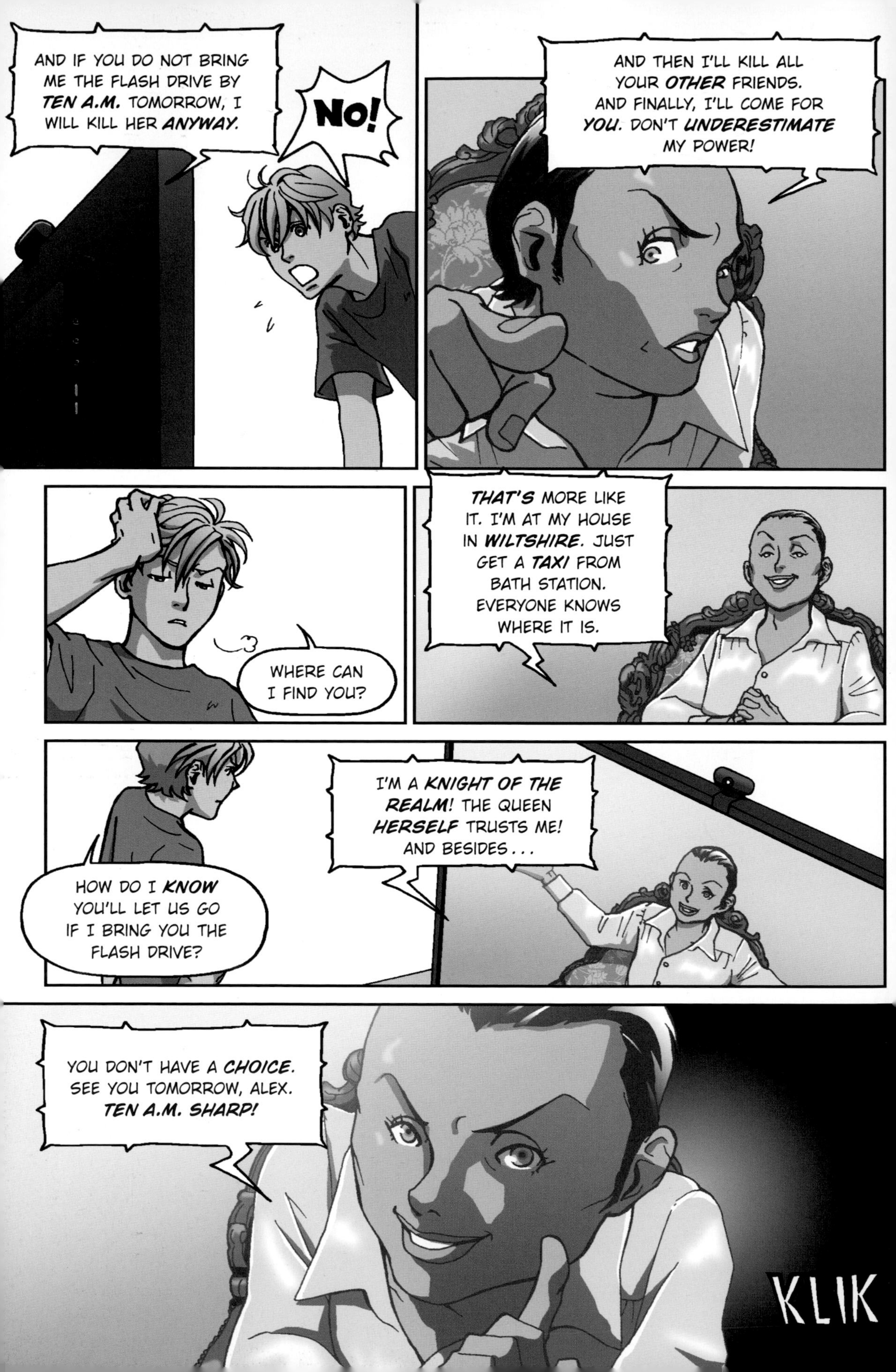
AND IF YOU DO NOT BRING ME THE FLASH DRIVE BY TEN A.M. TOMORROW, I WILL KILL HER ANYWAY.
NO!
AND THEN I'LL KILL ALL YOUR OTHER FRIENDS. AND FINALLY, I'LL COME FOR YOU. DON'T UNDERESTIMATE MY POWER!
WHERE CAN I FIND YOU?
THAT'S MORE LIKE IT. I'M AT MY HOUSE IN WILTSHIRE. JUST GET A TAXI FROM BATH STATION. EVERYONE KNOWS WHERE IT IS.
HOW DO I KNOW YOU'LL LET US GO IF I BRING YOU THE FLASH DRIVE?
I'M A KNIGHT OF THE REALM! THE QUEEN HERSELF TRUSTS ME! AND BESIDES . . .
YOU DON'T HAVE A CHOICE. SEE YOU TOMORROW, ALEX. TEN A.M. SHARP!
KLIK

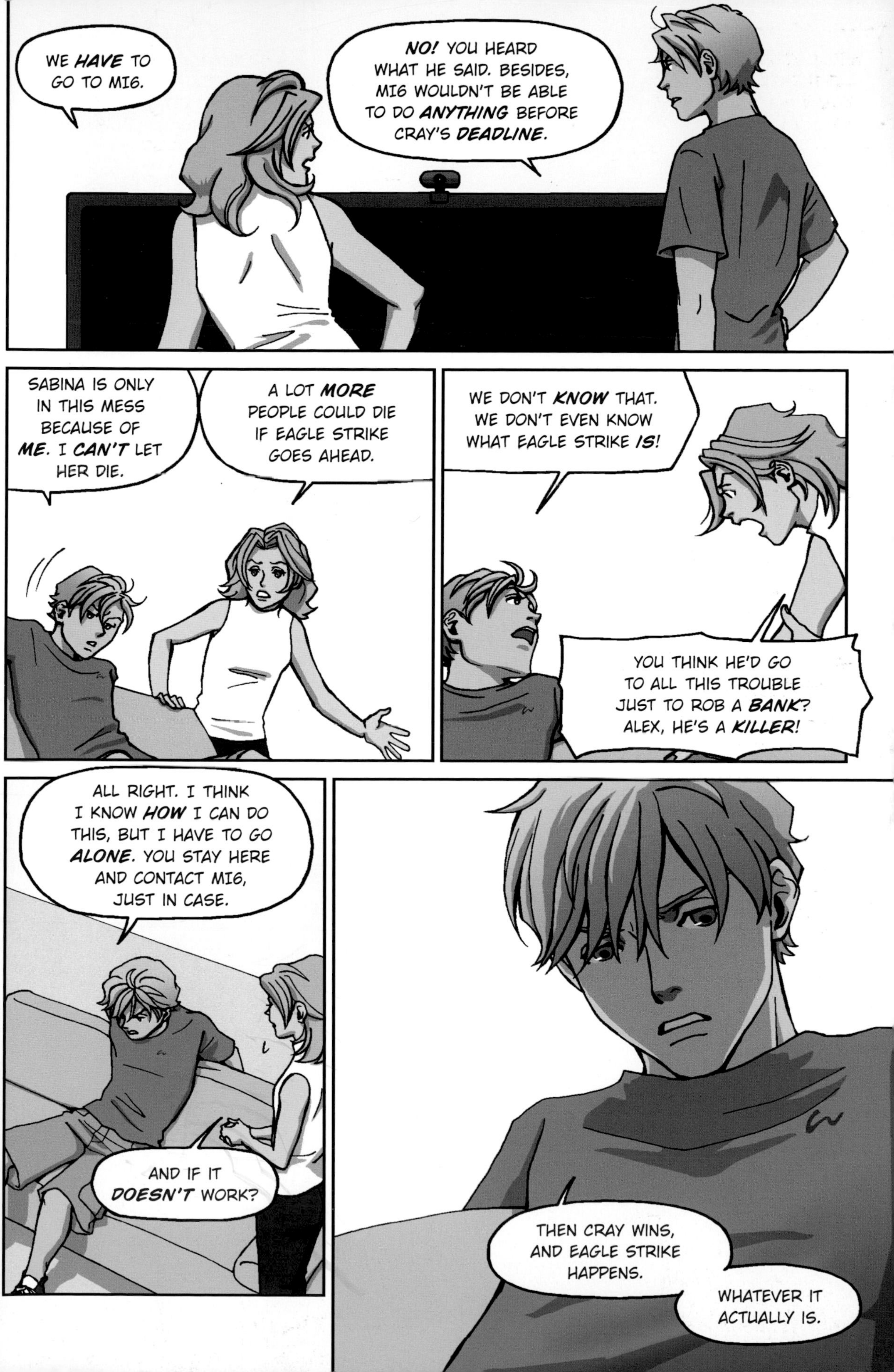
WE HAVE TO GO TO MI6.
NO! YOU HEARD WHAT HE SAID. BESIDES, MI6 WOULDN'T BE ABLE TO DO ANYTHING BEFORE CRAY'S DEADLINE.
SABINA IS ONLY IN THIS MESS BECAUSE OF ME. I CAN'T LET HER DIE.
A LOT MORE PEOPLE COULD DIE IF EAGLE STRIKE GOES AHEAD.
WE DON'T KNOW THAT. WE DON'T EVEN KNOW WHAT EAGLE STRIKE IS!
YOU THINK HE'D GO TO ALL THIS TROUBLE JUST TO ROB A BANK? ALEX, HE'S A KILLER!
ALL RIGHT. I THINK I KNOW HOW I CAN DO THIS, BUT I HAVE TO GO ALONE. YOU STAY HERE AND CONTACT MI6, JUST IN CASE.
AND IF IT DOESN'T WORK?
THEN CRAY WINS, AND EAGLE STRIKE HAPPENS.
WHATEVER IT ACTUALLY IS.

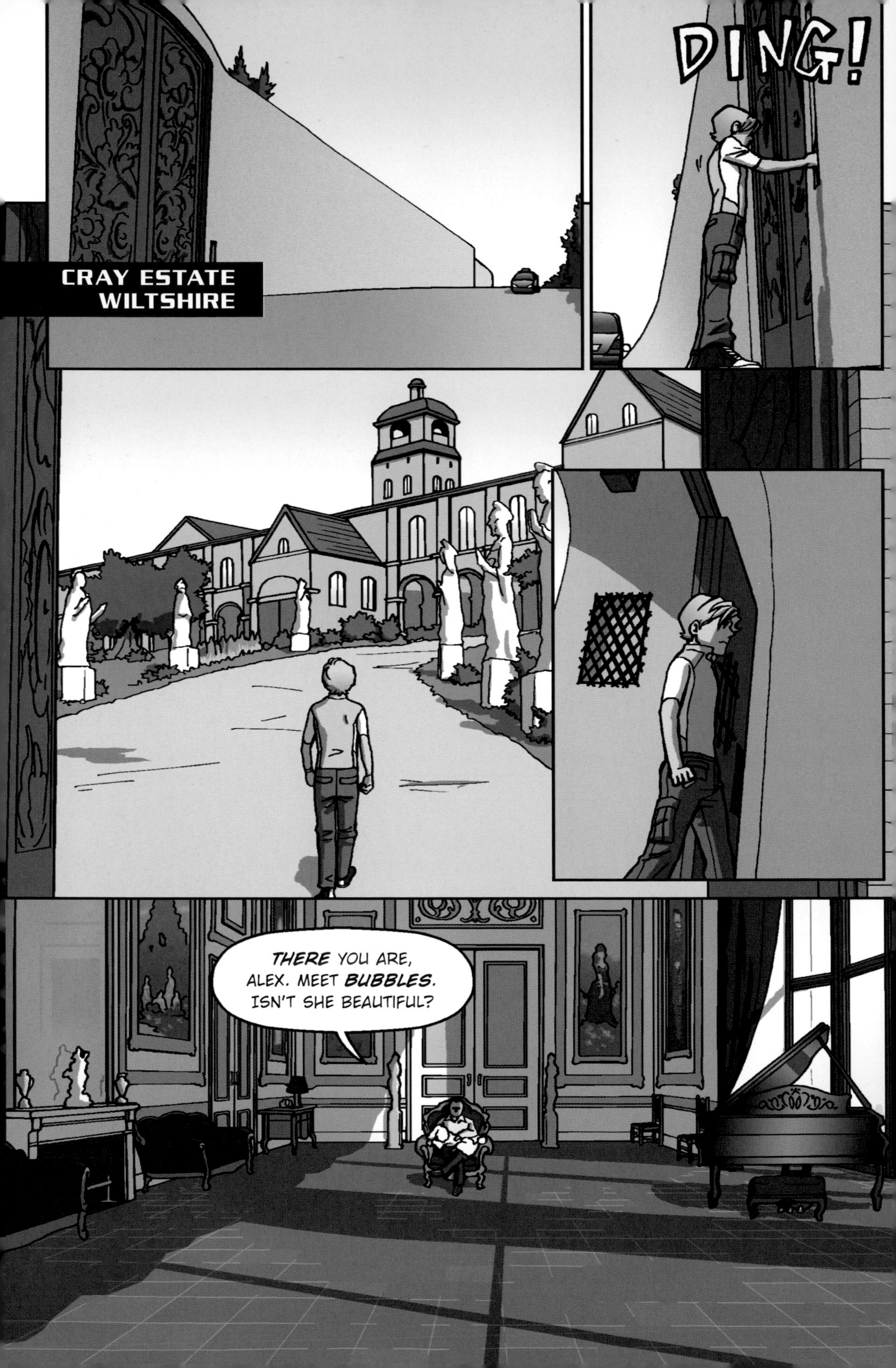
CRAY ESTATE
WILTSHIRE
DING!
THERE YOU ARE, ALEX. MEET BUBBLES. ISN'T SHE BEAUTIFUL?

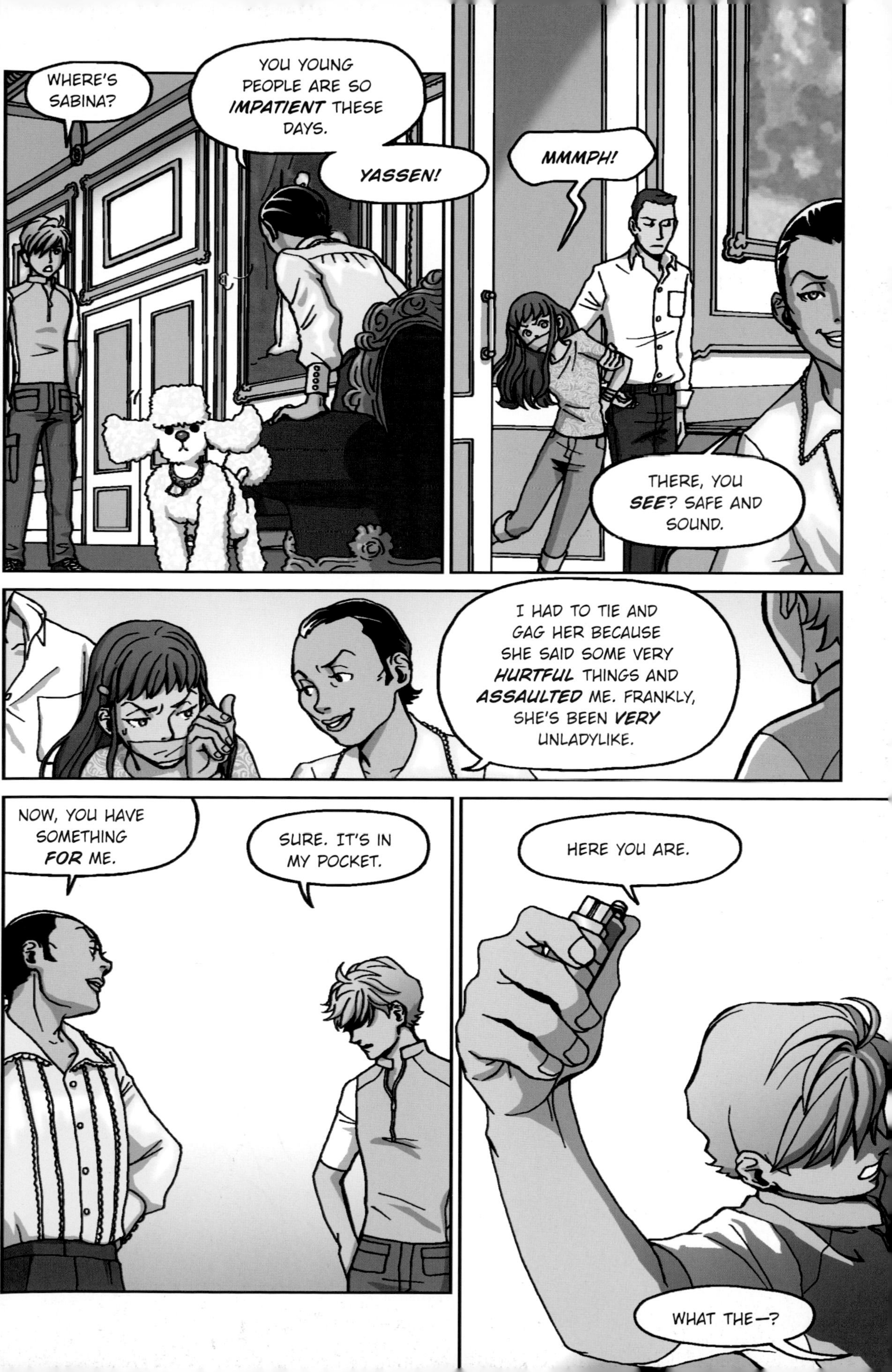
WHERE'S SABINA?
YOU YOUNG PEOPLE ARE SO IMPATIENT THESE DAYS.
YASSEN!
MMMPH!
THERE, YOU SEE? SAFE AND SOUND.
I HAD TO TIE AND GAG HER BECAUSE SHE SAID SOME VERY HURTFUL THINGS AND ASSAULTED ME. FRANKLY, SHE'S BEEN VERY UNLADYLIKE.
NOW, YOU HAVE SOMETHING FOR ME.
SURE. IT'S IN MY POCKET.
HERE YOU ARE.
WHAT THE—?

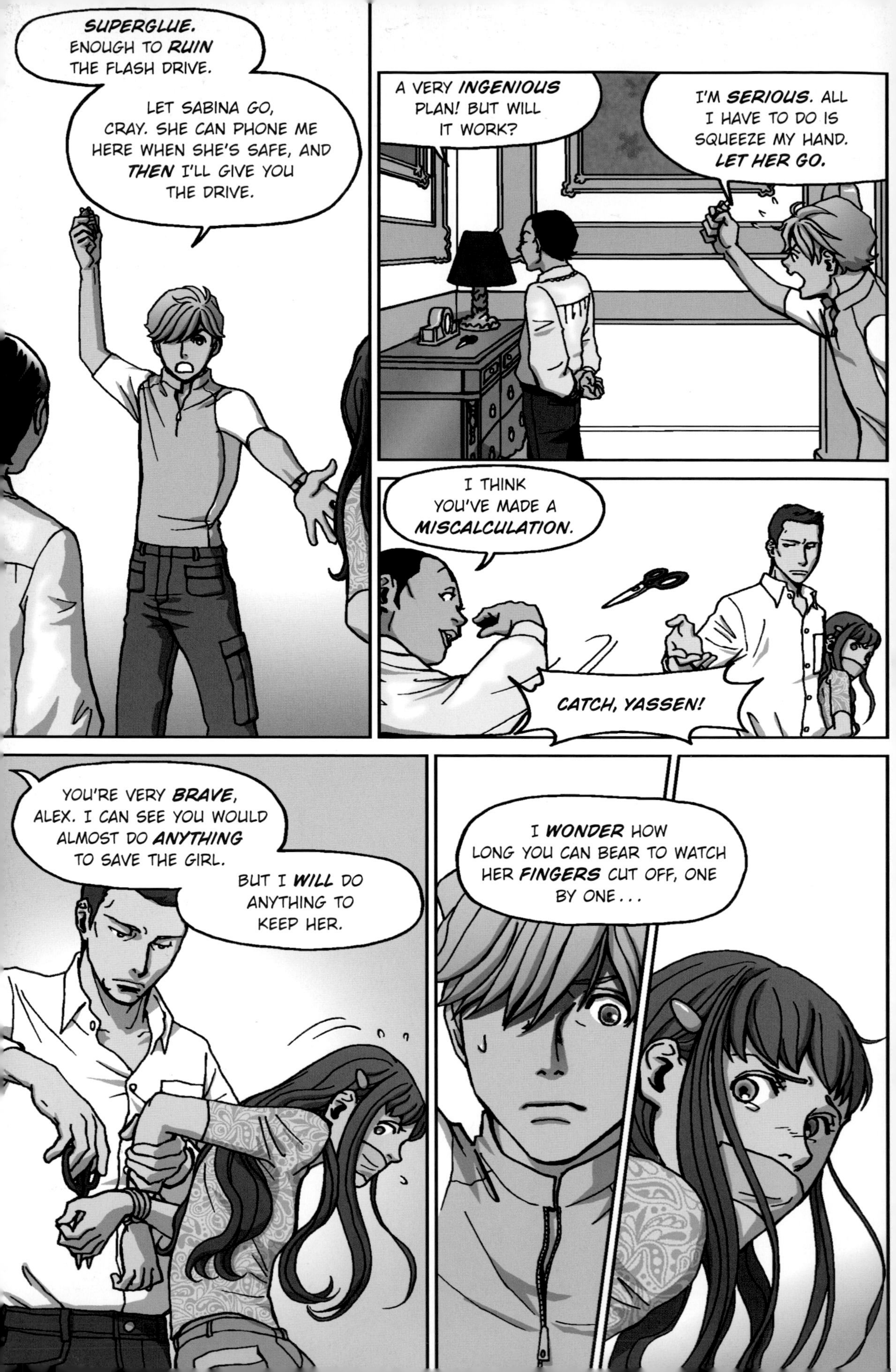
SUPERGLUE. ENOUGH TO RUIN THE FLASH DRIVE.
LET SABINA GO, CRAY. SHE CAN PHONE ME HERE WHEN SHE'S SAFE, AND THEN I'LL GIVE YOU THE DRIVE.
A VERY INGENIOUS PLAN! BUT WILL IT WORK?
I'M SERIOUS. ALL I HAVE TO DO IS SQUEEZE MY HAND. LET HER GO.
I THINK YOU'VE MADE A MISCALCULATION.
CATCH, YASSEN!
YOU'RE VERY BRAVE, ALEX. I CAN SEE YOU WOULD ALMOST DO ANYTHING TO SAVE THE GIRL.
BUT I WILL DO ANYTHING TO KEEP HER.
I WONDER HOW LONG YOU CAN BEAR TO WATCH HER FINGERS CUT OFF, ONE BY ONE . . .

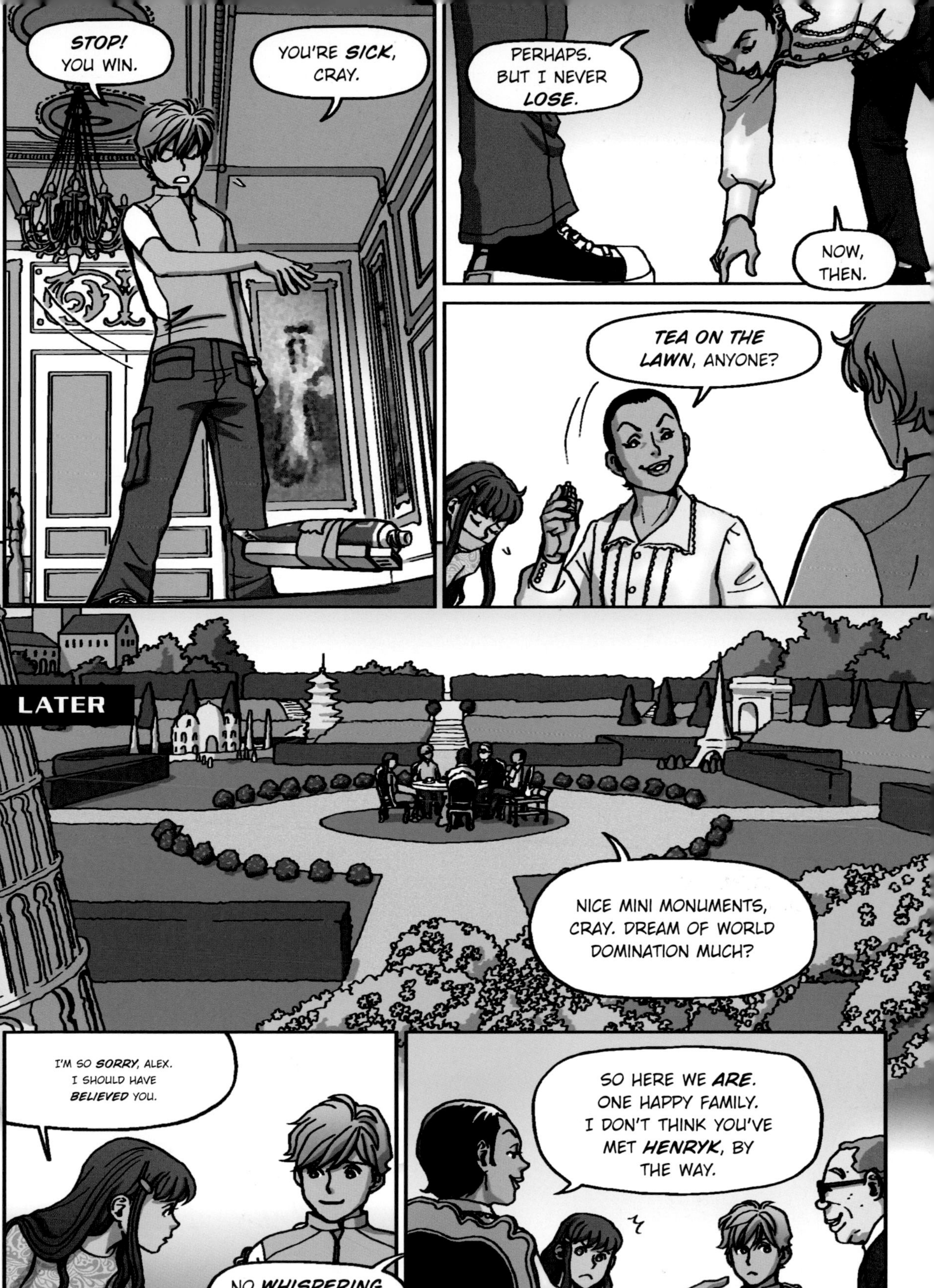
STOP! YOU WIN.
YOU'RE SICK, CRAY.
PERHAPS. BUT I NEVER LOSE.
NOW, THEN.
TEA ON THE LAWN, ANYONE?
LATER
NICE MINI MONUMENTS, CRAY. DREAM OF WORLD DOMINATION MUCH?
I'M SO SORRY, ALEX. I SHOULD HAVE BELIEVED YOU.
NO WHISPERING AT THE TABLE, THANK YOU.
SO HERE WE ARE. ONE HAPPY FAMILY. I DON'T THINK YOU'VE MET HENRYK, BY THE WAY.

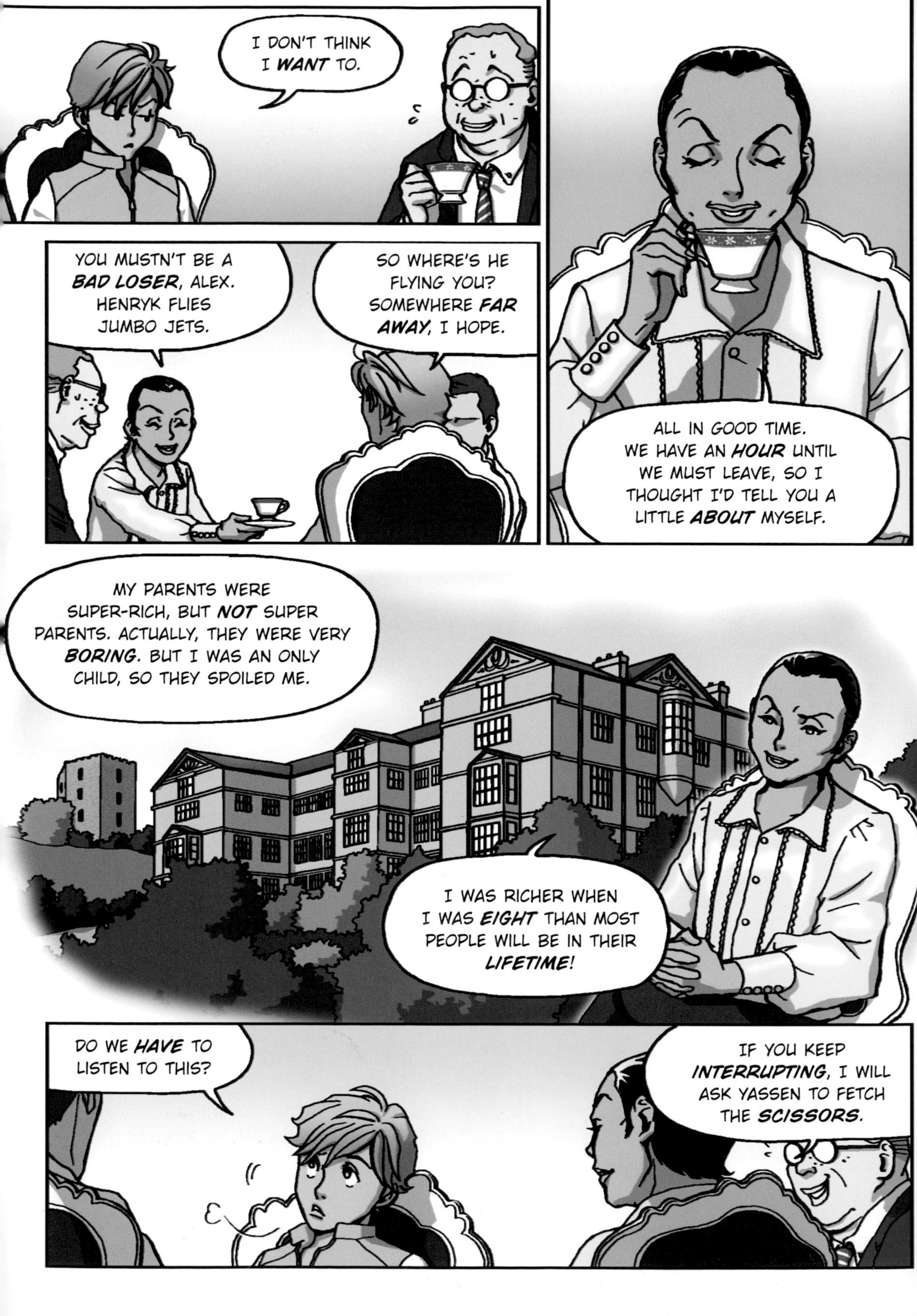
I DON'T THINK I WANT TO.
YOU MUSTN'T BE A BAD LOSER, ALEX. HENRYK FLIES JUMBO JETS.
SO WHERE'S HE FLYING YOU? SOMEWHERE FAR AWAY, I HOPE.
ALL IN GOOD TIME. WE HAVE AN HOUR UNTIL WE MUST LEAVE, SO I THOUGHT I'D TELL YOU A LITTLE ABOUT MYSELF.
MY PARENTS WERE SUPER-RICH, BUT NOT SUPER PARENTS. ACTUALLY, THEY WERE VERY BORING. BUT I WAS AN ONLY CHILD, SO THEY SPOILED ME.
I WAS RICHER WHEN I WAS EIGHT THAN MOST PEOPLE WILL BE IN THEIR LIFETIME!
DO WE HAVE TO LISTEN TO THIS?
IF YOU KEEP INTERRUPTING, I WILL ASK YASSEN TO FETCH THE SCISSORS.

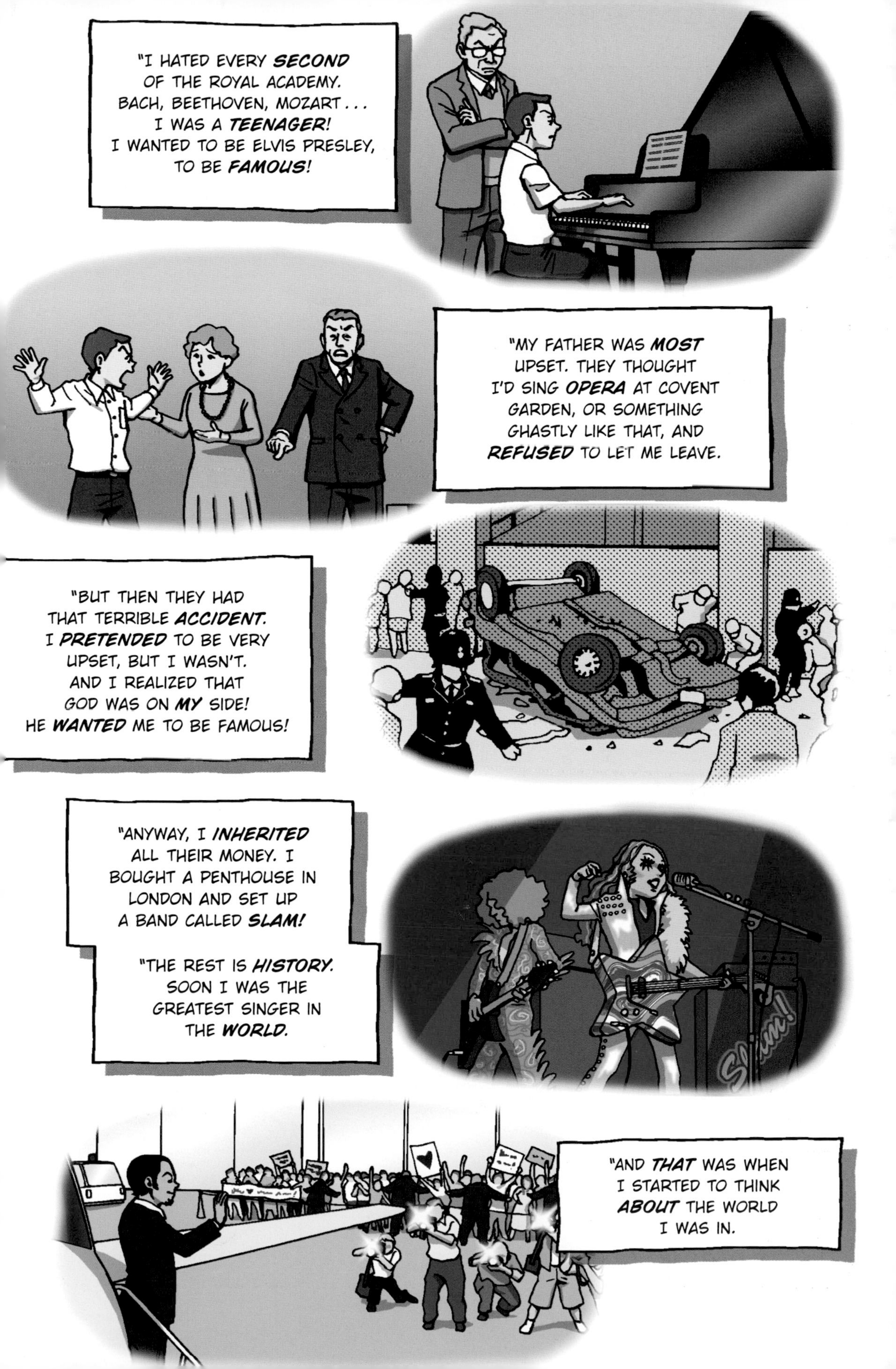
"I HATED EVERY SECOND OF THE ROYAL ACADEMY. BACH, BEETHOVEN, MOZART . . . I WAS A TEENAGER! I WANTED TO BE ELVIS PRESLEY, TO BE FAMOUS!
"MY FATHER WAS MOST UPSET. THEY THOUGHT I'D SING OPERA AT COVENT GARDEN, OR SOMETHING GHASTLY LIKE THAT, AND REFUSED TO LET ME LEAVE.
"BUT THEN THEY HAD THAT TERRIBLE ACCIDENT. I PRETENDED TO BE VERY UPSET, BUT I WASN'T. AND I REALIZED THAT GOD WAS ON MY SIDE! HE WANTED ME TO BE FAMOUS!
"ANYWAY, I INHERITED ALL THEIR MONEY. I BOUGHT A PENTHOUSE IN LONDON AND SET UP A BAND CALLED SLAM!
"THE REST IS HISTORY. SOON I WAS THE GREATEST SINGER IN THE WORLD.
"AND THAT WAS WHEN I STARTED TO THINK ABOUT THE WORLD I WAS IN.

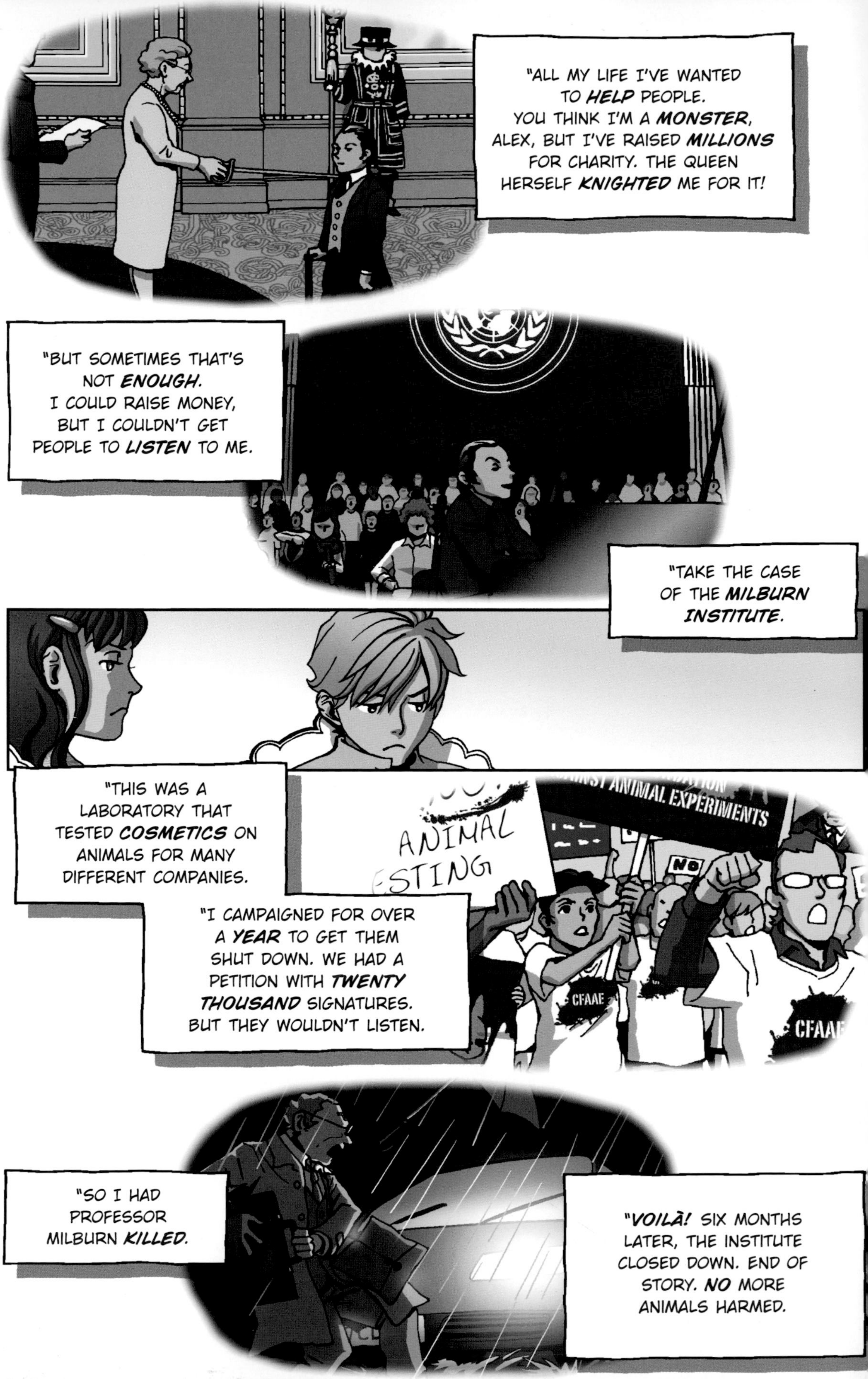
"ALL MY LIFE I'VE WANTED TO HELP PEOPLE. YOU THINK I'M A MONSTER, ALEX, BUT I'VE RAISED MILLIONS FOR CHARITY. THE QUEEN HERSELF KNIGHTED ME FOR IT!
"BUT SOMETIMES THAT'S NOT ENOUGH. I COULD RAISE MONEY, BUT I COULDN'T GET PEOPLE TO LISTEN TO ME.
"TAKE THE CASE OF THE MILBURN INSTITUTE.
"THIS WAS A LABORATORY THAT TESTED COSMETICS ON ANIMALS FOR MANY DIFFERENT COMPANIES.
ANIMAL EXPERIMENTS
ANIMAL
NO
CFAAE
CFAAE
"I CAMPAIGNED FOR OVER A YEAR TO GET THEM SHUT DOWN. WE HAD A PETITION WITH TWENTY THOUSAND SIGNATURES. BUT THEY WOULDN'T LISTEN.
"SO I HAD PROFESSOR MILBURN KILLED.
"VOILÀ! SIX MONTHS LATER, THE INSTITUTE CLOSED DOWN. END OF STORY. NO MORE ANIMALS HARMED.

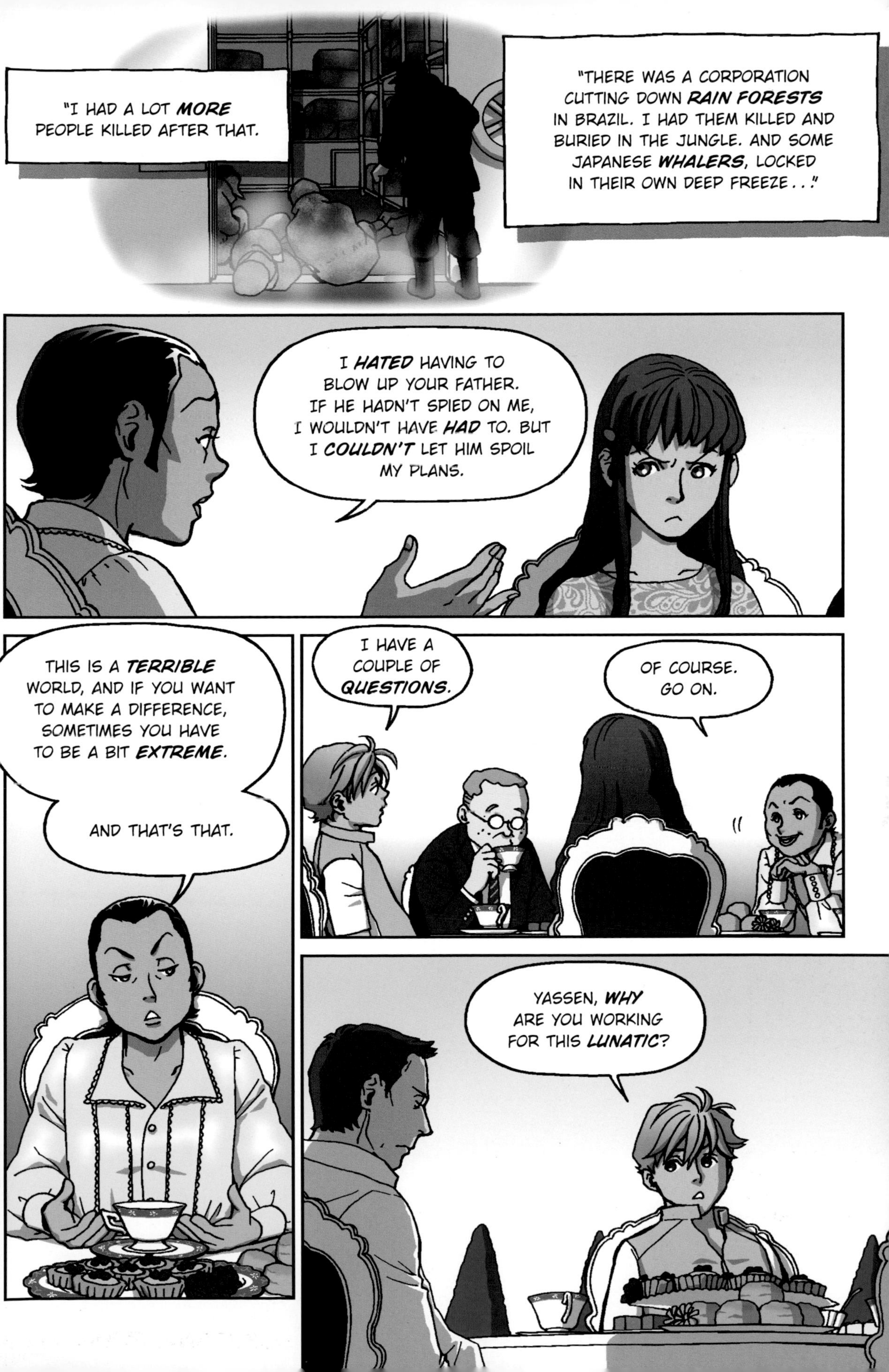
"I HAD A LOT MORE PEOPLE KILLED AFTER THAT.
"THERE WAS A CORPORATION CUTTING DOWN RAIN FORESTS IN BRAZIL. I HAD THEM KILLED AND BURIED IN THE JUNGLE. AND SOME JAPANESE WHALERS, LOCKED IN THEIR OWN DEEP FREEZE . . ."
I HATED HAVING TO BLOW UP YOUR FATHER. IF HE HADN'T SPIED ON ME, I WOULDN'T HAVE HAD TO. BUT I COULDN'T LET HIM SPOIL MY PLANS.
THIS IS A TERRIBLE WORLD, AND IF YOU WANT TO MAKE A DIFFERENCE, SOMETIMES YOU HAVE TO BE A BIT EXTREME.
AND THAT'S THAT.
I HAVE A COUPLE OF QUESTIONS.
OF COURSE. GO ON.
YASSEN, WHY ARE YOU WORKING FOR THIS LUNATIC?

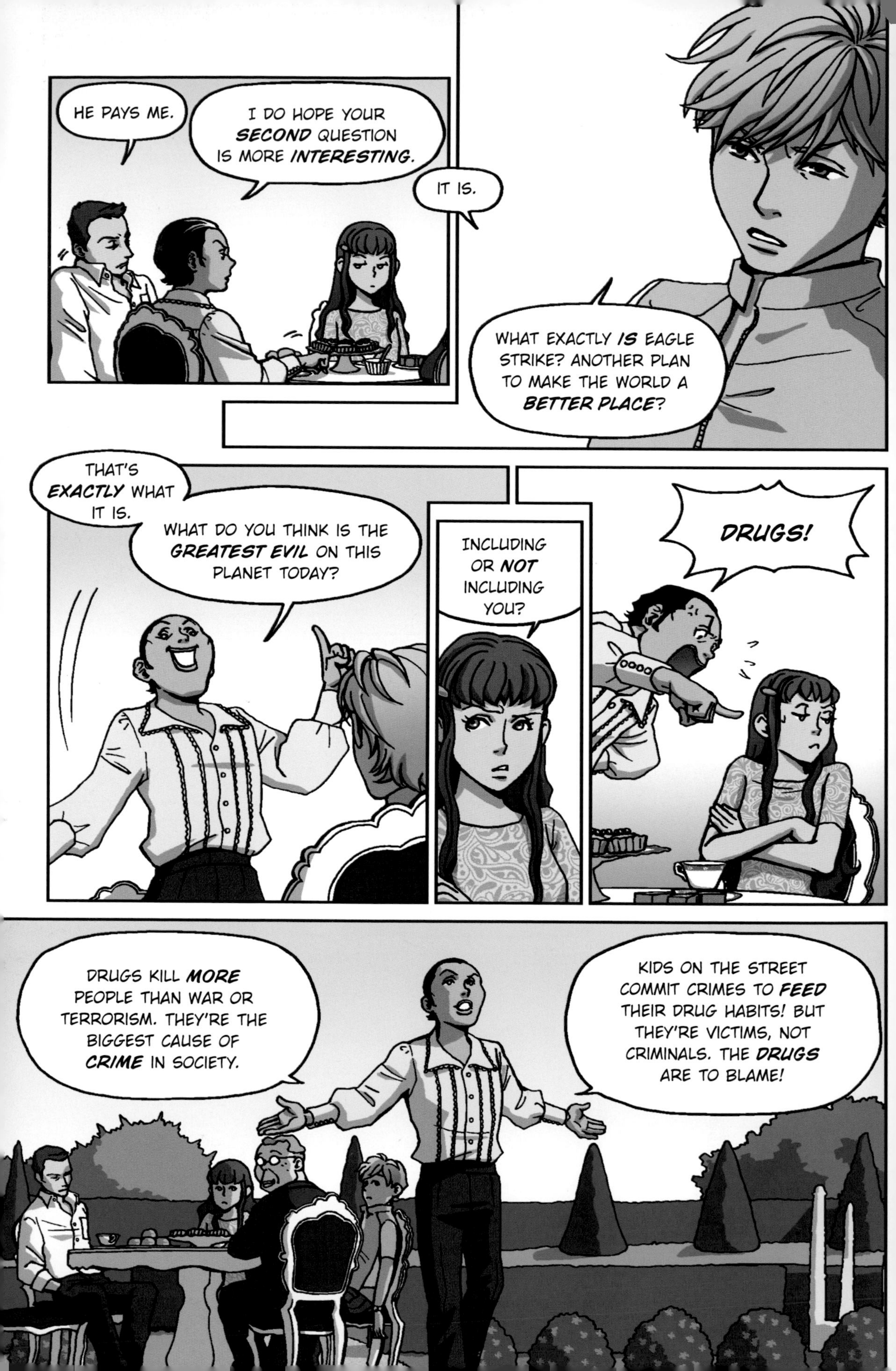
HE PAYS ME.
I DO HOPE YOUR SECOND QUESTION IS MORE INTERESTING.
IT IS.
WHAT EXACTLY IS EAGLE STRIKE? ANOTHER PLAN TO MAKE THE WORLD A BETTER PLACE?
THAT'S EXACTLY WHAT IT IS.
WHAT DO YOU THINK IS THE GREATEST EVIL ON THIS PLANET TODAY?
INCLUDING OR NOT INCLUDING YOU?
DRUGS!
DRUGS KILL MORE PEOPLE THAN WAR OR TERRORISM. THEY'RE THE BIGGEST CAUSE OF CRIME IN SOCIETY.
KIDS ON THE STREET COMMIT CRIMES TO FEED THEIR DRUG HABITS! BUT THEY'RE VICTIMS, NOT CRIMINALS. THE DRUGS ARE TO BLAME!

ALL MY LIFE I'VE *FOUGHT* DRUGS—DOING PUBLIC SERVICE ANNOUNCEMENTS, BUILDING TREATMENT CENTERS, WRITING ALBUMS ABOUT HOW *EVIL* THEY ARE.

BUT NOW I'M GOING TO *END* IT. THAT'S WHAT EAGLE STRIKE IS. IMAGINE A WORLD *WITHOUT* DRUGS! ISN'T THAT *WORTH* A FEW SACRIFICES?

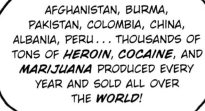

HOW?

EASY. *GOVERNMENTS* WON'T DO ANYTHING. THE *POLICE* ARE POWERLESS. *NO ONE* CAN STOP THE DEALERS. SO YOU HAVE TO GO TO THE *SUPPLIERS.*

AFGHANISTAN, BURMA, PAKISTAN, COLOMBIA, CHINA, ALBANIA, PERU . . . THOUSANDS OF TONS OF *HEROIN, COCAINE,* AND *MARIJUANA* PRODUCED EVERY YEAR AND SOLD ALL OVER THE *WORLD!*

THESE ARE THE PRINCIPAL SOURCES OF THE WORLD'S DRUG PROBLEM.

THESE ARE MY *TARGETS.*

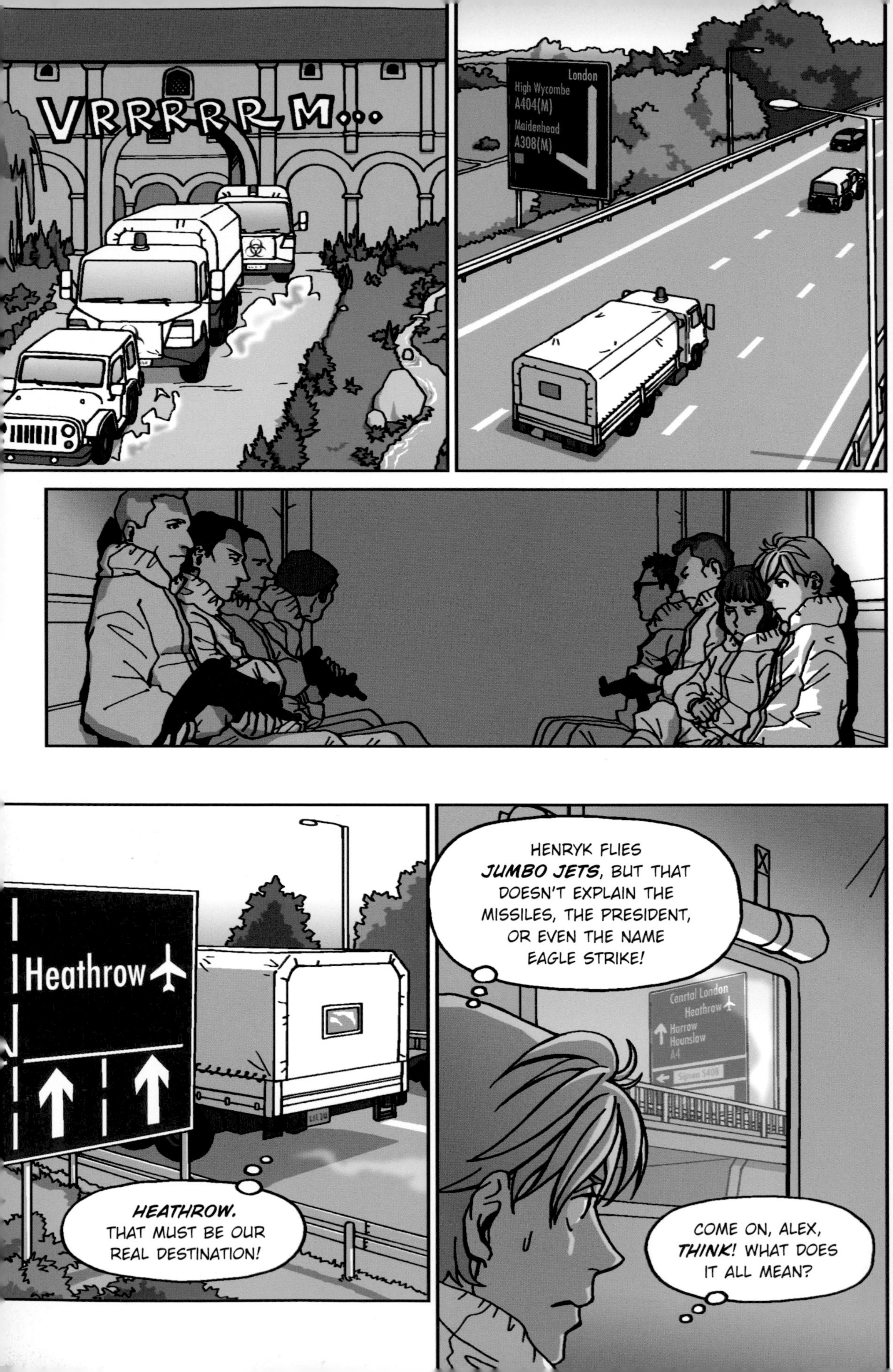
VRRRRR M...
London
High Wycombe
A404(M)
Maidenhead
A308(M)
Heathrow
HEATHROW. THAT MUST BE OUR REAL DESTINATION!
HENRYK FLIES JUMBO JETS, BUT THAT DOESN'T EXPLAIN THE MISSILES, THE PRESIDENT, OR EVEN THE NAME EAGLE STRIKE!
Cenrtal London
Heathrow
Harrow
Hounslow
A4
Sipson
COME ON, ALEX, THINK! WHAT DOES IT ALL MEAN?

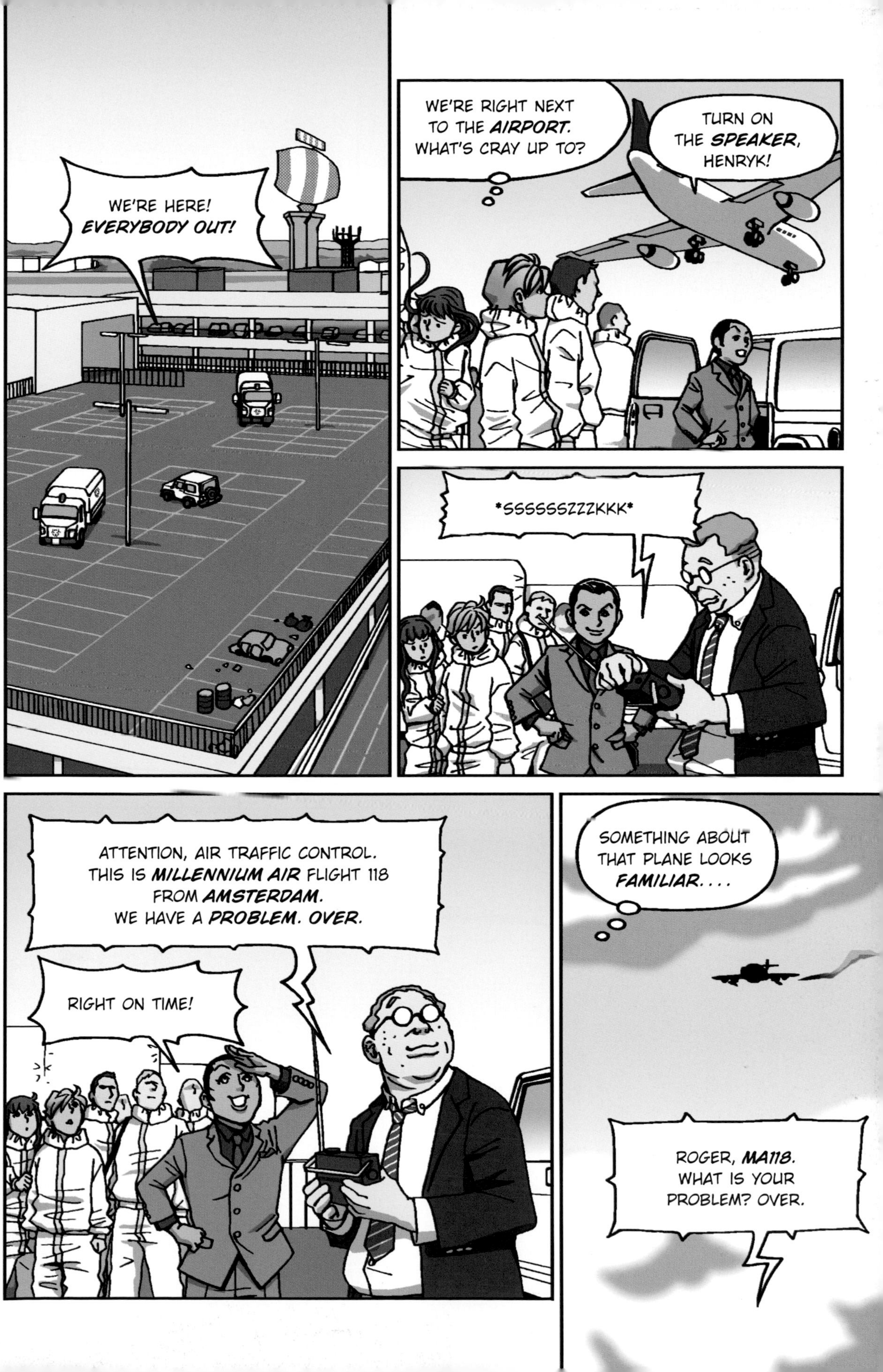
WE'RE HERE! EVERYBODY OUT!
WE'RE RIGHT NEXT TO THE AIRPORT. WHAT'S CRAY UP TO?
TURN ON THE SPEAKER, HENRYK!
SSSSSSZZZKKK
ATTENTION, AIR TRAFFIC CONTROL. THIS IS MILLENNIUM AIR FLIGHT 118 FROM AMSTERDAM. WE HAVE A PROBLEM. OVER.
RIGHT ON TIME!
SOMETHING ABOUT THAT PLANE LOOKS FAMILIAR. . . .
ROGER, MA118. WHAT IS YOUR PROBLEM? OVER.

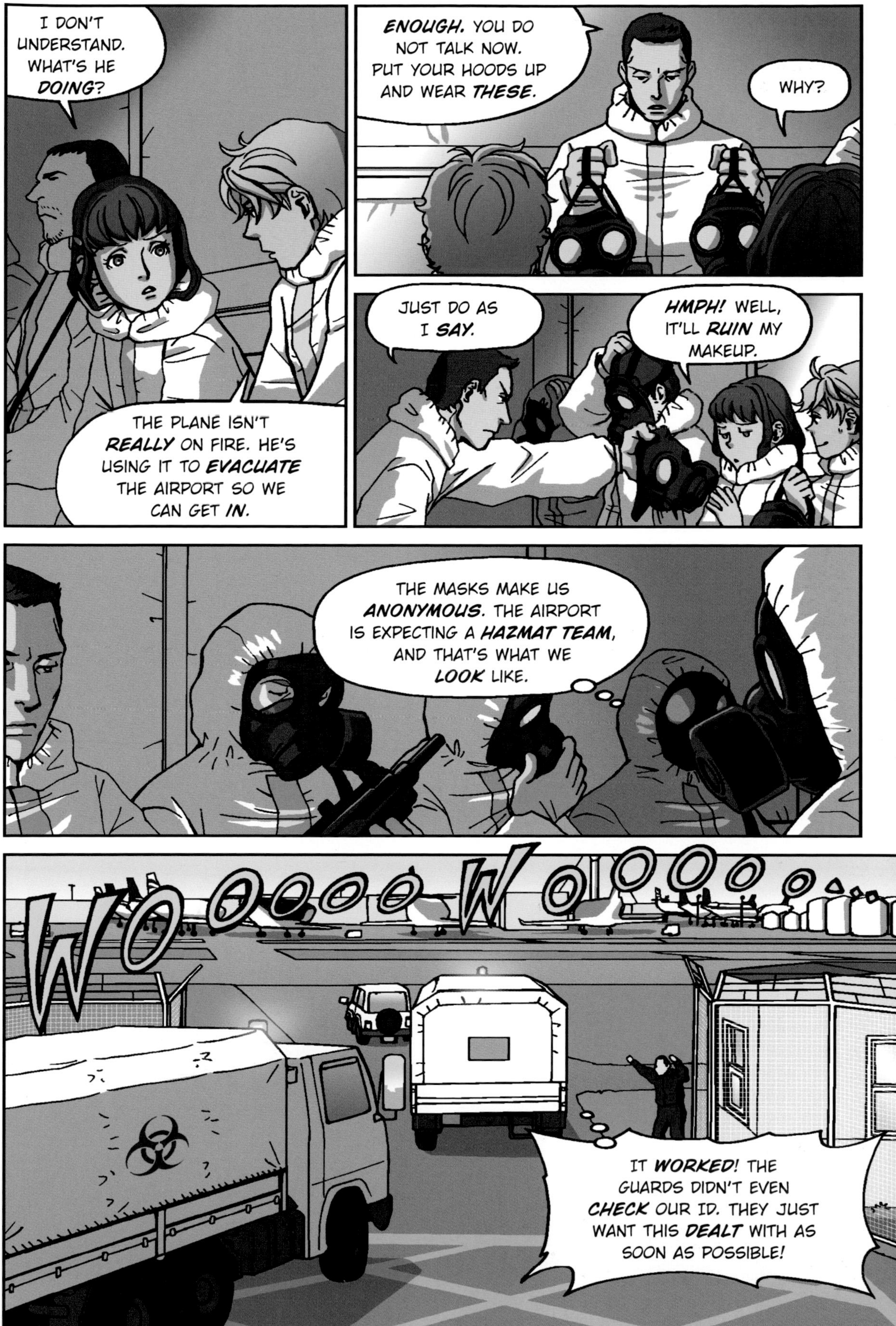
I DON'T UNDERSTAND. WHAT'S HE DOING?
THE PLANE ISN'T REALLY ON FIRE. HE'S USING IT TO EVACUATE THE AIRPORT SO WE CAN GET IN.
ENOUGH. YOU DO NOT TALK NOW. PUT YOUR HOODS UP AND WEAR THESE.
WHY?
JUST DO AS I SAY.
HMPH! WELL, IT'LL RUIN MY MAKEUP.
THE MASKS MAKE US ANONYMOUS. THE AIRPORT IS EXPECTING A HAZMAT TEAM, AND THAT'S WHAT WE LOOK LIKE.
WOOOOOWOOOOO
IT WORKED! THE GUARDS DIDN'T EVEN CHECK OUR ID. THEY JUST WANT THIS DEALT WITH AS SOON AS POSSIBLE!

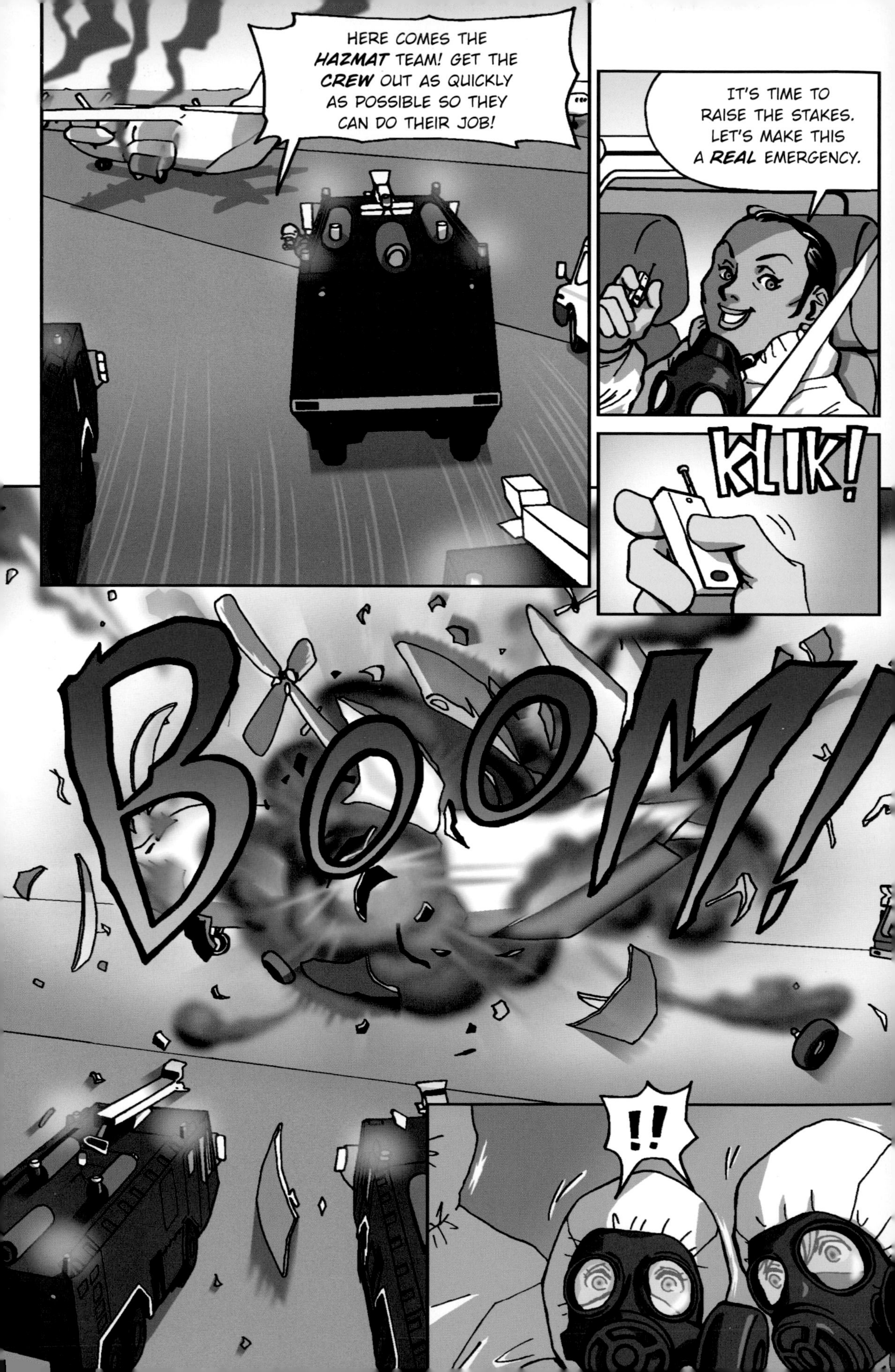
HERE COMES THE HAZMAT TEAM! GET THE CREW OUT AS QUICKLY AS POSSIBLE SO THEY CAN DO THEIR JOB!
IT'S TIME TO RAISE THE STAKES. LET'S MAKE THIS A REAL EMERGENCY.
KLIK!
BOOM!
!!

TOO LATE!

EVERYBODY OUT! THERE'S NOTHING WE CAN DO, LEAVE IT FOR THE *BIOCHEM* TEAM!

SO NOW IT'S JUST US AND A WRECKED PLANE. I BET CRAY TRICKED THE *PILOT*, TOO. HE PROBABLY EXPECTED TO GO TO PRISON, NOT *DIE* ON A RUNWAY!

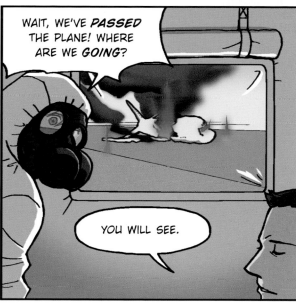

WAIT, WE'VE *PASSED* THE PLANE! WHERE ARE WE *GOING*?

YOU WILL SEE.

WE'RE *IN*, AND THE REST OF THE AIRPORT HAS BEEN *EVACUATED*. BUT I STILL DON'T UNDERSTAND WHAT IT'S ALL *FOR*....

!!

OH, NO.

NOW IT ALL MAKES SENSE!

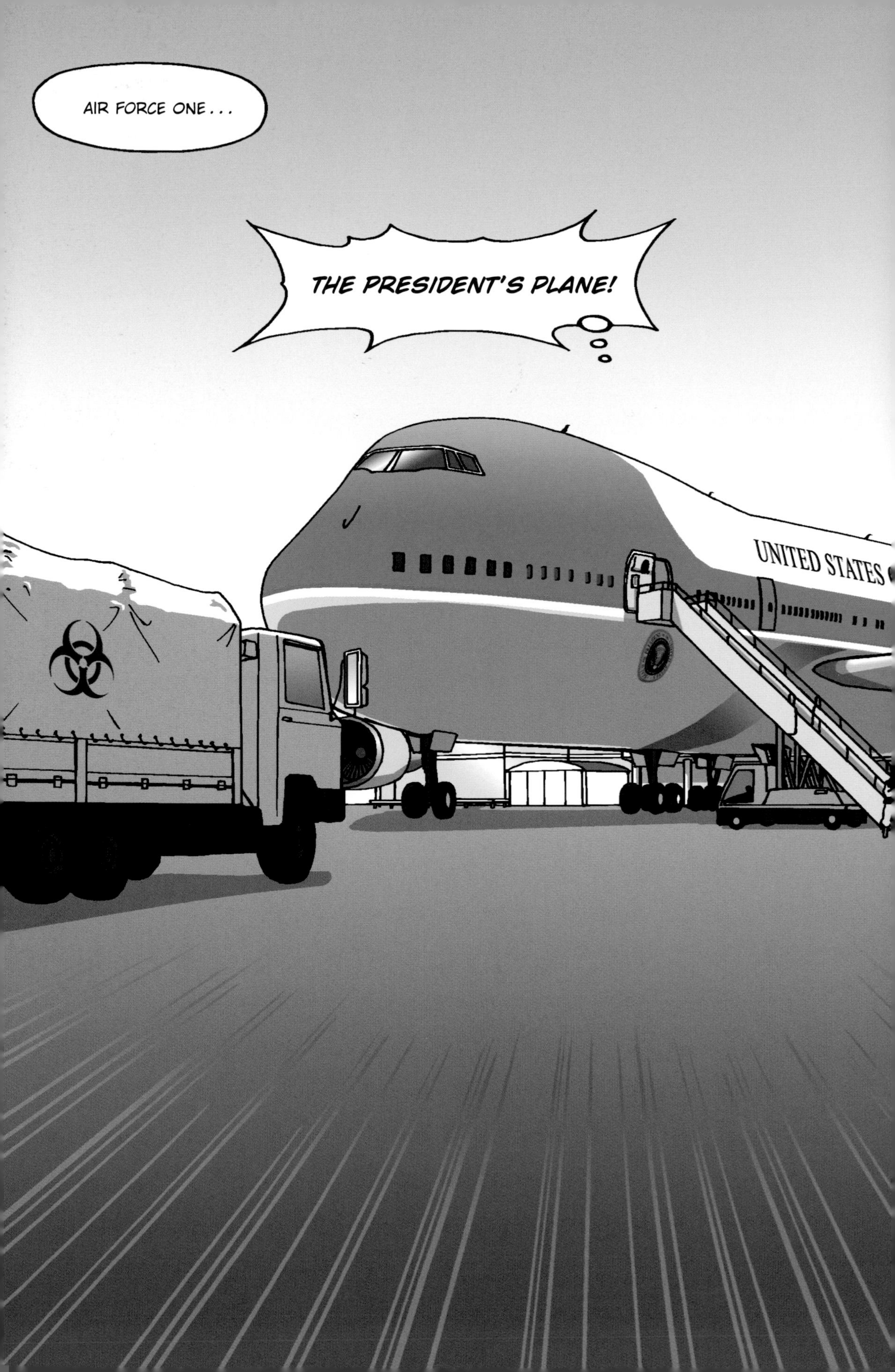
AIR FORCE ONE . . .
THE PRESIDENT'S PLANE!
UNITED STATES

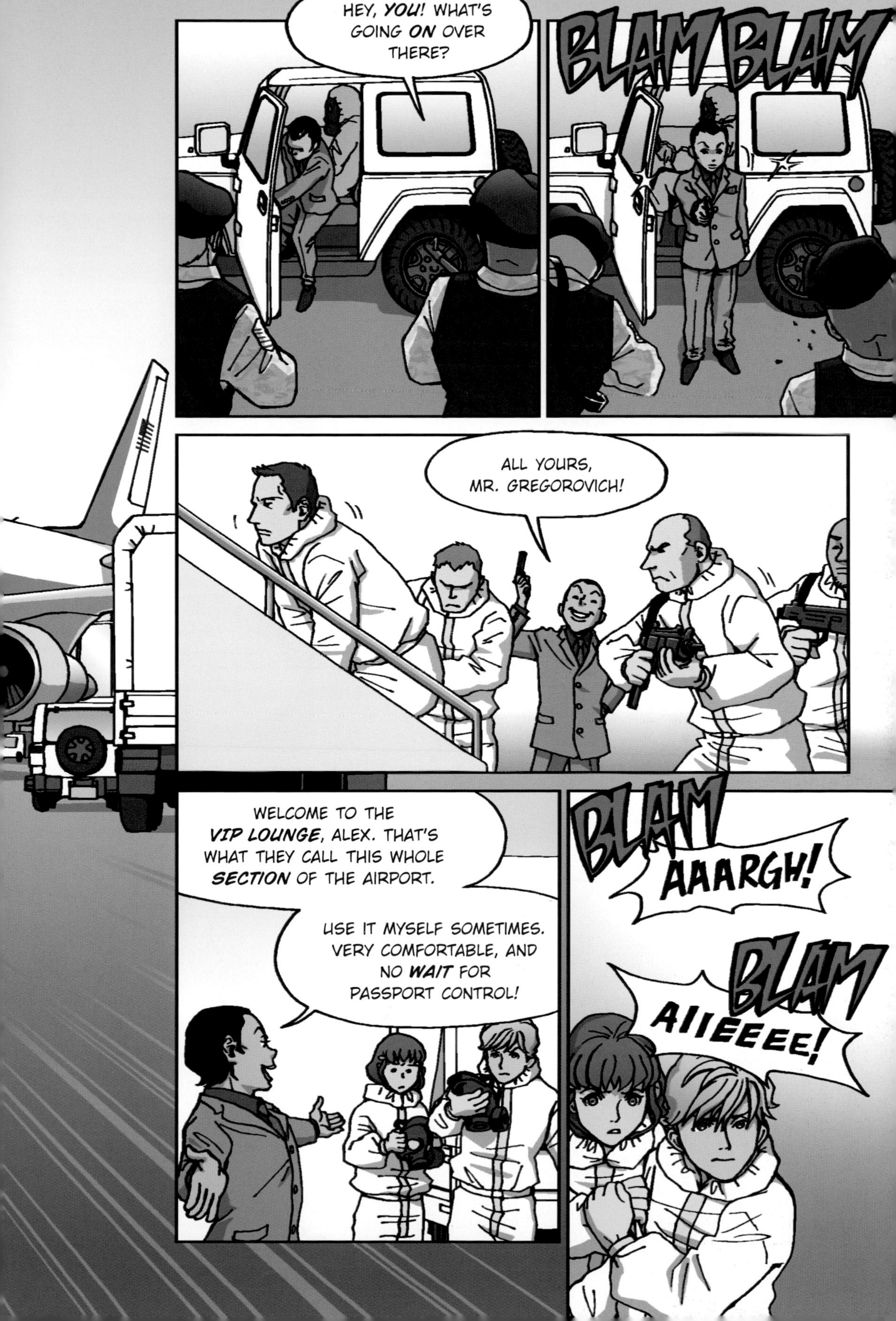

HEY, YOU! WHAT'S GOING ON OVER THERE?
BLAM BLAM
ALL YOURS, MR. GREGOROVICH!
WELCOME TO THE VIP LOUNGE, ALEX. THAT'S WHAT THEY CALL THIS WHOLE SECTION OF THE AIRPORT.
USE IT MYSELF SOMETIMES. VERY COMFORTABLE, AND NO WAIT FOR PASSPORT CONTROL!
BLAM
AAARGH!
BLAM
AIIEEEE!

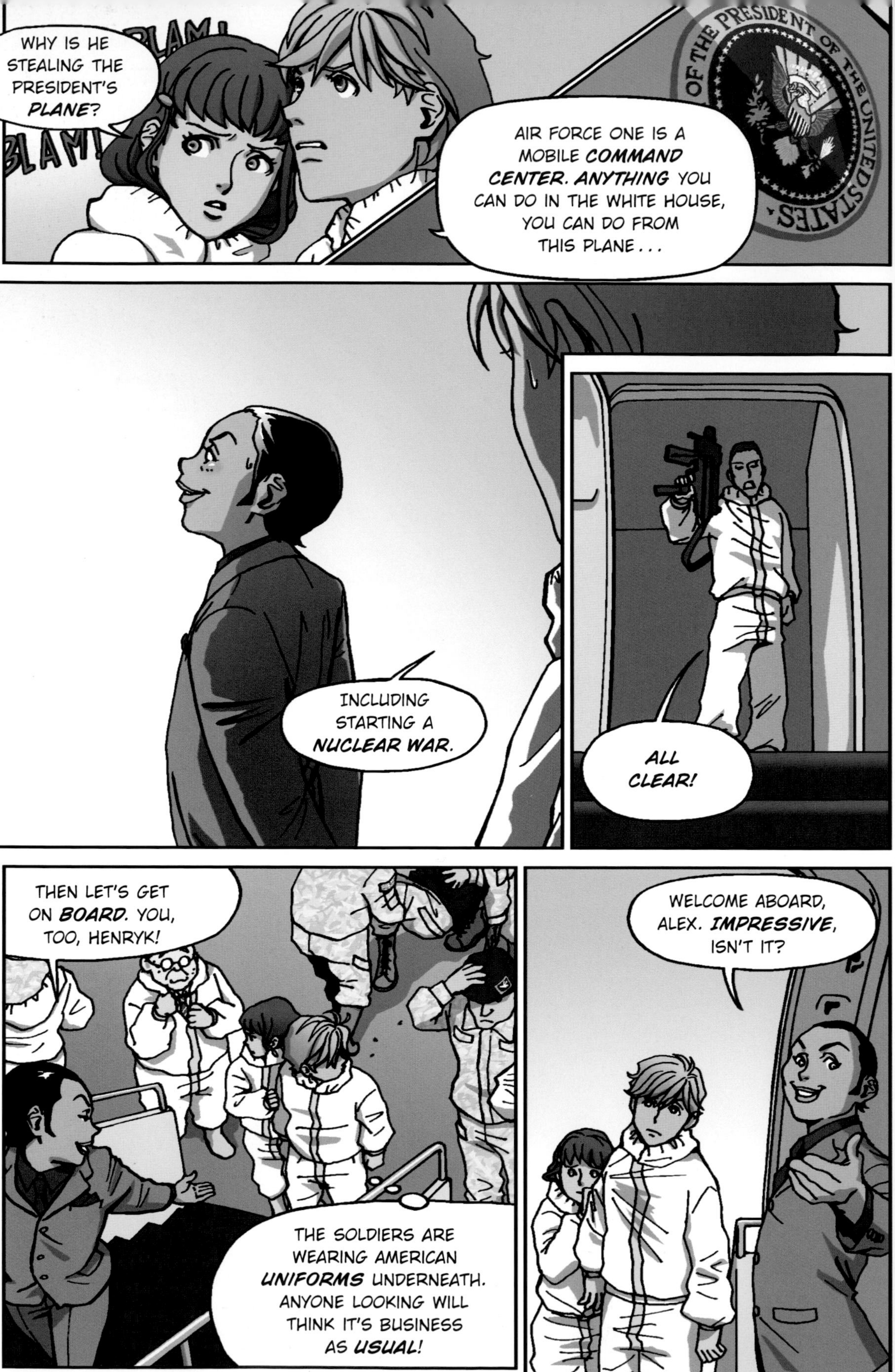
BLAM!
BLAM!
WHY IS HE STEALING THE PRESIDENT'S *PLANE*?
AIR FORCE ONE IS A MOBILE *COMMAND CENTER. ANYTHING* YOU CAN DO IN THE WHITE HOUSE, YOU CAN DO FROM THIS PLANE . . .
OF THE PRESIDENT OF THE UNITED STATES
INCLUDING STARTING A *NUCLEAR WAR*.
ALL CLEAR!
THEN LET'S GET ON *BOARD*. YOU, TOO, HENRYK!
THE SOLDIERS ARE WEARING AMERICAN *UNIFORMS* UNDERNEATH. ANYONE LOOKING WILL THINK IT'S BUSINESS AS *USUAL*!
WELCOME ABOARD, ALEX. *IMPRESSIVE*, ISN'T IT?

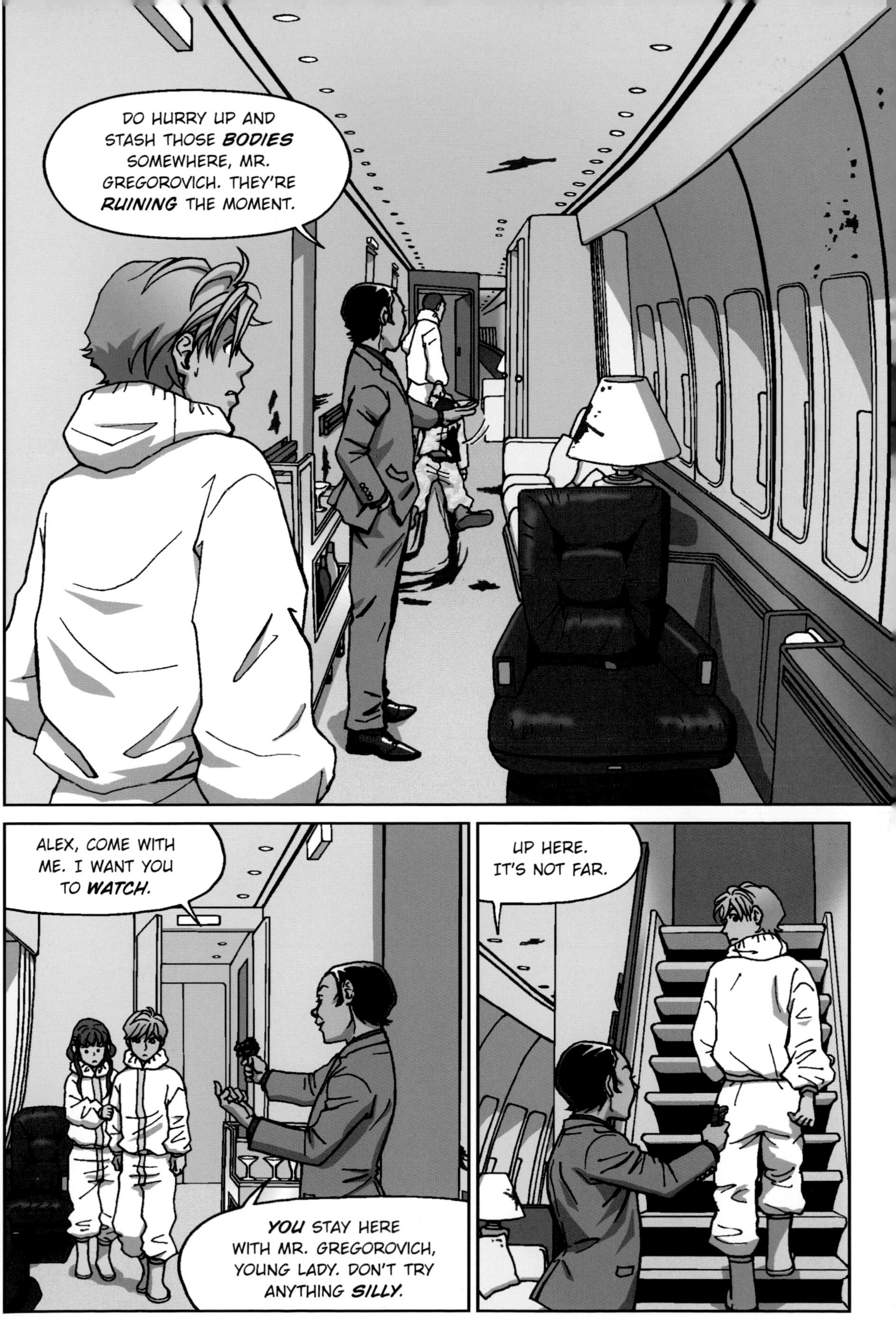
DO HURRY UP AND STASH THOSE BODIES SOMEWHERE, MR. GREGOROVICH. THEY'RE RUINING THE MOMENT.
ALEX, COME WITH ME. I WANT YOU TO WATCH.
YOU STAY HERE WITH MR. GREGOROVICH, YOUNG LADY. DON'T TRY ANYTHING SILLY.
UP HERE. IT'S NOT FAR.

THE **COMMUNICATIONS CENTER** OF AIR FORCE ONE. AND WE HAVE IT ALL TO **OURSELVES.**

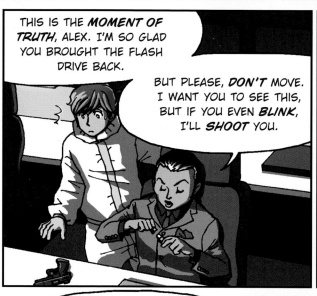

THIS IS THE **MOMENT OF TRUTH**, ALEX. I'M SO GLAD YOU BROUGHT THE FLASH DRIVE BACK.

BUT PLEASE, **DON'T** MOVE. I WANT YOU TO SEE THIS, BUT IF YOU EVEN **BLINK**, I'LL **SHOOT** YOU.

THESE COMPUTERS ARE LINKED TO **CHEYENNE MOUNTAIN**, THE UNDERGROUND **CONTROL CENTER** FOR AMERICA'S NUCLEAR WEAPONS.

THE LAUNCH CODES FOR THE MISSILES ARE **CHANGED** EVERY DAY AND SENT TO THE PRESIDENT BY THE NSA. A SATELLITE CALLED **MILSTAR** SENDS TWO COPIES.

ONE GOES TO THE **PENTAGON**, AND THE OTHER ONE . . .

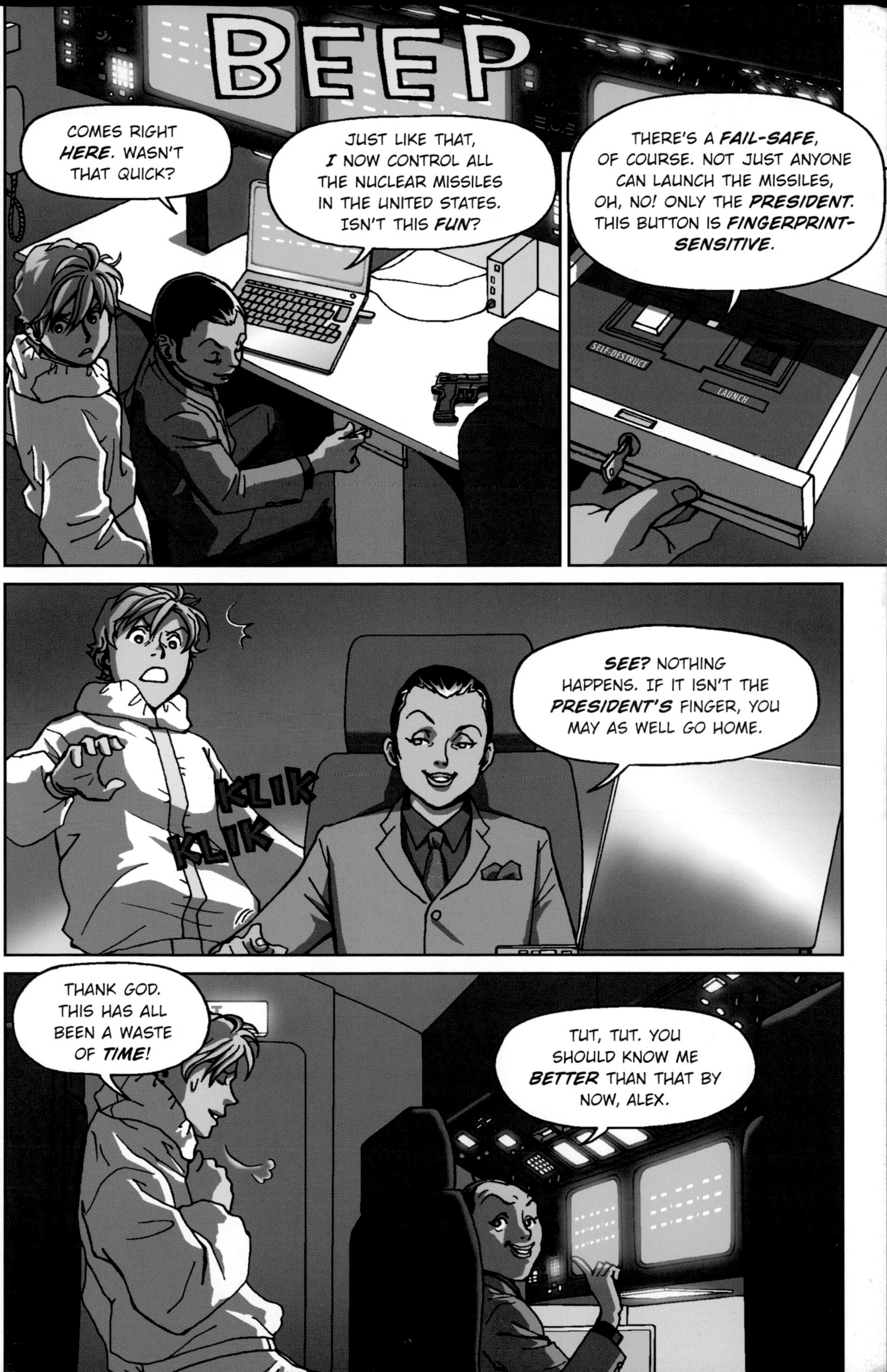
BEEP
COMES RIGHT HERE. WASN'T THAT QUICK?
JUST LIKE THAT, I NOW CONTROL ALL THE NUCLEAR MISSILES IN THE UNITED STATES. ISN'T THIS FUN?
THERE'S A FAIL-SAFE, OF COURSE. NOT JUST ANYONE CAN LAUNCH THE MISSILES, OH, NO! ONLY THE PRESIDENT. THIS BUTTON IS FINGERPRINT-SENSITIVE.
SELF-DESTRUCT
LAUNCH
KLIK
KLIK
SEE? NOTHING HAPPENS. IF IT ISN'T THE PRESIDENT'S FINGER, YOU MAY AS WELL GO HOME.
THANK GOD. THIS HAS ALL BEEN A WASTE OF TIME!
TUT, TUT. YOU SHOULD KNOW ME BETTER THAN THAT BY NOW, ALEX.

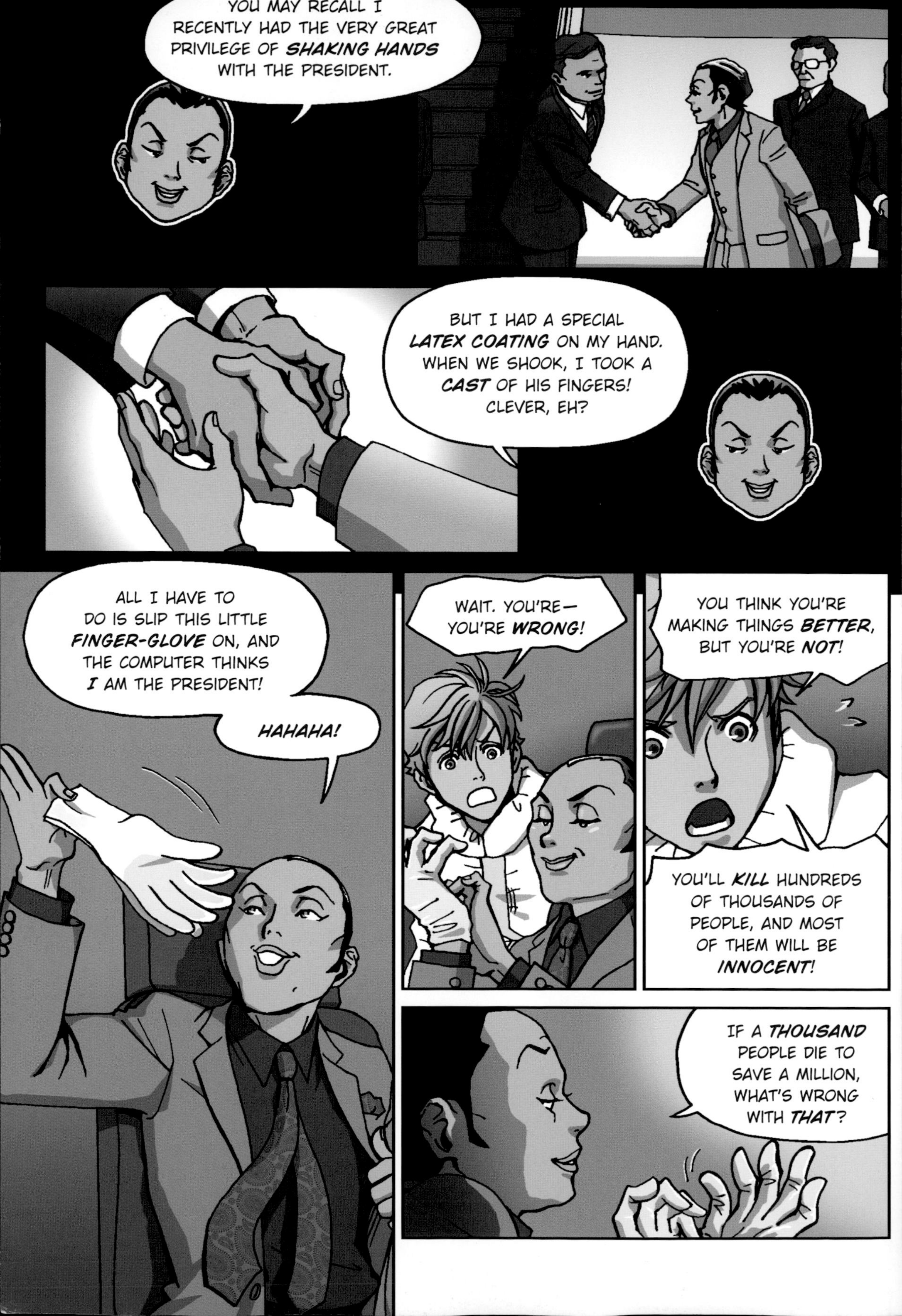
YOU MAY RECALL I RECENTLY HAD THE VERY GREAT PRIVILEGE OF *SHAKING HANDS* WITH THE PRESIDENT.
BUT I HAD A SPECIAL *LATEX COATING* ON MY HAND. WHEN WE SHOOK, I TOOK A *CAST* OF HIS FINGERS! CLEVER, EH?
ALL I HAVE TO DO IS SLIP THIS LITTLE *FINGER-GLOVE* ON, AND THE COMPUTER THINKS *I* AM THE PRESIDENT!
HAHAHA!
WAIT. YOU'RE— YOU'RE *WRONG*!
YOU THINK YOU'RE MAKING THINGS *BETTER*, BUT YOU'RE *NOT*!
YOU'LL *KILL* HUNDREDS OF THOUSANDS OF PEOPLE, AND MOST OF THEM WILL BE *INNOCENT*!
IF A *THOUSAND* PEOPLE DIE TO SAVE A MILLION, WHAT'S WRONG WITH *THAT*?

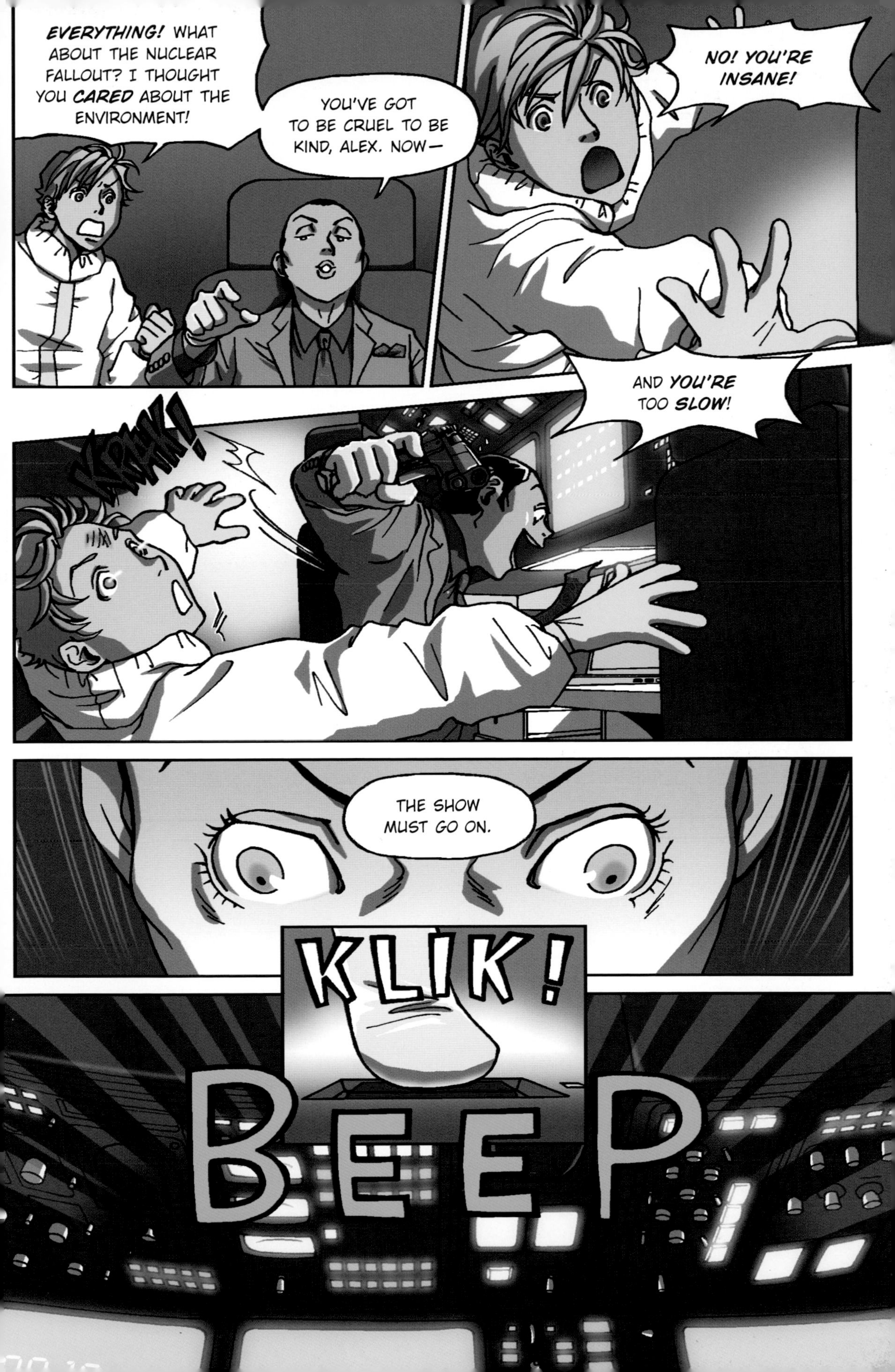
EVERYTHING! WHAT ABOUT THE NUCLEAR FALLOUT? I THOUGHT YOU CARED ABOUT THE ENVIRONMENT!
YOU'VE GOT TO BE CRUEL TO BE KIND, ALEX. NOW—
NO! YOU'RE INSANE!
AND YOU'RE TOO SLOW!
KRAAK!
THE SHOW MUST GO ON.
KLIK!
BEEP!

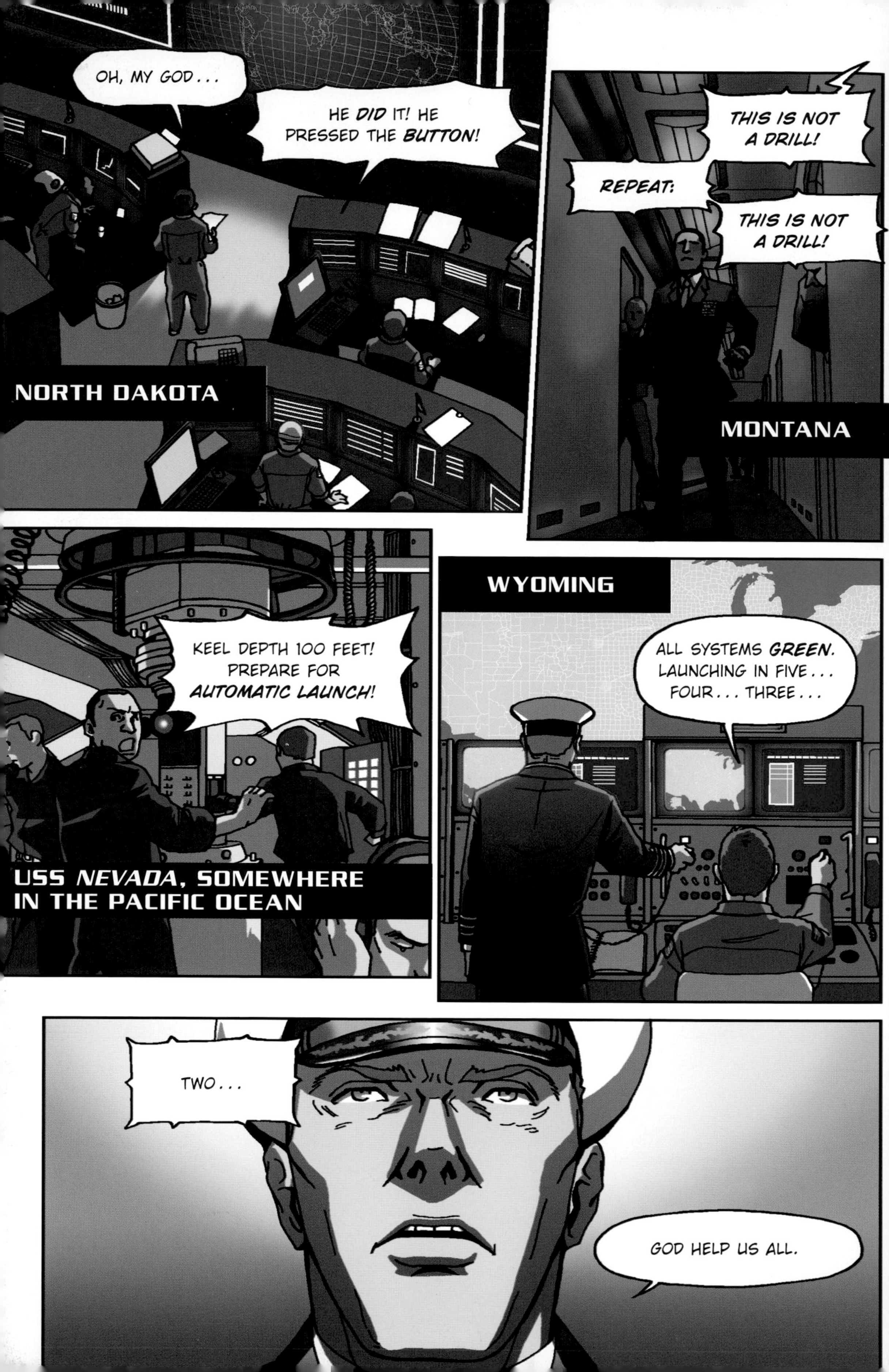
OH, MY GOD . . .
HE DID IT! HE PRESSED THE BUTTON!
NORTH DAKOTA
THIS IS NOT A DRILL!
REPEAT:
THIS IS NOT A DRILL!
MONTANA
KEEL DEPTH 100 FEET! PREPARE FOR AUTOMATIC LAUNCH!
USS NEVADA, SOMEWHERE IN THE PACIFIC OCEAN
WYOMING
ALL SYSTEMS GREEN. LAUNCHING IN FIVE . . . FOUR . . . THREE . . .
TWO . . .
GOD HELP US ALL.

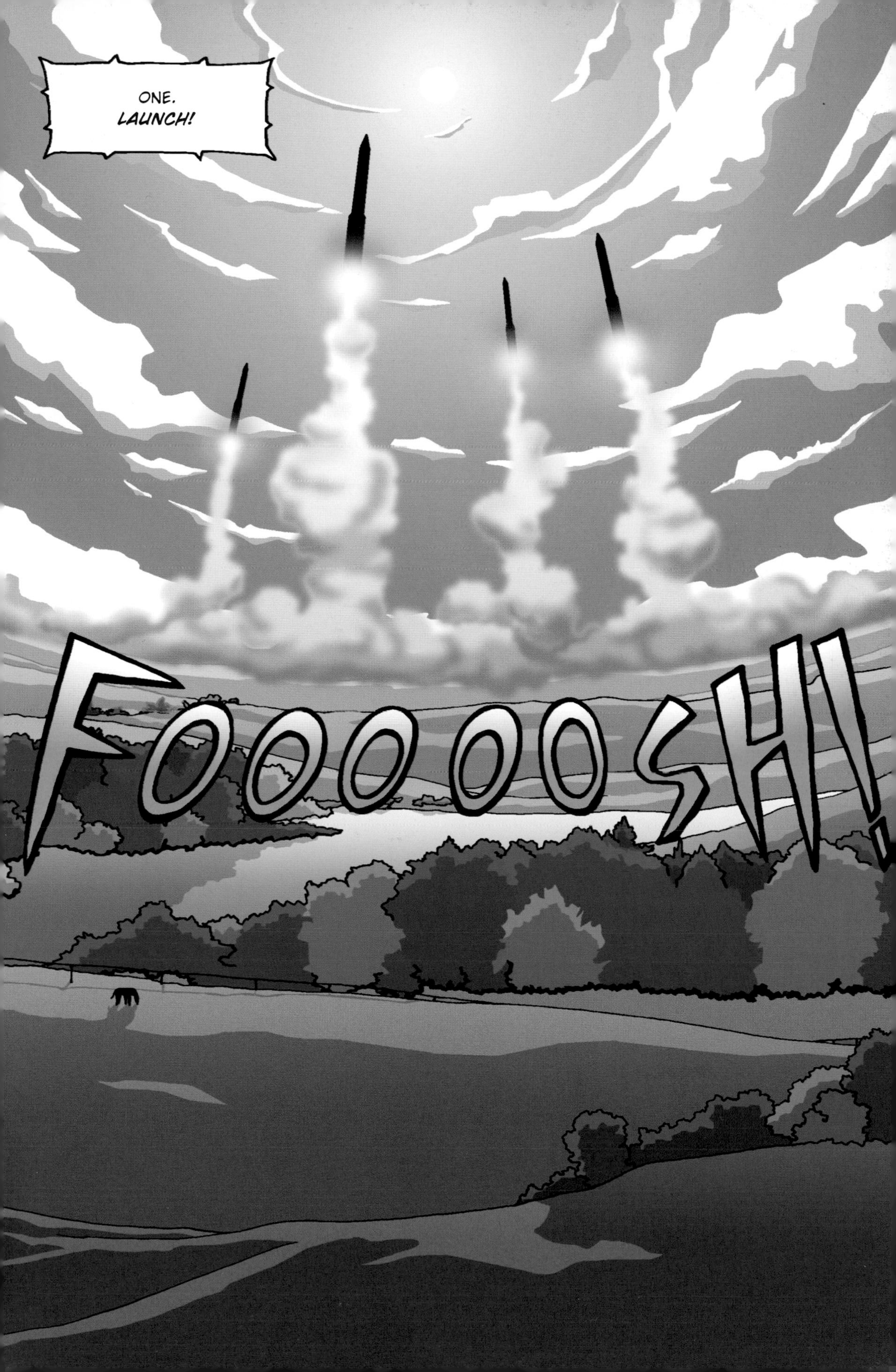
ONE.
LAUNCH!
FOOOOOSH!

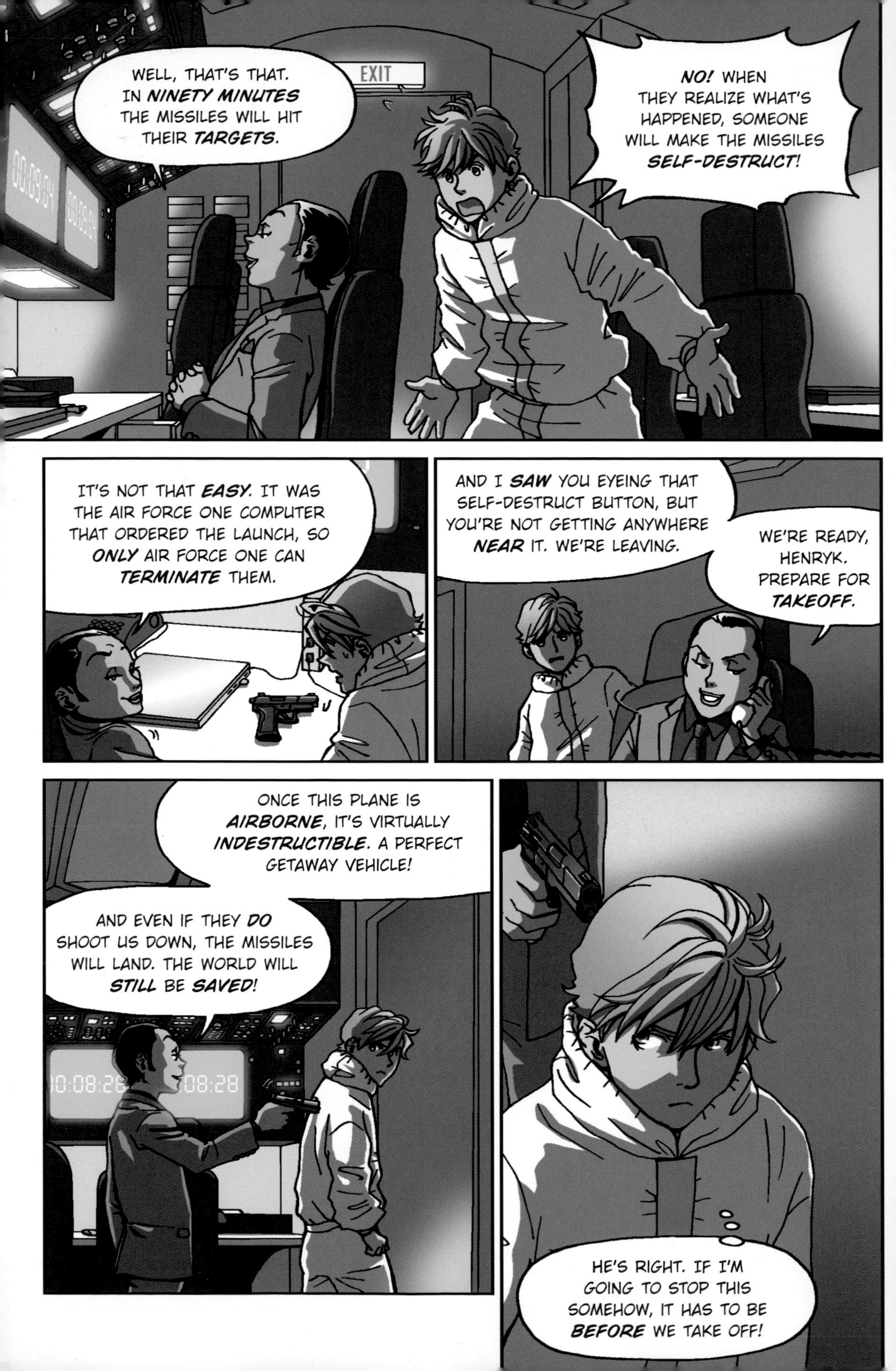
EXIT
WELL, THAT'S THAT. IN NINETY MINUTES THE MISSILES WILL HIT THEIR TARGETS.
NO! WHEN THEY REALIZE WHAT'S HAPPENED, SOMEONE WILL MAKE THE MISSILES SELF-DESTRUCT!
IT'S NOT THAT EASY. IT WAS THE AIR FORCE ONE COMPUTER THAT ORDERED THE LAUNCH, SO ONLY AIR FORCE ONE CAN TERMINATE THEM.
AND I SAW YOU EYEING THAT SELF-DESTRUCT BUTTON, BUT YOU'RE NOT GETTING ANYWHERE NEAR IT. WE'RE LEAVING.
WE'RE READY, HENRYK. PREPARE FOR TAKEOFF.
ONCE THIS PLANE IS AIRBORNE, IT'S VIRTUALLY INDESTRUCTIBLE. A PERFECT GETAWAY VEHICLE!
AND EVEN IF THEY DO SHOOT US DOWN, THE MISSILES WILL LAND. THE WORLD WILL STILL BE SAVED!
HE'S RIGHT. IF I'M GOING TO STOP THIS SOMEHOW, IT HAS TO BE BEFORE WE TAKE OFF!

WHERE ARE YOU *TAKING* US?

RUSSIA. A NEW LIFE FOR ME, AND A RETURN HOME FOR MR. GREGOROVICH. HE'LL BE A *HERO.*

I DOUBT THAT.

OH, *YES.* RUSSIA IS ON ITS *KNEES* BECAUSE OF DRUGS LIKE *HEROIN.* WE'RE BOTH GOING TO LIVE HAPPILY EVER AFTER.

WHICH IS *MORE* THAN CAN BE SAID FOR *YOU.*

DOORS TO AUTOMATIC, HENRYK.

THANK YOU. THIS IS YOUR CAPTAIN SPEAKING. . . .

PLEASE FASTEN YOUR SEAT BELTS AND PREPARE FOR TAKEOFF. THANK YOU FOR FLYING *CRAY AIRLINES.*

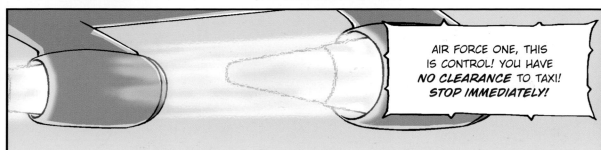

AIR FORCE ONE, THIS IS CONTROL! YOU HAVE *NO CLEARANCE* TO TAXI! *STOP IMMEDIATELY!*

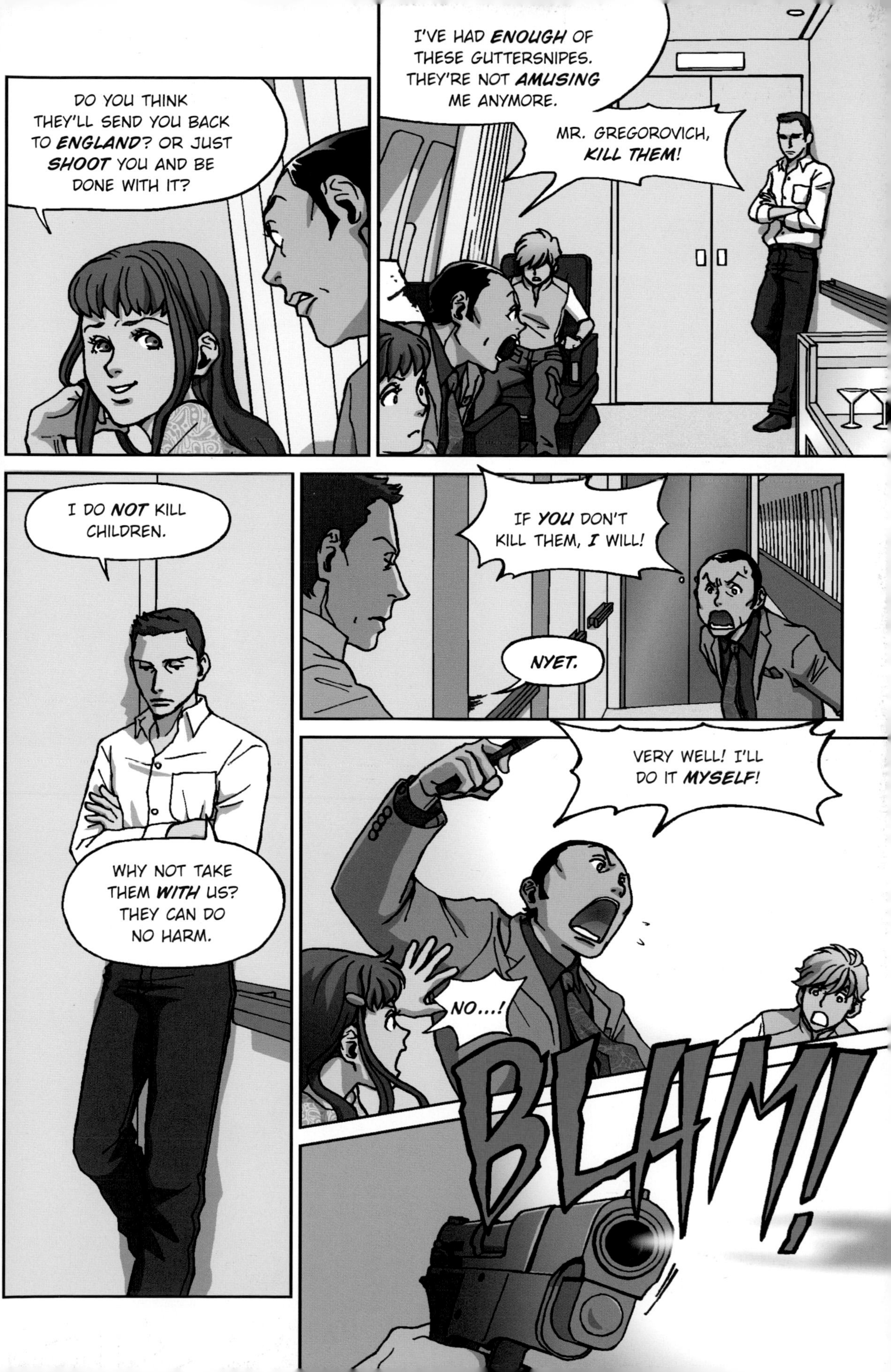
DO YOU THINK THEY'LL SEND YOU BACK TO ENGLAND? OR JUST SHOOT YOU AND BE DONE WITH IT?
I'VE HAD ENOUGH OF THESE GUTTERSNIPES. THEY'RE NOT AMUSING ME ANYMORE.
MR. GREGOROVICH, KILL THEM!
I DO NOT KILL CHILDREN.
WHY NOT TAKE THEM WITH US? THEY CAN DO NO HARM.
IF YOU DON'T KILL THEM, I WILL!
NYET.
VERY WELL! I'LL DO IT MYSELF!
NO...!
BLAM!

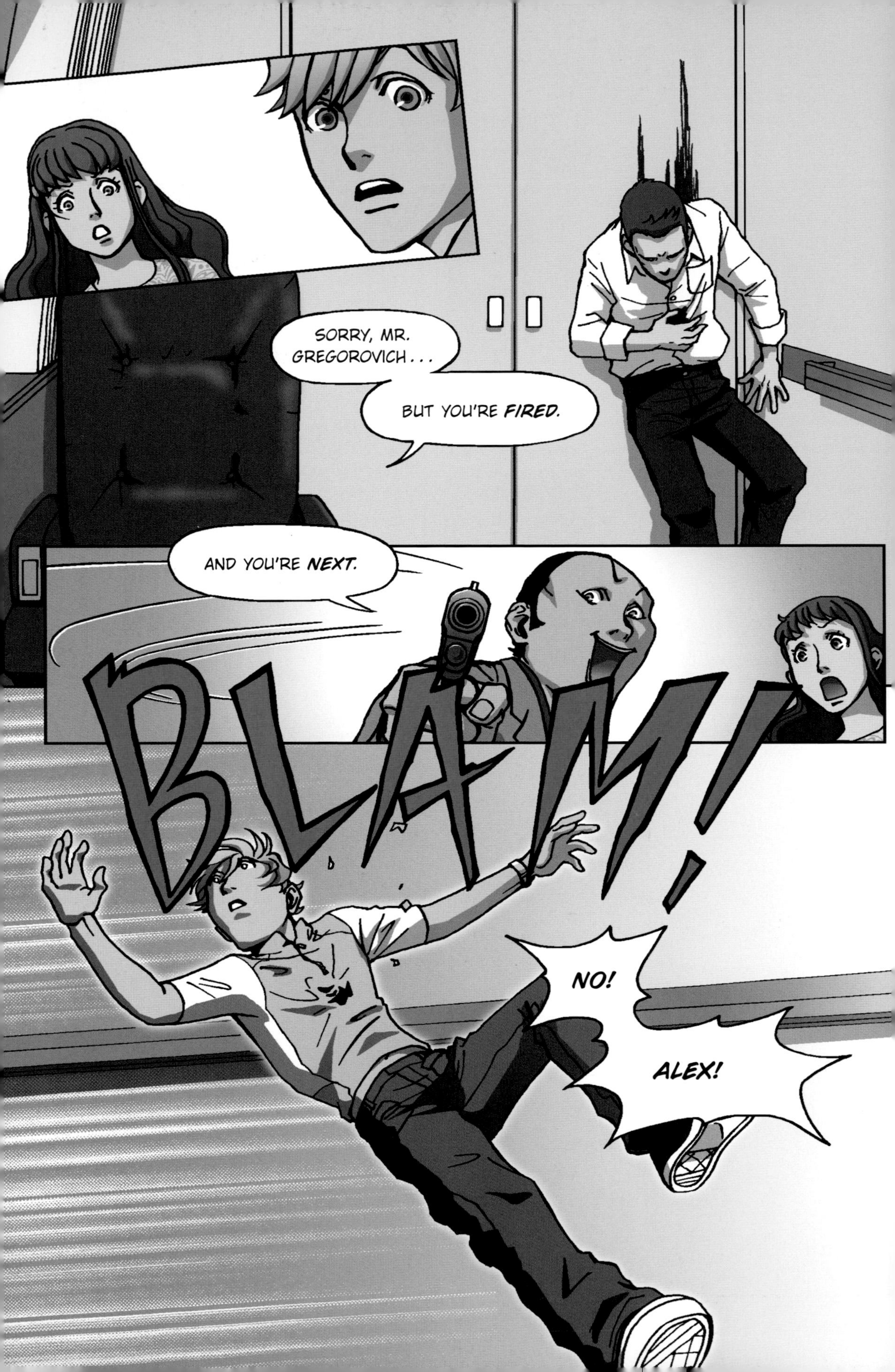
SORRY, MR. GREGOROVICH . . .
BUT YOU'RE ***FIRED.***
AND YOU'RE ***NEXT.***
BLAM!
NO!
ALEX!

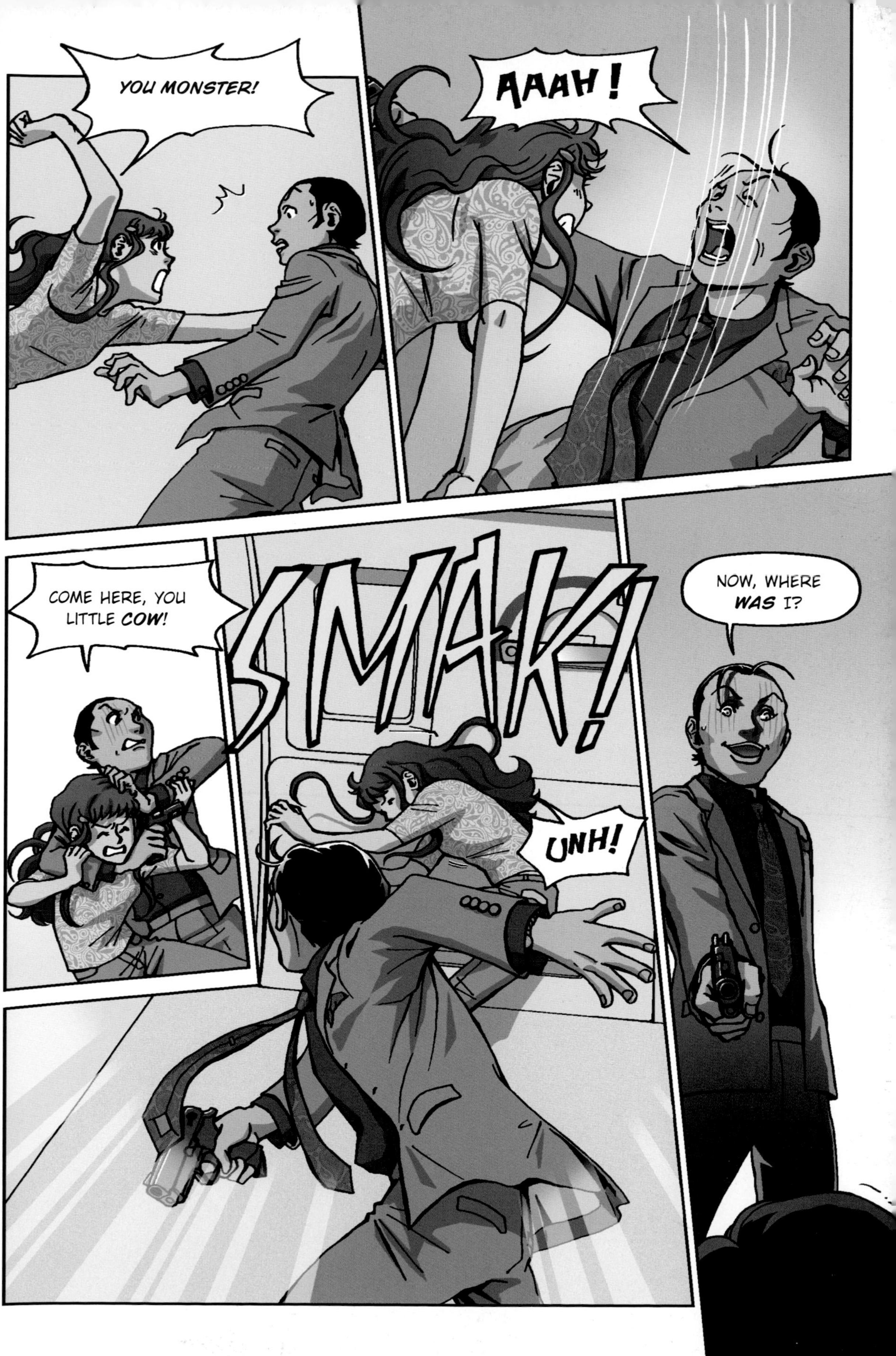
YOU MONSTER!
AAAH!
COME HERE, YOU LITTLE COW!
SMAK!
UNH!
NOW, WHERE WAS I?

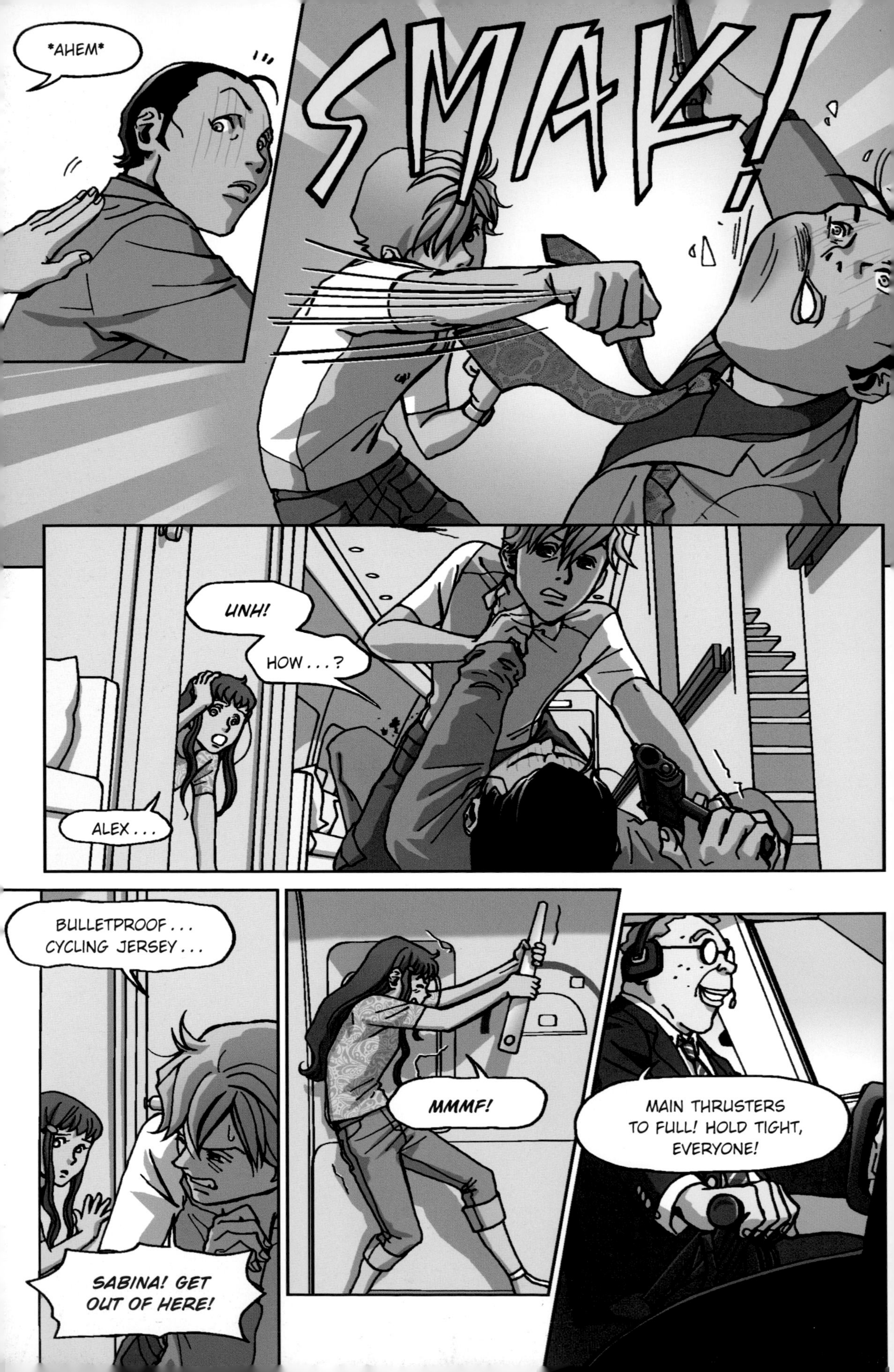
AHEM
SMAK!
UNH!
HOW . . . ?
ALEX . . .
BULLETPROOF . . . CYCLING JERSEY . . .
SABINA! GET OUT OF HERE!
MMMF!
MAIN THRUSTERS TO FULL! HOLD TIGHT, EVERYONE!

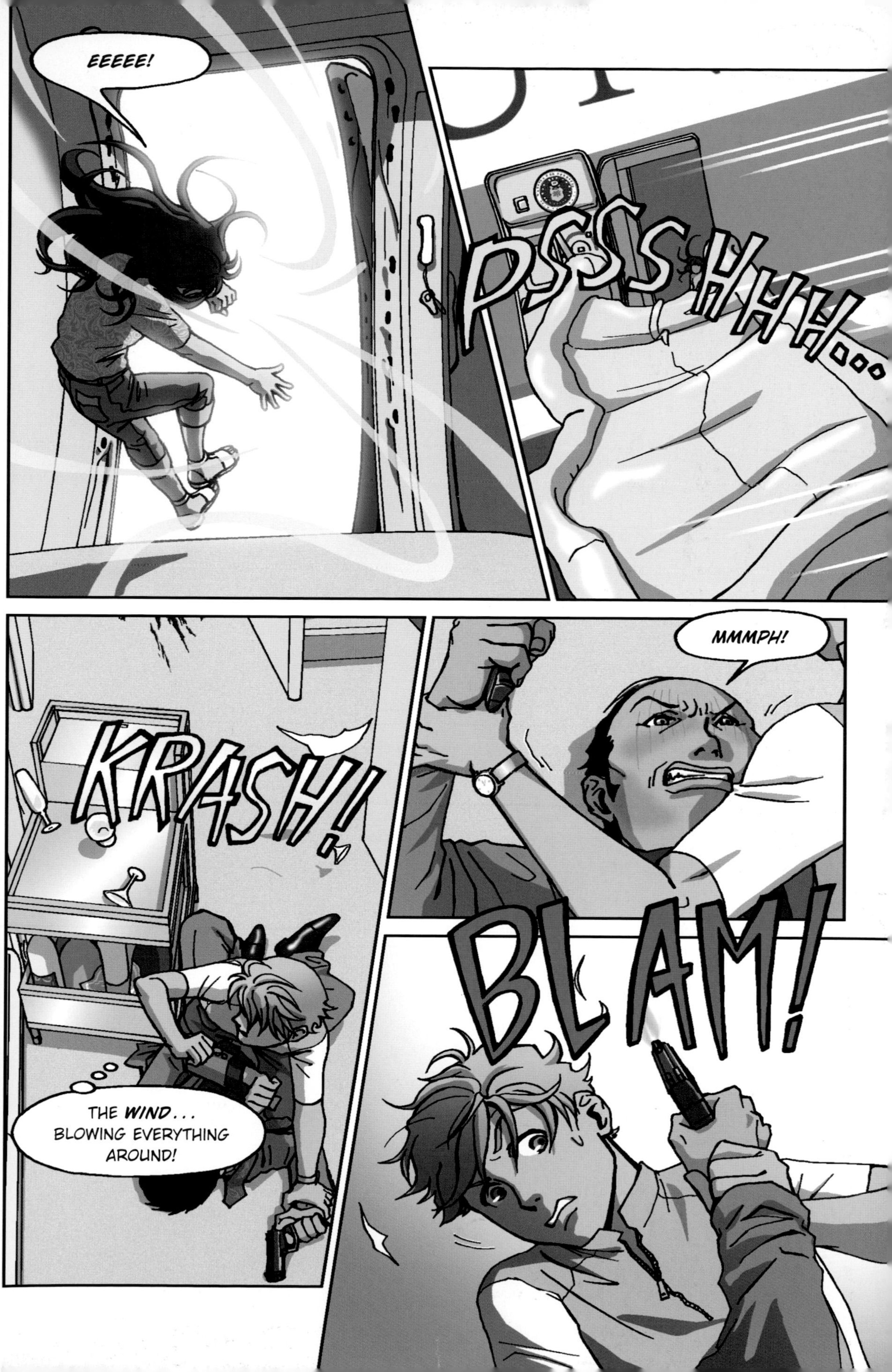
EEEEE!
PSSSSHHHH...
KRASH!
THE WIND...
BLOWING EVERYTHING
AROUND!
MMMPH!
BLAM!

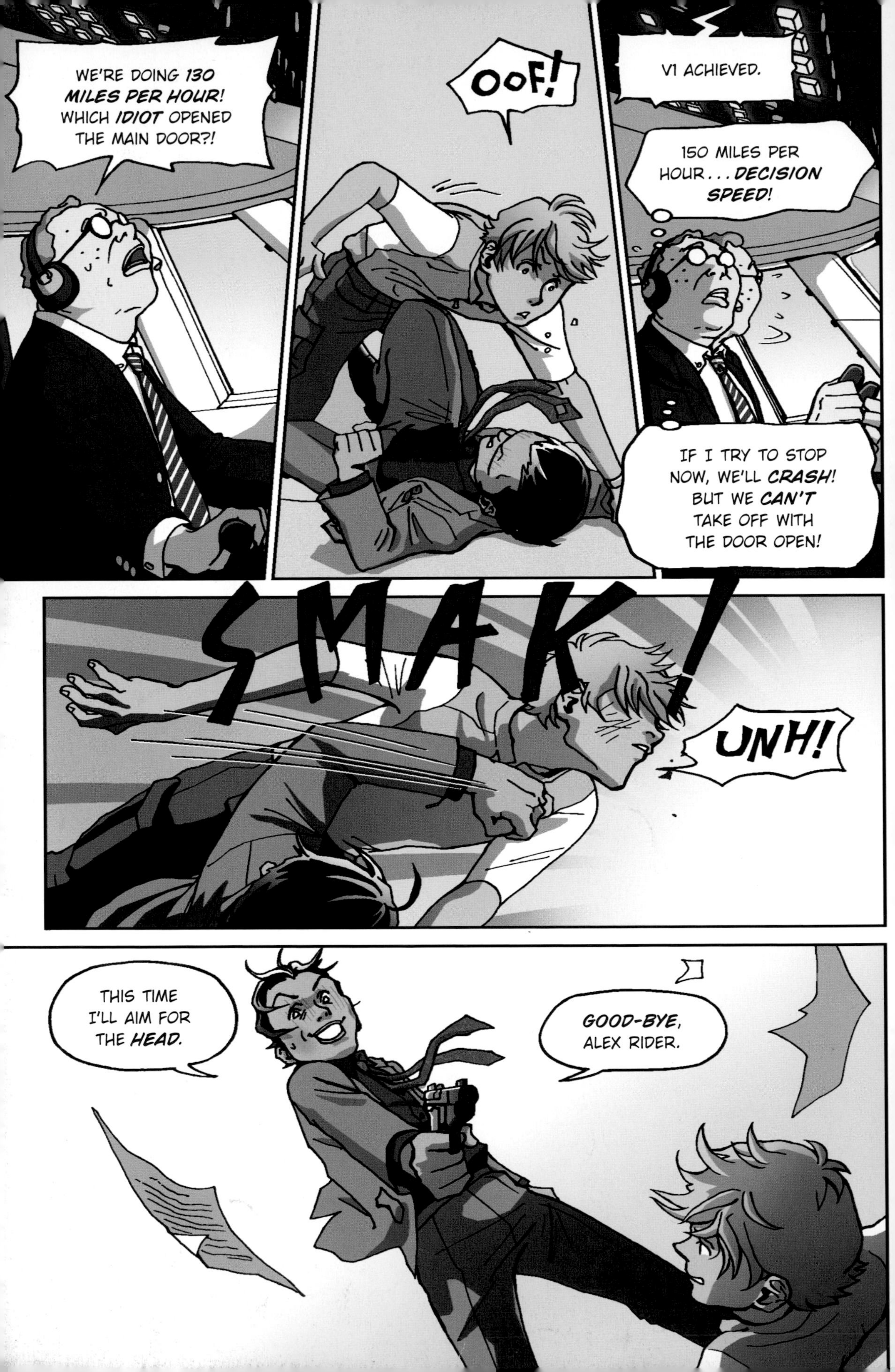
WE'RE DOING 130 MILES PER HOUR! WHICH IDIOT OPENED THE MAIN DOOR?!
OOF!
V1 ACHIEVED.
150 MILES PER HOUR... DECISION SPEED!
IF I TRY TO STOP NOW, WE'LL CRASH! BUT WE CAN'T TAKE OFF WITH THE DOOR OPEN!
SMAK!
UNH!
THIS TIME I'LL AIM FOR THE HEAD.
GOOD-BYE, ALEX RIDER.

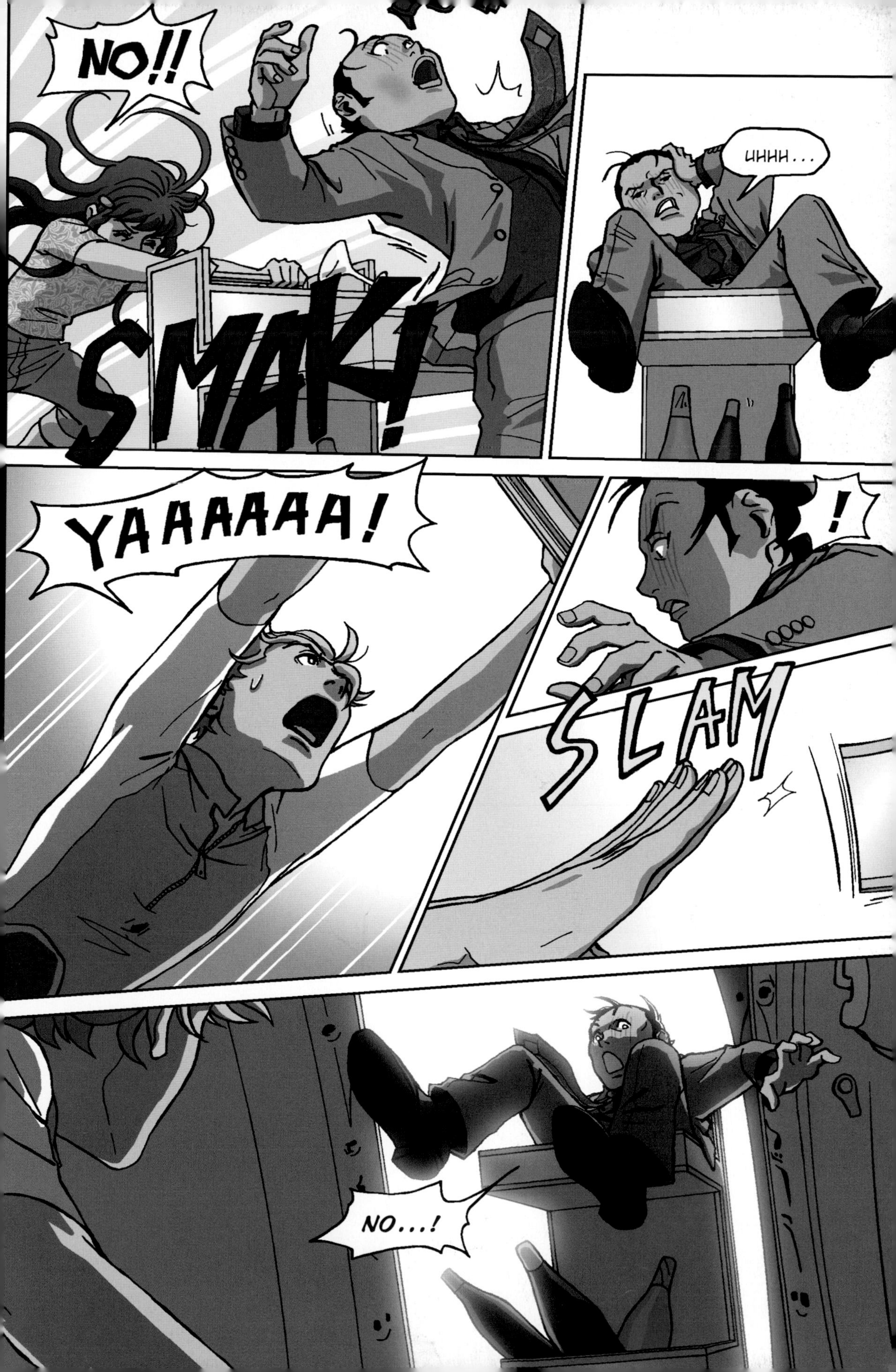
NO!!
SMAK!
UHHH...
YAAAAAA!
!
SLAM
NO...!

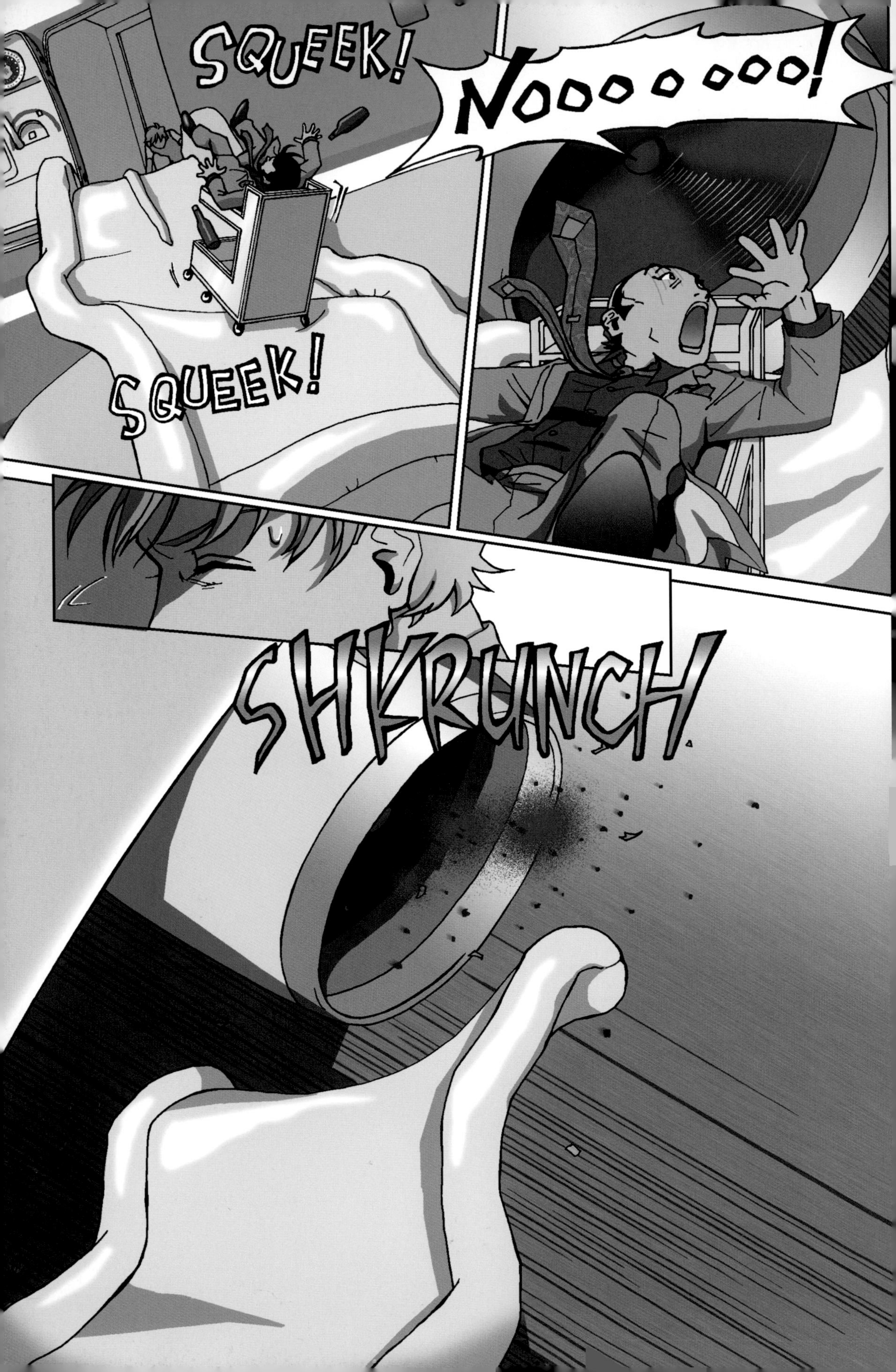
SQUEEK!
SQUEEK!
NOOOOOOO!
SHKRUNCH

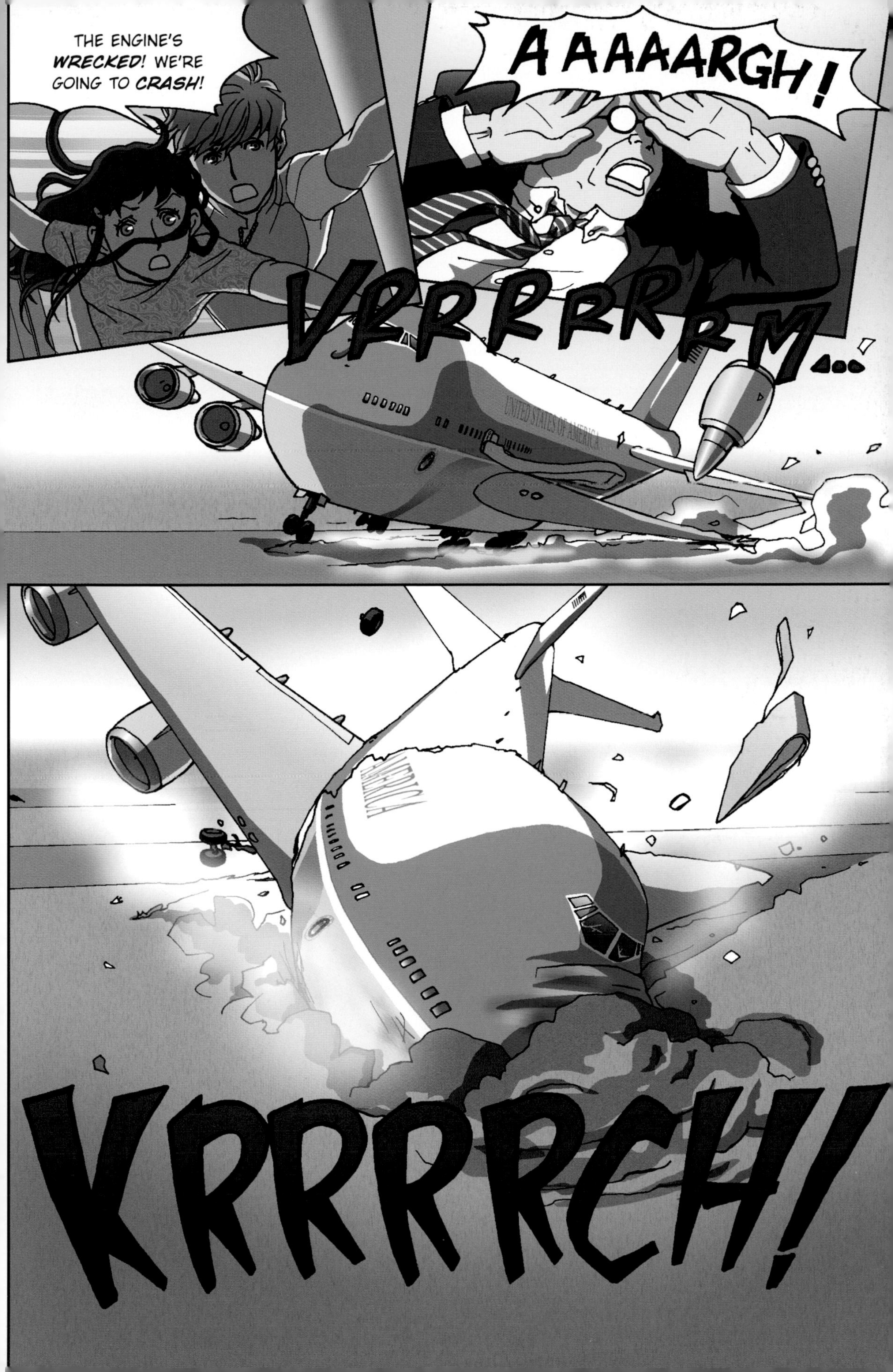

THE ENGINE'S *WRECKED!* WE'RE GOING TO *CRASH!*
AAAAARGH!
VRRRRRRM...
UNITED STATES OF AMERICA
AMERICA
KRRRRCH!

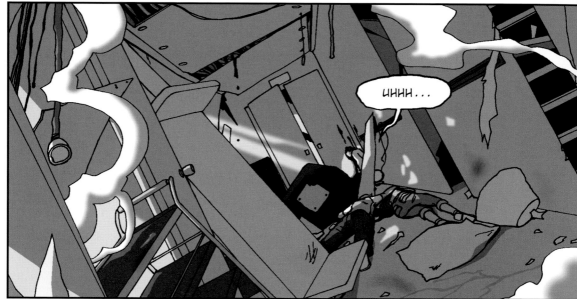

UHHH . . .

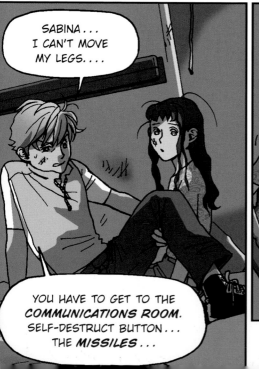

SABINA . . .
I CAN'T MOVE
MY LEGS. . . .

YOU HAVE TO GET TO THE
COMMUNICATIONS ROOM.
SELF-DESTRUCT BUTTON . . .
THE **MISSILES** . . .

OK . . .

YES, OF
COURSE . . .

ALEX.

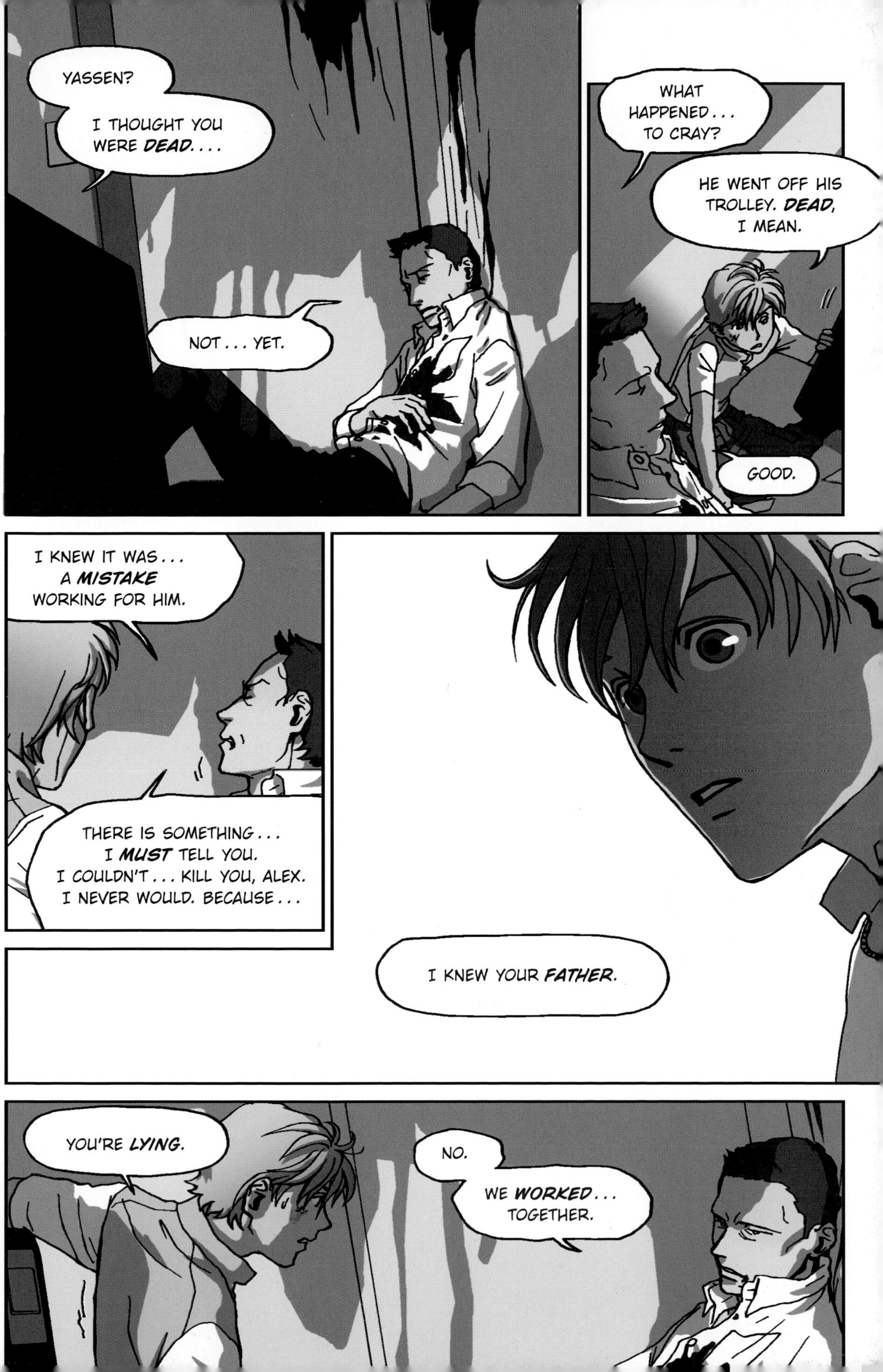

YASSEN?
I THOUGHT YOU WERE **DEAD**. . . .
NOT . . . YET.
WHAT HAPPENED . . . TO CRAY?
HE WENT OFF HIS TROLLEY. **DEAD**, I MEAN.
GOOD.
I KNEW IT WAS . . . A **MISTAKE** WORKING FOR HIM.
THERE IS SOMETHING . . . I **MUST** TELL YOU. I COULDN'T . . . KILL YOU, ALEX. I NEVER WOULD. BECAUSE . . .
I KNEW YOUR **FATHER**.
YOU'RE **LYING**.
NO.
WE **WORKED** . . . TOGETHER.

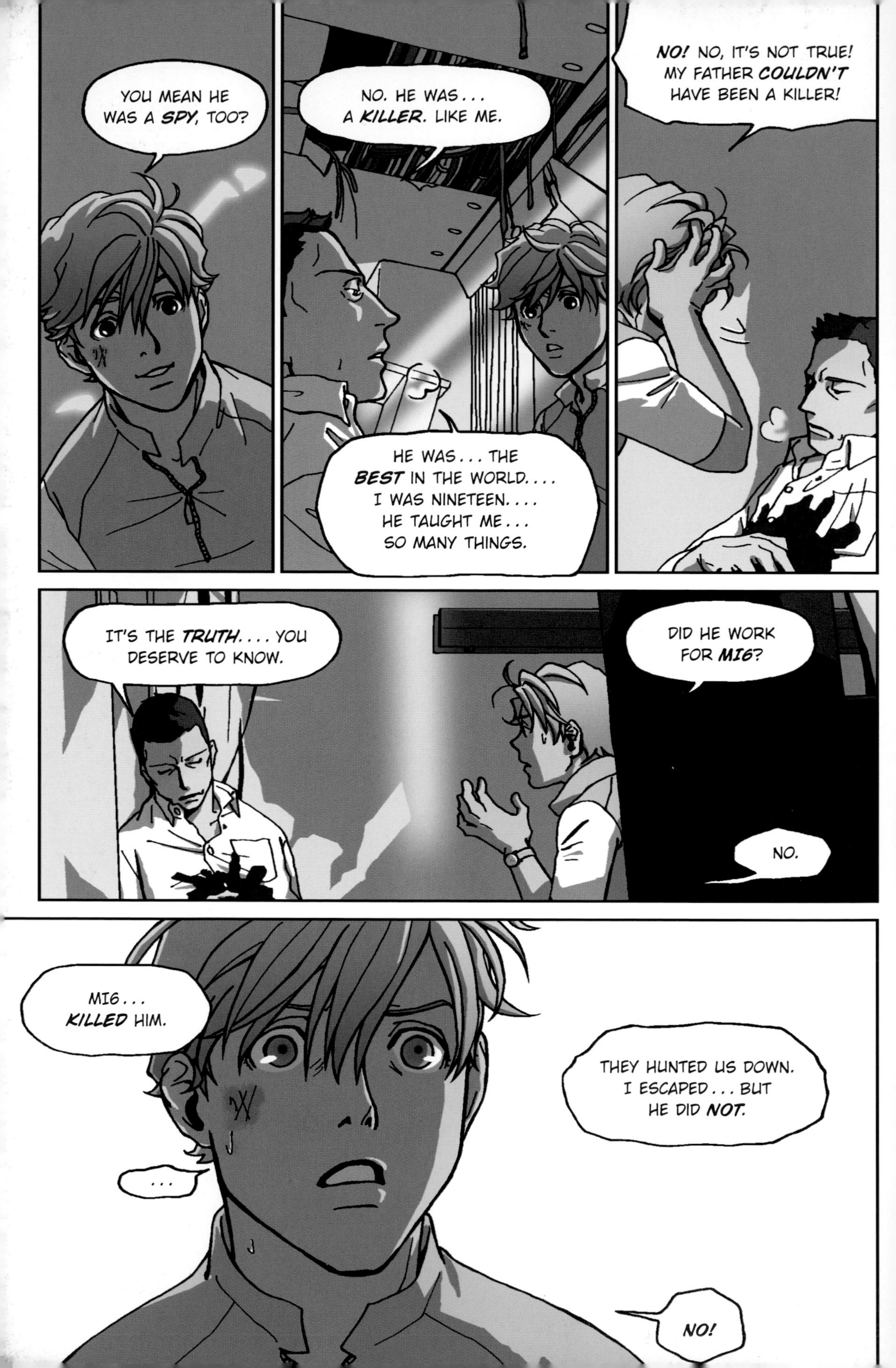
YOU MEAN HE WAS A SPY, TOO?
NO. HE WAS . . . A KILLER. LIKE ME.
HE WAS . . . THE BEST IN THE WORLD. . . . I WAS NINETEEN. . . . HE TAUGHT ME . . . SO MANY THINGS.
NO! NO, IT'S NOT TRUE! MY FATHER COULDN'T HAVE BEEN A KILLER!
IT'S THE TRUTH. . . . YOU DESERVE TO KNOW.
DID HE WORK FOR MI6?
NO.
MI6 . . . KILLED HIM.
THEY HUNTED US DOWN. I ESCAPED . . . BUT HE DID NOT.
. . .
NO!

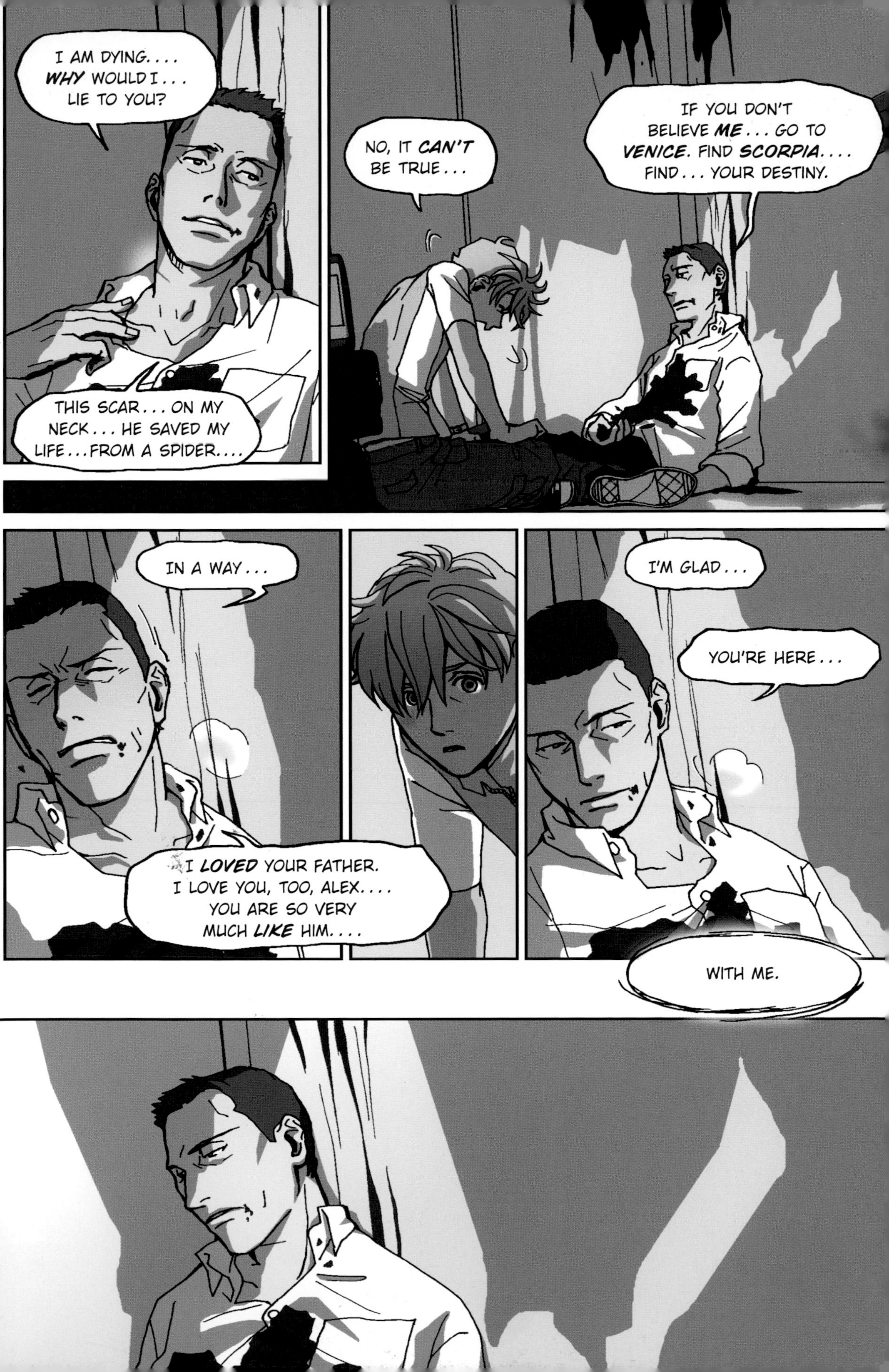

I AM DYING. . . . WHY WOULD I . . . LIE TO YOU?
THIS SCAR . . . ON MY NECK . . . HE SAVED MY LIFE . . . FROM A SPIDER. . . .
NO, IT CAN'T BE TRUE . . .
IF YOU DON'T BELIEVE ME . . . GO TO VENICE. FIND SCORPIA. . . . FIND . . . YOUR DESTINY.
IN A WAY . . .
I LOVED YOUR FATHER. I LOVE YOU, TOO, ALEX. . . . YOU ARE SO VERY MUCH LIKE HIM. . . .
I'M GLAD . . .
YOU'RE HERE . . .
WITH ME.

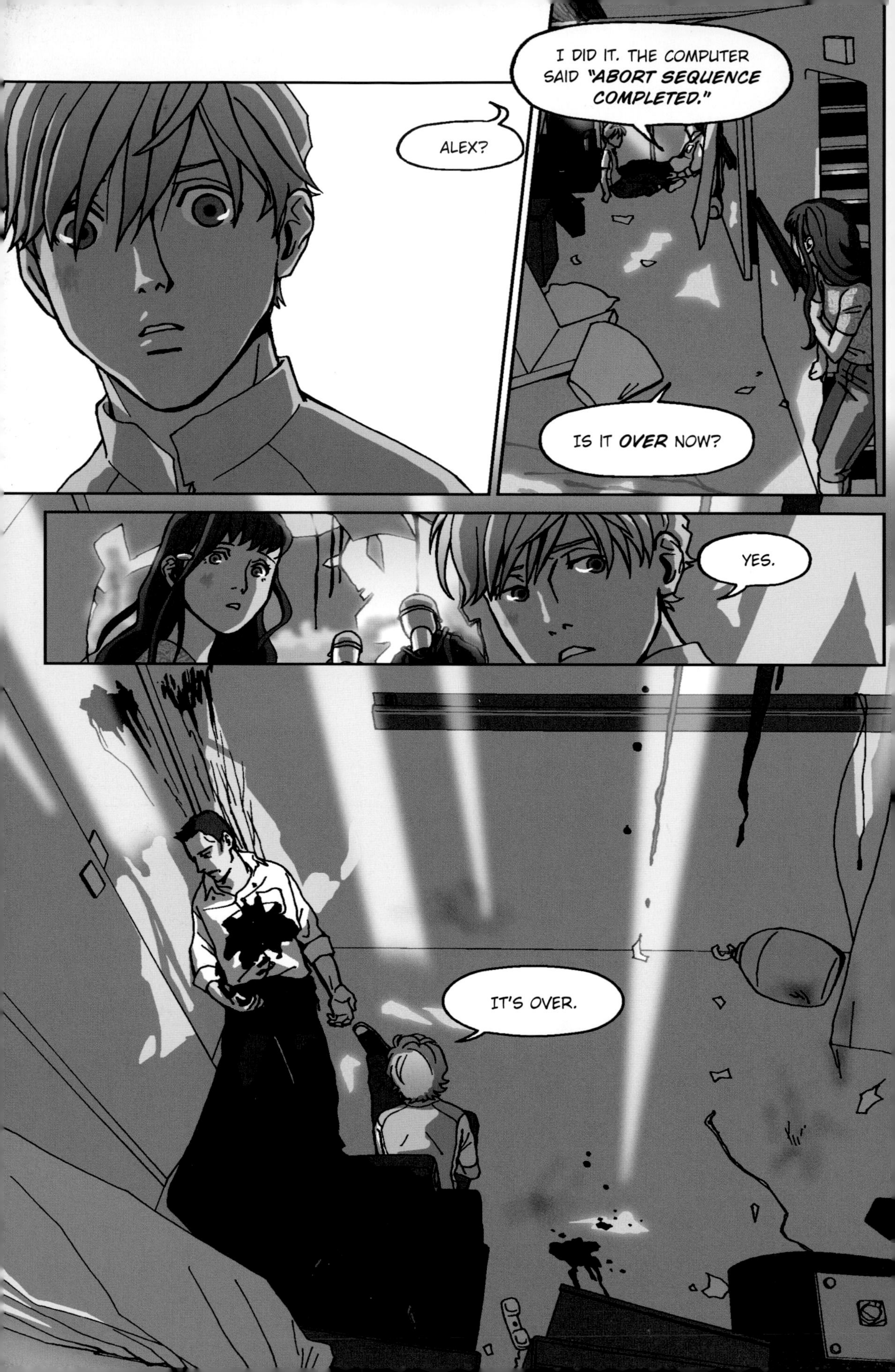
ALEX?
I DID IT. THE COMPUTER SAID "ABORT SEQUENCE COMPLETED."
IS IT OVER NOW?
YES.
IT'S OVER.

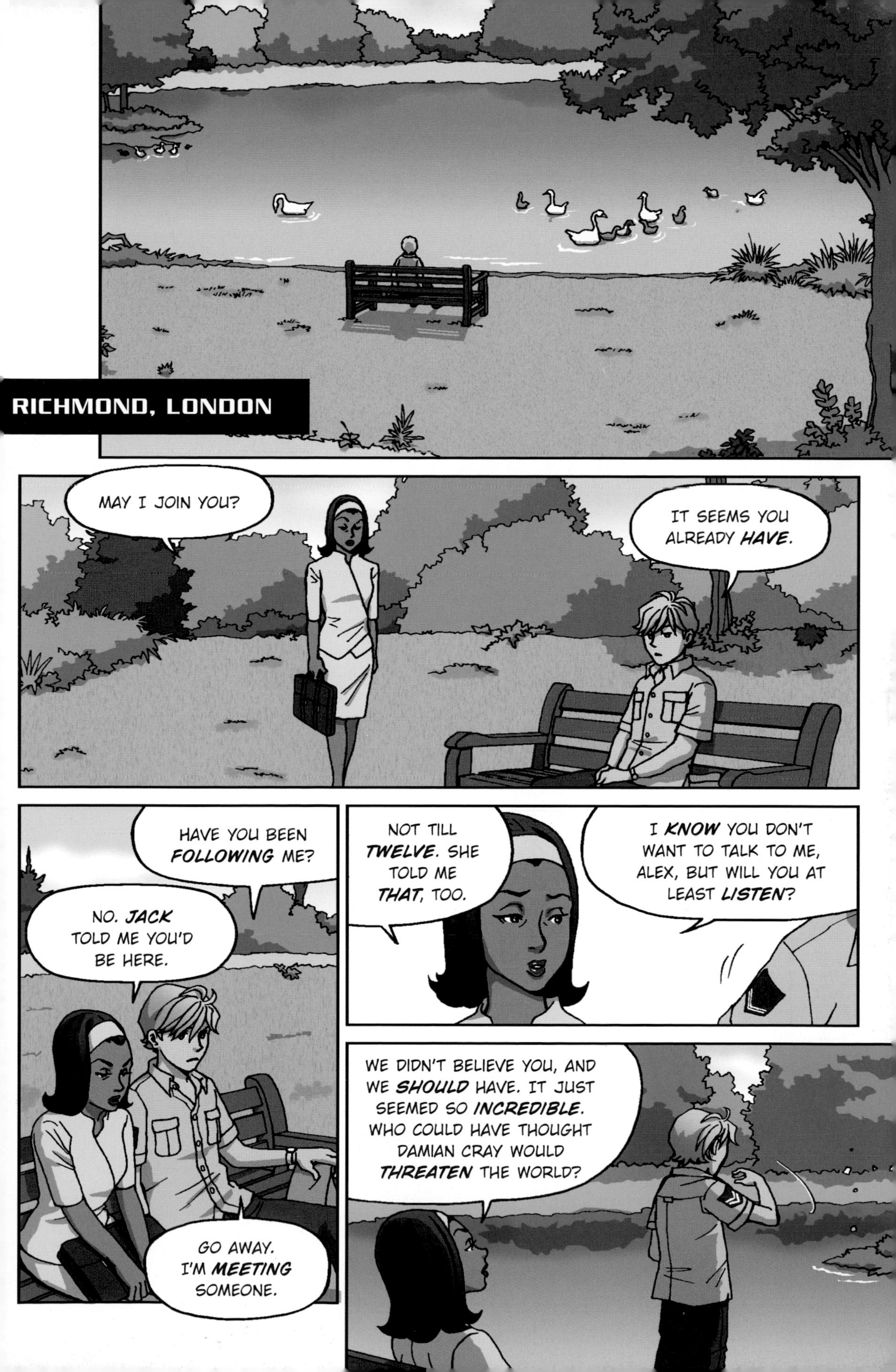
RICHMOND, LONDON
MAY I JOIN YOU?
IT SEEMS YOU ALREADY HAVE.
HAVE YOU BEEN FOLLOWING ME?
NO. JACK TOLD ME YOU'D BE HERE.
GO AWAY. I'M MEETING SOMEONE.
NOT TILL TWELVE. SHE TOLD ME THAT, TOO.
I KNOW YOU DON'T WANT TO TALK TO ME, ALEX, BUT WILL YOU AT LEAST LISTEN?
WE DIDN'T BELIEVE YOU, AND WE SHOULD HAVE. IT JUST SEEMED SO INCREDIBLE. WHO COULD HAVE THOUGHT DAMIAN CRAY WOULD THREATEN THE WORLD?

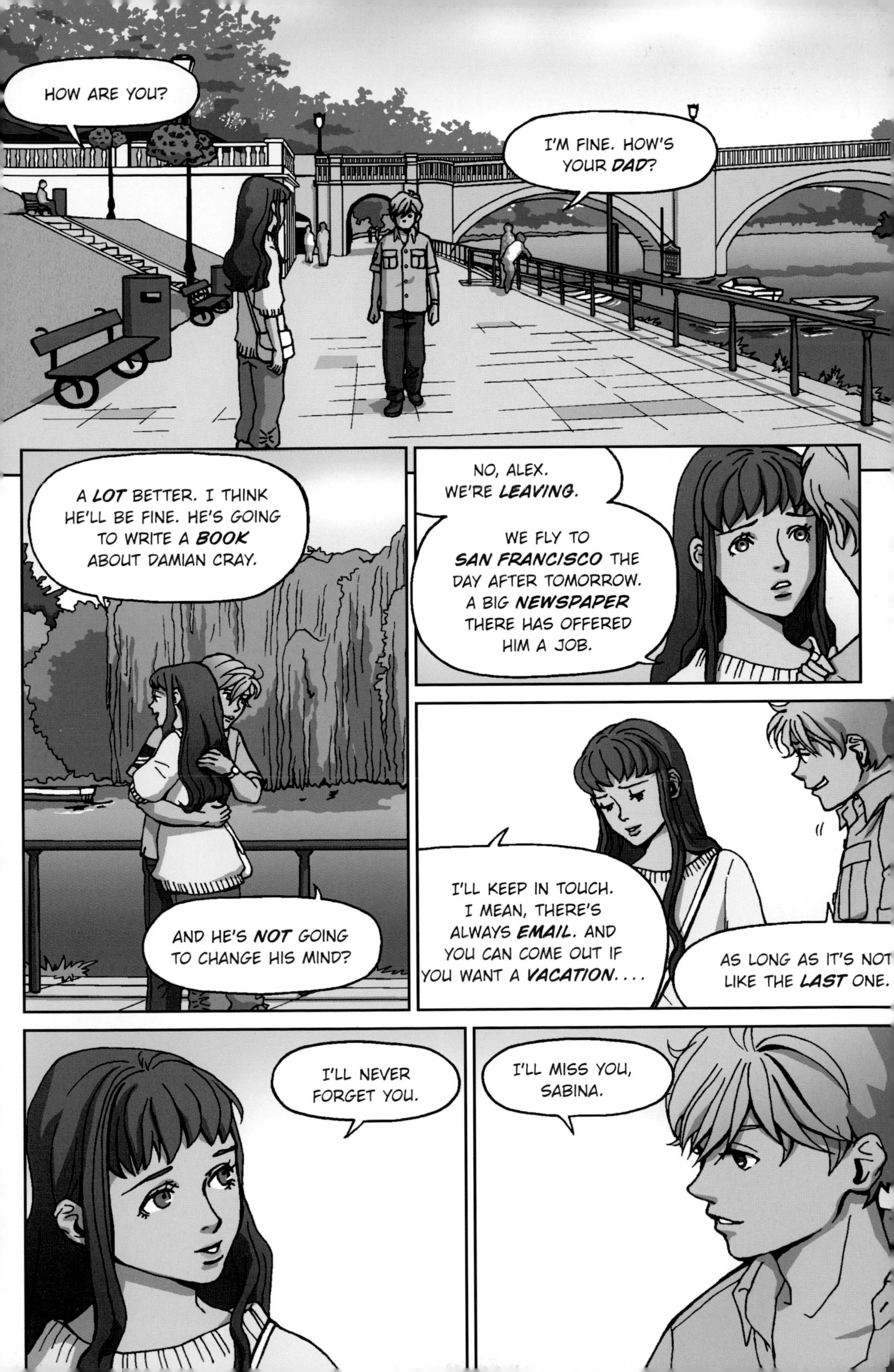
HOW ARE YOU?
I'M FINE. HOW'S YOUR DAD?
A LOT BETTER. I THINK HE'LL BE FINE. HE'S GOING TO WRITE A BOOK ABOUT DAMIAN CRAY.
AND HE'S NOT GOING TO CHANGE HIS MIND?
NO, ALEX. WE'RE LEAVING.
WE FLY TO SAN FRANCISCO THE DAY AFTER TOMORROW. A BIG NEWSPAPER THERE HAS OFFERED HIM A JOB.
I'LL KEEP IN TOUCH. I MEAN, THERE'S ALWAYS EMAIL. AND YOU CAN COME OUT IF YOU WANT A VACATION. . . .
AS LONG AS IT'S NOT LIKE THE LAST ONE.
I'LL NEVER FORGET YOU.
I'LL MISS YOU, SABINA.

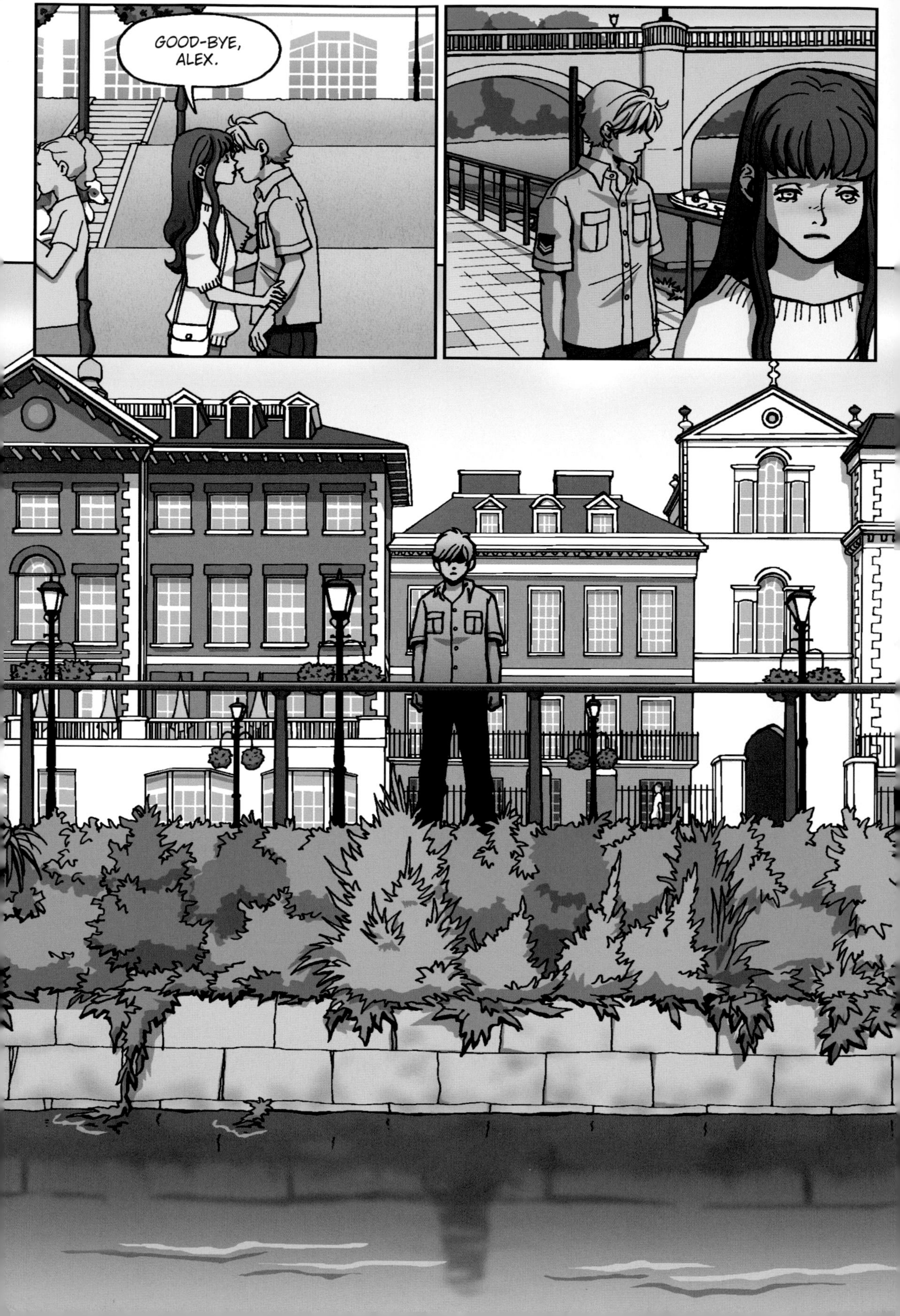
GOOD-BYE,
ALEX.